COME THE DAWN

CHRISTINA SKYE

A Dell Book

Published by
Dell Publishing
a division of
Bantam Doubleday Dell Publishing Group, Inc.
1540 Broadway
New York, New York 10036

ISBN: 0-440-21647-8

Printed in the United States of America

Published simultaneously in Canada

September 1995

10   9   8   7   6   5   4   3   2

OPM

In memoriam,

Paul M. Helmer
(1905–1994)

Prologue

It was said that Devlyn Jordan Carlisle could cajole a miser out of his last guinea and a nun out of her last rosary.

Men whispered that when he was a youth of thirteen, women began to follow him with their eyes—and then with more than just their eyes. London society dubbed him a consummate charmer and an utter cheat; a rogue who carried on a long tradition of recklessness which had started in 1355, when the first earl gave away his steed in the heat of battle so that his sovereign could ride to safety. In the ensuing carnage, Decimus Carlisle rendered up his life—and was ennobled by a grateful king.

For five centuries the Thornwood men hadn't two good guineas to rub together, but they always found a way to please—women, men, or country. Themselves, most of all.

About one thing London was in perfect agreement: the twelfth earl of Thornwood was the most rash in a long line of charming and impetuous men. With silver eyes, a striking face, and a charmed life, Devlyn Carlisle was a rake who could do no wrong—and no real good.

1

Alas, most of the scandalous gossip the ton whispered about him was true.

So when the news of Thorne's death was printed in the *Gazette*, after his chest was shattered in a muddy cornfield just south of Quatre Bras during the bloody encounter at Waterloo, every man within fifty miles of London heaved a sigh of relief—while every woman in the capital brushed away a tear.

Including a woman named India Delamere, the one person who had discovered the real man beneath all the careful layers of cool Carlisle charm.

1

"**C**ome out, villain!"

Sunlight lay in a pool of gold around the slender figure in the middle of the sloping green fields. A battered straw hat hung from a ribbon beneath her titian hair, and a silver-haired wolf perched tensely beside her booted right foot.

India Delamere, daughter of the Duke of Devonham, one of the greatest landowners in England, leveled the sights of her perfectly weighted pistol as the shrubbery beside Swallow Hill's ornamental pool started to shake. Who would be so insolent as to invade her family's estate at this hour? Even those fools who had been creeping around the hills plaguing her gamekeeper and destroying his traps would not be so bold in broad daylight.

Or would they?

"Come out this second, or I will shoot!" India's tone was adamant, prompting the wolf to growl menacingly.

When there was still no answer, she took a steadying breath and pulled back the hammer. "Very well, you leave me no choice. You now have three seconds until I lay a bullet between your eyes."

Only two minutes before, all had been peaceful. A
herd of geese had skimmed the pond while the great
silver wolf lay basking beside India in the sun. Then
the geese had fled in panic, and the wolf caught the
scent of an intruder.

"One. Two . . ."

The titian-haired heiress to one of England's oldest fortunes tossed back her battered straw hat and
focused through the crosshairs of her pistol.

And still there was no answer.

"Three!"

She fired.

The greenery along the lake shook. A handful of
leaves shot up into the air, and a groan emerged
from the nearest shrub as a broad-shouldered figure
dove through a gap in the greenery.

He landed prone between two rows of lavender.
"Hold your fire, blast it!"

"Ian?" India's fingers relaxed. The pistol dropped
to her side. "You silly ape, I might have shot you!"

India's brother rose, brushing dirt from his white
shirt. A lazy grin creased his deeply tanned face. "I
am most grateful that you *purposely* aimed for the
edge of that shrub and not its heart—which would
have been *my* heart."

"Why didn't you *say* something?"

"Because, my impudent sister, I was having far
too much fun baiting you." He brushed off his
hands and eyed the tear in his sleeve. "You really are
a complete and utter hoyden, India. I fear you are
more reckless at age twenty than you were at
twelve."

India slid the safety catch home and returned the
weapon to the fine doeskin pouch at her waist.
"What were you doing up here in the woods?"

Ian shrugged. "Following some tracks. Force of habit, you know."

India didn't believe it. Not for a second. Beneath those sleepy gray eyes, Ian was as relentless as a bloodhound, particularly when he felt someone was threatening his family. No doubt her older brother, Luc, had also been checking up on her, just as all her wonderful family had done without cease in the four months since her return from the Continent.

The Continent.

Even now the memory filled India with aching sorrow.

For the man she loved was dead. Devlyn Carlisle would not be coming back ever again. India couldn't deny the truth any longer.

So why did he still come to her in the suffocating silences of the night when her defenses were utterly gone? Why did she see him in the shadows of midnight and the mists of dawn, his smiling face as real as it had been in the weeks before Waterloo?

But the phantoms never stayed long enough. Far too soon those keen gray eyes turned sad, watching the carts and horses stream past, all madness and noise on the eve of war. As always, India had one last glimpse of his hard, beloved face, half in sun, half in shadow as he stood on the hill before turning to rejoin his regiment.

It was a memory she carried with her long after Devlyn Carlisle had disappeared over the rise, marching east to face Napoleon down in the muddy fields of corn.

There Devlyn Carlisle had died, his chest shattered by a French cavalry saber. But he had not left India. Whenever the wind whispered through the old beech trees at Swallow Hill, it seemed to take the timbre of Devlyn's husky laugh. When a gust of wind tugged at India's long hair, her breath caught in sharp, aching sadness, because this was exactly the way his hard fingers used to brush against her. Over a year had passed, but the memories still haunted her. And it was to confront those memories once and for all that India had returned to her family's Norfolk estate, pacing the vast, empty lawns from dawn to dusk.

But on this sunny September afternoon, India's memories were replaced by irritation at her brother. Frowning, she brought her fist to the slim hips covered by a pair of Ian's oldest breeches. "Tell the truth, Ian. You never could lie to me."

Her brother rubbed his jaw. "No? Well, perhaps I was coming to keep an eye on that ferocious pet of yours."

"Bosh. Luna and I are fine."

India sighed. Ian *had* been checking up on her, as the rest of her protective and entirely exasperating relatives had been doing ever since her return.

And all that time India had been careful to hide the real cause of her pain. Their pitying eyes would have been impossible to bear. So instead she haunted the lonely hills, licking her wounds in silence, while her family wondered what had happened to her in Brussels to put her in such a state.

Looking down, she smoothed the fur of the magnificent wolf that she had raised with such fierce protectiveness. She had rescued Luna from an angry mob of peasants outside Brussels. Now the creature followed India everywhere. At India's touch, the wolf gave a low, keening cry, almost as if aware of her dark thoughts.

India shook her head. "I could have shot you, Ian. These fools creep around the hills and do nothing but plague the gamekeeper, throwing rocks at the poor man and destroying his traps. It's all because of Luna." Hearing her name, the beautiful wolf looked expectantly at India, who ran one cheek along the silver fur. "I don't see why they're so frightened. Luna is perfectly harmless."

"For now perhaps," her brother said softly.

"But I've raised her since she was a cub. She wouldn't harm me or anyone else unless they attacked one of the family."

"You know that, but other people don't, India. They'll never give up fearing Luna because she is a wild creature. Because of that fear, they'll hate her. You must remember that, my love. Luna is safe, but only as long as she stays within the bounds of Swallow Hill."

India scuffed at a tuft of grass with one dusty boot. "I hate it when they throw rocks at her. I see them watching from the hills and I know they are just hoping for a clear shot. How can they be so bloody ignorant?"

Ian rested his hand lightly on India's shoulder. "It's the way of the world. We saw it in India with Father, and we saw it again in Egypt. I'm afraid there's not much chance of changing the way people think."

India saw the faint frown that creased her brother's forehead. "Are you going back, Ian?"

For a moment her brother's clear eyes darkened. "I can't say. Europe is still in chaos, even though Napoleon has been routed. There are still many who support the madman—even here in England."

"Surely not!"

"Princess Charlotte herself has expressed concern over what will happen to the man. There are many who whisper that the French emperor has been treated disgracefully and ought to be enshrined here in England rather than imprisoned on an island in the desolate reaches of the Atlantic." Ian looked down at the great wolf, his face harsh. "Often people fear what they shouldn't and admire what they ought to fear. You might be surprised at how many such men there are in England. But now I think we had better talk of something more pleasant."

"Well, I won't plague you with questions, since you're obviously sworn to secrecy." India looked out over the green lawns running down to the lake. "I suppose I shall have to give in and go to London, as Grandmama has been badgering me to do."

For months the Duchess of Cranford had been pestering her stubborn granddaughter to rejoin the social life of London. India had firmly refused, but knew she could not remain in this limbo forever. It was not fair to herself or to her family.

"It might be better than staying here and worrying yourself to death," Ian said softly.

"Oh, Ian, how can I? I can't bear the chatter and the inanity. Not now." She studied her brother, who had been in the thick of the slaughter at Waterloo. "You must know how I feel. I saw the wounded and dead in Brussels. So many of them." She looked away, hoping to hide the misery in her eyes.

Of course she didn't succeed. From her beloved brother, India Delamere could hide nothing. Though he took pains not to show it, Ian had seen every detail of her sadness.

"Maybe you need to do it for Grandmama. She's been in pain these days, India. Oh, she tries to hide it, but your trip would be do more for her than any medicine. Fretting over all those gowns, gloves, and balls would take her mind off this stiffness that grows daily in her joints."

India's eyes flew to her brother's face. "I didn't know, Ian. She always seems so indomitable."

"That she is, my dear. But she's in pain, just the same. And I'm afraid it is only going to grow worse."

India twisted her hands in the long flaps of the shirt she had stolen years before from Ian's wardrobe. "Then I shall have to let myself be poked and prodded like a pin cushion. How can I deny her, if it will distract her from the pain. But I won't stand for being paraded about London like a lump of horse-flesh at Tattersall's. I *certainly* won't stand for a passel of sharp-eyed knaves mauling me about."

Ian threw back his head and laughed. "Is that how you view us, my love? How positively lowering."

India gnawed her bottom lip thoughtfully. "Tell me, Ian, how do you know when—well, when you're in love? When you meet the one who is meant for you, do you feel it? Does your body shake and your heart sing, the way people always say?"

Her brother's eyes hardened. "I'm not sure I know, love. There's joy, of course, but I think it's the pain that tells us most. You feel a terrible sense of loss whenever you're not together—almost a kind of living death."

India's breath caught. "You've found someone, Ian. What a terrible fool I am. I've been so locked in my own world that I haven't seen *anything* going on around me." Impulsively, she pressed a kiss to her brother's cheek.

Ian's jaw locked, and then he laughed lightly. "You have a vast imagination, even for a Delamere."

But India wasn't deceived. "She's a fool, Ian. She isn't entitled to a minute of your concern. No woman of any sense could turn *you* down," India said fiercely.

"Do you think so, hoyden?" Ian gently ruffled his sister's hair. "And you so loyal, even after I threw you into the frog pond and broke your favorite painting set when you were six?"

India's lips twitched. "As I recall, I proceeded to break all your tin soldiers and then dumped you out of the hayloft in retaliation."

"So you did," Ian admitted, chuckling. "I still have the bruises to show for it."

"Then I propose we call ourselves even." India turned, hearing footsteps along the twisting path bordered by rose hedges.

"Ian? India? Where are you two? Don't think to go hiding from me!"

India frowned at her brother. "Grandmama? Why is she here?"

Ian looked faintly guilty. He knew that the duchess had already sent out invitations to a grand fete to be held at her London town house at the end of the following week. Although India did not know it yet, *she* was to be the guest of honor. "I suppose she is bent on some scheme or other."

"Not that dressmaker from London and crates of fabric, I hope."

Ian chuckled. "Most females would be panting for a creation of London's most select *modiste*."

"Not I," said India flatly. "The slippers pinch my toes and the stays are too tight for comfort."

But before India could continue cataloguing her complaints at the indignity of fashionable dress, the Duchess of Cranford was upon them, her eyes of robin's egg blue gleaming with animation. Her frail frame was perfectly upright and she leaned only slightly upon the silver-handled cane caught in a gloved hand. "I've been looking everywhere for the pair of you." The duchess shot an appalled glance at her granddaughter's male attire. "I thought we agreed that those clothes were to be burned, India Delamere!"

"No, we didn't. You demanded," the young woman said firmly. "I simply listened. Besides, these clothes are far too comfortable to burn."

"How do you hope to marry when you insist on running about dressed like a disreputable village urchin? Sweet heaven, you're covered with freckles and your hair is beyond taming!"

India shrugged. "I'm not interested in marrying."

There was a hint of sadness in her voice that made Ian and the duchess exchange worried looks.

"Not *interested*?" The duchess stamped her cane imperiously. "I've had three offers for your hand already this week, gel, and all of them were unexceptionable."

"Hmmm."

"Aren't you interested?"

"Hmmm."

"Don't you even want to know who they were from?"

"Not particularly."

Ian laughed and took each woman by the arm. "Come, let's not quarrel. Why not go back to the house and have some of that new souchong tea you had sent from China, Grandmama. After India's settled down, I'm sure she won't mind being fitted out for a few dresses."

"Humph. Don't forget the pelisses. And slippers and gloves and shawls and—"

Ian shot his sister a warning look.

"Humph," India repeated, but she did not pull away as Ian steered her past the rose hedges and up through the topiary garden to the beautiful stone house in the curve of the hill.

And though her face held a look of wariness, the duchess refrained from commenting when the beautiful silver wolf trotted happily behind them right into the house.

"It's too tight, Grandmama. I can't even *breathe*!"

"Nonsense. The dress is perfectly cut and the fit is superb."

India sniffed before her cheval glass. Patterned silks and exquisite Honneton lace spilled from hampers and cases spread over every corner of the second-story salon that the duchess had commandeered for their fitting session. India scowled down at the yards of écru satin that shimmered about her slender figure. "That's easy for you to say, Grandmama. *You* don't have to wear the thing."

"But the young mistress looks most enchanting," protested the dressmaker, removing a pin from her mouth. She was skillfully adding a final row of velvet braid to the gown's fashionably high waist. "The color is of the most fine to match my lady's hair."

The duchess's keen eyes ran over India's gown. "Passable," she said approvingly. "In fact, with that titian hair, I suspect you'll take London by storm, my dear. Of course, it's a pity there's nothing to be done about your freckles and those calluses all over your hands. Perhaps I'll try a pair of my chicken-skin gloves and a special rosewater cream for you to wear to bed at night."

"I won't, not even for you, Grandmama." India's face went mutinous. "Chicken-skin gloves, indeed! The idea is preposterous—this whole affair is preposterous, in fact. I don't want to go to London, I don't want to wear this gown, and I most certainly *don't* want a husband!" Her voice broke as she spun about, her fingers clenched on the fine lace at the window.

"That will be all for now, Madame Grès," the duchess said softly. "Froggett will show you to the servants' quarters for tea."

"Very good, Your Grace."

After the door had closed, the duchess moved to the window. As she suspected, tears glittered on India's radiantly healthy cheeks. "He's not worth it," the old woman said fiercely. "No man is worth your tears, India. Now you will tell me what happened in Brussels and why you came back white-faced and looking like your very heart had been torn out of your chest."

India took a long slow breath, her fingers twisting in the lace curtains. "I can't." Her eyes glistened with unshed tears. "I can't speak of it, Grandmama."

The Duchess of Cranford's white brow rose ominously. "Invitations have been sent out, India. There are five hundred people in London who expect to meet you next week."

"I *can't* go, Grandmama. I'm not ready."

"You've had well over a year to mourn this man, India. All that time I've watched and worried and held my peace. But the mourning must end. Whoever he was, he isn't going to come back."

"Man? I don't know what you mean," India said stiffly.

The duchess snorted. "Only a man could have put that stricken look in your eyes and taken away your laughter. You've gone and lost your heart, gel, and don't tell me you haven't. But now it's time to get on with your life. You owe it to your family and yourself, India. You've spent enough time buried in sadness."

India looked out the window. Down the hill lilies spilled in a pool of white against the green lawns of Swallow Hill. Here eight generations of Delameres had supported their sovereigns, pursued their wildly eccentric dreams, and left the world in some way richer than they had found it. Could she do the same?

India ran her hands along the velvet at her cuff. "I tell myself that every day, Grandmama. Maybe even *more* than every day. But then I hear a certain tone or I see a shadow—and suddenly I'm back at Lady Richmond's last party in Brussels. The carriages are clattering past and the soldiers are marching off to rejoin their regiments. And I can't seem to forget. Oh, I know he didn't love me because I was special." India put a hand on the window, oblivious to the priceless satin draping her slender body, indifferent as she always was to the vision she made with her vibrant hair and creamy skin. "I think he thought me—brave. But I'm not. Lately, I don't seem to have the heart left to do anything. I can't go to Lady Jersey's and titter about the Prince Regent's latest indiscretion as if nothing had happened. I've changed, Grandmama. *Everything* has changed." Her eyes darkened with memory. "After Waterloo, the wounded were crammed in carts and drays and wagons. There were no clean linens for bandages, no beds, and almost no suitable food." India shivered as she was swept back into the dark past. "We worked for hours at a time, losing most but saving some, fighting for whatever small piece of good we could do. And through it all I always thought—I always *prayed*—that I'd see one man walk out of the dust and smoke and turmoil. His step would be quick and his smile as jaunty as ever." Her voice broke. "But he didn't come, Grandmama. Not then or in the long weeks afterward. Now nothing will ever be the same again." India brushed at the tears she had concealed too long.

"Come here, you impossible child." The duchess tugged India into her arms. "Why didn't you tell me any of this sooner?"

"I couldn't. It all happened so—so quickly. And when the man I told you of didn't come back, I couldn't bear to discuss it. Not with anyone."

"My dear sweet gel," the duchess said huskily, smoothing India's hair. "You've come to womanhood by a rocky path, I fear. But face it you must. This man is gone. You have your whole life before you, no matter how impossible that seems now. You must find new joys and new challenges to live for, do you hear me?" The old woman made her voice stern. "You owe it to yourself and those who love you. You also owe it to the dashing man who's just waiting to have his heart stolen and his life overturned when you walk into that ballroom and pull him under your spell."

"Not for a second time," India said sadly. "Never again." She knew that kind of wild, blinding passion was forever beyond her. But her grandmother was right: she did owe a duty to her family and herself.

So she would go to London. She would wear her grandmother's chosen finery and attend all the balls and routs the duchess arranged for her. If a decent man of suitable family asked for her hand in marriage, India decided she would accept him, as long as he understood that her heart would not be given in the bargain.

For India Delamere knew she had no more heart to give. Not after she had given it to Devlyn Carlisle.

Outside the window came the low howl of a frightened animal. Instantly India turned, her eyes dark with anxiety. "That's Luna!" She shoved off her satin gown, revealing a pair of Ian's snug breeches.

"India Delamere, I told you no more of your brother's clothes!"

"Sorry, I must go, Grandmama." India grabbed up Ian's old white shirt and jerked it over her head, already halfway to the door. "If those repellent men have come back to shoot at Luna, I swear I'll fill their backsides full of buckshot."

The Duchess of Cranford shook her head as her stubborn granddaughter bolted out the door in a blur of leather and white cambric. Then slowly her lips curved up in a smile, for the white-haired duchess was recalling a particularly reckless exploit of her own that had taken place half a century before.

Shadows clung to the corners of the room and teased the tall figure braced at the mantel above the dancing fire. His eyes were the color of polished steel and his hair but one shade lighter than black.

But it was the mouth that set him as a man apart. Framed in tiny lines, the full lips showed that this man had once been quick to laughter.

But no more. Now the lips were tight and flat.

And there was no gaiety or joy about his hard shoulders or deeply tanned face, not this night of late autumn, 1816.

Home again, he thought, looking at the fine old prints, at the row of books and the intricate models of ships he had once made so patiently.

When had he made them? It seemed ten lifetimes ago.

He gripped the marble mantel and laughed then, the sound flat and bitter in the empty room. For he had begun to doubt he could ever truly go home again.

2

"Don't seem right. Not a bit right."

Resplendent in amethyst satin and puce velvet, the seventh viscount Monkton studied the glittering throng jamming the ballroom of the Duchess of Cranford's London town house. "Thorne ought to be here. He was always the charmed one. Don't know what he was doing on that blasted hill at Waterloo anyway." He sighed and stuck his quizzing glass back in his waistcoat pocket. "Nothing to see here. Same faces. Same tired stories. Not even any decent scandal this season." Suddenly he frowned. "Good lord, isn't that Wellington over there flirting with the Countess of Marchmont? Bad blood there, mark my words. Her husband isn't even a fortnight in the grave and she's prowling for new partners to fill her bed."

His friend, the Earl of Pendleworth, shook his head. "She prowled even *before* he was dead. But the problem with you, Monk, is you're spoiled. You always expect the best of people and most of them don't measure up."

"If I'm spoiled, it's Thorne's doing. He always knew how to do a thing devilish fine, Penn." As he spoke, Monkton's long face grew even more melan-

18

choly. "Don't seem right," he repeated. "Who else could race Alvanley to Brighton in his curricle, then be back in time to fight a duel of honor over an indiscretion with Repton's wife? The whole town's flat, I tell you. And I miss Thorne."

Lord Pendleworth's myopic eyes narrowed. "I beg you will conceal your *tristesse*, my dear Monk. From the things I saw during my brief time in Belgium, I've come to suspect that Lady Delamere had a tendre for Thorne, and it won't do to go dredging up her sadness with more memories. She's only just come back to London, you know. When I saw her yesterday on Bond Street, she was looking decidedly pale."

Monkton toyed with his embroidered waistcoat. "I don't mean to avoid the subject, if that's what you're hinting at, Penn. Thorne was my best friend. Besides, if the lady is so fickle to forget him already, I want nothing more to do with her."

"Monk, my idiot, it's been well over a year. Even a Delamere heiress must eventually think of her future. She must marry and marry well. The Duke of Devonham is a doting parent, but even his patience must begin to grow short. I've heard her grandmother's been trotting eligible suitors back and forth, but India refuses to look at any of them. All except for Longborough, perhaps."

Monkton snorted. "Longborough?" He studied a sober figure standing among the dowagers. "I don't believe it. The fellow's got no sense of color and even less notion of how to tie a cravat. Don't make a bit of sense to me how India could ever consider such a creature for a husband."

"Perhaps the lady looks for something other than the skillful fall of a cravat in a husband when she accepts a proposal," his companion said with awful irony.

"Being damned clever again, Penn. Don't like it. Can't follow a word in ten when you turn clever and speak in that prodigious cold tone. Wish Thorne were here. *He* always knew how to handle you. Stap me if I do." Shaking his head, the viscount heaved a long sigh. "And I don't give a damn what you say, here's to Thorne. Best friend any of us ever had. Never made me feel my wits were all to let. Always managed to lend a spare guinea without reading a lecture. Taught me how to tie my first Mathematical knot, too." Of the three, this last skill was clearly the highest accolade for Monkton. "Here's to you, Devlyn Carlisle, wherever you are. You're bloody well missed back here."

Out in the street, beyond the clattering carriages, beyond the jewel-clad women, beyond the urchins in tattered shirts lined up for a look at the gentry in all their splendor, a man stood surveying the Duchess of Cranford's brightly lit ballroom.

He was a tall man swathed in a heavy, caped riding coat. His eyes were brooding, their silvery depths aglint in the moonlight.

Travelers swirled around him. Grimy children begged for a spare pence. But the sober figure gave no notice. His eyes were locked on the windows of the ballroom at the far side of the square.

The Watch moved past, then stopped. "Lost, are you? New to London, mayhap?"

The man seemed to rouse himself. His lips took on a bitter smile. "Not lost. I've merely been . . . gone some months."

"Looking for an address, are you? Or information

about a certain resident? Someone you were fond of?"

The silver eyes narrowed. "I have all the information I shall need."

At the hardness in his tone, the Watch took an involuntary step back. "Well, then, I'll be off. Clearly, you're not in need of me."

There was no answer from the broad-shouldered figure in the shadows. He only frowned, studying the light at the far side of the square. Before him the road stretched dark, like a gorge that separated him from the man he had been before Waterloo.

For he was Devlyn Carlisle and he was alive, yet not quite alive.

He was returned, yet not truly returned. He fingered his chest, where a French cavalry sword had laid him low in the Belgian mud. There he'd lain for two days before his body was finally discovered.

Memories . . .

Always too many memories. And of *her*, not enough.

He slid his hat lower and moved into the glittering throng spilling toward Devonham House. He would have to work to make his way inside in this crush. All London had turned out to see the duchess's granddaughter, it seemed.

And though it was utterly rash, Devlyn could not keep from joining them.

As he turned down a side street, Thornwood's face slid into view, all hard lines and angles. And in the glow of the lamplight the scar at his jaw gleamed with cold brilliance.

White candles danced in the warm wind, ruffling the elegant lace curtains. The air was warm and the room was quiet, scented with a vase of roses from the duchess's conservatory.

Yet India Delamere shivered, unnaturally cold as she stood before the cheval glass, a pleated and tucked chemise hugging her slender body. Lace edged her neck and creamy shoulders. Long kid gloves lay nearby, along with her mother's pearl and diamond choker.

India knew she should dress. Her family was waiting below. The carriages had finally clattered past and all the guests had arrived.

And still India stood frozen, stroking the teal damask. Her father had told her the exquisite satin had come from the far workshops of imperial China, where the fabric had been loomed for the empress herself.

But the blue only made India think of a cool, boundless sky and the din of an army on the march. It made her remember Brussels at the end of spring, a city of desperate gaiety perched on the razor's edge of war.

And it made her think of a man with a hard mouth and eyes of slate-gray. A man who had kissed her, then marched away under that sky.

To some he was Thorne, the most dashing of a generation of dashers. But to his fellow officers, he was a legend as much for his charm as for his reckless courage. India would never forget her last sight of him, recently recovered from fever but determined to rejoin his regiment in the muddy fields of corn and rye.

Fields which would be long known as Waterloo.

Her hands tightened on the cool damask.

In the madness of those frantic weeks she had offered him her heart. Though Devlyn, too, had been struck, he had been resolute in protecting her honor. He had put her off with all his exquisite courtesy, and no one, it was said, could resist the charm of a Carlisle.

India hadn't been able to. Not then. Not later, when a nightingale singing in a garden full of roses had been the final spur to their blinding passion.

India had melted in his arms, all fire and yearning. Her honest desire had been more than Thornwood could resist and by the morning they were lovers.

He had been bound by her innocence and honesty, bemused and enchanted by her spirit. Had there been more time, that enchantment might have grown to something far deeper.

But Devlyn Carlisle had been a stranger to deep emotions.

In all his life he had had only a few moments of such wrenching contact. His mother had been more concerned with pin money than her son's needs, while his father had been too hardened a gamester to care for anything beyond his next game of faro. As a result Devlyn had learned to fear any feeling beyond his control or understanding.

And what he had felt for India Delamere went *far* beyond both.

India had glimpsed these things dimly, from the few comments Devlyn had made about his cold upbringing. Soon she came to see that they were moth and flame, fire and ice, she sprung from a warm and boisterous family and he from a succession of rigid servants who replaced an unfeeling mother and careless father. They had just begun to learn from each other's strengths when Dev was called back to his regiment.

So India had fought back her tears and smiled, then kissed him. Devlyn had given her one last, reckless, heartbreaking smile. Then he'd gone off to die.

And India's heart had died with him.

"India? Are you there, gel?"

The door creaked open. India sat up with a start as she saw her grandmother glaring at her from the dressing room. "I'm here, Grandmama."

"That blasted wolf isn't hidden in here, is it?"

India busied herself at the mirror, her face hidden. "Of course not. It's out in the stables, just as you demanded."

"Humph." The duchess frowned at India. "Why aren't you dressed? Here's the whole ton come out for a glimpse of you and you're mooning by the window!" Clucking loudly, the imperious old woman pulled the gleaming damask from India's bed and slid it over her granddaughter's ivory shoulders. "Whatever are you about, gel!" Her voice was tight with concern. "Your brother Luc is already below, with his wife at his side. And a lovely couple they make, too. Silver's figure is quite restored from her recent *accouchement,*" the duchess added, while she tugged and smoothed the lines of India's dress.

All the while India tried to smile, tried to summon the enthusiasm to face the crush of guests below. "How . . . lovely. It will be a delight to see Silver again. Are the twins still in the country?"

The duchess snorted. "Not a bit of it! Luc's packed the two into the nursery with their new nanny. He swears he and Silver can't bear to be away from the tow-headed rascals for even a night. Unnatural, if you ask me," the duchess added crossly.

But India knew that despite her frown, the duchess was delighted to be near her great-grandchildren. The imperious old woman simply considered it undignified to reveal such emotional attachments.

As the duchess fretted over her gloves, India listened to the strains of the waltz drifting up the stairs. There must be six hundred people thronging the ballroom, hoping for a glimpse of her elder brother, who was newly returned to London after being thought dead for five long years. The ton was also hoping for a glimpse of Luc's beautiful, russet-haired young wife, of course.

India hoped her brother would draw some of the attention away from her. She was little in the mood for small talk and idle laughter tonight.

She frowned at her face in the cheval glass. Too pale. Eyes too dark, cheekbones too sharp, and lips too wide. She had seen how men reacted to her mouth, eyeing it almost hungrily.

The gesture had always made her shudder.

All except *once*.

When one man had looked at her so, India had known instantly that this man was different. And when Devlyn Carlisle had kissed her, she had felt only heat and desperate longing.

Oh, Dev, why did you have to go? Why couldn't you have come back to me? Nothing will ever be the same again.

"India Delamere, where have your wits gone wandering?" The duchess shoved a fine sandalwood fan into her granddaughter's hands. "Your poor benighted brothers are downstairs trying to hold off half of London and here you are daydreaming."

India caught a deep breath and shoved her pain deep, where it wouldn't show. When she turned, her eyes were cool and her chin was high. She had her Delamere pride at least. "I don't know who he was or what he did to you," the duchess said fiercely, "but it's time you put the man behind you." Her fragile fingers closed over India's for a moment. "If he had *any* sort of decency, he'd have come back for you. Waterloo's over a year past!"

India sighed.

Her grandmother was right. Waterloo *was* behind her.

And she wouldn't let the world see her bleed. She was a Delamere after all. She had too much pride to wear her heart on her sleeve!

"Your brothers are waiting by the foot of the stairs. They'll squire you through the crowd. Those two friends of yours, Monkton and Pendleworth, are wishing to see you, as is Connor MacKinnon, Luc's friend. Let's not keep them waiting any longer, shall we?"

"You're so good to me, Grandmama," India said softly. "Luc, Ian, Silver—all of you. Far too good."

"Nonsense. I'm only doing what those two restless parents of yours would wish. You would think they had had enough adventuring around the world for antiquities by now." The old woman shook her head. "Meanwhile, just you remember we love you and want to see you happy."

If only I were, India thought.

But she raised her head and gave her titian hair a final careless glance, adjusting one teal satin sleeve to a rakish slant. "Very well, Grandmama, I believe I am ready. Let us go and find a few male hearts to break, shall we?"

Arm in arm, the two women descended the broad stairway to the glittering ballroom. Candlelight gleamed on the duchess's pearls and shimmered over the camellias pinned artlessly in India's up-swept hair.

At the sight of Lady India Delamere's flawless face

and smoky blue eyes, four score male hearts shattered in their brawny owners' chests.

The night was young. The brash Corsican was defeated and the world was free of his tyranny at last. Tonight all England was determined to celebrate.

And India Delamere, dying quietly inside, feigned smile after gay smile as she became the toast of glittering London society.

Somehow the evening passed.

Viscount Monkton was charming and vapid as usual, while his friend Pendleworth worked very hard at making India laugh. But they could not know that their mere presence was a wound to her heart, for she knew both had been friends of Thorne.

India had managed a steady flow of laughter, hoping that she had fooled her friends. In their wake had come Lord Longborough, resplendent in crimson and green damask, pressing her to retire outside to the gallery while he brought her a glass of iced punch.

And a proposal, too, India suspected.

She had prudently declined his escort, unable to face a matrimonial offer from Longborough or anyone else. Determinedly, she had danced a waltz with each of her handsome brothers, then a third with Luc's exotic friend Connor MacKinnon. After that she had refused all other offers.

Beside her two officers argued over who would have the honor of fetching punch and crab cakes for her. India tried not to smile at their foolishness and impudence. She was feeling strangely reckless after three glasses of champagne. There was too much laughter, too many jewels. The ballroom was hot, and everywhere she was crushed by jeweled and perfumed bodies.

Suddenly a wave of dizziness swept over India and she caught herself with a hand on the dashing lieutenant's arm. He gave her a delighted smile, while his brother officer looked on with an expression of burning fury.

India could only stare at the pair of them as if they were schoolboys. She felt so old standing next to them, letting the laughter and the gossip and the rich perfumes drift past her in waves.

So very old . . .

And yet she was barely twenty.

Perhaps she had seen too much in the days of anguish following Waterloo. Perhaps the lingering memory of the sickness and suffering after the great battle had changed her forever.

Sighing, India hid her momentary unsteadiness and released her adoring lieutenant's arm. She looked about for her brothers, desperate to make good her escape. Nearby the newly widowed Lady Marchmont tittered sharply, regaling a group of admirers with a blithe account of how she had lost five hundred pounds in a single hour of play the week before. One man suggested a way she could recover her losses—in his arms.

India turned away, her head throbbing. The air was too close, the laughter too loud, the perfumes too cloying.

As if in answer to her prayer, the crowd parted. Light from the gleaming chandelier slanted down on a crimson regimental coat looped with gold braid. Dancing candles played over a pair of broad shoulders and eyes of iron-gray.

Thorne.

India felt her knees sway.

It was impossible! The Earl of Thornwood was dead, cut down in the first fierce charge at Waterloo. Three of his fellow officers had seen his horse fall in a field overlooking the crossroads. Then had come the savage thrust from a French cavalry saber.

Dead.

She had read the reports herself.

Yet there he stood, light wreathing him all in gold, softening the harsh planes of his brooding face. He looked older, harder, sadder.

"—far too pale, my lady—"

"—must let me find you something to drink—"

Dimly, so dimly India heard the anxious questions. But her heart, her very soul, stayed locked upon the light-wreathed figure staring at her in taut silence across the crowded dance floor.

Abruptly, her grandmother's fingers circled her arm. "India, what's wrong? You're as pale as my narcissus buds."

India trembled. "He's come back, Grandmama," she said softly.

"*Who's* come back?"

"The man I told you about. He's *here*." Giddily, India spun back to the crowded floor, color filling her cheeks, joy burning in her unusual, uptilted eyes.

But the silent figure in the regimental coat was gone. Two matrons now stood chatting amiably beneath the dancing candles.

India caught back a cry, feeling her heart shatter.

She was reaching out to empty air when the polished floor rushed up to meet her.

And one pair of eyes darkened, watching from the shadows as she slid into her grandmother's arms.

* * *

Thanks to her brother's swift response, India's lapse was noticed by only a few. Ian had carried her into the study, and her name had barely begun to be whispered when a new item of gossip swept throughout the room.

The name of a soldier thought long dead.

"Is it really him?" two matrons whispered avidly, head to head.

"It *can't* be."

"But it is. There's no mistaking that cool smile. Just like Thornwood to come striding in, all arrogant charm, not a seam out of place. A perfect Carlisle, every wretched inch of him. As coldhearted as that gamester father of his. Even worse a rakehell, so I hear."

Fans waved, brows furrowed, and one name ran from mouth to mouth as the tall, broad-shouldered officer in scarlet regimentals moved silently through the ballroom. Devlyn Carlisle seemed to have emerged from the grave into the height of the London season, not a bit the worse for wear beyond a small silver scar at his jaw.

And he showed not the slightest bit of interest in the stir he was causing.

Only Monkton and Pendleworth, crowding close to offer their shocked welcome, noted Thornwood's stiffness and a grimness they had never before seen in his face.

"Dash it, Thorne, is it really you?" Monkton was the first to reach the slate-eyed officer. "But how—when—that is, stap me, man, we heard you were *dead!*"

The gray eyes narrowed. "Obviously not. But forgive me, have we met?"

"Of course we've met! It's me, Monkton. Don't tell

me you've forgotten who I am. Outside of enough, by Jove!"

There was a faint tightening in the full lips. "As it happens, that is exactly what I am saying. I have forgotten—Monkton, is it?"

"Forgotten? By Gad—"

Pendleworth's fingers cut off his friend's protest. "This is not the time or place for such a discussion, Monk." He studied the officer's hard, bronzed face. "At White's, shall we say?"

Devlyn Carlisle's brow rose. "Unfortunately, I must excuse myself. I have pressing duties tonight."

"But—"

Again Pendleworth interrupted his friend. "Quite understandable. Sometime soon, then."

But Monkton continued to stare after those broad, retreating shoulders, pale as if he'd seen a ghost. "He doesn't know me, Penn. And he's changed. The same, yet somehow not the same at all."

"I think that is part of what he was trying to tell us, Monk."

"But what are we to do? Can't let the man act a total stranger. It's—it's infamous!"

Pendleworth's eyes narrowed. "Perhaps we have no choice."

Hundreds of others also noted Devlyn's progress through the crowded room. Men shook their heads in grudging admiration, while beside them bejeweled women preened and tittered, hoping to summon a look of heated memory from that hard, tanned face.

But none came.

The Earl of Thornwood moved through the crowd like a shark through a school of ineffectual, irritating minnows. And one by one, the others began to notice the changes in him. He was harder now, and leaner. His eyes looked twenty years older, full of shadows and regret. And the few smiles he gave never seemed to reach those shadows in his slate-gray eyes.

Helena Marchmont, in particular, watched in silent fascination as Carlisle strode past. Her fan waved and her lips curved in a slight pout, both of which went unnoticed.

Nearby, the Duke of Wellington blinked once before picking up the threads of his conversation.

And the Duchess of Cranford, just emerged from the study, frowned as Wellington turned and made his way toward her.

"A lovely party, Amelia. I am delighted I could fit it in, since I will be staying in England for only a few days before returning to the Continent. But I trust that your granddaughter is not ill."

The duchess summoned up a false smile. "India? The girl's healthy as a horse. I expect it's just the heat and crush. She's unaccustomed to balls."

"She was in Brussels, I think? I seem to remember her from Lady Richmond's ball."

The duchess was amazed that the duke could recall such a detail in a night that must have been sheer chaos on the eve of Waterloo. "So she was. She stayed on afterward, too. I'm afraid the war left its mark on her."

"As it did on all of us," Wellington said grimly. "The victory was hard won, indeed. Still, she'll forget. If gossip runs true, Lord Longborough as well as several score of junior officers would be only too happy to teach her how."

The duchess frowned at the door of the study where India now lay resting. Longborough was a spineless fool and the junior officers not much better. What India needed was a man of courage and honor, a man with the adventurous spirit to match hers. The duchess remembered how the girl's joy had slid into shattering pain when she had looked across the crowded room that evening.

But why?

"You are certain there is nothing I can do to help?"

"Nothing. You are more than kind, but my grand-daughter will be fine. Just enjoy yourself. Of course, if you should happen to hear Lady Jersey spreading cattish tales about my granddaughter going into a decline, I would be most grateful if you would cut them off promptly, Your Grace."

"I'd be delighted. Ah, there's an old friend up from Sussex. I really should—" The duke stopped suddenly, his body rigid.

"Your Grace, is something wrong? You look most strange."

Wellington straightened his sleeve, eyes on the thronged ballroom. "It is . . . nothing. For a moment I thought I saw the face of someone I knew. Forgive me."

The duchess frowned, turning back to the study. She had sent a servant to fetch the family physician from Montagu Street. He was old, but thorough. He had tended India since her birth, though the girl had been sick only twice that the duchess could recall.

Behind the duchess came a peal of Lady Jersey's high-pitched laughter followed by Helena Marchmont's irritating titter. Shrews, both of them, the duchess thought. She only prayed that Wellington would do his part to scotch any gossip about India's condition.

But let a single soul try to say a word to *her*, the

duchess vowed. Every inch of her tiny frame went stiff at the thought. Family had always come first in her life, and any people attacking India would soon find themselves cut into tiny ribbons.

And the duchess would be only too delighted to begin with Lady Jersey and that fox-faced Helena Marchmont.

But India's illness did not become the byword of the evening that it had promised to become. A new source of curiosity had gripped the ton in the arresting sight of its greatest rake turned valiant soldier, newly returned from the dead.

Wellington, too, had noticed Thornwood. He nodded coolly to his former aide and for a moment their eyes met, turquoise to slate. Without another word the duke left the room.

Only Ian Delamere, standing just outside the study, noticed the faint nod that the duke had made before he left.

And it was Ian, his face hard with purpose, who ran Thornwood down in the broad alcove of the duchess's town house where the earl had gone to make his departure from the ball he obviously found of little interest.

"A word, if you please."

Thornwood turned slowly. His brow rose. "Yes?"

"Have you nothing to say, man?" Ian stared in amazement at the officer with whom he had marched through Portugal and the snows of half of Spain. "I thought you were dead. We all did."

"An obvious error, as you can see."

"But where have you been all these months?" Ian's eyes narrowed. "If it's something secret, of course, just tell me to go to the devil."

"Not at all." Devlyn's face was expressionless. "I am merely . . . tired."

Ian grabbed his wrist. "Damn it, I saw you cut down by that saber, Thornwood! Now talk to me."

"The cut was less than accurate. I was left . . . quite uncomfortably at the bottom of a pile of dead bodies. It was three days before I was discovered, so I am told."

"Told?"

Thornwood toyed with the white edge of one smooth cuff. "You seem determined to draw me into tedious explanations. Do I know you?"

Ian snorted. "I should bloody think so. We fought together at Badajoz and again at Vimeiro. You saved my life twice, and I certainly won't forget that."

The Earl of Thornwood's mouth hardened. "I see. That makes this all rather complicated, I fear."

"Damn it, Thornwood, stop speaking in riddles."

"I am merely being straightforward. I do not know who you are, nor anyone else in that room behind you. I am here because this seemed the quickest way to . . ."

"To do what?"

"To make the truth known."

"*What* truth?"

Thornwood sighed. "Must we discuss this now?"

"Right now. Right here." Ian's arms crossed at his chest. "I want to know where in the devil you've been."

"Very well, the truth is that the Thornwood you see is not the Thornwood you knew. The man you knew—the man all those other people in that ballroom knew—is gone forever, his memories and mind left in a muddy cornfield in Belgium."

"You're joking."

Thornwood's eyes went wintry. "Am I?"

"But, my God, man, you can't expect me to believe—"

"Frankly, I don't care what you believe. That is the truth, and you may take it how you will."

"So that's why you never came back."

Thornwood shrugged. "It was some months before I was even able to walk unassisted. As time passed, my wounds healed—all except the ones in my head." He smiled grimly. "So now you understand that I meant you no rudeness. It is simply that for me, there is no past. All I am, all I know began fourteen months ago as I emerged to consciousness swathed in dirty bandages in a smelly farmhouse near the border of France. And now I trust you will excuse me. It has been a long evening and I find I am tired." The earl took his gloves and hat from the footman standing impassively at the door. "I would appreciate it if you saw to it that your friends understood the situation. I would not choose to give willful offense, but neither would I care to offer false hope. The old Earl of Thornwood is dead," he finished flatly.

"I don't believe it."

"You *must* believe it." For a moment desperation swirled through Thornwood's eyes, but it quickly disappeared. "My past is gone. The sooner you and the others accept that, the better it will be for all of us. I simply want to be left in peace. Do not try to find me or talk to me, do you understand?"

After long moments, Ian nodded stiffly.

"Thank you for that, at least. And now good night."

As Ian watched Thornwood stride down the steps to a waiting carriage, he felt every nerve screaming. It was wrong, all of it. Thornwood, the man he had known through months of war, would never have been so cold and aloof.

Unless he had told the truth. Unless it was just as he had said, and the wounds of battle had destroyed the old Thornwood forever.

Ian didn't like it. He wasn't even sure he believed it. Then he frowned, thinking of India, pale and trembling as he had carried her into the study.

If Thornwood had something to do with *that*, by heaven he'd pay dearly, Ian swore. But he knew he'd have no luck prying anything more out of his stubborn sister, who insisted her lapse had been caused by a case of nerves exacerbated by the heat of the ballroom.

Nerves?

India Delamere had *never* been overcome by nerves in her life, Ian knew.

Which meant there were too many secrets she was keeping from him.

"Why, damn it?" Ian studied the silent hall and the open door. "Why, Thornwood? Why here and why now, of all times?"

But there was no answer. The steps were empty and the lean-faced officer had disappeared into his carriage.

Ian was still staring thoughtfully out into the darkness long after the last hoofbeats had faded away into silence.

3

"India? India, do you *hear* me?" The Duchess of Cranford looked down, frowning. "What's happened to her, Ian? She was fine when I left, but she appears to have fainted again."

"She was fine when *I* left, too," India's brother said worriedly.

At that moment India blinked and opened her eyes.

Two tense faces stared back at her—the duchess, frail and imperious, and Ian looking angry.

"Fetch Luc and his wife," the duchess ordered.

"No, I don't want to worry them. Please, I'll be fine." India struggled to sit up. "After all, this was to be their grand return to London. I couldn't bear spoiling their evening." She caught her grandmother's fragile hand. "*Please*, Grandmama."

"Very well," the old woman said at last. "But you must tell me what's amiss."

"I've disgraced myself again, I suppose," said India, who had occasioned comment too often to count, beginning when she was fourteen and had gone shooting at Manton's with Ian, much to her father's delight—and her grandmother's consternation.

At that moment her older brother strode in, frowning. "India?"

"I'm fine, Luc. Truly, you shouldn't have—"

"India? My dear, what happened?" Luc's auburn-haired wife entered the room close on the heels of her husband.

India sighed. "Everyone saw, I suppose. Tomorrow I will be the gossip of London. I can see it all clearly. 'Youngest Delamere struck down into a decline before the eyes of six hundred fascinated guests.'"

But the duchess patted her hand. "Nonsense. Very few people noticed, I assure you. What's important is how you feel now."

"I'm fine, truly. It was simply the heat and the crush of bodies."

The duchess frowned. She decided not to tell India about the evening's other surprise, the only thing that had kept her from being on everyone's lips right now. Not that it mattered. The girl probably didn't even know Devlyn Carlisle, who was at least eight years older than she was.

Luc Delamere sat down beside his sister, trying to keep the worry from his face. "You must come stay with us in Norfolk. Silver's been blending a new fragrance at Lavender Close and I know she'd be delighted for your company." He shot his wife a lazy grin. "The truth is, she gets decidedly irritable in this stage of her work and wants nothing to do with me."

India squeezed her brother's hand, noticing how happy he looked. She felt a trace of envy, then forced it away guiltily. Luc had endured years of pain and India could never begrudge him his happiness. "That is very kind, Luc, but I don't care to intrude, not when you have those two lovely rascals to keep you occupied. And don't *you* go thinking up invitations either, Grandmama. I shall do quite nicely back at Swallow Hill. All I need is exercise and fresh air. I shall pack a portmanteau and leave tonight, and take Froggett with me."

"You'll do no such thing," the Duchess of Cranford said indignantly. "Travel alone at night? I won't hear of it!"

"I'm afraid Grandmama is right, India. The roads are far too dangerous." Luc laughed grimly. "Given my years riding those roads, I should know the dangers. Wait till morning and we'll send you down by coach. I'd love to go myself, but buying supplies for Silver's new fragrance will keep us in town for another week at least."

"What about you, Ian?" the duchess demanded.

The broad-shouldered soldier with the deceptively sleepy gray eyes shook his head. "I'm afraid I cannot leave London just yet. I've—affairs of my own that keep me here for a fortnight."

"Another mission for Wellington?" Luc looked thoughtful. "Don't shoot me that cross look, Ian. I promise I won't try to worm it out of you."

"I wish you would all stop being so wretchedly *helpful*," India muttered, sitting up on the thick velvet cushions. "I'll be *fine*. All I need is some time away."

But it was a lie. India was afraid she'd never be fine again. Her family were all so kind and concerned, but she could never tell them the truth about everything that had happened during her months in Belgium. So, as she had always done before, India simply locked her pain deep and summoned up an entirely false smile.

The smile she kept for a world that had ceased to hold any interest for her.

"And as for leaving, tomorrow will do fine," she lied calmly.

Her loving relatives nodded, and some of the concern left their faces.

But as India accepted a glass of ratafia from Ian, she was already planning the contents of the single portmanteau she would carry when she rode out of London that night.

The moon sailed over the tile roofs and slid behind rows of twisting chimneys as India made her way silently downstairs. Clutching a cloak and battered hat beneath one arm, she crept past six generations of haughty Delameres, who stared down from their portraits in patent disapproval of her reckless plan.

Around her the house was quiet. The guests had all departed, well pleased with the evening's rich gossip. Once more the Delameres had lived up to their reputation for providing London with delicious scandal.

It was that knowledge that made India determined to leave London. She was too upset to bear the curious looks that were sure to come. She had finished stuffing a gown and two pairs of breeches into her bag and tugged on a voluminous and outdated gown, chosen precisely because of its ability to conceal the riding boots and old breeches that she wore beneath.

She was nearly to the front door when the study door was thrown open. She shrank into the shadows behind a robust statue of Diana that her father had brought back from one of his visits to Greece. Crouching low, she shoved her portmanteau out of sight just as Ian and Luc emerged from the study and walked slowly toward the front staircase.

"I wish it were so simple," Ian said. "But there's already been talk. It seems that the man is entirely aloof since his return."

"Odd business. He was anything *but* aloof before Waterloo." Luc's face was hard.

India frowned, wishing her brothers would hurry off so that she could be away.

"What does Wellington think?"

Ian smiled faintly. "Who in heaven ever knows what the Great Man is thinking? He's utterly unreadable when he wishes to be."

"Do you think his story is true?"

What story? India thought irritably.

Ian shrugged, red wool stretching across the hard muscles earned in skirmishes in Portugal and Spain. "I wish I knew. It's been chaos over there, Luc. Even now plots are boiling and spies are everywhere. Anything is possible and, lately, I've come to believe that where the French are concerned, no news is bad news."

"But surely with Napoleon's defeat all that has changed."

Ian laughed grimly. "Has it? Tell that to the people who believe the Corsican has been treated shamefully since his surrender. Tell that to Princess Charlotte, who has herself taken a great interest in Napoleon's welfare."

Luc frowned. "I had no idea. Is there anything I can do to help?"

Ian clasped his brother's shoulder. "Even if there were, I wouldn't ask it of you, Luc. You've had too much trouble of your own to be embroiled in any more. Besides, if there's a way of finding the truth, Wellington will manage it. The grim memories of Waterloo still eat at him, I assure you. Just as I'm afraid they eat at India."

Behind the statue, India stiffened.

Ian looked down at the fine Persian carpet. "She misses him far more than she'll ever admit. She loved him, Luc. As I told you, I saw the two of them together once in Brussels. I was carrying dispatches and in a terrible hurry, or I would have stopped. But it made no difference. She and Thornwood might have been a million miles away, for all they noticed me or anyone else."

India's fingers locked at her waist. Ian *knew. He had seen them together.*

She fought a wave of dizziness.

"I don't want her to hear this as gossip, Luc. That would be too cruel. See that she gets out of London and back to Swallow Hill. Meanwhile, I'll go over to Belgrave Square and find out what in hell Thorne's doing back in London."

Thorne? Back in London?

India locked her fingers to her mouth. He was *here*? The man she loved had not died amid the chaos of Waterloo? Could it be that he was even now less than ten blocks away, ensconced in his elegant town house in Belgrave Square?

A roaring filled India's ears, nearly drowning out the rest of her brothers' words.

"When do you mean to tell her?"

Ian frowned. "Not yet. I want to find out what Thorne's up to first. I won't stand for India being hurt any more. If it's over for Thorne, we'll have to find a way to break it to her gently. But if there's something more involved and Thorne is in some kind of danger, I want India well out of it, or she could become a target, too. Not that the little hellion would care about that. She seems to thrive on danger."

At that moment India slipped. Her foot struck Diana's marble knee.

The two men turned. Frowning, Ian strode toward the shadowed alcove where India lay crouched, her heart hammering. Suddenly the duchess's voice rang out over the stairwell. "Ian? Luc?"

Luc caught his brother's arm. "You don't mean to tell the duchess, do you? There will be hell to pay if you do, for Gran will want to know every detail. In fact, I'm astounded she hasn't already ferreted the truth out of India. Had it happened here in London, she would have known everything by now. But if India doesn't care to speak of it, I think we should keep her secret as long as we can."

Ian nodded. "Agreed. Although if India continues to go about looking so gloomy and pale, I don't guarantee to keep the promise for long. Do you think we should write to Father and ask him to bring Mother home?"

"Not just yet," Luc said thoughtfully. "Let's give it a little more time. But I understand exactly how you feel, Ian. It rips at my heart to see her so little like her old self. In fact, I've half a mind to go strangle some answers out of Thornwood myself."

"Better leave it to me, Luc." Ian's voice fell as they moved off, for the Duchess of Cranford had come out into the hall and was glaring at them.

Hidden in the shadows, India watched them go. Her fingers gripped the cold marble of the statue.

Thorne was alive? But if so, why had he not contacted her? Was he ill? Or had all his vows been forgotten so soon?

India knew there would be no rest for her until she had the answers from his own lips.

* * *

India pulled up the hood of her velvet cloak and hurried through the darkness, her eyes moving neither right nor left. The streets around her were quiet. Only a few bored coachmen dozed in their hackneys, while a pair of drunken exquisites stumbled over the cobblestones.

India barely noticed, struggling with a storm of emotions.

What had happened to Dev? Was he ill or suffering from deep wounds? Even if so, why hadn't he sent her a message? But she had no answers, of course. She strode over the cobblestones, oblivious to the admiring looks and murmured comments directed at her by an occasional link boy or footman.

Dev had described his town house to her, and India knew its location perfectly. She marched up the steps under the watchful eyes of a pair of stone lions, her heart pounding.

Just as she lifted the brass knocker, a frowning butler with silver-gray hair threw open the door. "May I help you?"

"I'm looking for Lord Thornwood."

"He is, er, occupied." Steady brown eyes took in India's dusty skirts and narrowed. "You would do best to send a note around to his lordship tomorrow. Now I bid you good—"

"I *must* see him." India brushed past the man into the broad foyer. Rows of keen-eyed Carlisles smiled down lazily from gilt-framed portraits. At the end of the hall a silver candelabrum burned outside a half-opened door. "There is no need to announce me."

"Really, miss, I must protest. This is not at all the thing. Who are you to push in here unannounced, demanding to see Lord Thornwood?"

"Who am I?" Something dark and wounded came and went in India's eyes. "I am his *wife*."

4

The butler's face paled. "Wife?" he repeated.

"Wife." India's fingers locked. "Please, where is he?"

"Er, through there, miss—er, my lady." In his surprise, the butler nearly stumbled over an ornate Hepplewhite end table to the right of the door. "But you can't—"

"Chilton, is that you?" A husky voice echoed from beyond the half-opened door. "Where is that port I asked you to fetch?"

It was a voice India knew well.

A voice she had thought never to hear again.

She swayed a little, one hand pressed to the wall, her face going pale. So it *was* true. The man she had seen in the ballroom had been no empty illusion. Up until that moment, India had thought it must be a mistake.

"Are you all right, miss?" the butler asked anxiously.

India took an unsteady breath and nodded, her head filled with a thousand questions. What would he be like? How would he have changed after all these months apart?

"Chilton, are you there?" Again the low, familiar

voice rang out. India shivered, remembering the first time she had heard that voice in the middle of a crowded and very muddy Belgian street. The tall officer had caught her bonnet, blown off in a stiff spring wind.

His look had been frankly admiring. "I find myself in a cruel dilemma, faced with two crimes. I am not sure which is the greater," he had added huskily.

A smile had tugged at India's lips as she watched him study her face, mesmerized. "Indeed?" she had asked softly. "And what crimes might they be?"

He had not spoken for a moment, his eyes narrowed. For the barest instant his fingers had brushed hers, and India had felt the touch churn all the way to the soft soles of her kidskin boots, mired deep in the mud of the Brussels street.

With slow grace he had bowed, proffering the charming straw bonnet with the tiny decoration of wild strawberry blossoms. "The first crime would be for such a lovely lady to lose this fetching bonnet." His gaze had risen, burning over her face. "But for me to return it would be even worse."

"And why is that?" India had asked unsteadily, feeling the heat of his gaze, tasting the raw power radiated by this stranger.

"Because then you would only use it to hide the most remarkable pair of eyes I have ever seen." His voice had darkened. "And surely the most beautiful mouth."

Even now India felt a knot form in her throat at the memory. Had they been merely words? Had Thorne's gallantry been only as lasting as their time together?

India's hands clenched. She refused to believe it.

His emotion had been as real as her own. There must be some other explanation for his absence.

But now everything would be wonderful. He was back, and all the pain would be past.

At that moment the study door swung open. A broad-shouldered figure stood silhouetted in the light from the room beyond. "Chilton, have you been at the port again?" The man took a step forward, his eyes narrowing. "Who is this woman, Chilton?" he demanded.

The cold, flat words brought India to a dead halt. She looked up at the sculpted jaw and lean face of the man in the doorway.

At Devlyn Carlisle, the man she had watched march off to war, the man whose death had tormented her for months.

The man she had married on the eve of the encounter at Waterloo.

India moved forward slowly, her heart pounding. "Dev, is it you?"

He froze, his mouth thinning to a hard line. "I beg your pardon."

India moved into the candlelight, her eyes misted with tears of joy. Slowly she put back her velvet hood, light spinning auburn sparks over her hair. "You're alive. You've come back to me at last." She reached out and caught his wrist.

But the man in the doorway only frowned down at her hand. His mouth hardened and he slowly pulled away. "I am afraid there has been some mistake."

India searched the lean face, the gray, cool eyes, seeing now the changes she had not noticed before. "It has been very hard for you, hasn't it? You look older, harder. I suppose I do, too." She laughed raggedly. "But none of that matters now. You're back, and I have so much to tell you." For a moment regret darkened her eyes, then she smiled once more. "Still, there will be time enough for questions and explanations. For now, let me simply touch you and convince myself you're really alive."

Her hands reached out, settling on the hard muscles beneath the crimson jacket. She felt him flinch at even her light touch.

"Dev?"

He muttered a curse, staring at the pale fingers spread against the dark wool. "My name is Thornwood."

"Not to me."

"We are—closely acquainted?" the man before her asked roughly.

"You are my husband and the man I love," India said with quiet dignity. "Don't you know me?"

Thornwood pulled his arm from beneath her hand and frowned at the butler, who was watching with avid curiosity. "That will be all, Chilton," he said curtly. "Leave us now."

"Of course, my lord."

"What's wrong, Dev? What cruel game are you playing?"

"It is no game."

India still expected him to throw out his arms and pull her against him, his eyes gleaming as they had in Brussels.

She had expected it, but no joy came, and the pain of the discovery was like a sword cut to her heart. How could he stare at her so coldly with no shred of memory or emotion in his eyes?

"I'm afraid there has been a grave misunderstanding, Miss—"

"Lady Delamere. In truth, Lady Thornwood. As if *you* didn't know."

"Have you come like the others, all agog to snag a bit of gossip about the newly returned earl?" Thornwood's voice was harsh with cynicism.

"Not for gossip. I have come to see the man I love. The man I thought loved me. The man I married in Brussels just before Waterloo." India's voice trembled. "Yet now I begin to wonder if you can possibly be the same man."

"My dear woman, a dozen females have already been to see me tonight. Each one claimed a prior and very intimate acquaintance." Thorne's voice filled with cynicism. "You must excuse my skepticism, even though *you* are the first to claim marriage."

India swayed, her thoughts in turmoil as she studied the familiar features which now seemed to belong to a cold, hostile stranger. "But it's true."

"Is it? And where is this ceremony supposed to have taken place?"

India's hands tensed. "Don't joke. Not about this, Dev. It's not like you."

"But perhaps you don't know anything about me, madame. Perhaps I am not who you think I am."

"How can you speak to me so? I have waited so long. Any moment I thought you'd come striding through the smoke and chaos, jaunty as ever. But no matter how I kept waiting and hoping, you never came." Her voice caught and a small, broken sound tore from her throat.

Thornwood cursed harshly. "I think you had better come inside and sit down."

"I don't *want* to sit down. I want to touch you. I want to kiss you," she said huskily.

A vein hammered at the Earl of Thornwood's forehead. "I can see there is something I must . . . explain."

India brushed at her eyes, tears glinting in the candlelight. "Explain? What do you mean?"

"Not here," the man with her husband's face said grimly. For a moment there was infinite sadness in his voice. "In the study. I find that I require a drink." He bowed tightly. "After you, madame."

India moved inside, her body tense. Pain dulled her fine eyes as she dimly registered the rows of shelves covered with well-worn books from floor to ceiling. Here and there were scattered exquisite wooden models of Spanish galleons, Chinese junks, and sleek English square-riggers. Newspapers spilled across one corner of a vast mahogany desk, alongside visiting cards, correspondence, maps, and vellum invitations.

Something tore at India's heart. She remembered laughing at Devlyn's description of the ordered chaos of his study. It was like him somehow, at least like the man he had been, reckless and exuberant and endlessly clever about anything he put his mind to.

Not at all like this hard-eyed stranger in front of her.

"Sit down, Lady Delamere."

"I'll stand, thank you."

"Sit *down*." He studied her rigidly. "Please."

India sank into a tufted velvet wing chair opposite the cluttered desk.

"Forgive me, but I shall try to put this as plainly as I know how, Lady Delamere."

"Lady Thornwood," India corrected fiercely.

His eyes glinted for a moment. "As you say." Silently the earl tipped several inches of brandy into a glass and drank deeply. Only then did he turn back to India. When he did, the mask had fallen back into place, shielding his feelings. "Delaying will only make this more painful. I am Devlyn Carlisle, yes. I am a week returned to London, yes. Beyond that, however—" He turned away, studying the rows of gleaming cut crystal decanters on the wine table as if they were utterly unfamiliar. Indeed, he looked at the whole room as if it was unfamiliar, India thought. "In short, I came home, and yet I did not come home. I have no recollection of being Devlyn Carlisle. I have no recollection of what made this man laugh or cry. Or love . . ." As he spoke, his long fingers traced the edge of his jaw, where a scar gleamed like a silver crescent in the candlelight. "I was cut down at Quatre Bras, so I am told."

At his words, a ragged sound spilled from India's lips, but the earl resolutely ignored it, his eyes taut on the goblet in his hands. "Afterward I had no memory of the French blade that wounded me, or of the three days I spent in a pile of wounded bodies. Perhaps it is just as well, too. I was left for dead and was too weak to correct the impression. Eventually an English officer found me and carried me off to an overworked surgeon, who wrestled me back from death. All this I know only from reports. My own memory begins several months later, when I awoke covered in dirty bandages in a smoky farmhouse somewhere near the French border."

"But what happened to take you there?"

"I cannot tell you that. Beyond those few facts, I can tell you nothing at all. All those months are missing in my mind. You claim that I am your husband and I cannot dispute it. You claim we were in love, and I cannot dispute that either. But the deepest truth is that I am not that man, nor ever will be again. I am a stranger to you—even as I am to myself."

India's hands began to tremble. "You . . . remember nothing?"

"Nothing." Thornwood shook his head grimly.

India could only stare at him. Could what he said possibly be true? Did he truly remember nothing of their meeting in Lady Richmond's rose garden after that chance encounter on the street, and the whirlwind courtship that had followed? Had he forgotten the shock of sweet passion, the swift flare of hunger, the wrenching pain of parting? Was this truly no more than a cool, unruffled stranger who looked out at her from those well-loved features?

India trembled, her fingers locking over the plush arms of the wing chair.

The movement made Thorne frown. "I am sorry to break it to you this way, my lady. If what you say is true, this must be a grave shock."

Again the emotionless words, every one a knife tearing at India's heart. "But it has been well over a year. You *still* can't remember?" Something cool touched her fingers. India looked down to see a wineglass pressed to her hand.

"Drink. Then we will talk," the unsmiling stranger who was her husband ordered.

India took a sip, letting the comforting heat burn down her throat. Blindly she watched Devlyn, who had turned away to pace the firelit room.

Every movement was achingly familiar, yet now she imagined there were subtle differences. "What happened, Dev? What happened to us?"

"A war happened, madam. A lifetime intervened." He gave a harsh laugh. "During that time I nearly died. Sometimes I think I *did* die, between the wounds I bore and the fever that came afterward." Again his long, powerful fingers traced the silver scar at his jaw.

"But surely that will change." India looked at him in confusion, fighting desperately to retain some shred of hope in the face of this detached flow of words. "Eventually, you will remember. Little things at first, then more."

"No." He cut her off harshly, his eyes burning. "Don't delude yourself. The doctors shake their heads and cluck, but they make no assurances." He ran his hands through his dark hair, where sparks of gold glowed from the firelight. He looked up then.

The wrenching desolation in his eyes made India's breath catch.

"So you see, I'm afraid I can be of no use to you, Lady Delamere. You will of course have your man of business call on me and present the proper documents. If the marriage is legal, some sort of settlement will be made."

"It was legal," India said tightly.

He studied her face, his expression hard. "I see. Was the union consummated?"

India flung herself to her feet, color staining her cheeks. "You *dare* to ask such a thing?"

"I must. You claim to be my wife, may I remind you? Unconsummated, a marriage is an easy matter to break through annulment. But consummated, or with heirs, the business will be a great deal messier."

This sharp recitation was more than India could bear. "Messy? Is that how you think of it? I waited for you! I watched every load of wounded carried back into Brussels. I searched the roads at dawn and stopped every English soldier, desperate for even a scrap of news. Week after week, I waited." Her lips trembled and she caught back a ragged sob. "All that time I stayed and worked, tending wounds I could hardly bear to look at. It was little enough to do when I hoped that one of the soldiers might have some news about you. Sometimes I thought I saw you walking out of the dust, that old teasing smile on your face. And then the fevers came. Even then I worked on until one day I was struck down, too." India's face was pale as she continued. "They say I came very close to dying one night, my lord. Shortly after that . . ." Her eyes glittered, pools of pain. "Never mind. Just tell me how you can look at me and call our past—our marriage—*messy*."

Devlyn Carlisle muttered a low curse and strode toward her. "Sit down. There is no purpose in—"

India drove her trembling fists against his chest. "Don't *touch* me." She was on the edge of breaking, and she knew it. But she would never show her pain to this hard stranger with the face of the man she had loved. "You have made yourself more than clear. I—I must go."

"It is late, madam. Stay here and rest awhile longer. Then I will fetch a hackney. You are in no condition to go anywhere right now."

India pushed him away, and in the process her fingers splayed, driving against the breadth of his chest. She flinched as a jolt of memory slammed through her.

Memories of warm, hard muscle.

Memories of strong hands and low laughter.

And the gentle, aching pleasures he had shown her in a quiet garden rich with roses while around them a desperate city prepared for war. As the moon climbed through the velvet sky, they had tasted enchantment itself, fighting to hold back an implacable dawn which would tear them apart all too soon.

Trembling, India drove away the memories. They were too difficult to bear. "I must go now. Don't hold me, I beg of you." There was a fierce tension in her shoulders as she struggled desperately for control.

Thornwood stiffened. "I am sorry."

India's ragged laugh was full of despair. "Sorry? What good does sorry do?" She took an awkward step backward. Her eyes were luminous with unshed tears as she stared at him. "Good-bye," she said. "Good-bye, Devlyn Carlisle. Do not come to see me. Do not try to contact me, not ever again. I am now as dead to you as you are to me. I must finally learn how to accept that." Then her chin rose and she made her way proudly to the door.

5

Over the next two days, the Earl of Thornwood sent five messages to India at the Duchess of Cranford's town house.

Each message was returned to him unopened. When he sent his man of business to speak with the auburn-haired heiress, he, too, was sent away.

At each impasse Thornwood's temper grew steadily worse, and finally he called at the Duchess of Cranford's town house in person.

His reception was far from welcoming.

No, Lady Delamere was not receiving.

No, she would not accept a written message from the Earl of Thornwood.

No, there was no way he could possibly speak to her, the old butler announced imperiously, then closed the polished oak door in Thornwood's face.

Fuming, the earl stalked back to Belgrave Square. If it was war the female wanted, it was war she would have. Once in his study, he pulled forth quill and vellum, and after a moment his bold scrawl raced over the page.

The note was not to India, however, but to Ian. Thornwood disliked being devious, but he saw no other way to reach this stubborn woman who appeared to be his wife. And reach her he would, for their tense encounter in his study had left him more shaken than he cared to admit.

The past was the past, he had told himself grimly, but the empty words did not banish the sight of India Delamere's pale face or trembling hands.

Nor did they banish the odd, hollow pain that day and night gnawed at his heart.

The streets around Belgrave Square were lit by moonlight, quiet save for the steady clip-clop of a single passing carriage when the Earl of Thornwood's study door was thrown open.

"What do you *want* of me?" India Delamere stood stiff and furious in his foyer, color flaming through her cheeks.

"I am delighted to see you received my message. Let me take your cloak."

India's hands clenched on the swirling flow of midnight-blue velvet. "There is no need, because I will *not* be staying." She flung the silk-lined capelet back over her shoulder angrily. "I asked you to leave me alone, but you refuse. What game are you playing?"

"No game," Thornwood said tightly. "I merely wanted to assure myself that you are . . . faring well."

"Wonderfully well, thank you."

"Why have you not sent your man of business to see me?"

India shrugged. "I shall notify you of my decisions in due time. And now, if you are quite finished, my lord?"

"Not just yet." Thornwood's fingers circled her wrist, unconsciously reprising the gesture she had made here only three days before.

Had it been only three days? To Thornwood it seemed a cold and painful lifetime.

"Stay for more of this insulting interrogation? I think not. You told Ian you had to speak with me on a matter of great urgency, and so I came. Obviously, it was just a lie."

"No, there *is* something else." Thornwood drew his hand slowly from his pocket. "I was going through some old papers and I found this letter. I don't remember, but you mention I was away running messages for Wellington in the countryside." Thorne's eyes were unreadable as he held out a folded sheet of paper. Between the folds was pressed a delicate glove of fragile lace. "Do you recognize it?"

"My glove." India's face paled.

"It was in the letter you sent to me." Thornwood's eyes narrowed. "You wrote that this glove has been in your family for two hundred years. It seemed only right for me to return it to you now that . . ."

India took the bit of fragile lace. "Now that our vows are ended?" She laughed tightly. "How very touching. Thank you so much for your courtesy, my lord."

"Lady Delamere, don't."

"Don't what? Don't be hurt? Don't feel that the ground has turned to quicksand and any minute I'm going to sink under a weight so vast I can never fight free of it?" For a moment tears misted India's eyes. "Don't waste your worry on me. I'll survive this, just as I've survived everything else, Lord Thornwood. And in the meantime I will thank you to stop interfering in my life!"

India spun about and was nearly at the door when a small figure wandered into the hall, a battered doll clutched in one hand. Golden curls tumbled over the girl's long, tucked nightgown, and her eyes were full of sleep.

"I heard voices," the girl said anxiously. "Angry voices, just like before. Why are you shouting? And why is the pretty lady crying, Papa?"

A muscle flashed in a hard line at Devlyn's jaw as he looked down at the little girl whose nightgown trailed over the floor, three inches too long and two sizes too large. "The pretty lady is *not* crying, Alexis." He looked up at India, his dark eyes implacable with a silent command. "You weren't, were you?"

India stared at him, her heart pounding. Papa, the girl had called him! Sweet God, what other secrets had this man hidden from her? But of course, he was right, it wouldn't do to show her turmoil before this innocent child. India gave a bright and entirely false smile. "Your father was quite right, my dear. I simply had something in my eye."

The little girl nodded knowingly. "I understand. That happens to me quite a lot, too." As she spoke she hugged her well-worn doll to her chest. "But why were you talking so loudly? I could hear you all the way up the stairs."

"Grown-ups do that sometimes, Alexis," Thorne said gravely. "But now I think it's time you and Josephine went back up to bed. Nurse will be looking for you."

The little girl frowned. "Nurse will sleep till midday. She put something from that bottle in her tea again. It always makes her talk strangely and bump into walls when she walks."

Thorne's face darkened. "Bottle? What bottle?"

At his harsh tone, the girl shrank back against India's skirts, her hand unconsciously stealing into the soft folds. "It's all right," India murmured. "I'm certain that your papa isn't angry at you, my dear."

The little girl sniffed but did not let go of India's skirt. "I suppose you're right," she said finally. "He does shout a great deal. It seems to happen whenever he gets those letters with the red wax seals. Then I hear him talking about blunderers and fools and cloth-brained imbeciles." Her head cocked and she looked up at Thornwood. "What's a cloth-brained imbecile, Papa?"

"Not now, Alexis," Thorne said, frowning. "It's time you were in bed. And I do wish you would stop calling me Papa. We've discussed all this before, you know."

India's eyes widened. A bubble of relief pressed through her chest. So he was *not* the girl's father.

A moment later two more childish faces appeared in the corridor. The taller was a boy of roughly twelve with the clear and steady gaze of someone far older. Beside him stood a gray-eyed girl of about nine, who was frowning at her sister. "How many times have I told you not to bother Lord Thornwood?" The girl put her arm around Alexis. "There's no one in your room, you know. There never is. It's all just another one of those dreams you have."

"There *was* someone there," the little girl said, her lip trembling. "I saw him. He had terrible eyes and huge teeth and a big black mask to cover the scar across his cheek. He was there, I tell you, standing right at the foot of my bed."

The boy clicked his tongue. "You were just dreaming, Alexis. Now come upstairs with Marianne and me and stop troubling his lordship. You wouldn't want him to be sorry he brought us here from Brussels, would you?"

"Of course not, Andrew." the young girl said in a

pitiful voice. She looked up at Devlyn, her face troubled. "You aren't, are you? Sorry that you took us in after our parents—" Her voice broke.

Devlyn sank down until his face was level with hers. Very carefully he brushed back a strand of hair from her cheek. "Of course not, Daffodil. Who else would teach me how to play Spillikins and Chase-the-mouse? Just think of all I'd be missing."

The little girl nodded soberly, then took a step out from behind India's skirts. "I'm glad," she said softly. "Because if we hadn't come here, I don't know what we would have done."

"So *that's* where you've gotten to."

The three children spun around as a dour-looking individual came charging down the stairs, a shawl flying at her shoulders. "You're not to be trusted, not the lot of you! I can see I shall have to be more strict with you in the future, so I can break this outrageous behavior of yours once and for all!"

So this was the children's governess, India thought. The woman's cheeks *were* unnaturally flushed, no doubt from the drink that Alexis had so innocently described.

"What you will do, Miss Porter, is see the children to bed," Thorne said curtly. "And tomorrow morning you will present yourself at my study at precisely seven o'clock, when we shall discuss your future here. Or the *lack* of one."

The woman's eyes widened. She started to make an angry reply, but contented herself with a little hissing puff of breath before turning to shoo the children before her back upstairs.

India felt her heart catch as Alexis gave a sad wave before disappearing.

"By now you will understand that they are *not* my children," Thornwood said harshly. "I found them wandering quite parentless in a little village outside Quatre Bras. I took them in and saw to their needs. When no relative could be found, I brought them back here with me to London. But they are in sad need of discipline, I'm afraid." He plunged his hands through his hair and laughed darkly. "But my little dramas can hold no interest for you. The hour is late, Lady Delamere, and your presence here is questionable, to say the least. I suggest that we discuss our problem tomorrow. At your residence, perhaps?"

"There is no need." India raised her chin. "I wish to have no further contact with you. You were quite right, Lord Thornwood. I can see now that the man I knew, the man I loved and married, died at Waterloo. I have no interest whatsoever in the stranger who has come back in his place."

Thorne frowned. "Enough of this skirmishing. We are two adults. I'm certain we can be civilized about this whole tangled affair."

India gave a harsh laugh. "Civilized? If you knew anything about my family, you would realize that being civilized is not a Delamere strong point. In fact, you ought to be glad that I do not have my pistol about me." She turned toward the door. "Now, good night, my lord. Of rather, good-bye."

"This is folly," Thorne growled. "I insist you come back inside. I'll send my man out to fetch a hackney to carry you home."

"My safety is no concern of yours." Trembling, India pulled free of his hand. "You would do better to spend your time taking care of those three poor children upstairs rather than worrying about *me*." With that she stormed past Thornwood toward the front hall.

For long moments the earl stood motionless, firelight dancing over his broad shoulders. He heard the tap of angry feet, followed by the woman's voice raised firmly to a shocked Chilton and then the slam of the front door. He scowled and poured himself a glass of claret, which he drained too quickly for enjoyment or mental clarity.

And then he threw the goblet into the fire. The fragile walls of glass shattered into a thousand pieces, their sharp edges winking from the roiling flames. It was madness, all madness. He knew that full well.

But some things could not be changed.

When the Earl of Thornwood strode from the library toward the kitchen a few seconds later, there was nothing but angry determination in his steely eyes.

6

India could have sworn she was being followed. She turned sharply, tugging her cloak closely about her while she studied the shadows of the nearby streets.

There was nothing.

She hurried on, her lacquered walking stick tight in her hands, ready to be used as a weapon if it became necessary.

Again and again her thoughts were drawn back to a hard, tanned face and a silver scar that coiled about one jaw. Thorne's voice had been so utterly cold, so lacking in affection that she could not believe he was lying. He seemed completely the stranger he said he was, a man whose memories had been wiped clean and whose heart was gutted. India shivered, remembering the endless rows of wounded, carried back in carts from the horrors of the battlefield at Waterloo. Had a man fallen there and been left to die, beneath a pile of other wounded . . .

Yes, India could believe that such horror might well strip the mind clean of memory. And what was she to do now? She had moved through her life half asleep since the day Devlyn Carlisle had left her in

Brussels, her mind and heart numb. In the wake of his death, she had closed herself away from happiness of any sort. India saw now that she had set about creating her own version of death in the last months. Locked in a world with no hope and no joy, she had given up being alive.

She gave a wild, ragged laugh. Her husband, come back from the dead, had taught her a painful lesson. And now she was coming alive again, accepting the reality of her own nature, which had always been fiercely independent.

Maybe it was better this way, India told herself. She was bone and blood a Delamere, and her birthright made her reckless and proud, driven by different passions from others of her acquaintance. And India now vowed there would be no more grieving for her!

She would start by attending the masquerade at Vauxhall that Ian had mentioned to her several days before. If her brother balked at taking her, she would simply go by herself!

India was smiling with pleasure at the thought when she rounded the corner and found two surly individuals blocking her way.

"What's this we have here, Graves?" The taller of the two, his face nearly hidden beneath a battered brown hat, idled toward India.

"A nice bit of pigeon for the plucking, that's what," his companion hissed, laughing. He brushed one hand along India's shoulder, close enough for her to smell his breath, sour with whiskey.

India's fingers tightened on the walking stick. "I advise you to move out of my way."

"Oh, ho," the bigger man said, easing closer. "So we are to be out of the lady's way, are we? Not just yet, I think. And not without the purse that no doubt lies hidden beneath yer skirts."

India raised her walking stick and leveled it at the man's chest. "Be gone with you, or I shall have to use this against you."

"Behold me quaking in my shoes, my lady," her attacker muttered. He was smiling when he reached out to the walking stick or at least to where the walking stick should have been. But in a twinkling the polished wood was there no more. Instead it was flashing through the air and slamming down against his shoulder. Cursing, the man twisted sideways and toppled to the cold cobblestones.

India turned to glare at her second assailant. "Take your friend and be off with you, or I shall do the same to you."

"I'd like to see yer bleeding try it."

India frowned as the man inched closer. She had learned her skills years before on the sandy plains outside Delhi, where her father had been host to an Indian master of ancient fighting techniques. India had learned well, and soon could handle the most innocent stick with deadly accuracy. Even Ian did not slight her abilities, and they continued to enjoy sparring together. India was planning her strategy when a new figure hurtled out of the shadows behind her.

A pistol glinted in the faint moonlight. "Move away from her."

Thorne? India turned, brow raised. What was *he* doing here? The man must have followed her all the way from his town house. Truly, it was the outside of enough. India had been taking care of herself quite nicely without his help.

But Thorne seem to be the one having difficulties at that moment. The tall man in the battered hat had recovered from India's jab and come growling to his feet. Now the two men were closing in on Thorne.

"Run," he ordered, his eyes never moving from his attackers. "Damn it all, get yourself to safety, woman."

India could only sigh at this example of utter folly. What honor would she have if she left now? Instead of picking up her skirts and fleeing as he expected, India pulled her stick from beneath her arm and stood watching for the best moment to attack.

"What are you doing? Get yourself out of here, I said!" Thorne's breathing was labored as he circled the two ruffians.

India's stick rose through the air again, chill and swift in the moonlight. It hammered down on the man to Devlyn's right, sending him to his knees. A moment later Devlyn finished off the other attacker with a right hook and a sharp left undercut.

The two lay on the cobblestones grunting in pain as Devlyn brushed off his coat, scowling at India. "I told you to run."

"And I decided to stay. It would have been two against one, hardly fair odds."

"You're a *woman*, blast it. You shouldn't even be out alone, much less fighting with such riffraff."

"You would prefer than I ran away and allowed you to be slain?"

"It's not a question of preferences, damn it all!" Devlyn took her arm, trying to tug her down the street. "We'll speak of it later. This is no time and place for—"

India shoved his hand away. "On the contrary, this is precisely the time, Lord Thornwood. I am to

run away, clutching at my skirts, strangled with terror—is that what you expect of me?"

"Blast it, I never said—"

"That is *precisely* what you said."

Thorne's face hardened. "At any moment those
two are going to come around. We will not be here
when they do so, however. Now let's *go!*" He eyed
the darkened houses around the square.

"You have no right to give me orders."

"No?" Devlyn's eyebrow rose in a mocking slant.
"You tell me I am your husband. Should I choose to
exercise my legal rights, giving you orders would
only be the *beginning* of what I might do to you, my
lady."

"You wouldn't *dare!*"

"Do not think to try me."

India's fists slid to her hips. "I am going home. Do
not interfere anymore in my life." She spun about in
a whirl of muslin, but had gone only a foot when a
shadow lurched past her. Without warning, a pistol
barked and she cried out, pitching forward onto the
cold cobblestones.

Thorne fired, but the footpads were already out of
range, vanished into a dark alley that led to the
north. Cursing, he caught India in his arms and
scanned her face.

She was pale, her jaw tight. When Thorne looked
down, he saw that a line of blood darkened her
gown.

"Little fool," he said harshly. But his hands were
trembling as he started back toward Belgrave
Square, and he had the uncomfortable feeling that
the woman in his arms couldn't even hear him.

The surgeon seemed to take forever. Devlyn was
on his hundredth trip between the upstairs bed-

room and the front door when the older man arrived, looking rumpled and anxious.

"It's the youngest girl, I take it? I trust her fever hasn't returned. A pity, because she seemed to be doing so much better when I last saw her."

"No, it's not Alexis this time. A woman has suffered a pistol wound."

"By God, London grows more dangerous by the day!"

Thorne led him up to the bedroom where India lay, her eyes closed. She seemed far too pale, and was barely breathing. He looked at the doctor. "Well?"

"Most irregular." The doctor cleared his throat. "The propriety of this—"

"*Damn* the proprieties! Just pull her through this, and you can name your price."

The doctor rolled up his cuffs as he bent to his bag. "My price does not change per patient, Lord Thornwood. Now I suggest you go fetch a glass so that I can prepare some laudanum for my patient when she wakes. She's had a nasty bump on the head, unless I'm mistaken." The doctor frowned when Dev did not move. "Go on. And don't come back for at *least* twenty minutes!"

Thornwood went to the study, emptied a glass of brandy, then found another glass for the doctor. When that was done, he ran his hands through his hair and stared down at the fire.

Long moments passed before he roused himself. His hands tightened and he made his way to the bookshelf, where he pulled out a volume entitled *Miscellaneous Tracts on Natural History*. As the book left the shelf, there was a click, and the whole bookcase slid away from the wall.

Thornwood caught up a branch of candles and made his way into the darkness, where a passage led down to a storage room just off the kitchen. No doubt in centuries past the route had conveyed and smuggled goods in and out in secrecy.

Now it was used for a different sort of mission.

At the base of the stairs, Thorne stopped and waited. At the far wall a door eased open. A man stepped into the gloom.

Thorne stared critically at the man in the shadows, a man with black hair and gray eyes.

A man with what could have been Thorne's own face.

"Did you get those papers off without being seen?" he asked tightly.

"Right as rain. There should be an answer in several hours. Shall I—"

Thornwood shook his head. "No, this time I'll go. It's safer. I don't think I could stay here anyway. Not with her beneath this roof." He looked out the room's single window at the now quiet streets. "It was all my fault, of course. I should have *made* her take that bloody hackney, instead of trying to follow her. And this damnable shoulder of mine slowed me up."

"You're lucky to *have* a shoulder after the pounding you took at Quatre Bras," the other man said grimly. "Besides, you couldn't have known she'd be followed and attacked."

"But I *should* have. Someone is always watching the house, after all. Why should this night be any different?" Thorne turned and slammed his fist against the wall.

"You had your orders. We all do, Thornwood."

"Maybe I'm tired of the orders and the secrecy.

Maybe it's time the war was finally over for me, Herrington."

The man named Herrington frowned. "But it *isn't* over. It won't be until those diamonds are found. You know what Wellington said. In the wrong hands they could reverse all the gains won at such cost at Waterloo. Meanwhile, this whole plan depends on utter secrecy, Thornwood, and you know that as well as I do. Otherwise neither of us would be here, and I would not have to play at being a blasted aristocrat while you ghost about, trying to track down those lost diamonds of Napoleon's."

The man by the window cursed softly. The light of the candles danced about his face, and a look of rage filled his eyes. "Wellington talked me into finishing this last mission, but I'm not going anywhere tonight. Tonight, for the first time in far too long, I'm going upstairs to stay with my wife."

"But that last report said—"

"Damn the report!"

The Earl of Thornwood caught up the branch of candles and strode back up the passage, leaving his near-double to frown and shake his head.

He stood in silence, drinking up the sight of her.

Her red-gold hair glinted against the pillows. Her face was creamy and soft, and the full lips made passion race as wild as ever through his blood.

And Devlyn Carlisle just stood in the doorway, drinking in the sight of her.

He shouldn't be here, of course. Wellington had been all too clear about the importance of this mission. But she *was* his wife. She had kept the marriage secret as they had agreed, and Dev yearned to explain the dangerous masquerade that Wellington had forced him to play.

But he could explain nothing. She should not even be here. Any involvement brought her terrible danger and threatened Wellington's whole plan. Devlyn thought again of the general's face when they had last met, and of the cold despair that had filled his eyes. Only that thought made him bite back a curse and hold his tongue.

There could be no explanations. Not tonight. Maybe not ever, since she would probably refuse to speak to him ever again.

The surgeon finished tying off a bandage and looked up. "She's lost a fair amount of blood, but she seems to be resting calmly now. I've bound the wound, but I dare say she'll run a fever in the night. You may give her some laudanum if it becomes necessary." The surgeon looked anxiously at Devlyn. "My lord? I think you'd better sit down. You look most unwell."

Thorne knew it was true. The sight of India, so still and white, was nearly more than he could bear. He had never meant to bring her sorrow, but it seemed that from the first moment of their meeting he had done little else.

He sat down heavily on the chair beside the bed. Crystal clinked beside him.

"Drink this." The surgeon pressed a glass of brandy into his hands, and Thorne tossed it back in one movement, letting the alcohol burn down his throat.

It did nothing for the chill in his chest, however, nor for the anger that threatened to choke him. He reached out and took India's hand, which was curled above the white sheets. "She looks so pale," he said hoarsely.

"I daresay. But she'll manage nicely. Not that I don't worry about the possibility of fever. It's common after wounds of this sort, even though I took care to dig out the scraps of fabric caught in the wound."

Thorne's hands tightened.

"Don't worry, she didn't feel a thing. Thankfully, she was unconscious all the while. But someone will need to watch her through the night in the event she turns restless."

"I'll be here."

"I could find a woman to come in and keep an eye on her. I have a number of very reliable females who—"

"I will watch her." There was no mistaking the steel in Thorne's voice.

Understanding crept into the doctor's face. "Very well. See that she has this laudanum every four hours, and send word around to me if she grows worse. Otherwise, I shall stop by to see her in the morning."

Thorne nodded absently, all his attention focused on the woman in the bed. As the doctor left, a shadow slid over the floor.

Reports unseen, missions forgotten, the aristocratic Earl of Thornwood was bending forward to plant the softest of kisses against his sleeping wife's cheek.

"No, he *must* be there. Try over among the wounded!" Several hours later India Delamere, her face flushed with fever, struggled against the white linens, her hands moving in restless patterns.

Thornwood sat forward instantly, mindful of the doctor's warnings. He caught India's hands and held them still, brushing a long strand of red-gold hair from her cheek. But she fought him, her body tense with visions only she could see.

"The wagons are bringing more wounded through the square. I have to look for him, Maria. No, I don't care about that. I'm going *now!*" She fought to sit up, desperately shoving at Thorne's fingers, her eyes wild.

He realized then that she was reliving her own hellish version of Waterloo. She had stayed, faithful and resolute, watching for him among the desperate cartloads of wounded and dying carried back from the battlefield.

An icy chill settled at his heart. No wonder the woman had nightmares, Thorne thought darkly.

He touched her cheek, whisking away a haze of moisture. "Damn it, India, fight," he growled.

But there was no answer, not then nor in the long restless hours of night that followed.

And so Devlyn Carlisle sat back and thought about Brussels, about minutes of gaiety seized amid the looming shadows of war. He thought, too, about the story he had told India, which had been not too far from the truth. He *had* been hit in the muddy cornfields, felled by a French saber. There he had lain, one more among the dead and dying, until an old French peasant searching for her son had come across him trying to push feebly to his feet. By then his jacket and boots had been stolen by battlefield scavengers, and the woman had taken him for a French officer. She had helped him back to her cart and taken him to a tumbledown farmhouse, where she had nursed him with what bits of food she had. The vegetables were fresh and the broth was nourishing, and slowly Dev had regained his strength.

But his memory had taken months longer. He spoke French with the easy skill of a native, owing to the secret missions that had kept him among the populace in France in the uncertain days before

Waterloo. As a result, the farmer and his wife had never known that he was anything but a wounded French officer.

Nor had Dev.

Not until the day he had seen a band of English officers riding past. The sight of their crimson coats had stirred some fragment of his shattered memory back to life. Slowly the past had crawled back to him, piece by painful piece.

And the first thing he had done, even before reporting to Wellington, was to look into India's safety. But the lodgings she had held in Brussels were empty and the landlady knew nothing of her whereabouts. It was then that Wellington had come across him on the street, and their reunion had been as warm as any that the granite-eyed duke was able to give. Over claret and a warm fire, Wellington had filled Thornwood in on all that had happened since he was wounded, including the news that India Delamere was well.

But the Iron Duke had lost most of his aides at Waterloo, and he immediately pressed Devlyn to accept one final mission of the gravest importance.

The task?

Tracking down a lost hoard of nearly a thousand diamonds.

All that evening Thornwood had refused to be involved, resisting Wellington's sharpest arguments. All he wanted was to recover and return to his Norfolk estates, where he meant to begin making a life with India. But before Thorne could act on his resolution, Wellington had brought the startling news that India had already gone.

Disconsolate, Thorne had stayed on one day, then two, then ten. Every hour rumors of an attempt to restore Napoleon to power grew more serious. In-

dia, meanwhile, was happy and well, restored to her
family and living in Norfolk. The reports tortured
Thornwood, torn between loyalty to his wife and a
more urgent loyalty to his country.

After two weeks of Wellington's unceasing pressure, Thorne finally relented. No Englishman knew
France better, and he told himself that being apart
from India a little while longer would be best for
her.

So it was that for the next four months Dev had
crisscrossed Europe from Vienna to Cádiz, secretly
pursuing the lost hoard of priceless gems that had
been stolen from the French treasury in 1792, during the darkest days of the Revolution. Many of
these stones had fallen into the private coffers of
Napoleon, protection against an uncertain future.
Before Waterloo the emperor had traveled everywhere with a locked wooden chest under the con-
tinual guard of his two most trusted officers, and it
was Wellington's belief that this chest held the diamonds stolen from the French treasury. But no
chest had ever been found after the battle nor
among the emperor's possessions at his surrender.

And now Napoleon's supporters were once again
on the move. Whoever held those diamonds could
equip an army to support the French leader and
free him from confinement on the lonely island of
Saint Helena. Even now Napoleon had many supporters in England, men who saw only his triumphs
and ignored their cost in human blood. Princess
Charlotte herself had turned a favorable ear to arguments that the general should be returned to France
with honor.

Wellington was right, Devlyn knew. Until the lost
jewels were found and Napoleon's shadowy supporters were revealed, there could be no lasting

peace in Europe and no security for a war-weary England.

Thornwood looked down at India's pale features, his eyes filled with shadows. There was another reason that Dev had relented to Wellington's urgent pleas—one even the duke did not know. He had a sharp suspicion that the killer of the parents of his three young wards was one of the group trying to restore Napoleon to power. Their father, an old friend of Thorne's, had ridden out without Thorne's knowledge, rashly determined to see their investigation brought to a close.

And that same night young Lieutenant Graham and his wife had died a violent death while their children slept quietly upstairs.

Guilt gnawed at Thorne even now. Had he been with Graham that night instead of rushing head-long into his own investigation, desperate to get back to India, his friend might still be alive.

Thorne's fist tightened, lined and hard against the soft white linen. He had learned the hard way the high price of recklessness, both his own and his best friend's. He would never forget that lesson again.

Meanwhile, all the wishing in the world wouldn't bring Alex Graham and his wife back. Thorne would never rest until he saw their killer run to ground.

After that Devlyn swore there would be no more missions. He was done with shadows and secrets. It was time he settled down on his family's rolling fields in the fen country of Norfolk. He had walked along the silent pools as a boy, watching how they snaked like polished silver beneath the autumn sun. They had brought him peace then, and they would bring him peace again, he hoped.

Because when he walked there, Thorne meant to have India beside him. But until then he would have to find some way to keep this infuriating, stubborn, and incredibly spirited woman safe from harm.

Every day he spent in London made that task harder.

His town house was being watched and his connection with Wellington was suspected. Wellington's solution had been simple but masterful. He had plucked James Herrington from a quiet country militia in Devon, and with Herrington in place in Belgrave Square, Dev was free to come and go in secrecy. The story of his loss of memory provided Herrington with a perfect excuse for any errors he might make, while also throwing Devlyn's enemies off guard. A man with no memory could present little threat, after all. For this reason, no one could know the truth until the mission was finished.

Not even India.

A muscle went taut at Thorne's jaw. *Especially* not India. A Delamere through and through, she had always seen too much, felt too deeply, and could never hope to lie without blazing the truth from her huge, expressive eyes.

Outside, a carriage clattered past in the street. To the east, dawn crept through the graying sky and stole in through the curtains of the room where India lay sleeping, her dark dreams finally past. Thornwood took her hand, his face grim.

The lie must stand. A suspicious eye would soon spot the differences between himself and Herrington. To aid his masquerade, Herrington had allowed his hair to be darkened and his jaw to be scarred like Thorne's. That new scar would pass scrutiny, but the older one at Herrington's brow would not. Nor would the slight difference in the men's accents.

Which meant that Thorne must keep to the shadows. As soon as India showed signs of waking, he must be gone, leaving Herrington to take his place, for if he spent any more time with India, she would be certain to notice the little differences.

So would others.

And that kind of slip might cost *all* of them their lives.

7

Over the next few hours the Earl of Thornwood watched, helpless, as India again slid into fever, her mind tormented by dark and painful memories. Each restless cry was a testimony to the horror of those long days after Waterloo when she had kept her vigil for him.

The sight gnawed at Thornwood, but even then he did not reveal himself in any way. To do so would be too dangerous for them both.

So he held his silence, helping her to a glass of water, a moistened cloth at her brow, or to laudanum when her dreams grew too fierce. Finally, as the sun hung high over the smoking roofs of London, he saw her sit stiffly upright.

"He's there, Grandmama. I told you he'd come back." Her hands reached out to nothingness and a single tear streaked down her cheek. Devlyn realized he was witnessing the scene at the Devonham ball earlier that night. Even then she must have sensed his presence.

"Sleep my reckless one. Don't make this any harder for us."

Something came and went in India's face. "Devlyn, is it you? Truly you?" Her trembling fingers

traced his brow and then she gave a little sigh. Her
body swayed as sleep overcame her once more.

Dev eased her back against the sheets, though it
was the last thing he wanted to do. He had waited
too long to pull away her clothes, layer by layer, and
feel the swift, sure rise of her passion.

But he could do no more.

Not while this last desperate mission remained
unfinished.

Afternoon sunlight washed over the handsome
old house at the corner of Belgrave Square, where
Devlyn Carlisle made his way through one of its
hidden passages, unseen by the rest of the house.

His careful work had begun to show results. India's fever was nearly gone and she now slept restlessly in the quiet rear room overlooking the little
walled garden.

Devlyn frowned. It was foolhardy to stay now that
she was on the mend. He hadn't given her any laudanum for six hours and she could wake at any moment.

If she did, Devlyn knew the emotion in his eyes
would betray him.

Behind him came the creak of a door. He turned
quickly.

"How does she do?" Herrington asked.

"Much better. She's still sleeping, and the wound
is beginning to set."

"You're running a risk being here like this."

"All life is a risk, James." Thorne's eyes darkened.
"You should know that. Half of your regiment was
cut down at Waterloo."

"More than half," the ex-officer said harshly.
"Which is the *only* reason I consented to this mad
masquerade to begin with. I hate it, Thornwood.

Thank God I didn't have to attend that crush at the Duchess of Cranford's or I would have given away everything. This is not my world and I feel damned uncomfortable passing myself off as someone I'm not."

"Don't let it worry you," Thorne said lightly. "You're doing a magnificent job."

Herrington looked at the woman on the bed. "Something tells me she wouldn't be fooled for a second."

At that moment India gave a sigh and turned to her side.

Instantly Thorne was on his feet and moving toward the door, while Herrington stepped in front of him. But Dev could not resist one final look, slow and searching, as if he could gather up every shred of memory and draw it into his heart.

Slowly India's eyes opened.

In the same moment Thornwood was gone.

"Yes, the wound is doing nicely. Very nicely indeed." Clucking his tongue, the doctor stood up and closed his bag. "You must be one very healthy young woman."

"The credit belongs to you. My side doesn't even hurt." India moved slightly and winced. "Not a great deal, at least." She tensed as a shadow fell across the floor.

"Doing well, is she, Richardson?"

"Superb, Lord Thornwood. A perfect patient." The doctor rolled down his cuffs and picked up his bag. "I only wish *all* my patients were so strong. What you need now, young woman, is bed rest for two more days and then restricted movement for several weeks after that. I'll trust that you take my advice. Otherwise, I'll have to come back to repair the damage."

India managed a faint smile. "I'll be careful, I assure you."

Thornwood was on his way to see the doctor out when three eager faces appeared.

"Eavesdropping, are you?"

Andrew Graham shook his head, looking vastly guilty. "Not a bit of it. We couldn't hear a single word."

"We tried, though." Alexis pushed inside, clutching her old doll to her chest. "I'm glad you are here," she said to India. "Maybe you'll stay here forever. Then you can be our new mama."

Andrew glared down at his sister. "You just can't go around asking someone to be your mama, Alexis!"

The little girl pouted. "I know that. I asked her to be my *new* mama. Our real mother is dead." The small lips began to quiver. "Sometimes I don't even remember her." Her fingers trembled, then tightened on the old doll.

Andrew bent down and gave his sister a hug. "Of course you miss her. We *all* miss her. But that still doesn't mean you can order someone to take her place."

"Why not?"

"Because—hang it, it just isn't *done* that way."

"Then how *is* it done?" his sister asked impatiently.

The boy looked uneasy. "It's just different, that's all."

Again Alexis's lip quivered. "I didn't order anyone." She looked at India. "I didn't, did I?"

"It wasn't precisely an order," India said, a dimple

appearing at her cheek. "And if it *was* an order, it was the very nicest one I've ever heard."

"There, you see." Alexis shot a triumphant look at her brother. "I told you I didn't order."

The Earl of Thornwood cleared his throat. "You may have five minutes with Lady Delamere," he said stiffly. "Then it is up to the nursery and back to your lessons."

A collective groan broke out, but Thorne was adamant. "Five minutes, no more. After I show the doctor out, it's upstairs with all of you."

As soon as he was gone, Alexis shot to India's side. "How did it happen? Did a spy shoot you? Was it one of Napoleon's men? Papa—that is the earl—tells us there are spies everywhere, even here in London."

Andrew cleared his throat. "I'm sure Lady Delamere knows all about the nature of English-French relations, Alexis. Besides, we mustn't tire her."

"Oh, I'm sure Lady Delamere isn't tired," Alexis said brightly. "It *was* a spy, wasn't it?"

India smiled faintly. "Actually, it was a pair of footpads."

All three children sighed as one, imagining a scene of wonderful danger and perfect heroism.

"And to think we missed it." Alexis shook her head. "It would have been a capital adventure."

India's brow rose. "I didn't think so at the time."

"We're all very sorry you were hurt, of course. Were there twenty of them, all brawny men with guns?"

"I'm afraid there were only two."

"Only *two*? And the earl couldn't get rid of them?" Alexis looked disappointed. "I thought he could take on a whole regiment with his bare hands."

"Without doubt," India said quickly.

"Do you think so?" Alexis smoothed her doll's hair. "He was wonderfully brave when he brought us back from Brussels, you know. Some bad men rode up with pistols and he did the most wonderful things with a whip he pulled from his saddlebags. Maybe footpads in London are different from footpads in Brussels."

"That's enough talk for now, Alexis. You remember what the earl said." Andrew put his hand on his sister's shoulder. "We have to go upstairs and work on our lessons now."

"But I hate drawing and sewing," Alexis protested.

Her older sister gave an irritated sniff. "I want to go see Astley's Amphitheater and the Menagerie. Then I want to eat ices at Gunter's. I've also heard there's a real steam train in London."

"So there is," India affirmed. "I've seen it, as a matter of fact."

Andrew's eyes grew wide. "You *have*? Did it run on a track? Was it very noisy? Do you know what the ratio of coal to energy output was?"

India laughed and shook her head. "I'm afraid you are far beyond me there."

Andrew frowned. "We're not likely to go to any of those places. The earl is very busy, and the last thing we want is to make things more difficult for him."

"Especially when he seems so—so moody," Marianne added. "It's positively strange how he'll leave in the afternoon silent and distracted, then come back later in the day and be the most cheerful man imaginable." She frowned at India. "Andrew thinks it's because of the wounds he received at Waterloo."

"I suppose it might be." India smiled faintly. They

were an engaging lot, these wards of Thornwood's. Rather scruffy, however. Alexis's petticoat was dragging inches below her dress, and the older girl, Marianne, wore slippers that were torn in one toe. Andrew definitely needed a new jacket, since his shoulders strained at the gray twill. Yes, she would have to talk to Thornwood about new clothes. They could hardly continue to go around in this state.

After Andrew had herded the other two upstairs, India sat for a long time watching the sun play over the linden tree in the small rear garden. There was a hot throb at her side, but otherwise she was fairly comfortable. Her real pain came from the knowledge that she was lying beneath Thornwood's roof.

She let herself slide into a recollection of the last time she'd seen him. The streets had been in chaos and he had pulled her into a quiet doorway, kissing her with fierce, desperate hunger. Then he had pulled away and smoothed her hair, calling himself a bloody fool for nearly shoving off her gown in the middle of a downtown Brussels square. With an unsteady laugh he had warned her that she'd made a bad bargain in marrying him.

India had cut him off with a pretended jab to the jaw.

And so the moment of madness, of blind need and desperate sweetness, had passed. But India had remembered the look in his eyes always. She had been sure there was enough yearning there to last both of them a lifetime.

She had been wrong. Cruelly wrong.

Now he was all coldness and formality, as if an utter stranger, and the certainty of all she had lost tore at her heart. Wounded or not, she knew she could not stay here a moment longer.

She threw off her covers and pushed unsteadily to

her feet. Ignoring the dull pain in her side, she tugged her gown over her chemise and made her way to the rear servants' stairs. There, at least, she would be less likely to encounter Thornwood.

She had just stopped for a steadying breath at the bottom step when a low voice rumbled out of the shadows behind her.

"What in God's name are you doing out of bed?"

India turned slowly. All she could see was the grim line of his jaw and the dark strand of hair curving low over his forehead. "I'm leaving, of course. I can only be a bother to you here. Besides, you have your hands full with the children."

The air shimmered with tension. "On the contrary, my lady. The only place *you* are going is back to bed."

India's hands tightened on the stair rail. *"I won't."* She swayed slightly, pain gnawing at her side.

Thornwood took two angry steps toward her and caught her wrists in his fingers. His face was all hard planes and his eyes burned with anger.

India blinked dizzily. His hands locked against her waist and slowly he pulled her against him.

Her breasts were crushed against the crisp linen of his shirt. She felt every blazing inch of his fury, at war with his iron discipline.

She shivered, pressing closer, driven by old needs rekindled without warning. He was her husband, blast it! It was time he remembered that!

India closed her eyes, slightly dizzy. A subtle scent was rising on the heat of his body. Leather, she decided. Leather and cloves.

"What are you doing?" Thornwood growled.

"Concentrating. When you can't forget, all you can do is try to remember." She laughed raggedly. "I

seem to do a lot of that." She took a deep, apprais-
ing sniff. "Leather and brandy and something else."

Thornwood cleared his throat. "It's time you were
upstairs."

India went very still. One hand rose to the scar at
Dev's jaw. "Did it hurt?" she asked softly.

His body tensed. After a moment he shrugged.

A flood of memories swept through India. With
them came a need so keen it hurt. She leaned close
and pressed a soft kiss on that small silver scar.

"Don't." This time Thorne's voice was hoarse. His
indifference was gone, and most of his control, too.
India heard the note of pain—and the hoarse edge
of rising desire.

Something dark and wild, an instinct com-
pounded of memories and loss, pulled her onto her
toes. Slowly, carefully, she traced the locked line of
his mouth.

Iron fingers gripped her wrist. "No more. You are
going back to bed."

"Bed. That sounds . . . interesting." India's lips
parted. She slid her tongue over her lower lip.

Thornwood cursed, his hands angry and unrelenting as he caught her up in his arms and carried
her up the narrow, dark stairs. And his anger called
out to her own, sparking the Delamere pride that
demanded she penetrate the walls of his forgetful-
ness.

It was dangerous, of course. But India Delamere
had always had a love for danger.

She tilted her head, studying Thorne's rigid jaw.
Carefully she ran her hand along his shoulder and
twined her fingers through his hair.

His jaw hardened.

She pressed a lingering kiss to his neck.

He stiffened, cursing darkly. "It won't work, you know."

"Won't it? Don't you remember anything, Dev?" India's voice was low with desire. "Not even that last night in Brussels? There was a full moon and all the roses were in bloom. There was a nightingale singing in the beech tree and we stopped to listen." She laughed huskily. "Only we didn't actually end up hearing, did we?"

"Don't." A pulse hammered at his neck. "You won't succeed."

"Won't I, Dev?" India whispered.

And then she inched closer still. Her cheek brushed the hollow of his neck and her swollen nipples shifted across the soft linen of his white shirt.

"You can't hope to make this work, damn it."

"Remember, Dev. Remember the smell of those damask roses. Remember the soft night wind and the sounds of that distant waltz. Remember *me.*"

"Don't you understand?" He was at the top of the stairs now. With one booted foot he kicked open the door to her room. Then he stood deadly still, looking at her.

Just looking at her.

"You are a complete fool. Any other man would topple you onto that bed and jam himself between those white thighs of yours."

"What about you, Lord Thornwood?"

Thorne looked down and his eyes darkened. The curve of one crimson crest lay only inches from his hand, a ripe, tempting shadow upthrust against her cambric gown. "Maybe I'm no different," he said hoarsely. "Maybe I'm far worse." With a curse he strode to the bed and followed her down, trapping her beneath him and driving one thigh deep between hers, until her skirts rode all the way to the top of her lush thighs.

His eyes burned over her. "You're not wearing trousers beneath your skirts now, my lady. With one thrust I could have you naked. You would be panting and wet when I shoved home inside you. Does that thought frighten you?"

Something came and went in India's eyes. "Yes," she said slowly. "But it frightens you, too. I can feel it in the tremor of your hands. You want me, Devlyn Carlisle, and that frightens the hell out of you. I want to know why."

"You can't hope to understand, and I'm a fool for even being here."

"How do you know *what* I hope for?" Her breasts were warm and full, pressed to his chest. Her hair spilled in a red-gold cloud across the pillow.

"I don't. That's the problem, isn't it? It's all gone, every trace of that past we had. And until you start to accept that, Lady Delamere—"

"India."

"Lady Delamere."

Her finger brushed his lip. *"India."*

"It makes no difference. Whatever we did, whatever we had, is gone. The memories you describe belong to another man. Somehow you must accept that." His voice hardened. *"Both* of us must."

But forgetting was the very last thing India wanted to do. It wouldn't have worked anyway. She had carried this man in her heart too long already.

She looked up at the dark hair curving across his forehead and felt something twist inside her chest. Her pulse began to hammer. "Kiss me, then." Her lips parted in lush surrender. "Kiss me and *prove* that you've forgotten."

"Fool," he growled. "What does it take to convince you?"

"The truth," she whispered. "Just the truth. Why does that frighten you so much, Devlyn?"

His eyes burned over her. "Why?" he repeated harshly. "Because I'm still a man. And no man with eyes could see you and not want—"

India felt him shudder. But she would show him no mercy. She slid to her elbows and felt her gown slip from her shoulders as she ran her fingers through the hair at his neck. "Not want what?"

"This," Dev grated. "And this." He found the soft float of cambric and wrenched it back, revealing the perfect swell of high, full breasts. His fingers opened, catching all the satin heat of her.

"God," he whispered blindly.

And then his mouth covered the crimson skin that taunted him, framed in cambric and lace. His lips tightened, hot and demanding, until every stroke drew a ragged sound from India.

Her eyes opened, hazed with desire.

And finally with triumph.

"You—remember. You *must*."

"Do I?" His hands took up the drugging strokes, calluses endlessly erotic against the warm, sensitized skin. India closed her eyes, burrowing against him, hungry for the pleasures he had taught her what seemed a lifetime ago.

"And what about you, my lady? Do you make a habit of offering *every* man you meet the pleasures of your honeyed body?"

His cold words were a lash at India's heart. Her breath caught, and heat filled her face.

Her hand rose.

She struck him on the face with all the strength she possessed.

Thorne did not move, not even when welts began to rise against his darkly tanned skin. "Shall I take that for a yes, my lady?" he said mockingly.

"You repulsive, arrogant—" But her hand stilled in its next attack. "You meant for me to do that," she said slowly. "You *meant* to make me angry. That was the only way you could be safe, since you could not count on your own strength to say no."

His hard gray eyes neither confirmed nor denied the accusation.

"And you've succeeded," India said coldly. "I hate you, Devlyn Carlisle. With all my heart I hate you. I only hope you're happy in your success."

She turned her head away, trying to hide the angry tears that crept from her eyes. "Get out. Or are you waiting to gloat?"

Without a word he turned. His boots hammered toward the door.

India bunched the pillow, her hands shaking. Behind her the door shut softly. "Was it all a dream? Was all my waiting nothing but a cruel joke?"

But Devlyn had seen the tears. He had heard the low, ragged words poured out against the pillow.

Every one left a deeper wound than the French saber which had very nearly ended his life.

8

"She was trying to leave. She would have made it, too, if I hadn't happened to come up the servants' stairs at that very moment." Devlyn thrust his hands into his pockets and stared at James Herrington as they stood in the storeroom that led off the broad kitchen area at 61 Belgrave Square. Devlyn's face was hard.

"Do you think she recognized you? After all, it's been me there briefly all the other times since she woke from the fever."

Something came and went in Devlyn's eyes. "I doubt it. She was half unconscious by the time she made her way down the stairs, the little fool. And then—there were distractions," he said grimly. "I was a fool to stay."

He turned abruptly to close his leather saddlebags. "You're going to have to watch her like a hawk, Herrington. Those children upstairs, too. I've asked a domestic agency to send around three ladies to interview as governesses. One of them will no doubt be acceptable—though my notion of acceptable may be different from the ton's. If I can't trace the man who brokered those jewels any other way, we'll have to use the children. One of them must remember some detail of what happened that night in the farmhouse outside Quatre Bras. If my instincts are right, that's when the traitor got away with the diamonds. I expect Alex Graham had tracked them down, and so they killed him."

"If those unfortunate children remember anything it would be a miracle," Herrington said darkly. "After all, they had just found out their parents were dead."

"They might be our very last clue, I'm afraid. So far none of my sources in Dover and Le Havre has been of any help. Whoever these men are, they are disturbingly clever."

Herrington shook his head. "It could be dangerous for children."

"Do you think I don't *know* that?" Thorne slammed the saddlebags down on a worn pine table. "They're *my* wards, after all. Young Graham was my best friend. He had gone to that farmhouse without me."

"You couldn't have known that—"

"That he'd be followed and murdered, his wife along with him." Thorne finished packing the saddlebag and jerked the strap closed. "He took a bullet meant for me, Herrington. If I'd been with him, I could have stopped his reckless attempt to tie everything together at once. Now he's dead and I can never forgive myself for that."

Herrington sighed. "When will you be back?"

"God knows," Thornwood said flatly. "Wellington has come up with a list of names for me to run down in Dover. If there's difficulty, I'll have to cross over to France."

"Are you finally close to knowing who is managing things here in London?"

Thorne made a sharp gesture with his hand. "It's better if you don't know, Herrington."

"Of course," the other man said, flushing slightly. "I didn't mean to presume to—"

"It's a natural enough question. Still, you'll understand if I say no more. Not yet, at least. There are too many gaps."

As Dev turned, there was a knock at the door. He stepped quickly into the stairwell, leaving Herrington to open the door to a flustered Chilton.

"Someone is asking to speak with you, my lord. *Demanding*, actually. It is the young lady's brother," he added breathlessly.

"Very well, Chilton. I shall be up shortly. You'd better show our guest into the yellow salon."

After the butler left, Dev moved out of concealment. "So Ian Delamere is upstairs, is he?" A smile crossed Thorne's face. "What I wouldn't give to be able to tell him the truth. He could be a wonderful ally in this whole business. Of course, it's out of the question."

Herrington frowned. "You're leaving me to handle an irate brother?"

Devlyn swung the saddlebags up over his shoulder. "I'm afraid it's all up to you, James. Ian's tough-minded, but he's fair. I'm certain you can handle him. You've done a brilliant job with everyone else so far."

"Your confidence is gratifying," Herrington said rather grimly. "But I doubt I'll fool those children much longer. Needle-witted, they are, just like Graham was. A damned bloody shame." Herrington took a deep sigh. "I only hope Lord Delamere doesn't decide to practice some of his exotic fighting skills on my face before I can explain what happened to his sister."

* * *

"Confound it, Thornwood, give me an answer! Is my sister here or not?" Lord Ian Delamere stood scowling in the Earl of Thornwood's sunlit salon. His hands were bunched to fists and his broad shoulders were tense inside an immaculately cut jacket of blue broadcloth.

"Yes, she's here." The "Earl of Thornwood" tried to hide an edge of uneasiness. "I was just about to send a message around to tell you."

"You bloody well took your time, Thornwood. I demand to know what my sister is doing under your roof."

"Recovering from a bullet wound, as it happens."

"Sweet God, man, you're jesting?"

"I only wish I were. I was seeing her home last night when two footpads waylaid us."

"Seeing her home? What was she doing *here* last night?"

James Herrington, in his uncomfortable role as Devlyn Carlisle, ran a hand through his dark hair. "It's rather a long story. Why don't you have a glass of brandy while I, er, explain."

"Don't bother with the brandy," India's brother snapped. "All I'm interested in is an explanation. On second thought, let's skip the explanation, too. I want to be certain that India's well."

"Of course," Herrington said, trying to hide his relief. "The surgeon's called twice today. The wound was a clean one and the bullet exited smoothly."

"Thank God for that." Ian frowned. "By heaven, I'll blister her backside for this mad episode. She's got to learn that London is not the wilds of Norfolk. She cannot go kicking up her heels as she chooses."

"If you'll come this way, I'll take you to her."

Ian followed, his expression anxious. At the foot

of the stairs he heard a trill of gay laugher and the sound of youthful voices. He shot his host a questioning glance, but Herrington simply motioned him toward the open door.

There India sat, bolstered by pillows, the sun gleaming on her hair, creating glints of gold and silver among the glossy red. Beside her were three children, their feet trailing over the edges of the bed. Their faces were caught in intense concentration.

"No," Andrew was saying. "The balloon ascension was from Hyde Park, I'm certain of it. They could see all of the city spread beneath them. It must have been a ripping experience. That's what I would choose."

"Not me," his sister argued. "My choice would be to visit Astley's Amphitheater and then go to Gunter's for sweetened ices."

The two looked expectantly at Alexis. "Well?" Andrew prompted. "What would be *your* favorite day, Alex?"

Under India's coaxing, each of them had been busy arguing over their very favorite activity in London. Now Alexis sat chewing her lip, looking uncertain.

"Go ahead, my dear, you can tell us."

"Well, it's not an activity. Not really." Alexis stroked her doll and bent her head as she spoke. "My favorite thing would be to see the earl smile more often. He always seems so distracted now. Sometimes he comes up to the nursery late at night, though, and then he's different. He tickles me behind the ear and throws me up into the air. He even brought Marianne a wooden rocking horse once. Yes, that would be my very favorite thing, but I don't know how to go about it."

The others were quiet, struck by the generosity of the little girl's wish and feeling selfish for their own answers.

It was then that they saw the new arrivals. Alexis immediately flushed, while Andrew came uncomfortably to his feet. "My lord! Er, we mustn't stay. Although Lady Devonham is very kind, I'm afraid we have been pestering her."

"Nonsense." Though India's face did indeed look a little pale, she merely laughed. "I was growing bored to tears here by myself. I ought to be thanking *you* for the visit. But let me make introductions. This great, scowling creature is my brother Ian. Ian, meet Andrew, Marianne, and Alexis, wards of the earl."

Alexis walked in front of Ian, wooden doll dangling behind her. Her head cocked measuringly. "You are *very tall*, aren't you?" she said to the gray-eyed cavalry officer.

Ian smiled and bent down on one knee beside her. "Now I'm not. Now I'm just as tall as you are. What do you think about that?"

After a moment the girl's cheeks dimpled. "I think that you are not only tall but very nice."

India laughed from the bed. "Don't be fooled, my dear. He broke my painting set when I was just about your age and then he had the utter gall to throw me into our pond."

Marianne giggled. Even Andrew smiled slightly. But Alexis's face stayed very serious as she studied Ian, almost as if she could look through him and plumb the deepest secrets of his heart.

"You are very much alike, I think." She nodded approvingly. "And now you want to know what happened to your sister. It was footpads," she explained. "There were twenty of them at least. The earl fought them all off with his bare hands. Your sister helped, too, of course," she added quickly. "She must have beaten off ten by herself, which makes her very brave, don't you agree?"

Ian looked at India, pale but smiling on the bed. "I think this is probably the bravest woman in the world."

Alexis nodded gravely. "You *are* nice. I think *both* of you are nice." Then she turned suddenly commanding. "Let's go, you two. Lady Delamere will wish to be alone with her brother." Alexis looked at Herrington, standing uncomfortably in the doorway. "I think you had better come with us, too, my lord."

The "earl" nodded and took Alexis's hand. "Why don't you tell me more about this favorite day of yours?" he said gravely. "While you do, we'll go down to the kitchen and find out what Cook has in the way of cookies. Would you like that?"

Alexis's face brightened. "I'd love it more than anything. And if they're *very* nice, we'll let Andrew and Marianne come along, shall we?"

"Of course." Herrington laughed as he led the children from the room.

After the others had gone, Ian stood for a long time studying his sister. Her face was pale but composed. Only he would have noticed the faint haze of tears in her eyes and the tension in her shoulders. Uncertain where to begin, Ian held his tongue, leaving the explanations up to her.

Her fingers pleated and unpleated the edge of the bed linens. "Don't scowl, Ian."

"Was I? So sorry."

"Where can I start?" she said finally. "It was Dev, of course. It happened in Brussels, and suddenly everything was—out of my control. I meant to tell you, but you were always away on some mission or other. Then there was Waterloo." Her eyes locked on the doorway. "When it was over and I knew I had lost him, I couldn't bear to speak of it. Perhaps I thought if I didn't say the words, they wouldn't be true and he might still come back to me."

Ian's heart twisted when he saw her cheeks, slick with tears.

"But now he has come back and it doesn't make any difference. He's forgotten everything, Ian. He might as well be a stranger. How can I possibly bear it?"

Her voice broke and her brother bent low, putting his forehead against hers. His hand ran gently across her cheek. "It can't be forever, India. Surely the memories will return."

"Perhaps," India whispered. "But I don't think I can bear to wait. How can I look into his eyes and see nothing there, only the flat, indifferent gaze of a stranger? Especially after all we were to each other?" She caught a ragged breath and brushed awkwardly at her cheeks. "Now you'll think I'm a disgrace for spoiling your beautiful jacket this way." She brushed Ian's exquisitely tailored broadcloth.

But her brother snorted fondly. "You're no such thing. A hoyden and a minx, but never a disgrace." Then his smile faded. "And as for Thornwood, I think you must learn to wait. He has come back to you, his body intact at least. We can only pray that his mind will return also. And now," he said gravely, "I want to know *exactly* what you were doing wandering about the streets last night and how in heaven's name you managed to get yourself shot by a pair of footpads."

"I had to see him, Ian. I couldn't bear that we would run across one another among a crowd of strangers outside the British Museum or in a crowded ballroom. And it was worse than I could have imagined. There was *nothing* in his eyes, nothing in his face. I thought his death had destroyed me, but this—this is like a waking death." Her hands tightened on the linens. "I know I need to rest while this wound heals, but I don't know if I can stand the pain of staying here and seeing him like *that.*"

Her brother frowned. "You shouldn't be up and about for several more days."

"I can manage it," India said grimly. "I *have* to."

"No doubt you'd try, but I can't let you. Irregular as it is, you must stay here until the doctor pronounces you fit to travel."

"But—"

"No buts. You need time to regain your strength. Is that agreed?"

His sister made a muffled sound of protest.

"India?"

"Don't worry, Ian. I won't do anything rash."

Her brother smiled faintly. "That was the same thing you said the day you decided to jump from the barn with a set of silken wings. I believe you wanted to see if you could fly."

India smiled faintly at the memory. "Well, at least I got my answer. Thankfully broke only one arm when I hit that pile of hay."

Her brother looked at her lovingly. "Reckless has always been your middle name, India. Sometimes I think it curses all of the Delameres." Ian sighed. "All I ask is that you be careful."

"I'll try." India touched his hand. "I'm nearly afraid to ask what Grandmama has to say about all this."

Ian's eyes rolled. "Better not to ask. I expect that

she will pay you a visit later this afternoon. She means to find out if the earl is related to the Hampshire Carlisles. She called them a dreadful, scurrilous lot and said if he has *any* resemblance to them, she'll see you carried home herself."

"Is there *anyone* in England that Grandmama does not know?" India asked wonderingly.

A stern answer shot from the doorway. "No one that counts, my dear." And then the duchess herself appeared, silver cane in hand, her back stiffly erect as she studied her granddaughter. Ian pulled a chair closer to the bed and helped her to sit down.

"Vastly irregular," the duchess snapped. "Even for a family such as ours, which doesn't know the meaning of the word. You are feeling well?"

India nodded.

The duchess looked unconvinced. "I spoke with that surgeon of Thornwood's. The man assures me the wound is clean and in several days you'll be able to leave. Meanwhile, he insists it's best for you to stay here. I suppose I have to agree with him." She cleared her throat. "I even met those three children. An odd business, to be sure, for them to have fallen into Thorne's care. They are in dreadful need of manners, of course, but rather engaging in an odd sort of way. Especially that youngest girl." She made her voice carefully casual. "By the way, you will be happy to know that the earl is *not* related to the Carlisles I knew in Hampshire. A good thing, too, since Henry Carlisle was an out-and-out bounder if I ever saw one."

India suppressed a smile as the woman looked imperiously about the room. The bed was piled high with pillows, and books lay within easy reach at a nearby table. Crisp white curtains flapped at the window beside a row of framed prints of scenes from the palace gardens at Versailles.

The duchess nodded in approval. "Very nice. Yes, you'll have to stay here awhile longer, India. I shall come to see you every day, of course. So will that ungainly brother of yours." She slanted Ian a disapproving look. "As long as he isn't off on some secret mission or other."

An outsider might have thought her unduly critical, but India knew this was an old argument and she merely smiled. Then the duchess sniffed as India vainly tried to hide a yawn. "You've done too much, gel, I can see that clearly enough. I'll be off now and I'll take this brother of yours with me. If you need anything, *anything at all*, you're to send a message to me. I can have that crotchety old Montvale look in on you, too, if you like."

"That would be fine," India said, her voice rather faint. In truth, she *was* struggling to keep her eyes open. By the time her grandmother and brother left the room, her head was already nestled against her pillow.

The duchess sat stiffly, eyes narrowed, while the carriage lurched around the sunny square.

"Well, Grandmama?"

"Well, *what*, boy? Do you think to discover some mystery?"

"I am merely wondering what is making you so thoughtful."

"Humph." The duchess moved the tip of her silver cane in a restless circle. "There's something here I can't put my finger on. Something odd."

Ian's jaw hardened. "What do you mean, Grandmama? Do you think that Thornwood has gone past the line with India? If so, by God, I'll—"

The duchess waved her hand impatiently. "No, no, the man was cool as a Scotland salmon. That's exactly what bothered me. Any normal, red-blooded male would be more than a little unsettled by being in the same house with your sister. That girl's a beauty, right and proper, and yet the man seemed as cool as if he'd been closeted with an old hag like myself."

The duchess frowned, staring out the window at the smoke that rose from the chimneys and coiled around the tile rooftops. "No, there's something very odd in this, mark my words. One way or another, I mean to find out what."

9

The next two days passed slowly. India alternated between resting and reading to the unruly trio of children, who seemed constitutionally unable to agree on anything. If Alexis wanted poetry, Marianne and Andrew wanted adventure tales. If Andrew wanted history, then Alexis and Marianne wanted poetry. If Alexis wanted *Sleeping Beauty*, then the other two wanted Sir Walter Scott's latest work. India had had little experience dealing with children, but she found she enjoyed Thorne's wards. They were frank, relentlessly curious, and all too capable of making the same faux pas that she often feared committing herself.

Meanwhile Thorne's doctor had come every day as promised. The earl himself had been an unfailingly pleasant, if distant, host. But it was that very pleasantness—and distance—that left India's throat tight and her eyes burning with tears after their every meeting. Since their explosive encounter on the staircase, there was nothing in Thorne's eyes beyond affability. He even looked different, India thought sometimes. Every scrap of passion and emotion seemed to have vanished, until India wondered if she had only imagined their tense encounter.

But each hour left her more desperate to be gone from his house. On the second night, when her old dreams returned in shattering force, India knew it must be soon.

She ran wildly.

Charging horses streamed around her, neighing wildly in a city gone mad. In the distance she could hear the pounding of Napoleon's cannons, ranged six to one against the troops of Wellington. Already the wounded had begun to trickle into Brussels, white-faced and exhausted beneath layers of gunpowder and grime. They said little, but they did not need to. There were far too many words in their eyes, which carried the dark horror of the battlefield.

But the man India waited for did not come. After long hours helping the wounded in makeshift tents, India had finally gone back and curled up in a little window seat that overlooked the major thoroughfare. And there she had slept.

Now, nearly two years later, she relived that same dream in all its fury. She relived the night in a moonlit garden where each had gone to escape the heat and din of a crowded ballroom. Devlyn had caught her taking a stone from her slipper and had gallantly insisted on bending down to restore the shoe to her foot. There the magic had begun, the kind of magic that strikes but once in a lifetime. As the moon gilded Devlyn's dark hair and shimmered over his hard features, a net of light crept over India, touching her soft curves and enhancing the fullness of her mouth. Bent before her on the ground, Devlyn Carlisle had stared up speechless, struck by a storm of sensual awareness. His hands had tightened with the urgency to possess her. Standing above him, India had caught a jerky breath, feeling a thorn press into her hands. But it was a small pain compared to the vise at her heart as she realized she was staring into the eyes of the man she would love forever.

On and on the dream bore her, carrying wild fragments of those weeks they had spent in Brussels. Then in a blur the days fled past, and she twisted sharply, reliving the moment she had looked into her landlady's worried face. "Forgive me," the woman had said in hasty French. "There is an officer below to see you."

India had flown down the stairs, only to stop when she saw not Dev but one of his fellow officers.

His eyes were glazed, his face covered with soot, but he took her hand and kissed it gallantly. "I have but a second," he had said apologetically. "Then I must be off again." His fingers had tightened. "I am sorry, but he wanted me to tell you, should anything happen. I was with him, you see, when the charge was made. I saw his horse go down and then the saber cut he took at his chest. No one could have survived, not after a wound like that."

A wild rushing filled her ears. The room had tipped sharply. The next moment the world had gone dark around her.

Now, as so many other nights before, India relived that same horror of losing someone to whom she had given her heart and her future. The memories left her pitching on the bed, while her hands reached out blindly to a future she could never have and a happiness she could never quite forget.

Concealed in the shadows, Devlyn Carlisle watched India twist in restless dreams. He was dust-stained and tired from long hours on horseback, but he could not resist one glimpse of her before taking himself off to rest. He drove one hand through his hair, frowning as he fought a raw urge to pull her into his arms. The heat of his body would soothe her.

But Devlyn knew he could not touch her again. He had come too close to revealing himself twice already. Any more mistakes would put them both in gravest danger, and the interests of their country along with them.

But God, how he wanted her. The need to possess her was as great as it had ever been. Desire surged through him, hot and mocking. He could smell her soft scent on the air, something with violets and a faint hint of sage.

From one of the bedposts hung her battered straw hat, a white band of cutwork linen across its brim. How like her it was, Dev thought. Beautifully made, with elegant proportions, it was still perfectly suited to action and use.

Temptation overwhelmed him. He moved close, caught her restless fingers and pressed a kiss upon her palm, wishing he could do far more.

But he could not. Only exhaustion made him risk this much.

He took one last, lingering look then turned from her, pushing away his own dreams and striding back into the night as silently as he had come.

The moon was a fragile curve of silver between the drifting curtains when India awoke. She was exhausted, her whole body faintly aching. She sat up slowly, rubbing her eyes as she fought through the storm of old memories.

Somewhere downstairs came the faint rise and fall of voices. After a moment India recognized

Thorne's low rumble, harsher than usual. Moving to the door, she listened intently.

"But I don't understand why not. You are quite free now. You must have nothing but leisure since this wretched war is done."

"That might be, but your husband is barely three weeks in the grave, my lady."

"What does it matter *how* long Frederick has been dead? I never loved him, if that's what you're thinking. Come, my lord. It will be unforgettable. Kiss me and I'll show you." The woman's voice was slow and sultry.

India frowned, knowing she had heard that voice before. She was considering its identity when she heard Thorne's curt answer.

"It is very late, Lady Marchmont. Your beauty is obvious, but I'm certain you can find many other men who will be willing to accept your generous offer."

India heard the stamp of a foot and the crack of shattering china. "I don't *want* any other man. I want you, Thorne. And what I want I invariably get," the countess purred.

"Not this time."

"No? We shall see." There was a sultry laugh and then the rustle of silk.

Fire filled India's eyes. So the notorious Lady Marchmont had set her sights on Thornwood, had she? If India had anything to say about it, the beautiful widow would be disappointed with this night's work.

Smiling darkly, India picked up her gown and set to work.

* * *

"Come, Devlyn, surely you can feel some sympathy for me. I am a young, passionate woman. My husband's death has left me bereft and lonely."

Her companion laughed grimly, trying to pull free of her trapping fingers. "I doubt that you were *ever* lonely, my lady. In fact, I think you must have men lining up in search of your favors."

"Perhaps I have, but that does not mean I have accepted any of them," the dashing widow murmured. "Not until tonight," she added suggestively.

At that moment coal buckets clanged from the doorway, and a vision in grime stumbled into the room. The woman's face was dark with soot and her hair was bound by a dirty mobcap.

India maneuvered her two tin buckets filled with an array of brushes and dusters toward the fireplace, stopping only long enough to drop a quick curtsy. "Ah, there you two be. Don't let me disturb you. I'll just work around you, so I will. Can't ever let that soot build up, you see. I had a niece in service what didn't clean the fireplaces for two days and the next thing the whole family was laid low with a putrefying contagion of the lungs. Aye, just you go on about your business and pay no heed to me. I'll just be about my cleaning, right over here."

India clattered through the room, dropped her buckets noisily on the marble hearth, and began laying out her equipment before her.

But Helena Marchmont was not about to have an audience for her attempted seduction. "Really, this is the outside of enough! See this creature gone, my lord."

"But you heard what she said, Helena. Hygiene standards must be maintained, after all."

Angry light flared in the widow's eyes as she studied the grimy figure bent over the fireplace. "Have you worked in service long?" she demanded sharply.

The voice beneath the mobcap was muffled. "Long enough, miss. Mebbe three months in London, I've been."

The widow's eyes narrowed. She bent her head sideways, hoping to get a better look at this odd, forward servant. But somehow the look was always denied her.

The earl cleared his throat. "As you can see, Helena, our, er, talk had best be postponed."

The widow was opening her mouth to protest when a bucket clattered at her foot. The next moment a greasy cloud of soot and coal dust drifted over her white satin slippers. The countess gave an angry cry and jumped back, but the movement sent coal dust wafting over her silk gown. "You did that on purpose!" she said shrilly.

"Oh, I do beg pardon. Right clumsy I can be sometimes. It's these old bones acting up. Rain tomorrow and no mistake. Why, just last month I was telling my niece—"

"We have no interest whatsoever in you *or* your stupid niece," Lady Marchmont hissed. "Now go fetch a clean cloth, so I may tidy my ruined slippers."

"Oh, I'm certain I couldn't do that, not now. It's these fireplaces I must be tending. It wouldn't do to have the whole household down with a contagion. Next *you* would be sure to take ill, my lady." India continued relentlessly. "They do so say as how sickness takes a dreadful toll on a woman's looks. Aye, it can leave her gray and haggard, old before her time."

With a little cry the widow shrank back, her

hands going protectively to her carefully rouged face.

Her companion managed to suppress a smile. "I really do think you had better be on your way home, Helena. I'll send a footman to escort you." He reached for the bellpull, and in a suspiciously short time the butler appeared.

"Yes, your lordship?"

"Lady Marchmont is just leaving, Chilton. Do see that her cloak and gloves are brought up, will you?"

The countess spun about. "But I haven't said that I—"

She never finished.

With an ominous clatter, the little mahogany table to the left of the widow went toppling forward. Crystal decanters of claret, port, and whiskey hurtled through the air, their crystal stoppers flying and their contents splashed across the widow's already blackened skirts.

The countess shrieked, staring down at the litter around her. "This dress cost me fifty guineas. I'll have every bit of it out of your wages, just see if I don't!"

The earl put his hand firmly at Lady Marchmont's back and pushed her toward the door. "I shall see the damage is reimbursed, never fear. Meanwhile you had better hurry home. In those wet skirts you run a risk of serious influenza."

"Putrefying contagion, too," India added hopefully.

Helena Marchmont turned and glared at the servant bent before the fireplace. "If I didn't know better, I would swear there was something familiar about that woman."

"Impossible." The earl's voice was crisp with sarcasm. "Unless you've begun associating with a very different class of people, Helena."

The widow's angry answer was lost as she was swept outside. And her departure came none too soon, for India Delamere, hands covered with soot before the fireplace, found she was unable to contain her laughter a moment longer.

"She did *what*?" Thorne turned from the narrow camp bed hidden off the cellar, his face thunderous. He had been on the verge of lying down for a few hours of much needed sleep when James Herrington had come in search of him via the secret passage.

"She routed Helena Marchmont, that's what. And a more perfect battlefield maneuver I never saw."

"Did the countess recognize her? If she did, the story will be all over London by sunrise."

"There's no chance of that, I think. Your Lady Delamere did a laudable job of concealing her features beneath a mobcap and a layer of coal soot. A proper hag she looked."

Devlyn frowned. "She's not *my* Lady Delamere."

"No?"

"No!" Devlyn shook his head. "And if word gets out, she will be ruined."

"I'll leave it to you to tell her so, for I doubt I'm up to another encounter. Not after escaping Helena's clutches."

Thorne grinned. "Predatory, was she?"

"I could have sworn I was a rabbit and she was looking me over, measuring me for my pelt."

"Oh, it wasn't the size of your pelt she was interested in," the earl said cynically.

Herrington laughed ruefully. "I daresay." He

looked down at Thorne's mud-stained boots. "Been to Dover, have you?"

"Dover and half a dozen other places. Not a bit of luck in any of them, however. No one seems to know anything about this shadowy band of men called l'Aurore who vow to create a new 'dawn' with the return of Napoleon to power."

"What will you do next? Nothing involving the children, I hope. They're a plucky lot, and I'd hate to see them come to any harm."

"I will see that they don't." Thorne shrugged into his jacket. "Meanwhile, I suppose I shall have to teach that little hellion upstairs a lesson."

"You mean Alexis?" Herrington asked innocently.

"No, not Alexis." Thorne's jaw set in a hard line. The movement sent his small silver scar into bold relief. "I was speaking of India Delamere, of course."

When Thorne strode into the study several minutes later, his silver eyes were snapping and his mouth was taut. India was sitting on the wing chair, her face smudged with tears of laughter. She had managed to straighten some of the chaos of the room, but glass bits still sparkled from the carpet.

"You are a fool to be out of bed," he said harshly. "Leave this and go upstairs."

India's face tilted back. "If I was a fool, my foolishness saved you from a most indelicate scene, my lord." Her lips pursed. "Unless, of course, you were *enjoying* what Lady Marchmont had to offer. If so, I apologize for interrupting such a lovely opportunity for seduction."

"Don't be ridiculous," Thorne snapped. "I was glad of your intrusion, but not at the risk of your health. Nor at the cost of your reputation. Helena

Marchmont would have the story all over London, if
it didn't leave her looking like a fool."

"I think she *is* a fool. As for me, there is no need
for any concern. Your physician did a fine job." India touched her side thoughtfully. "I can almost forget the wound, except for a certain tugging when I
move too quickly. See?" She pushed to her feet, as if
to demonstrate. "And as for my reputation—"

But her sudden movement drew her skirt against
the sharp irons at the edge of the fireplace. There
they caught, and India swayed, thrown off balance.
In an instant Thorne's arms were around her and
she was folded against his chest.

His hands tightened as his silver eyes burned
down into her face. "You were saying something
about your *reputation,* my lady?"

10

Thornwood's fingers slid slowly into India's hair, driving the red-gold curls free of the old mobcap. "You bloody little idiot." The words were a husky whisper against her cheek. "Do you never think that you may fail at a thing?"

"Never," India lied, feeling the thud of his heart against her chest and the heat of his skin. Dizzily, she raised her hand, desire shimmering through every corner of her body. "You may let me go now. I am quite recovered."

He spoke so low, India might have imagined his response. "You may have, but it seems I have not." And then Thorne's lips were buried in her hair while a groan tore from his throat.

India stood entranced, unable to believe what she was hearing. Did some fraction of memory remain, deeply hidden? Excitement spurred the hammering of her heart as she eased her hand high on his shoulder and allowed her head to fall back.

Devlyn pursued the advantage, angling his head to kiss the naked, exposed curve of her throat.

"Dev?" she whispered.

"No, don't say anything," came the hoarse command. His lips hardened, possessive and demanding. His hands circled her hips and he pulled her intimately against him. India felt the unmistakable jut of his manhood against her soft thigh.

A little sigh escaped her throat at the perfection of the contact, which had lived in her memory for so many painful months. Desire burst like a summer storm and without conscious thought she pressed closer, in search of more of his heat.

Devlyn's fingers tightened on her hips. Cursing, he drove back her head with his mouth and took hot possession.

India's lips softened beneath his. She could not fight this intimate embrace so long dreamed of, even when his tongue drove into the silken recesses of her mouth.

With a ragged breath she kneaded his shoulders. Her own lips tightened, working against the hot length of his tongue. Her body was on fire now, tense with need, moist in secret places that demanded his touch. She couldn't think, couldn't breathe. All she knew was Devlyn and this terrible, exquisite hunger for his touch.

Their bodies clung. India bit him gently, driven by a dark female instinct to claim him as he had claimed her. Dimly, she heard the rustle of linen. A cool wind drifted over her shoulders.

Her breasts tumbled free of the bodice of the old gown. She moaned softly, feeling his hands, warm and big and strong, close over the tight, aching crests.

And when he pulled her between his legs where the awesome rise of his manhood pressed boldly, India felt a shudder of need sweep through her.

Dimly, so dimly she heard his harsh curse. Then his mouth covered her full breast. She murmured, mindless, wanting.

He teased her, a master at exacting the wildest pleasure. This was Dev, she told herself blindly, come back from the dead. His memory could *not* be gone. There was too much fury in his touch, too much mastery. Somewhere deep in his mind he *had* to harbor the memory of the weeks they had spent together.

Without conscious thought, India slid lower, searching restlessly. Her breath caught when she found him, huge and hard and thrusting beneath her fingers.

A moment later she was caught up in his arms while he pounded up the stairs to his bedroom. He carried her to the bed, his eyes harsh with desire. "You've won, my lady. I hope you're happy."

The room was veiled in darkness except for a bar of moonlight spilling through the open window. India moved beneath him as he bent low, his hands locked on each side of her. Her eyes were bright with need, her lips flushed with the bite of his mouth. Her breasts gleamed faintly, thrusting hungrily where he had freed them from her gown.

But he did not move, not even then.

"Dev? What is it?"

At those husky words of passion and need, Devlyn Carlisle closed his eyes and breathed a graphic curse. She was his wife, perfectly open to him, perfectly naked in her desire.

And he was nothing but the worst sort of fool to fall prey to his hunger again. Every second he spent with her was dangerous. He could not possess her as his body raged to do. Not until this wretched masquerade for Wellington was at an end.

His jaw hardened. Need made him blind, and the only thing he could think of was sliding up her skirt and driving against her soft thighs until he heard her husky cry of passion.

His hands opened. Slowly his head fell to the curve of one full breast. India moaned and bowed her back, pulling him closer.

That clear token of her love ripped Devlyn's heart whole from his chest. He could go no further, not until he was free to give the explanations that must follow such a scene of stark intimacy.

To do more now would shame them both.

So Thorne told himself—and he tried vainly to make his angry body believe it.

His eyes were unreadable as he released her and came slowly to his feet. At first, India didn't realize his intent. Her eyes widened, pain and uncertainty darkening their beautiful blue-gray depths.

"Dev?" Her voice was a ragged sigh. "Where are you going?"

"It's late." Somehow he managed to speak with tolerable clarity. "You must be exhausted and I need to regain my control. What I did was madness. You are a guest beneath my roof, Lady Delamere."

"I am your *wife!*"

A muscle flashed at Dev's jaw. "So you say."

"You still won't admit it?"

"I am a man, only a man. Here in the moonlight and shadow I came very near to taking advantage of you."

"You merely took what I offered freely, in love."

"Then you are a greater fool even than I." Devlyn closed his eyes, trying to shut out the sight of her. But his memories were sharp, more cruel than any vision. Her hair spilled gold and red across the pillows. Her breasts were tight and full, capped a deep rich red, hungry for the touch of his lips. Thorne knew exactly what she would do if he touched her again. She would moan, shifting her body and opening to his jutting erection, welcoming him when he spread her and put an end to her need.

A fine sheen of sweat glimmered on his brow. "Yes, I want you. And that wanting makes me the worst sort of villain," he said harshly. "Desire makes me presume upon a memory I do not share."

India struggled backward, her voice breaking. "Even now, you remember nothing?"

"Nothing." His face could have been carved from granite, half in moonlight and half in shadow. "You are very beautiful, Lady Delamere. Your body would be a mortal temptation to any man. That, I'm afraid, can be my only excuse."

Her hands fisted. She slid away from him, her eyes wild with pain. The impersonal slide of his gaze made her raise her hands to cover her nakedness. "Get out!" she said raggedly, her face pale with shock.

She was right to be furious, Dev thought bitterly. He had done the unforgivable, thought the unthinkable, said the unspeakable. And there could be no explanations, not now while it mattered.

Not until he found Napoleon's treasure trove of lost diamonds and saved his country from sliding back into war.

And so he bowed coolly in the moonlight, his face blank and hard as any of those lost gems. Staying, he knew, would only cause her greater pain. That knowledge made him turn away and stride from the room.

In his blind desire to rid her of his painful presence, Devlyn did not notice the first of the tears that spilled like cold diamonds onto India's cheeks.

* * *

Devlyn sat tensely before the fireplace an hour later, his eyes locked on the dancing flames. His thoughts were still grim as the scratch of small fingers against the door to his study made him look up.

Alexis stood swaying anxiously from foot to foot, her worn doll clutched tightly under one arm. "I-I'm sorry to bother you, Papa. That is, your lordship. But, I thought you'd want to know."

"To know what, Daffodil?"

"That she's gone."

Devlyn moved to the door, frowning. "Gone? Who is gone? This isn't more of your imaginary intruders, is it?"

"No, it was her. The pretty lady," Alexis said impatiently.

"Lady Delamere?" Devlyn bent down beside the small girl.

"Yes, that's the one." The girl's head crooked. "Why are you wearing different clothes from when I saw you earlier? You're all dusty." She raised a hand and touched his brow. "And the scar on your forehead—it's not there."

Devlyn bit back a curse. "It's just a trick of the firelight, Alexis."

The girl frowned, trying to see beneath the dark curve of hair that had slid over his brow. "But I didn't see the scar."

Devlyn raised her face to his. "How do you know Lady Delamere has gone away?"

"I saw her. She had one of Marianne's old cloaks about her shoulders. I was watching from the stairway when she left." The little girl was quiet for a moment. "She was crying."

Devlyn's jaw hardened. He caught Alexis up in his arms and carried her to her room. "Stay here with

Marianne. Chilton will keep an eye on things while I'm gone."

"But where are you going?"

"I am going after the most impossible woman in the world."

Alexis watched her guardian stride from her room. Her fingers plucked nervously at her old doll. "Be very careful," she whispered. "He is out there again. And now he is watching all of us."

11

India plunged down the rear steps of Thornwood House, her heart hammering. Any moment she expected to see Chilton emerge, or Thorne himself, his face tight with fury.

No matter. She could not stay further. Every hour risked a graver wound to her heart. How wrong she had been to hope that the brush of her lips could make Thorne remember. She remembered the aching moments when he had stood above her, drinking in her nakedness. His expression had been fierce, but not with memory or recognition. Only lust had tempted him in that silent, shadowed bedroom.

What a fool she had been! India plunged through the darkness, her walking stick tight at her side. She looked about for a passing hackney, but her greatest urgency at that moment was to be away from Thornwood House. After that she would worry about her own safety.

The hooves of a team clattered behind her. India turned eagerly, then felt her shoulders gripped tightly.

"You shouldn't have run from me." Devlyn's scar

gleamed in the moonlight, stark against his hard jaw.

"No? Did you wish to have more time to gloat?"

"I gave you my reasons, damn it."

"Maybe I don't *want* reasons. Now let me go before I—"

The next minute India was caught up in Thorne's arms as he strode to the carriage he had left waiting down the street. He nodded tautly to the coachman who slid open the door.

"Where are you taking me?" India demanded as he pulled her inside and jerked the door closed. Dev tapped on the wall of the carriage and the horses shot forward.

"I haven't decided. *No* walls seem to hold you."

India muttered angrily and shoved at his chest. "You can't do this!"

The movement sent her soft hips grinding over his rigid thighs. His eyes hardened. "I'm a man, not a saint." He stifled a curse, his fingers tightening on her shoulders. "Stay still or you'll be sorry."

"I already am," India hissed, thrown by the carriage as it rocked around a corner. Pain slammed through her side, and she went rigid.

Scowling, Devlyn leaned back and caught her against him, cushioning her from the jolting movements of the carriage with his body.

But the pain India felt in her side was nothing compared to the heat that swept through her at the intimate press of his arms and the tension of his thighs jutting beneath her.

All she wanted was to be *free* of him. Now, before the heat in her blood grew unbearable. "Can't you even let me escape in peace?"

"Not like this. You could have been killed," he said harshly.

"Maybe there are different ways of dying." India took a ragged breath. "But I won't go back. Nothing you do can make me." Heaviness gathered in her chest like the dawn mist that clung to the Norfolk marshes.

"You will. I'll see to it."

"Will you? The minute you turn around, I'll be gone. I won't be your prisoner."

"Because of what happened in my bedroom? If so, there is no need to worry. That particular scene will never be repeated, I assure you."

The cool edge to Thorne's voice fired India's fury. Was his control so perfect that he could simply shove her out of his thoughts like coal dust from a dirty grate?

Her hands tightened.

Some reckless instinct made her yearn to teach this stubborn stranger that he was not so impervious as he imagined. As the carriage swayed, India moved toward him. She did not stop to think, but followed that first angry instinct, her breast sliding over his chest.

Instantly his body tightened.

A promising start, India thought. Her eyes narrowed as she moved to the next stage of the attack gradually unfurling in her mind.

Her fingers moved over Thorne's shoulders.

"What do you think you're *doing*?"

"Testing your resolve, my lord. After all, you assured me your control was complete." Her eyes glittered, belying the careful calm of her voice. "But is it really?" Her hand inched into the dark depths of his hair.

"Don't," Thorne said harshly.

"Where is all that wonderful control you spoke of?" It was reckless and dangerous, but at that mo-

ment India didn't care. All she knew was a blind
urge to see Thorne's control shattered. Maybe then
she could glimpse the real man hidden beneath the
layers of reserve.

"Don't overestimate your luck, my lady." His
voice was like granite.

"Afraid you won't succeed?"

"Don't do this. You will only make us both sorry."

But India closed her ears, reckless as only a Delamere could be. She was nearly facing him, locked
across his thighs. Slowly she bent her head until her
face was inches from his. Her eyes locked on his
mouth, sharply carved in moonlight and shadow.
Silently she raised her hand to his chest.

And in that instant her plan began to backfire, for
India found every gesture kindling memories of
heated pleasures he had taught her all those months
ago in Brussels. Before she realized the extent of
her danger, she was lost. What had begun as reckless provocation turned into ragged need.

Her eyes locked with Thorne's.

"You have no idea what you're doing."

"I have every idea."

"Do you think so?" Thorne said hoarsely. His
hand fell, found the cool line of her neck, and slid
lower. In taut silence he worked beneath the layers
of muslin until he met the heat of one full, hungry
breast. As India moved restlessly against him, he
bared her to his gaze. "Do you still think so? And is
this what you wanted of me, my lady?"

This time there was anger as well as desire in his
voice. Dimly India realized that she had pushed him
over the edge.

She knew a moment of fear. They were alone in a
carriage, on a deserted London street. She was
without anyone to help her. But anything was better

than this emptiness. A hundred years of pain would be worth one night of knowing he hadn't forgotten her.

"Still in the mood for danger?"

She was. And, God help her, she was in the mood for *him.* So India did not pull away from his possessing fingers, nor the lips that followed in their wake.

Suddenly she was bent over his arm as his mouth covered the hungry line of her nipple. She moaned, desire moving through her like a storm, leaving her weak and flushed.

And Thorne knew it. Like a hunter, he plotted his course, noting every moment of her weakness. With a single motion he slid her gown lower. His mouth turned demanding, nipping gently, drawing forth her husky cry.

"If it's danger you wanted, it's danger you shall have, my lady."

"And—your memory?"

"Memory, be damned," Thorne said hoarsely. "Maybe I want what *he* had, this man whom I cannot remember. Maybe I need it more than you can know." His hands molded her hips. A moment later linen and cambric were shoved aside and he found the heat of her, yielding and sweet beneath his strong fingers.

"Dev, no. Not unless there's more than touch. Not unless you *remember.*"

"It's too late, my lady. Maybe touch is the only way to bring back that stranger you used to know."

Long months before, he had been gentle, restrained, patient as he brought her inch by inch to an understanding of her own body and all its textures of desire.

Now the patient teacher was gone. Against her

body India felt the angry line of Thorne's desire and knew that this was no teacher, but a man. A man too long denied. But India wanted him too much to stop now. His recklessness goaded her own, which always simmered too near the surface. She felt his mouth nip at her neck and then an exquisite tingling as his teeth left a love mark on her naked skin. Her hands went to his throat, shoving away the buttons that kept his body from hers.

But Dev was stronger. He opened her thighs, groaning softly when he felt the lush, wet heat of her arousal. "My God," he said hoarsely.

A shudder ran through India. Outside, the clatter of the carriage, the rush of the wind, the neighing of the horses, all were swept away, lost in the sensual haze washing over her. She fell deep into a world of darkness, texture and sensation. And because Dev's touch was sweet and too long denied, she did not fight him as she was pulled relentlessly along those swift, dark currents.

Somewhere in the night a clock tolled twice. It brought India the memory of another clock in another time when two lovers had stood listening to the last chime fade away, their fingers tightly locked.

"I'll come back," Devlyn had whispered huskily. "I'll find you, my reckless Delamere, even if I have to march past Napoleon himself to do it." India thought of those fierce words as she studied Thorne's shadowed face. Dear God, what if it was true? What if he couldn't ever remember? What if her Dev was lost to her forever, leaving only a man with Dev's likeness?

"Stop," she said raggedly, shoving at his hands even as pleasure gnawed at her logic. "I can't, not like this."

Devlyn's jaw hardened. "Yes, now. So that I can see exactly what I've lost. So I can hear your restless cry of passion. I've waited too long for that."

India shivered at the harshness of his voice, truly a stranger's now, as his hands eased slowly into unthinkable places. How could she allow him such a caress? It shamed every memory of the man she had loved.

"No, not like this. Not with you—as a stranger."

She heard him curse raggedly. The next minute his fingers stilled, although they did not leave her.

"A stranger?" His laugh was bitter. "But I've told you exactly what I was from the start. I'm Devlyn Carlisle and yet none of him. I'm simply a man, my lady, a man who's fallen under your spell, intoxicated by your sweet passion. But I shall stop," he said darkly, "if you tell me you want that. If you convince me now." He waited, body rigid, breath checked.

India felt the hard thrust of his manhood and knew that he was not half so controlled as he appeared. And then she realized he had wedged his arm painfully against the small compartment at the center of the carriage wall so that her side would be elevated. In spite of the pain of that position, he had done this without question, protecting her bandaged side from scraping the sharp corners of outthrust wood.

Stranger or not, he had protected her without comment or hesitation.

Whoever this man was, he would not hurt her. His honor was clear, as was his honesty.

Some last shred of reason broke inside her then. She shuddered, driven by need and something far deeper then need. It might have been the force of memories as exquisite as they were tormenting, or it might have been the yearning of a heart that had met its match. Perhaps it did not matter why.

She moaned softly and moved against his fingers.

It was the sign Thorne had waited for. Eyes glinting, he eased deep inside her, every second wild with pleasure and endless torment.

"I want you," he said harshly. "Right here and right now. With you welcoming and sweet, right out of a man's darkest dreams. But that wouldn't be enough for you, would it? You'll always want answers and memories I can't give." His jaw hardened as passion filled her eyes. "But maybe *this* memory is all I need." His thumb found the tiny hidden bud of her desire.

Instantly India cried out. Her body shimmered, tossed headlong into a blinding wave of desire. Again and again he moved, gentle and expert. And India melted against him, accepting the wild wonder that grew and grew until it took over her body, a body that accepted the dark care of a stranger's hands, just as she accepted him and this blinding passion he taught her, knowing that somehow, someway he would keep her safe.

Even when her Delamere blood boiled and the very *last* thing she wanted was to be safe.

The watcher stood in the shadows, looking toward the darkened room on the second floor. The door was bolted and the curtains pulled. One by one the lights went out in the grand house. And still he did not move. His thoughts were dark, his mouth set in a harsh line.

It was not over yet, he swore. As he spoke, his fingers crushed the rose he had taken from the thronged ballroom, a blush-pink bloom whose petals reminded him of India Delamere's creamy cheeks.

Petal after petal fell silently on the cold cobblestones and then were ground ruthlessly beneath his boot.

Soon the last prize would be within his grasp.

India's eyes opened. A hundred different emotions warred in her head as she studied Devlyn's dark features sculpted by moonlight.

She caught a ragged breath. "Devlyn, I—"

"No, don't." His voice was low, tight. He eased away and sat stiffly on the opposite seat. "Don't misunderstand. It was for you, but also for me, Princess."

"Princess?" Her voice was unsteady.

"You might as well be. That Delamere pride is part of you, obvious in every gesture and look. But tonight I needed to feel that blind passion course through you. I needed to see if your softness and your heat would fill the silence and all those dark holes." He cleared his throat. "You know about the darkness. I've seen that in your eyes, too."

She shivered. "It was chaos. The wounded just kept coming . . ."

Thorne's mouth hardened. "I won't shame either of us by apologizing for something I don't regret in the slightest. And yet . . ." His hands tightened as he looked out at the passing streets, silent and lonely in the last hours before dawn. "One thing I swear. It won't happen again. *Never.*"

Slowly, India sat up. "So, it's all to be forgotten, as if it never happened?"

"Exactly. It's the only way. What just took place never should have—and it never will again."

Abruptly, Thorne sat forward. "You're bleeding again."

India looked down, surprised to see the dark stain at her side. "So I am," she said mechanically.

Thorne muttered harshly, pulled his cravat free, then pressed it against her side. "Don't move. How could I have been such a fool to—" He shook his head. "Maybe you're right. Thornwood House is no longer safe for you." He pulled away the tangle of linen and stared down at the dark speckles of blood, then returned it to her side. "More of a bloody fool than I thought," he muttered. Leaning out the carriage window, he shouted "Devonham House, coachman. And be quick about it!"

A moment later the team turned and lurched off to the north. Devlyn sat in tight-lipped silence, his hand against India's side.

"What if your memory doesn't matter?" India said unsteadily. "What if I'm willing to take you any way I can have you, Devlyn Carlisle?"

"But not for long, I'll warrant. You've too much dignity for that. And even if you accepted me, do you think I could agree, knowing I could give you only part of me? Knowing that every second we were together was built on lies and omissions that must eventually tear your heart in two?" he said bitterly, reaching out to catch her hand. With exquisite grace he raised her palm to his lips. "Not like a thief in the night. No, by heaven, not in this damned hole-in-the-wall manner."

The carriage lurched to a halt outside the elegant town house belonging to the Duchess of Cranford.

After opening the door, Devlyn looked at India for long moments. Then without a word he swept her up into his arms.

"I'm perfectly able to walk."

"But *I'm* not able to let you," he said harshly. "It is a small enough service to render, after all."

Her body was stiff as he strode up the steps. The door was thrown open by a sleepy footman. "Who—" The startled servant rubbed his eyes. "My lady?"

"Yes, Thomas, I'm home again. You needn't stay, however."

"But, my lady, you're *bleeding!*" The young footman's eyes swept accusingly to Thornwood.

"Of course she is. She doesn't know the meaning of rest." Devlyn felt the damp trickle of her blood at his hand. "I'm taking her up to her room."

"But—"

The earl did not wait for an answer. He strode inside and on toward the stairs. But at the foot of the great winding staircase Devlyn was stopped by an imperious butler. "Well, man, where's her room?"

The old retainer, dignified and silent, did not move.

"Her room, blast it. Don't you understand English?" He felt a tug at his shoulder and looked down at India.

"Don't bother," she said softly. "It's Tuesday."

"Tuesday? What in bloody hell does *that* have to do with anything?"

Her frown told him what she thought of his language.

"A thousand apologies, Princess. Now tell me why the day should be of any interest right now."

"On Tuesdays Beach does not speak, of course."

"Of course," Devlyn muttered. "Why didn't I know that? Since your butler does not deign to speak, why don't *you* tell me where your room is?"

"Up the stairs and to the left."

But Devlyn got no more than a few steps when his way was again blocked, this time by a plump woman with a string of keys jangling at her waist. "I beg your pardon," he said, "but I need to get up the stairs."

The woman did not move. Indeed, she gave no sign that she had noticed his presence.

Devlyn started to speak, then stopped. He stared down at India. "Don't tell me. It's Tuesday and she—"

"Oh, not because it's Tuesday." India's voice was softly protective. "Mrs. Harrison never recognizes the presence of a male after midnight on the second week of the month. It has something to do with an uncle who had promised her passage to the West Indies, where she was to meet her future husband and be married. Unfortunately, her uncle died in a state of violent inebriation and his heir refused her any assistance. As a result, Mrs. Harrison's chance at love was shattered. I suspect she has never quite forgiven either man."

"Mrs.?"

"Just a formality. She never married," India explained.

Devlyn frowned. To India Delamere this all seemed entirely commonplace, but he was stunned. In his family servants had been treated well, but impersonally. Certainly his mother and father had never made the slightest effort to remember the likes and dislikes or personal history of their staff.

It struck Devlyn that he had never had any particular attachment to those who had served in silence as he grew up. He began to think his life was made a great deal poorer by that loss.

He was wondering what else was in store as he sidestepped the motionless cook and made for the beautiful staircase that spiraled up to the second floor.

But when he put one foot on the stairs, India's voice caught him up sharply. "No, don't!"

He looked down, one dark brow cocked. "What now? No, don't tell me. Napoleon is visiting and no one else may use the staircase when the emperor is in residence."

"Of course not." India's eyes narrowed. "I see," she said gravely. "You are poking fun at our little rituals. I suppose they must seem frivolous to an outsider. Others have told me so often enough."

Pain darkened her eyes and instantly Devlyn regretted every sharp word. He had a furious desire to know who had dared to say a cutting word to this unique creature in his arms. Devlyn would gladly have run the cad through with a blade at that moment.

"No, not frivolous. It's just that they require a bit of getting used to. Now perhaps you will tell me why I must not climb the staircase?"

India looked down at the elegant little enameled timepiece pinned to the bodice of her dress. "Because it's after twelve o'clock."

Devlyn waited. No doubt this was supposed to mean something to him, but he had no idea what.

"It's nearly time, you see." She looked expectantly at the staircase.

Devlyn also looked. A tall figure appeared at the top of the stairs, clad in the pristine crimson livery of the Duchess of Cranford. As Devlyn watched in amazement, the man hooked one leg over the banister and began a perfectly balanced, hair-raising descent that brought him in a matter of seconds down two flights of steps. At the bottom he slid off handily and came to a halt before India.

He made a careful bow. "My lady," he murmured, then moved off toward the kitchen.

It was only then that Devlyn noticed the servant's awkward limp as he tapped across the gleaming marble of the alcove. "An accident?"

"Albert and his family have been with us forever. He accompanied Papa on many of his archaeological excursions abroad. But he was badly wounded at Ciudad Rodrigo in the thick of the fighting. Papa called in the best of physicians, but the leg was still lost. Papa insisted on giving him an easier job, but Albert wouldn't hear of it. Every night he insists on patrolling the house to see that all is secure. With all those flights of stairs so devilishly difficult, Ian and I hit upon this method to ease his way." She looked up at Devlyn, her face utterly sincere. "It *is* better for him, don't you think?"

The Earl of Thornwood could only stare down in amazement. In his whole life, had he ever given half this much thought to the people who cleaned his dishes, laid his fires, or cared for his clothing?

He nodded gravely. "Yes, you are quite right, Princess. It *is* a much better system. It was very clever of you and Ian to have thought of it."

"I'm glad you agree. It is safe to go up now. We will have no more activity for a quarter hour."

Devlyn's brow rose. "What happens then?"

"That's when Albert returns by the little basket chair that we fitted to the staircase. He is most adept at using it by himself, but he would be uncomfortable if we were watching."

Devlyn fought to hide a smile. "Of course, we must not be present," he said gravely.

"Not that you have to *carry* me at all," India began. "I am well able to walk. It is but a bit of blood and my side feels quite well, I assure you."

"Out of the question. I'm taking you up and seeing you placed physically in your bed. There you are to stay until the surgeon pays a visit tomorrow."

"Oh, I shall, shall I?"

"Yes, you'll do *exactly* that." At that moment something brushed against Devlyn's leg. A large gray shape ghosted around him and blocked the stairs. What now, Devlyn thought.

He looked down at feral green eyes, a long wide nose, and gleaming white teeth.

Sweet heaven, it was a wolf and the huge creature was crouched to strike!

12

Grimly, Devlyn swung around, placing his body between India and the wolf, wishing desperately for a weapon of some sort. Even a walking stick would be better than his bare fists against those teeth.

"Down, Luna. It's quite all right, he's a friend."

Luna? Devlyn heard a last low growl give way to a whine. Good God, was this wild creature her *pet*?

India looked up and smiled. "It is terribly selfish of me, I know, but I couldn't leave her behind. I found her nearly dead in Brussels when I was—when I was traveling about."

Traveling about.

Dev understood instantly. When she had been looking for him. Dear God, what sights she must have seen in the chaos and devastation of those nightmare weeks following Waterloo. And how like her to be concerned with a helpless creature even when she had so much trouble of her own.

Thorne's fingers tightened unconsciously. He felt a burning urge to pull her close and kiss her fiercely.

Except that the great beast would probably bite off both his legs, Devlyn thought darkly.

"Is something wrong?"

"Wrong? Why do you say that?"

"Because the way you're holding me is going to leave bruises tomorrow."

Instantly Thorne relaxed his fingers, cursing slightly.

But India's gaze was thoughtful. Before Devlyn could say a word, she turned her head. "Go ahead, Luna," she ordered softly. "Show us the way."

As the great silver-haired wolf turned and loped up the staircase, Thorne followed speechlessly, struck by the feeling that he had stepped into a bizarre dream. "How old is she?" he asked, watching the magnificent creature move over the priceless Persian carpet.

"A little over two years, I think." India frowned. "I couldn't bear to leave her behind in Norfolk, but it has been rather an ordeal for her here in London. I hooked her to a leash and took her to Hampstead Heath one afternoon for a run, but she ended up scaring away all the sheep. Then two despicable old men had the arrogance to try to shoot her. I couldn't allow *that*, of course."

"Of course," Dev said, managing to keep his voice calm. "You shot them instead, I take it?"

"I *would* have if I'd had my pistol. Instead I simply stirred up the sheep a little bit." A dimple appeared at India's cheek. "Well, perhaps more than a little. When I was done, the great bleating creatures had charged everywhere. They knocked down those two beastly men before they could do any harm to Luna, so all was well in the end."

Two hundred sheep sent hammering off in terror over Hampstead Heath? No doubt their owner would not see things quite the way India did.

Dev had to bite his lip to avoid laughing aloud at

the thought of the ensuing chaos. He began to wish they had had someone of her utter resoluteness with them at Waterloo. No doubt she would have sent Napoleon screaming back to Paris in terror before a single shot was fired.

India frowned at him. "I'm sorry that you think us comical."

"Oh, I don't. Unusual. Adventurous. Resolute. But never comical."

"Oh." A long pause. "But really, there's no reason to carry me. I would—" Her face flushed. "I would prefer to walk."

"And make that wound bleed again? Not bloody likely."

Devlyn moved past a marble alcove decorated with life-sized Greek statues, Hindu deities, and thirty-foot Italian Renaissance tapestries. "Where now?"

India pointed down a corridor filled with landscape paintings. At the far end stood a mahogany chest covered with polished chunks of Baltic amber, an exquisite miniature of an old Spanish galleon, and a collection of snakeskins.

Devlyn shook his head. "I feel as if I've walked into the British Museum. Is there *anything* your family doesn't collect?"

India's face was pale. He realized she was fighting exhaustion and pain.

"We collect whatever intrigues us," she said firmly. "The materials or costs are irrelevant. All that matters is their honesty. Honesty carries its own beauty."

Devlyn frowned a little at her words, knowing they were a question he could not answer. Not until he'd found Napoleon's cursed diamonds.

He stopped at an open door.

"This is it," India said. "You can put me down now."

Thorne did nothing of the sort. Instead he stood studying the large room. One glance would have told him this had to be *hers*. Upon one long lacquer table lay an array of precious Pacific coral. Nearby a line of seashells circled a working astrolabe from a Spanish galleon and a beautifully illuminated medieval book of days in jewel-tone colors. A miniature hot air balloon, rendered in stiffened silk and fine slivers of bamboo, sat on a table under the window. Beside the model lay a notebook covered with sketches of various basket structures and rigging types.

Thorne stared down at the woman in his arms. "The sketches are yours?"

"Of course," India said. "Ian and I have been working on some modifications."

Devlyn cursed softly. "Don't tell me you've been *up* in one of those things?"

India's brow rose. "They are entirely safe, as long as one has calculated the proper amount of ballast. Of course, if you allow too much, you'll crash. And if you allow too little—"

Devlyn shook his head. "I don't want to hear it. Balloon ascensions," he muttered. "Next I suppose you'll tell me you're thinking about jumping out of one of the things with a pair of silk wings to see if you can fly."

India shook her head seriously. "Oh no, not *wings*. But there is a new device designed by a man in France. It has a curving canopy and dangling strings. He calls it a parachute and I've been trying to persuade Ian to—"

"I don't want to hear! If nothing else, your family ought to find you a husband just to keep you from afflicting damage on yourself and everyone within three counties."

India stiffened. "I see. That, I suppose, is your notion of why a woman should take a husband."

"It appears to be better than *most* of the reasons women choose for marriage," Devlyn said grimly.

"Well, as you seem to have forgotten, I *have* a husband, and I find your manner loathsome. Put me down this instant."

"Gladly." Devlyn deposited her in a heap on top of a pile of pillows. "Hot air balloons," he muttered furiously, as he turned and strode to the door.

But his exit was cut off by the arrival of the Duchess of Cranford, looking more fragile than usual, her tiny body half concealed beneath a heavy shawl. "And just what exactly do the two of you think you're doing?" She closed the door behind her, mindful of curious servants below on the stairs. "It is nearly one o'clock in the morning."

Devlyn thrust his hands into his pocket. "Well, *she* tried to—"

India cut in. "He positively doesn't know the *first* thing about—"

"Be quiet, the both of you." The duchess glared at the two of them. Her eyes narrowed as she saw the small bloodstain on the side of India's gown. "Obviously you have no more sense than a caged baboon, India. I'll tend to that wound of yours in a moment. Meanwhile, you will stay in that bed and not move a muscle, is that understood?"

India opened her mouth, then closed it. Sighing, she nodded, knowing that any attempts to argue with her grandmother would ultimately be useless.

Next the fragile old woman glared at Thorne. "And as for you, my lord, I shall expect to see you cooling your heels downstairs in my study precisely on the first stroke of eight o'clock. Is that understood?"

"I shall try to fit it into my schedule," Thorne said tightly. "Has anyone ever told you that you are perfectly Machiavellian, Your Grace?"

The duchess smoothed her shawl. "More times than you might imagine, young man." Her eyes focused on the distance for a moment. "William Pitt once told me that had I been born a man the course of Europe might have been changed." She laughed softly. "As for your Machiavelli, I continue to read him once every year just to keep myself in good form."

Devlyn looked impressed. "In the original Italian, of course?"

The duchess's brow rose. "But of course. Doesn't everyone?" Then she made a shooing motion. "Now be gone with you. My granddaughter and I have work to do." With that curt order, she turned to India.

Devlyn left, feeling like an ungainly chicken sent clucking from its master's path. On his way down the stairs he passed four avidly curious footmen, the cook, who froze at the sight of him, and a silent butler. Behind him, he heard the creak of Albert's wicker basket being pulled into place.

Thorne wasn't sure if *he* had gone mad or this whole household had.

13

Dawn had barely broken over the murky swells of the Thames when twelve grim men assembled at the residence of the hero of Waterloo. Even now, months after the battle, the Duke of Wellington was every inch the commanding general, and the men gathered soberly in the quiet drawing room recognized him as such.

The tall, hook-nosed officer began without preamble. "You are all aware of the unsettled situation in Europe. Even now there are many who wish their emperor"—Wellington said the word scornfully— "to be returned to his former glory. It is our job, gentlemen, to see that that does *not* happen." His sharp eyes bored into the grim faces. "You may recall that on the night of 15 September, 1792, the French treasury was ransacked. Over the course of several evenings a band of thieves went back and forth along the roofs and by the time the theft was discovered, the Garde-Meubles National on the Place de la Concorde was nearly empty. Of eight thousand diamonds that had been in the treasury, not a single diamond was left. Only fifteen hundred have *ever* been recovered. It is said by many that those jewels were stolen by the order of Napoleon himself. Some he arranged to be "rediscovered," and come legitimately into his public use, but we have reason to believe that the greater part of the remaining stones entered Napoleon's private coffers. On several occasions these gems were seen to be loaded into an iron-bound chest that accompanied him everywhere on campaign—along with his beloved Cologne water," Wellington said with a sniff.

"Though we made every inquiry, this chest was never found, neither before Waterloo, nor in the months following. This loss presents grave dangers, for there are those who support Napoleon even in England. Reports lead us to suspect that the jewels have been shipped here to our shores, where they will be used to raise political support for freeing Napoleon from St. Helena. Even Lord Holland has mentioned his dislike of the treatment of Napoleon and now there are wild stories that the British governor of St. Helena has attempted to poison the Corsican. Absurd, of course, but public opinion has already been swayed. Should this clever campaign continue, Napoleon's supporters may be able to negotiate his freedom. And who are these men? They are a shadowy group who call themselves l'Aurore, or 'the dawn.' No doubt, they compare their general's release to the dawning of a new age. Those of us at Waterloo know it would be not a dawn but a harsh and blood-red sunset. But they are clever and capable, these men, and with those diamonds to finance them they might well succeed in their plot."

There was a rush of shocked breaths as Wellington continued. "We must not let that happen, gentlemen. We *will* not let it happen. Too many lives have already been lost to this tyrant. That case of jewels must be *found*. Meanwhile, no one beyond this room is to know of our task, *no one at all*. There are too many details that have escaped already."

The duke moved to the large table at the end of the room and pulled open a parchment map, which sported three large arrows. "These are the areas where the jewels are most likely to be brought in, conveyed by the usual smugglers and malcontents." Wellington looked at one of the men. "Torrington, you will take this area. Report to me as soon as you have news. But for God's sake, do it discreetly and give no one reason to suspect what it is you're looking for. Otherwise, we'll be besieged by a hundred false reports of lost French diamonds."

Wellington moved to the other side of the map and continued briskly. "Wilmot, you'll take this area. And utter discretion, I remind you. Delamere?" he said to the quiet man at the far end of the table.

The tall officer with the broad shoulders waited expectantly.

Wellington tapped the third arrow. "You'll take this area in Norfolk. Home terrain should be easier for you. Don't overlook any clue, even if it means dealing with the most unsavory types. As a matter of fact, they are the most likely to have news of these wretched jewels."

Ian Delamere nodded. The sleepy look had left his gray eyes.

Wellington snapped the map together and used it to tap the table forcefully. "Now everything depends on us, gentlemen. We have to find those jewels, or we will face more bloodshed and chaos. That is something I pray we may avoid. Notify me of your progress."

The duke turned to the window, his back toward the room, as the men filed out silently. Even after the last had left, he did not turn, his eyes locked on the street.

Then a door on the far wall opened. A man in a caped greatcoat entered, his head hidden by a chapeau bras. He did not speak, but his light step brought Wellington about.

The duke's eyes narrowed. "Who the devil are you? What do you—" Abruptly, his mouth twitched in the beginnings of a smile. "I should have known. But that hat is quite repellent, Thorne." He took a step forward. "It *is* you, is it not?"

At these words, Wellington's visitor pulled off his hat and stripped away his cloak. His face was angular and bronze, full of extraordinary power. It was a face that would have neared classical perfection had it not been for the scar atop his jaw and the lines of tension carved into his brow.

"So it is you, Thorne." Wellington shook his head. "You do enjoy taking risks, don't you?"

"But of course," the man with the shrewd silver eyes said, easing back the black eye patch that had concealed a good deal of his face. "After all, it wouldn't do for me to be seen frequenting your residence."

Wellington laughed grimly. "That's true enough. Your memory is gone, I believe, and you've left soldiering behind." He poured a glass of port, which he offered to his guest.

Their eyes met, grim.

"What news brings you?"

Devlyn Carlisle, frowning, turned the fine crystal tumbler. "There is talk along the docks about a cache of amazing jewels that will soon enter England via the Thames. And not just any jewels, Your Grace. Of course, they will never be put up for public auction. Their sale will be handled in secrecy, and only select men will be invited to offer a bid."

Wellington frowned. "By that, you mean only those who know not to ask any questions."

"Just so."

"It's a damnable business! Of course they *must* be the lost French Crown diamonds!" Wellington began to pace the room. "But where, Thorne? And when?"

"I cannot say. Whoever is behind this is being devilishly closemouthed. But any cargo coming in or out of London via the Thames falls within my domain and I'll hear of them sooner or later. You've put men on the other possible areas?"

Wellington nodded. "You don't believe they will come in from Norfolk or the Isle of Wight, then?"

"It would be more difficult to move them overland in secrecy, but not impossible. Still, some intuition tells me they will come in by water. Remember, these men called l'Aurore are pressed for time, too. The public is fickle. If they wait too long, their cause will no longer be fashionable."

"If that madman raises money for another army, France will be thrown into chaos. We might soon be looking at another Waterloo."

Thorne's eyes hardened as he finished his port, then set the crystal sharply onto the table. "Not if I can help it. I've died *once*, and I don't intend to die again. I have affairs of my own that I must attend to. Carlisle Hall is nearly derelict, and—" He bit back his words. "I know how important this is to England, but I don't relish seeing my ancestral home in Norfolk fall to ruin in the process."

"Two more weeks, Thornwood, that's all I ask." Wellington looked at his visitor. "I must return to the Continent, and by then it may well be too late for *any* of our clever schemes."

"Very well. Two weeks to succeed or fail." The earl held up his glass. "A toast to our success, then, and to the confusion of our enemies."

The tumblers met with a clink and both men drank deeply. In that moment their eyes were hard with memories of gunpowder and blood and the mud churned up by a hundred thousand marching feet.

Thornwood was the first to clear his voice. "May I offer my felicitations on your impressive appearance at Lady Jersey's recent ball?"

Wellington's brows rose in a frown. "What do you know of that?"

Thorne bowed low, a gesture filled with a hint of self-mockery. "Do you not recall the graceless old dowager seated next to you at the end of the evening? You spoke of poultry farming in Sussex, I believe, and the difficulties of provisioning troops on the march."

"Good heavens, man, do you mean that was *you?*"

"None other. It was most amusing. Even Ian Delamere didn't recognize me." Thorne's mouth curved in a grin. "I suppose the veil helped."

"You go beyond the line, Thorne. What if you had been discovered?" Wellington shook his head. "You would have destroyed all our work."

"Ah, but I wasn't discovered, and I made it my business to acquire a great deal of useful gossip that night. I now know exactly who is in the market for singular jewels—and whose sentiments toward the French might be more than warm."

"You found that out in one night? I wish *I* might know your methods."

"Nothing simpler. Just by listening, Your Grace. It

is amazing how much people will say to an old woman whom they think slightly deaf and more than a little senile."

"And you still refuse to tell me where you are staying now that Herrington has moved into Thornwood House?"

Thorne's eyes darkened. "You wouldn't wish to know, Your Grace. Let us just say that I am . . . not what I appear."

Wellington sniffed, half in disapproval, half in admiration. "You always were a man who went his own way. You worked best that way in Spain, as I recall. Damned good with disguises, too."

Devlyn Carlisle's smile faded. "I've had to be." He stared down at the dusty greatcoat, thinking about his unhappy youth, his uncaring mother, and his inflexible father. He had learned young to hide his emotions and conceal his true hopes from the world. As he'd grown older, the act became second nature as he'd watched his reckless and profligate father let the estate fall to ruin. All the family's financial stability had come from Thorne and his planning, though the world had no idea of that. For years he'd played a role, feigning lazy nonchalance and every fashionable vice. And he had always succeeded in the masquerade.

Right up until the day he'd met a woman with flame-red hair and probing eyes. In a matter of minutes India Delamere had seen right through his facade of boredom.

"And what of Lady Delamere? She bore the news of your death badly, I fear. But it will not do to see her until this business is over, Thorne. She would soon recognize Herrington as the masquerader he is." Wellington's eyes narrowed. "You do understand that, don't you?"

Thornwood shrugged. "Lady Delamere will get over me soon enough. She has infinite resources at her disposal, given her scores of admirers."

"She is to marry, you know." Wellington spoke the words with utter casualness, though his eyes were keen on his officer's face.

Thorne's fingers tightened. "Longborough?"

"So everyone says. She does not look like a woman in love to me, however."

"What has *love* to do with it? It is an alignment between two fine houses," Thorne said coldly. "Yes, that is one of the things we English do best, after all." He shrugged. "I wish them well of each other. He is a mercenary opportunist and she has been spoiled by having too many men dancing in attendance. The two should suit admirably," he growled.

Wellington looked as if he would speak, but his visitor was already reaching for his greatcoat. "I must take my leave. My little band will be growing restless."

"Keep me informed. Be careful, but be swift, Thornwood. We haven't much time left. Two weeks is my guess."

"In two weeks kingdoms have been toppled and fortunes secured," Thorne said.

And hearts have been irrevocably broken, he thought bitterly as he made his way back down the narrow passageway and out into the night.

When Thorne presented himself at the Duchess of Cranford's front door the next morning, he was not surprised that there was no hint of recognition in the impassive butler's eyes. "You with to see Her Grace, the duchess? Whom may I say is calling?"

"Thornwood," Devlyn said curtly.

"You are late, my lord," came the icy answer.

Late? Did the whole *world* know his schedule? Dev thought irritably.

"If you will come this way, I shall ascertain whether the duchess is at home to visitors. It is too early for *normal* calls, of course."

Devlyn damn well did understand. After the wild events of the night before he had had no success at sleeping. Then he had been off to see Wellington at the first tinge of dawn. As a result he was in no pleasant mood to endure Beach's dour looks. But he bit back his retort and followed the butler to the sunlit salon. He was admiring the rows of potted exotic plants and exquisite orchids that were the Duchess of Cranford's principal hobby when he heard footsteps behind him.

"The duchess is indisposed. She is not at home to visitors," Beach said icily.

"But she—" Devlyn stopped. Of course it would not do to argue with a retainer. He was far too well bred for that.

What sort of game was the crusty old woman playing? As Devlyn strode back out into the street, he vowed that he was bloody well going to find out.

14

"I don't like it, India. Not one bit."

Her hair fetchingly covered by a lace cap that enhanced her fragile features, the Duchess of Cranford stood staring down at the Earl of Thornwood's disappearing back. "I told him to be here at eight o'clock, and he has come." She looked thoughtfully down at the streets already bustling and crowded this unseasonably warm September morning. "But it will do him good to learn some humility, especially since I have yet to have any answers from *you*, young woman. You escaped me last night because you were dead on your feet." She confronted her granddaughter with the piercing blue eyes that had sent more than a few English statesmen into a panic. "You won't be so lucky now."

India smiled fondly at her petite dynamo of a grandmother. "I simply wanted to be home, Grandmama. Oh, Lord Thornwood was passably nice and the children were wonderful, but there's nothing like being here with you."

The duchess's eyes narrowed. "Did anything happen I need to know about, young woman? If so, I'll drag the man here by the scruff of his neck and see that he—"

"No, nothing, Grandmama," India said quickly.

She too had had a sleepless night, tormented by memories of Devlyn's touch and the shattering emotion that always seemed to grip her—for good or ill —whenever she was in his presence. No, the best thing was to have nothing more to do with Devlyn Carlisle. She would simply set about securing a divorce. He had made his *own* feelings all too clear, after all.

But India was not yet ready to confide this to the duchess, nor even to her beloved brother Ian. First she needed time to heal.

And time to learn how to forget, if that was possible.

"You're too docile by half, gel." The duchess stared knowingly at her granddaughter, who had run before she could competently walk. The duchess had fetched India's first doll after the girl had thrown it away in anger when it would not speak back to her the way she ordered. Later the duchess had wiped India's tear-streaked face after the girl had taken her first tumble from the tall oak tree at the Devonham estate in Norfolk. This sudden docility was *not* part of the girl's character. "Well, no explanations?"

"Really, Grandmama, you are off the mark this time." India looked at her grandmother and waved airily. "Whatever there was between us is past. It was nothing but a silly infatuation, I realize that now. Lord Thornwood holds absolutely no interest for me. In a way I am glad for his return, because it has shown me just how wrong I have been. Now the only thing on my mind is how to make up for lost time."

Her eyes narrowed speculatively. She studied one toe encased in a vibrant yellow satin slipper. "I rather think I shall begin by attending a meeting of the Balloon Ascension Society this afternoon. Two French representatives are going to present the proper procedure for strapping a basket to the rigging."

The duchess muttered something inaudible.

"And tomorrow," India continued, "I shall attend the evening festivities at Vauxhall."

"Out of the question," the duchess said firmly. "That place is a meeting ground for every cutthroat, footpad, and villain in London. It is no spot for a respectable female, and I will *not* have you going there."

India did not look at all deterred by this argument. "Is it really? How very interesting, Grandmama. I think I shall enjoy myself vastly."

"You didn't listen, India. With your mother and father off on another one of their jaunts, you are in *my* keeping. I have every intention of seeing that you are safe. That, my gel, means *no* visits to Vauxhall."

India pursed her lips and fingered the pristine white embroidery on the sash at the raised waist of her morning gown. "There is no need to be stuffy, Grandmama. Of course, I shall take Ian with me. You will have to admit that *he* would make an acceptable chaperon."

The duchess looked undecided, but she preferred to see India in the company of her brother. The duchess well knew that if she forbade India the trip, the girl was likely to slip out alone at the very first opportunity.

The old woman sighed. "Very well. If your brother is available, there can be nothing exceptionable in that."

"I shall ask him this very afternoon," India said, jumping to her feet.

"You'll do no such thing, gel. It's back into that bed with you."

"But, Grandmama—"

"Enough! The doctor said you need several more days of rest."

"Then he's a querulous old fool. I'm fine!"

"Into bed. *Now.*"

"Oh, very well. But only since I am going to Vauxhall."

"*Only* if that wound is set. Strong as you are, you must not keep tearing it open." The duchess frowned. "I cannot fathom what sort of activity you indulged in to make the dressing come free last night."

India looked away to hide a flush. At her feet, Luna sat up and licked her hand. "Nothing of any great importance, I assure you." India's words were muffled as she stroked the great wolf's fur. "It was just an . . . an experiment."

The duchess's eyes narrowed. "And did your experiment yield the results you planned?"

"I'm afraid so," India said softly. "But now I know what to expect. Because of that I shall be careful that it *never* happens again."

The meeting of the Select Company of the London Society for Balloon Ascensions was postponed until the following afternoon due to a flare-up of the founder's gout. Bored and restless, India was returning from her fourth covert trip to the duchess's library the next morning when she heard the big brass knocker thunder at the front door. Some instinct made her slip into the drawing room as Beach moved regally to the door.

Devlyn Carlisle waited outside.

"May I help you?" the butler intoned.

"The Earl of Thornwood to see Her Grace, the Duchess of Cranford," came the crisp answer. "I trust she has recovered from her—indisposition."

"If you will step in, I shall ascertain if Her Grace is receiving."

India knew she shouldn't do it. It was conniving, ill-bred, and utterly reprehensible.

She did it anyway.

As soon as Beach had led Devlyn upstairs, where the duchess was to see him, India made her way to a storeroom that opened onto the high, domed conservatory. In one corner, there was a wedge of plaster missing behind a luxuriant potted rose. If she slid her ear close, India could hear every word that Thorne and her grandmother said in the room next door.

And that is what she did.

"It's no use making that long face at me, boy. I've gotten no real answers from that granddaughter of mine, so I mean to have answers from you." The duchess frowned down at a potted fern and snipped off a dozen straggling fronds. "Go ahead, I'm listening."

Thorne leaned back against a wall of glass and studied the duchess lazily. "Answers? What sort, I wonder?"

"Young jackanapes! As if you didn't know perfectly well. Answers about what has been going on between you two in the last three days, of course! And probably before that, though I can't guess when, since India just came to London."

Thornwood plucked an infinitessimal speck of lint from his beautifully fitted jacket of royal blue. "I rather fancy it would be better for you to ask your granddaughter those questions."

"I *have*, blast it, and she's told me nothing. That's why I'm asking you."

Thorne shrugged. "There is nothing between us. I suffered losses to my memory after Waterloo. Whether I shall ever remember is a question none of the medical men seems to be able to answer."

The duchess looked up from packing dirt around a pot of flowering strawberries. "Damn nuisance that must be."

Thorne smiled reluctantly at the woman's crusty language. "That's rather the way I look at it, Your Grace."

"But you still haven't answered my question. What went on between the two of you while India was at Belgrave Square? That girl has been restless as a goose after the first frost. And don't tell me it's because of that wound at her side, because I know better. She's appallingly healthy. Always has been."

"Perhaps," Thorne began carefully, "it has to do with something your granddaughter said. It seems that we became . . . rather close in Brussels."

"*Close?* What does that mean? Were you in love with her?"

"It would seem so. Unfortunately, as I have no memory, I can neither confirm nor deny the tale. But I have nothing to add, Your Grace. Any questions will have to be answered by your granddaughter." A muscle tightened at his jaw. "Of course, whatever association we might have had must now be considered severed."

"Indeed?" The duchess put down her trowel and stared at Thorne. "And just why is that?"

"I should think it was obvious. I am not the same man she knew. Any further association would only bring her pain."

"And possibly because you have other business to attend to right now?"

Thorne's head snapped up. "What?"

"My dear boy, I have a perfectly good set of eyes in my head. Your father, though a rapscallion, was often engaged on diplomatic missions for the Crown and I have my reason to suspect that you are involved in exactly the same business."

"Who told you—"

"For one thing I noticed you and Wellington's secretary in very deep conversation outside the Royal Academy yesterday. In addition, that same very formal secretary of the duke's has already called three times this week at your town house."

"You've had my house *watched!*"

"Of course." The duchess was unperturbed. "India is my only granddaughter, after all. Now do you mean to tell me what is really going on?"

Thorne stiffened. "Your inquiries are unwanted, Your Grace. I might even go so far as to call them dangerous."

The duchess's eyes glittered. "Indeed? Is that a threat, you arrogant stripling?"

"Not quite." Thorne traced the petals of a strawberry bloom. "It is rather a suggestion that you be careful."

"Bosh," the old woman snapped. "I've lived too many years to start being careful now, and I won't countenance anything that troubles those in my family. Do you understand me?"

"I understand perfectly, Your Grace. But may I also add a word of advice? There are things you cannot understand—duties and responsibilities which I am not at liberty to discuss. I will say no more. But I trust you will consider the deepest meaning in my words and see that others of your household behave accordingly."

The duchess smiled slowly. "Duty and responsibility? Hardly the sort of words I expected to hear from a Carlisle. Of course your father was a complete fool until he reached the age of forty. Then he finally began to show some sense. Unfortunate that he married a woman who seemed determined to run through his whole fortune in the course of the first year of their marriage."

Thorne's shoulders stiffened and then a reluctant smile crept across his face. "She very nearly did it," he said wryly. "Among her other projects was building a menagerie. She brought in two hundred peacocks and five tons of marble from Italy so that a palace in the Grecian style could be built overlooking the river." He shook his head. "My father had a competence that should have been passed on nicely, yet all I seem to remember is stables empty of horses and salons empty of paintings."

And a house empty of laughter, he thought.

The keen old eyes studied him. "And you'll be different?"

"You may be certain I will," Thorne said darkly.

After a moment the duchess nodded. "Very well. Then there's one bit of advice I shall give to you. My granddaughter will be attending the fireworks at Vauxhall in the company of her brother. She will be in the costume of a shepherdess, with a mask of blue satin. It is a devilish place, and should she find herself in danger she might perhaps be glad of a helping hand."

Devlyn's brow rose. "Are you setting yourself up as a matchmaker, Your Grace?"

The duchess's face was utterly unreadable. "I leave that up to you to decide, dear boy."

*   *   *

After the duchess and Thornwood had left the great domed conservatory, India crept out of her hiding place. As she did a cold wind brushed across her face. Since the conservatory was always kept carefully closed to protect the duchess's prized orchids, the cold air was unexpected.

Frowning, India made her way to a long corridor of glass that led to the back of the house, where she finally found the source of the draft. Two of the rear windows, usually locked, were thrown open. Moving closer, India looked out over the twisting chimneys. As she did, something moved down the slope of the roof in the shadow of a chimney.

India froze, searching the rooftops but the motion was not repeated. Finally she convinced herself it had all been her imagination. But when she turned to make her way back inside, she saw the perfect print of a shoe outlined in sand on the floor. The same sort of sand was scattered along the floor and sprinkled over the windowsill.

Her hands tightened. So it wasn't enough that Thornwood wormed her plans out of the duchess! Had he also sent someone to spy on her in her grandmother's house?

A fragile stem of violets snapped beneath her tense fingers. She would *not* be spied upon by Devlyn Carlisle. Nor would she stand for his interference in her life. Not after he had made his feelings for her so very clear.

Her eyes darkened with mischief. Thorne expected her to be at Vauxhall as a shepherdess, did he? Very well, she would see to it that he had a surprise or two coming.

*   *   *

In the hectic activity of the next hours, India forgot about the footprint and the opened windows. Her costume for Vauxhall was yet to be finished and the seamstress was still busy adding gold braid to the low neck and sheer billowing sleeves. The lovely gown was of the finest silk gauze and would have been entirely scandalous if worn alone.

The fine fabric was all the rage, the dressmaker assured her, and no one knew tonnish dress and taste better than the imperious Madame Grès.

But as she stood studying herself in the cheval glass, India had a sudden thought of what Dev would say if he saw her in this dress, with her hair caught up in a cascade of curls and her face provocatively covered by a red satin mask. Of course he expected her to be dressed as a shepherdess wearing a blue mask.

That costume was now out of the question. India was not about to make Dev's interference any easier. No, she would be Nefertiti, the imperious Queen of Egypt. She smiled at the sheer white and gold dress, draping her slender body perfectly. To complete the exotic look, one shoulder was left bare.

The seamstress sat back with a sigh. "Mademoiselle is *épatante*. You will have many men at your heels tonight. *Vraiment*, this necklace was an addition of the most brilliant."

India fingered the intricate choker of lapis beads and gold amulets with Egyptian hieroglyphics. The necklace had been given to her by a fierce Bedouin prince who had hoped to make India his seventeenth wife. Her father, the duke, had not been amused by the offer, as India was barely twelve at the time. In the interest of diplomacy, however, gifts had been exchanged and horses traded. The momentary unpleasantness had passed, and they had left the Bedouin camp that night on terms of greatest friendship.

India touched the heavy lapis beads, smiling reflectively. The prince had told her she would be a woman above women and that no man could possibly resist her. As the sensuous silk clung to her body, India found herself wondering if those words were true. If so, did she truly want to ensnare Devlyn or was this foray merely to repay him for all the pain he had caused her?

Neither question left her comfortable.

Irritably India straightened the bodice of her dress, which had a disconcerting habit of sliding lower than she liked. Being fashionable was all very well, but she was used to country ways and roaming about in her brother's old shirts. To have her chest so much exposed left her decidedly uneasy.

"You are truly a picture of perfection, my lady," the *modiste* assured her. "You will make the gentlemen mad with admiration."

Yet was it only *one* gentleman that India wished to make mad? But she would not think about that now.

She had given the gown to the seamstress for final alterations when there was a knock at her door. Beach was once again speaking, now that Tuesday had passed. India smiled at the impassive retainer who had been in this house for years, overseeing the lives of three generations of Delameres with a martial hand.

"I'm afraid Lord Thornwood thinks that we are all bedlamites," she said. "Strange, I had never considered us eccentric."

The butler looked disapproving. "I'm certain that

it is hardly the earl's place to make judgments about the members of your family, my lady."

India planted a quick kiss on the man's lean cheek. He flushed faintly and then cleared his throat. "I'm sorry to trouble you, my lady, but there are three children below clamoring to speak with you. I'm given to understand that they are wards of Thornwood."

India laughed brightly. "Here, the three of them? What rascals. But how perfect. I shall see them of course. Beach, would you be a dear and ask Mrs. Harrison to bring out some of her walnut cake? It will be perfect, for they always look hungry."

The butler nodded. It would be no problem today, since the cook had also resumed *her* normal schedule. Then the old retainer cleared his throat.

"Yes, Beach?" India said.

"I'm afraid there is a problem, my lady. You will of course have recalled that today is Wednesday?"

"Damn and blast," India said comfortably, knowing the butler would not be surprised by her language. "That means no fires are to be lit in the kitchen in observance of Cook's sister's passing into spirit."

"Exactly."

India's eyes glinted as they always did when her ingenuity was called upon. "Then we shall have to set the little iron cooking stove up in the conservatory and I will make tea myself."

The butler looked scandalized. "But, my lady, it is not at all the thing."

"Nonsense, Beach, I was never one to stand on ceremony. Please see it is carried up to the far wing."

"Very well. But I shall stay to ensure that you don't send the house down in flames around us."

"You are a fearsome martinet, do you know that, Beach?"

The butler merely snorted.

"By the way, did you notice that two of the windows in the conservatory were opened? Was someone working in the storeroom this morning?"

"Not that I am aware of. I shall ask the footmen, my lady. If they are shirking their duties, I shall soon know of it."

"I'm certain none of them meant any harm," India said quickly. In these times a job was hard to come by. The last thing she wanted was for one of the domestic staff to be sacked, which is exactly what Beach would do if he discovered the staff had been lax about their duties. "Perhaps Grandmama was taking some air and forgot to close the windows. I shall speak to her about it myself. Never mind, Beach."

After the butler left, India noticed a scrap of white beneath the edge of her armoire. Bending down, she found a torn piece of paper anchored beneath one carved foot.

Her hands tensed as she read the hastily written words.

STAY AWAY FROM VOKSAL
OR YOUL B SORY

A traitor in her own house? Or had someone come in through the open windows in the conservatory?

India shoved the note into her drawer, frowning.

One thing at least was certain. She *would* go to Vauxhall. And she *would* have a splendid time of it!

15

Three eager faces awaited India in the yellow drawing room. Andrew was studying a perfect miniature of a Spanish galleon, while Marianne eyed an exquisite piece of coral brought back from the South Sea Islands by India's father. Alexis was seated in a large armchair near one window, her feet rocking happily as she studied the beautiful prints on the walls. As usual, her battered doll was clutched under one arm.

As soon as India appeared, the little girl swung to her feet in excitement. "She's *here*. I told you she would see us, Andrew!"

"Of course I would see you," India said, bending down as the little girl enveloped her in a warm and rather grimy embrace.

Laughing, India scooped Alexis up and pulled her onto her lap as she settled gracefully on a gilt settee. Alexis frowned at the Egyptian-style feet carved in the shape of griffins.

"So you do not care for the furniture? I assure you it is all the rage in France."

"Is it so?" the little girl asked, unconvinced. "The animals stare at me quite fiercely until I feel my stomach start to rattle."

"Nonsense," her brother said abruptly. "Alexis, you are being wretchedly rude in criticizing Lady Devonham's furniture."

"I didn't mean to," the little girl said, her lip trembling. Her hand slid into India's. "They are just a little surprising. Still, I expect one would grow comfortable with them after a while. Like that beautiful wolf of yours. Luna, isn't she named?"

At the sound of her name, the sleek animal eased forward, ears erect. "Yes, this is my beautiful Luna. She does seem to get into a great deal of trouble, but I couldn't bear leaving her in Norfolk."

Andrew settled himself gingerly on a long divan covered with a leopard skin. Beside him lay two ornate pillows capped with griffins, which he studied rather dubiously himself. "Your family must be keen collectors. How lucky you are to have traveled so many places."

"I suppose so. My brothers and I were always scurrying here and there helping my father track down some treasure or other. Whenever a temple was in disrepair, Papa was always the first to hear of it. When a monastery's collection of rare books was to be sold, he managed to be first on the scene. Yes, it was an interesting life."

Alexis frowned. "But you didn't like it."

Amazingly, the little girl was right. India stroked Luna's smooth fur, thinking about the footloose life she had enjoyed with her family. But she had always felt something was missing. Now that she was cast back into the rigid rules of London society, she felt ill at ease, as if people were just waiting for the next example of Delamere eccentricity to surface.

"Not exactly, imp." India ruffled Alexis's hair and decided to change the subject since the girl was far too quick. She looked at the wooden doll clutched beneath Alexis's arm. "But you've never told me the name of your friend."

"It is very rude of me. This is Josephine, the empress of France," Alexis said gravely. "Josephine, curtsy to Lady Delamere. You have lost the war, and because of that, you must be very humble when you present yourself." As she spoke, Alexis made the doll sweep into a low curtsy.

India fought to hide a smile. Once again she was struck by the strange mix of gaiety and maturity that these three children exhibited. It came no doubt from having lost their parents so young and then experiencing the turmoil of the weeks following Waterloo.

"Very gracefully done, Your Majesty. Would you care to take a dish of tea with me in the conservatory?"

Alexis's eyes widened. "But most certainly Josephine would. And if it is to be permitted, so would my brother, my sister, and I."

Andrew looked uncertainly at India. "We do not mean to be a bother. It was simply that we hadn't seen you since you left."

"Why *did* you go?" Alexis demanded. "You didn't even come to say good-bye. It made the earl very angry."

"It was time for me to leave." India smiled, ruffling Alexis's long golden hair. "And your visit is no sort of bother, I assure you. I've been feeling dreadfully flat this morning and I'm delighted to have a bit of company. Now come along, you three. We will take a turn among Grandmama's potted orange trees before we have our tea. But when she comes upstairs, be certain to tell her how much you admire her orchids. You will be in her good graces forever, I assure you."

The three nodded conspiratorially.

The scene in the conservatory ten minutes later would have made any proper London society matriarch gasp. The three children sprawled next to India on a rare old Turkish carpet, which Beach had unrolled among the rows of roses and flowering oranges. At a safe distance away, a teakettle bubbled happily on a wrought-iron brazier. Since no society matrons were anywhere in sight, the four were having a wonderful time.

"The widow Marchmont came to visit again." Marianne frowned as she delicately slipped a last crumb of walnut cake onto her tongue. "All she does is make calf's eyes at the earl."

"I don't like her," Alexis said. "She treats us as if we were wild animals who belonged behind bars in a menagerie."

India noticed that Andrew did not censor his younger sister as he usually did. "Andrew? You are remarkably thoughtful."

The boy looked torn for a moment. He had eaten three mince tarts and four slices of walnut cake and was just beginning to look comfortably full. India made a mental note to speak to Thorne about the children's diet. She suspected that his cook was buying expensive cuts of meat and seeing all of them went to the servants' quarters, while the children grew thin. She also determined to speak to Mrs. Harrison about some nourishing recipes that the children would enjoy.

Andrew cleared his throat. "She *does* seem to be forever calling on the earl. And she *is* a little stiff in our presence, I suppose." Since Andrew was not one to criticize lightly, those two simple sentences spoke worlds.

Alexis sniffed. "That's not what you said when she

ordered Chilton to kill your mouse. You said that
you wished her to blazes and you just dared her to
raise a hand to your pet."

"Well, I was blisteringly mad. To think that she
thought she had a right to interfere." A look of
worry creased his brow. "Of course, it is very possible that she may soon have *every* right if her campaign succeeds."

The three children turned very quiet, their faces
glum.

"Do you mean to say that Lady Marchmont has
set her cap at your guardian?"

"It appears that way," Andrew said sadly. "And
she is very much an experienced woman of the
world, I believe. The earl is often moody. I think it
is because of Waterloo. All of this makes him
very . . ."

"Vulnerable?" India said.

"Exactly. But that is why we thought of coming to
you. You seem to—to understand him even when he
does not himself. And he listens to you."

Hardly, India thought. She pushed to her feet,
struck by the appalling notion of Thorne wedded to
Helena Marchmont. The woman was a notorious
libertine who, it was said, had shared her bed with
half the rakes of London before her elderly husband
had the good fortune to die in a hunting accident.
India could not believe that Helena Marchmont and
Thorne would suit. Certainly, the children would
suffer in such a match.

Still, what business was it of *hers?* "I fear your
guardian must make his own decisions."

Alexis's fingers tightened on her doll. "But *you*
would suit him much better. He laughs when you
are there, and his eyes go all distant and soft. He
even sits in his study holding that hat of yours."

So *that's* where her straw bonnet was. India had not been able to find it after her return. But why did Thorne want it? "I'm certain it means nothing, Alexis. You must not read too much into a simple gesture."

"Alexis is right," Andrew said abruptly. "Lord Thornwood keeps the hat on a hook beside his desk. I saw it there when I went to talk to him yesterday. He has been proposing to send me away to Eton and I told him I did not want to go until Alexis and Marianne were a little older. After I left, I remembered a message for him. When I turned back, he had taken the hat down and was holding it to his face, almost as if to smell it."

India felt a flush creep into her cheeks. "You must be mistaken."

Andrew looked at her face, but wisely held his tongue.

"Well, I think he's a fool," Marianne said. "Lady Marchmont is a terrible hag without her rouge and lip color. Not like you," the girl said firmly. "You would be beautiful without any creams or powder. Even first thing in the morning."

India felt her throat tighten with emotion at the three loyal faces before her. Their lives were so uncertain and now the one man who could protect them would be shut off to them if Lady Marchmont had her way.

"Very well," she said with sudden resolve. "What is it you want of me?"

"We rather thought we would try and scare the widow off," Andrew said. "Nothing dangerous, of course. We'll simply free my collection of pet mice."

Marianne giggled. "And I have a dead horned beetle that I will put in her reticule. It is most revoltingly lifelike, I assure you."

India bit her lip to keep from laughing at the thought of the imperious Lady Marchmont reaching into her bag and pulling out what she thought to be a horned beetle. "And what is to be my part in all this, you rogues?"

"We were hoping that you'd keep the earl occupied while we made our preparations," Andrew explained.

India knew a moment of doubt. She did not care to be in Thorne's company any more than she had to. It was true that she had already been planning her own campaign of revenge, but she felt guilty in allowing the children to be involved. "I shall try," she began uncertainly, "but your guardian is not likely to be interested in spending much time in my company."

Although Alexis opened her mouth to protest, Andrew cut his sister off. "You are very good, my lady. We can ask no more of you than that."

The three sat looking very glum. Thoughts of having Lady Marchmont as a stepmama drove away all the sweetness of their adventure in the conservatory.

Then India clapped her hands. "But I have the very thing to cheer you up. Have you ever seen a balloon ascension?"

"Balloon ascension?" Three sets of eager eyes swung toward her.

"I've been reading about such things," cried Andrew. "Is there one planned?"

"In Hampstead Heath today, directly after a meeting of the Society for Rational Investigation of Natural Phenomena. Would you like to attend?"

The three children jumped up, shrieking.

"I will accept that as a yes," India said, laughing. "And I shall be delighted to chaperon you. But you must tell your guardian where you are going. It will not do to lie to him."

"I'll send around a note," Andrew said quickly. "But it doesn't matter. He won't be back for most of the day and maybe even the night. He does that often, you know. It is rather strange, I suppose, but most grown-ups seem to act strangely." The boy flushed. "Oh, I beg your pardon, my lady. I did not mean to say that you—"

"It's quite all right, Andrew. Sometimes I agree with you." India frowned, recalling Dev's cryptic comments to the Duchess of Cranford. He had said something about duty and responsibility, she remembered. Could there be more going on here than she imagined? After he had nearly lost his life at Waterloo, could they continue to demand more of him?

Anger flooded through her for a moment. It would be just like Dev. His sense of honor had always carried an element of recklessness. "Very well," she said briskly. "If you will write a note for your guardian, we may be off." She looked down at her little timepiece and nodded. "We still have three quarters of an hour before the ascension is to begin. This will be an important day in the annals of scientific investigation, after all. The experience will no doubt have a most improving effect on all of our minds."

But there was a distinct note of mischief in her voice as she led the children downstairs.

"They've gone *where?*"

The governess who stood anxiously before the Earl of Thornwood was the fifth that he had hired for the task of instructing his wards. Her hands twisted nervously. "Off to Hampstead Heath," she repeated breathlessly.

"Hampstead Heath? Why in heaven's name *there?*"

"I believe, my lord—" The woman caught a quick breath. "That is, I conclude that they are off to a balloon ascension. Master Andrew sent a message around with a footman from Devonham House."

Thornwood cursed softly. He should have known. This had all the earmarks of one of India's escapades. The next thing he knew, she would be taking them off on a ship to interview Napoleon at St. Helena.

He paced the floor angrily, hands locked at his back. Andrew at least should have known better. Thorne had told the boy that he was responsible for his two younger sisters. He would be well and truly punished for this piece of disobedience.

"Very well, Miss Linton. That will be all. I shall handle this business myself." He frowned as Chilton tapped at the door of his study. "Yes, what is it?"

"A servant with a message, my lord. She is from—" The butler cleared his throat, managing in that short sound to convey great disapproval. "She is sent from Lady Marchmont."

"Oh, very well, show her in. Show all of London in!"

Lady Marchmont stood before her cheval glass smoothing her fingers over the transparent gown that her maidservant had just fetched for her. "You saw to it that he got the message?"

The servant nodded anxiously. "Yes, my lady. I told him all you said. How you would be at Vauxhall tonight and would wait for him in the Great Walk at the stroke of midnight."

"Excellent," the countess murmured. She pirouetted, well pleased by the thrust of her full breasts, clearly visible beneath the translucent silk. Her green eyes narrowed. "And you gave him the other message just as I told you? The one about the children?"

"Yes, my lady. I told him they had gone with Lady Devonham to the balloon ascension at Hampstead Heath."

"Perfect," Lady Marchmont purred in triumph. "Just let the Delamere vixen try to work her wiles upon him *now*."

Behind her the maidservant cleared her throat.

"Yes?" the countess said impatiently. "What is it now?"

"It's just that, well, the earl seemed different, my lady. Nervous like. His eyes kept going to the next room. 'Twas almost like something was hidden there what he didn't want me to see."

The widow snorted. "Nonsense. You are just imagining things. Now be off and fetch that chocolate for me. I told Cook I wanted it here thirty minutes ago, and I will see the woman sacked if she isn't more prompt in the future. You *too*," the countess snapped.

"Yes, my lady. Right now, my lady." The woman bobbed a quick curtsy and fled from the room. She had been wounded too often by the countess's angry barbs to risk another attack. And she well knew that when the Countess of Marchmont was in this wild frame of mind she could do anything.

Anything at all.

"Oh, Andrew, this is a perfect adventure!" Alexis clapped her hands in delight as the carriage drew over a hill, revealing a sea of other vehicles thronging the heath for a view of the ascension soon to begin.

But India was already having very different thoughts about bringing the children. The hills were packed with farm wagons, racing curricles, and spectators of all sorts. Sharp-eyed pickpockets jostled amid ladies of dubious virtue, drunken lords, and noisy villagers.

India studied the loungers and canine observers anxiously. "This is not the best day to observe the ascension. Perhaps we should leave. The weather looks uncertain and there are too many carriages before us for us to have a good view."

All three children cried out in protest. "There's a path." Andrew pointed where a farm cart had just moved. "I'm certain we can make it through."

India sighed. The boy was utterly intent on seeing the ascension. What kind of an ogre would she be to deny him this simple pleasure? "Very well. But you must not leave the carriage. I'll have the coachman turn so that you can look out through the window."

"Look," Andrew called excitedly, as they pulled to a halt. Through the trees the bright canopy of silk lifted skyward. "They're about to fill the balloon. It is a very dangerous moment."

"Why?" Alexis demanded, wriggling about on the seat.

"Because the gas they use is extraordinarily flammable."

"Flam—what does *that* mean?"

"It means, imp, that the whole thing could explode at any moment."

Alexis slid closer to her brother. "I'm going to hold my breath."

India had the same thought. In truth, she had lied to Thorne about her experiences, which were still only a dream. Now the glowing silk make her blood stir, and she yearned to drift silent and free over the hills and hedges.

At that moment India heard her name called by a figure in a purple waistcoat embroidered with cabbage roses. "Monk, is that you?"

"Quite. But we never expected to see *you* here." Beside the viscount, holding the reins of the curricle with exquisite skill, sat a man whose exotic cheekbones and lazy smile were very familiar to India.

"What, are you here too, Connor MacKinnon?" India smiled at the inscrutable friend of her eldest brother, Luc. She remembered their adventure freeing Luc and his wife from a villain bent on seeing Luc dead. "Don't tell me that you are interested in balloon ascensions."

"Not I, my lady. I'll choose a pitching deck and driving rain over one of those contraptions any day. I'm just here to keep an eye on Monkton."

Beside him, the exquisite in purple satin began to sputter. "Not a bit of it! I had to force you to—" He snorted in disgust as Connor MacKinnon's emerald eyes lit with lazy humor. "Villain. You've spent too much time at sea, that's your problem, MacKinnon." The viscount surveyed the crowded slope. "Don't suppose you've seen Thorne?" he asked casually.

India's smile fled. "Not . . . today."

"Odd. I don't see him anywhere. Been acting devilish strange since he got back, if you ask me." He looked at the children pressed to the window in India's carriage. "Not the best place to bring a brood of children, you know. Nasty mix of people here. But no matter. Between MacKinnon and myself, we'll keep you safe."

At that moment a farm cart and a coach full of

noisy young gentlemen pulled into place behind them. India sighed. "Since it seems we cannot leave now, I shall be glad of your assistance."

Suddenly the crowd roared. The balloon canopy expanded to its full height and drifted above the trees. India's breath caught as the bright silk dipped and swayed. And so it was that she did not at first notice Andrew slipping over the side of the carriage. By the time she did, it was too late, for her cry was drowned out by the excited shouts of the spectators.

She pulled on her cloak, calling sharply to Lord Monkton. "I must go. Keep an eye on the girls!"

"You *can't* go! Not at all the sort of place for a lady."

But he was too late. India had already disappeared, swallowed up by the boisterous crowd.

16

Shading his eyes against the early afternoon sun, Thornwood studied the milling humanity spread over the sloping hills in front of him. He felt his irritation turn into raw anxiety. For the third time since his arrival, he waved aside a woman displaying the better half of her chest and then tossed a handful of coins to the pair of urchins in ragged clothes who had followed him all the way up the hill.

What in heaven's name was India about to bring the children to a place such as this? His fingers tensed on his reins, causing his great bay to dance skittishly. Every inch of ground seemed to be jammed tight with wagons filled with excited spectators. Dev picked his way to the top of the hill and there a terrible sight met his eyes. Young Andrew, his face white with fear, had one arm draped over the edge of the basket. Whatever the boy was saying was drowned out by the roar of the crowd. No one had seen that his arm was caught fast in the balloon's rigging.

At that moment Thornwood's attention was caught by a man trying to pick his pocket. Deftly, he caught the grimy wrist and twisted it aside. "I suggest you try your profession somewhere else."

The man scowled, but hurried away.

When Thorne looked back, the basket was bumping and straining across the ground only seconds from ascent. And halfway over the edge of the basket, one slender ankle clearly exposed, hung a woman. Her long auburn hair streamed wildly beneath the currents of the balloon.

Devlyn glared up in disbelief as he watched his wife rising over the hundreds of cheering spectators, a bright and entirely delighted smile on her face.

Somehow India managed to keep a smile locked firmly on her lips in spite of the fact that her fingers were clenched with terror on the flimsy wall of the basket.

At least Andrew was safe. She had managed to pull him free of the rigging just before the balloon swept free of the ground.

Now *she* was caught.

How in heaven's name had she managed to get herself into this coil? Jostled by the crowd, Andrew had stumbled forward and in the process his wrist had caught in one of the balloon's riggings. Desperately India had jerked at the ropes until he was finally able to pull free, but in the process her sash had become caught and she had been left with two desperate choices.

Was she to allow the balloon to rise with her sash entangled, resulting in her being stripped naked before a sea of onlookers, or to work her way into the basket herself and take an unplanned flight with the astonished operator?

She chose the latter. After her terror had faded

and she had grown accustomed to the pitch and
sway of the little basket, she began to see a strange
beauty to the scene. Below her the figures slid away,
growing smaller and smaller until they were no
more than ants against the green heath. There was
no sound except for the whistling of the wind, giving her the effortless sensation of a bird in flight.

"Is it always this way?" she demanded of the bal-
loonist.

"If one is lucky," the man said. "Aye, it was a fair
enough ascent." His leathery face creased in a
frown. "But you shouldn't oughtter have jumped
aboard like that, miss. It was too dangerous by
half."

"I'm afraid I had no choice. There was a boy
caught in your rigging. When I tried to free him, my
sash was caught."

The man's eyes widened. "A close thing, that, and
no mistake." He cleared his throat. "In that case, I
suppose you did right. Bloody brave, too, beggin'
your pardon." He stuck out a hand, "Glad to have
you aboard. I'm Smithson."

India returned the quick handshake, then looked
up, studying the brightly colored silk and the solid
rigging that ran from the basket up to the balloon
canopy. "I know a little about the process, Mr.
Smithson, but not about the rip line. What exactly
does that do?"

"Well, it's like this, young lady," the man began,
obviously delighted to expound on his expertise. "If
you look right over there you'll spy a rope running
from this basket here up to the top of the balloon.
When I pull on it just a little, it forms a hole in the
upper part of the balloon and that means we de-
flate. But dear me, it has to be done properly, so it
does. Why, I remember last year in Yorkshire I went

up with a friend of mine, who made a mull of things. Almost lost his arm, he did."

India's eyes widened as she listened to Smithson's hair-raising adventures. At the same time, far below, a rider was racing through the crowds in pursuit.

"Pull the rip line! Tighter, my lady. Aye, that's it." Fifteen minutes later Smithson had his hands full controlling the air valves and sandbags for ballast.

They were beyond the heath now, skimming in magnificent silence over the thatched roofs of a small village. Smithson had judged it was time to set down, but one of the valves was stuck and he was having trouble with the rip panel. Without that release of hot air they would never make it down safely. On top of that, one of the sandbags had come loose, tearing down to the ground far below. With any more loss of ballast a controlled descent would be impossible.

India shivered slightly. At this height it was decidedly cooler than the ground and she wished she had her cloak. But being cold was the least of her problems, she knew. Smithson was struggling to keep an eye on the landscape while maneuvering the rip line when India saw one of the sandbags heave sideways and toss against its ropes. Quickly she bent out over the basket and tugged it inside in the nick of time.

"Nice work, miss," Smithson said tightly. "But I think I've got this line nearly free. Hang on tight. I'm going to try to set down."

One moment they were soaring effortlessly on a silent sea of wind and the next hot air was rushing out the top of the balloon. The basket shuddered beneath India and then the ground seemed to rush toward her. "The *trees*, Mr. Smithson!"

"Aye, my lady, I see them. With a bit of luck we'll just manage to—"

The man muttered a curse as the basket skimmed a row of elm trees and dragged free. A farming field was beneath them. They hit with two jolts, wind wrenching the silk out in a wild cascade.

India breathed a huge sigh of relief. "I do believe that was the most exciting thing I've ever done, Mr. Smithson. Possibly also the most dangerous."

The man nodded, a twinkle in his eye. "And I do say as how you're the best assistant I've ever had, miss. In fact, anytime you're wishful of having another flight just you let me know." He looked about at the lonely field and rubbed his neck. "And you may be certain I'll have a word with that lazy apprentice of mine when he appears. It's him as to blame for not securing those sandbags and nearly killing the pair of us. I only hope he followed close enough with the wagons so we don't have to spend the night in this field."

As he spoke, a rider broke from the clearing atop the hill. India frowned as a figure thundered down the narrow track, took a fence at the gallop, and pounded through the fields of clover.

Her eyes widened. It *couldn't* be. Surely, this was the worst possible ending to a day that had been full of disaster.

The Earl of Thornwood vaulted from his horse and strode angrily toward the gondola. He bent forward, lifted India angrily from the basket, and set her down hard on the ground.

"Thorne, I—"

"No, not a word. I don't want to hear a single wild attempt at explanation." A muscle flashed at his jaw. "I couldn't believe my ears when Lady Marchmont sent word that you were going to the ascension with the children."

"How wonderfully helpful of the widow to pass along the information," India said icily. "I can only wonder how she seems to be so well informed of my affairs."

"She happened to see you and the children leaving your house," Dev said flatly. "Her coachman has a brother who works in the stables across the street and he happened to mention where you were going."

"How very convenient," India said, her eyes narrowed. "And I suppose she just happened to mention this bit of news to you?"

"She sent me a note, quite properly thinking I would wish to know what dangers my wards were being dragged into."

"Andrew sent a message back to you."

"If so, I didn't receive it."

"The children were quite safe. Except for—"

"Safe? I saw with my own eyes what happened, and I won't have it, do you hear?" Thorne's eyes were glittering, his whole body tense.

"But I didn't expect to—"

"That's just the point, isn't it? You never do think about anything. An idea simply captures your fancy and you bolt like an ill-trained horse. Or perhaps," Thorne continued angrily, "like that wild wolf you insist on keeping as a pet."

"Leave Luna out of this."

Thorne laughed coldly. "Luna. An appropriate name. The two of you are both struck with moon madness, if you ask me."

"Begging your pardon, sir, but the lady was not at fault." Smithson was eyeing Thornwood, not liking the tone he was using to the companion who had just proved herself so useful in what could have been a disastrous flight.

"I'll thank you to hold your tongue, my good man. This is between Lady Devonham and myself."

"You are rude," India hissed, her hands going to fists. "Perhaps you've always been rude and I've never seen it before. All your thoughts are devoted to yourself, what makes *you* happy, what makes *you* comfortable. Do you have any idea how those children feel cooped up in a dismal house with a dismal string of governesses who don't care a fig about their happiness or welfare?"

Thorne's eyes glittered. "I've paid well to have them attended."

"Paid! Yes, that's right you've paid. But money can't buy affection. Money can't buy time with the only person they trust. Are you such a fool that you can't see that?"

"I think that these matters are best discussed in private," Thorne said curtly. "And then you may begin to explain to me how in God's name you managed to create such an imbroglio."

India took a step back, her face pale as ice and her blue eyes glinting with fury. "Explain? I think not, my lord. It would be pointless to waste another word on you!"

Smiling grimly, Thorne reached down and began to roll his cuffs over his long muscled forearms. "No matter. We'll have plenty of time to talk while I take you back to your carriage."

India's face filled with color. "You wouldn't *dare*." She took a step backward, her body rigid.

The next moment, Dev's hard hands were at her shoulders.

"I'll not stand here and see the lady harmed, do you hear me? Let her go this minute."

But Smithson might as well have been talking to one of the Elgin marbles. Thorne's fingers tightened on India's shoulders as he saw the anger in her face, the rigid line of her body, the high color in her cheeks. Her hair was blown in a wild red cascade about her shoulders. Suddenly Thorne remembered how she looked, slanting over the edge of the basket. The little fool might have been tossed out and even now been lying with her neck crushed.

Her breast pressed soft and warm at the inner curve of his elbow and he felt the curve of her hips beneath her soft muslin gown. His body tightened with a storm of angry need. Sweet heaven, how did she manage to strip him of sanity again and again?

In Brussels he had thought her charming, adventurous, with great joy and wit, but now Devlin saw that she was far more than that.

India Delamere was a woman who would never be broken to his bit or any other man's. And that very recklessness of hers stirred some answering sense of adventure in him, something Devlyn had thought long buried beneath the cold facade that long months of war had given him.

But now, with one brush of India's soft hips, with one glimpse at her full satin curves, he came perilously close to forgetting duty and honor and country.

He tried to hate her for that. He worked hard at summoning up that anger. But Thorne was too honest for the strategy to work for long.

No, his real anger was for himself for failing to realize his danger while it was still early enough to extract himself. Now he could no longer ignore his feelings. When she was away from him, he found himself dreaming of her honesty and vibrancy, counting the minutes until he would see her next.

All his duties went unattended, and his mind performed in the most perfunctory fashion. He was acting, in short, as green as a lovesick boy up to London for his very first season on the town.

He had heard all kinds of wild stories about the Delameres, of course. The family was spoken of in awe and hushed whispers. Their wealth was beyond measuring and their eccentricities beyond numbering. Dev had soon seen the jealousy and envy in the cold little tales circulated through the ton. The eldest Delamere son had vanished for five years, only to reappear without a word of explanation. The duke and his wife were just as bad, spending more time digging in foreign ruins than seeing to the proper education of their unruly children.

And India?

Thorne had heard about the wild heiress and the legions of suitors whose hearts had been ensnared by her red-haired beauty. He hadn't believed the stories. Not at first. But he was starting to believe them now. No matter how his own feelings were involved, he had a duty to his three wards, who had known too much pain already.

His face was hard as he caught India up over one shoulder and spun about.

"Put me down this minute, Devlyn Carlisle!" India's fists hammered against his back, but he did not stop. Smiling grimly, he vaulted up into the saddle with India before him, cradled tightly against his chest.

India didn't say a single word as they rode in silence back to Hampstead Heath. Every stride of the horse threw her against Thorne's hard chest. Every jump and gallop made his hard thighs press intimately against hers. She tried to ignore him, tried to tell herself her heart was cold and empty and he was nothing but a stranger.

But it didn't work.

He could never be a stranger to her, no matter how hard she tried to make it so. Brussels had happened. The war had happened. Like it not, their love had bloomed against that dark stain of chaos. And bloomed again in the darkness of a carriage on a quiet London street. Now India feared she would never be able to let go of her dream, though it would only make them both wretched.

As the black trees slid past and the scattered cottages grew to tiny villages and finally to the town that huddled on the edge of the heath, India felt a hot ache gather in her throat. She closed her eyes, tasting a fierce sense of loss, more bitter than any she had ever known. She had lost this man once and grieved for him for months, feeling her life had ended. Then she had found him again, only to lose him a second time with her discovery that his memory had been taken from him.

Now it seemed that India would lose him for a third time, and this time the loss would be final. He was not the man she had known in Brussels, clever, generous, and with a restless wit. That man was gone. His cold profile rose before her, rigid and stern, everything the man she loved was *not*.

India was honest enough to know they would never suit. She came from a long line of adventurers who had delighted in dangerous independence ever since the very first Delamere won a title for flouting William the Conqueror's orders and slipping away from the main line of fighting at the Battle of Hastings. He had then made his own attack from the rear, a piece of insubordination that would have cost him his head had his foresight not carried the day. In the end her ancestor had been knighted the first Earl of Devonham. In succeeding centuries the earldom had been replaced by a dukedom, won for a similar stroke of reckless bravery at the Battle of Agincourt.

No, India knew that she would never be content with a man so different. The past was finally closed for her. She must put Devlyn Carlisle out of her mind forever.

But her face held no emotion when Thorne reined in his horse among the straggling remnants of the spectators on the heath. Without a word he handed her down to Viscount Monkton, while the children watched anxiously. She spoke tersely, trying to produce a smile and not really succeeding, as Monkton shot thoughtful glances between the two.

And then with a flutter of satin and a cloying onslaught of rose perfume, Lady Marchmont advanced upon the scene, enormously elegant in a damask mantua and a feathered bonnet. "So there you are, my lord." But the countess was studying India as she spoke. Her eyes filled with malice beneath half-lowered lids. "I'd feared that you had disappeared on some adventure and had quite forgotten about me and these brave little wards of yours."

Thornwood gave her the merest nod, turning instead to hand over his horse to a waiting groom.

"But my carriage is just down the hill. I'd be more than delighted to escort you and these delightful children back to London." Her face took on a totally false smile as she stared at India. "Of course, I include you in the invitation too, my lady." She managed to slant a cutting look at India's dusty gown and the wild curls flowing about her shoulders. "No doubt you will wish to rest after the rigors of your adventure," she murmured.

India's chin rose. Delamere pride raged hotly through her veins. "I would not *dream* of inconveniencing you, Lady Marchmont. Especially as I'm certain you and the earl have so very *much* to discuss. I shall take my own carriage."

"I'd better go with her," Connor MacKinnon said tightly. "She's a look of wildness about her, and I know that look all too well from Luc."

"Who in hell are you?" Thorne shot an angry glance at the exotic stranger seated beside Monkton.

"I'm a friend." MacKinnon's eyes glinted. "A friend who does not care to see the lady hurt. You would be well advised to remember that, Thornwood."

"Hurt? She does a brilliant job of that all by herself," Thorne said tightly.

Monkton shook his head as Thornwood took his wards firmly by the hands and headed for Lady Marchmont's coach. "What in the name of heaven have those two managed to do now?"

MacKinnon smiled slowly. "I rather think they've managed to fall in love, Monkton. Only it's not all bells and fireworks the way they thought it should be." He looked thoughtfully at India, moving stiffly up the hill. "She'll lead him a merry dance, that's for certain. Meanwhile, I'd better keep an eye on her. Luc will have my hide if anything happens to his baby sister."

Monkton ran a hand through his hair, for once unmindful of the fashionable disorder that he had worked so hard to create that morning. "Not going to end well, mark my words. Both of them are too stubborn by half." He shook his head as Thornwood handed up the last of the children and then climbed up after them into Lady Marchmont's coach. "I'll have to talk to Penn about it. Must be *something* we can do."

India did not cry once on the way back to London. Tears stung her eyes and heat bit at her throat, but she angrily forced them away. The man was not worth a single tear, she told herself fiercely.

All her juvenile mooning for Devlyn Carlisle was at an end. She saw him now for exactly what he was —selfish, coldhearted and arrogant.

She had months of unhappiness to make up for, India vowed as the London streets rushed past.

She would begin this very night at Vauxhall.

17

"No, not that way. If you crimp the girl's hair any tighter she'll look like a complete quiz." The Duchess of Cranford stood before a cluttered dressing table issuing orders to a harassed lady's maid struggling to comply with an utterly contradictory stream of demands.

India sat impassively in the midst of the turmoil. She felt almost detached from herself, as if she were watching a total stranger be dressed, adorned, poked, and discussed. She bit back a sigh and smoothed the beautiful embroidery of her white chemise. The cut work was fine and delicate, cool against her skin.

And yet it might as well have been rough, unbleached linen.

"Very well, Hawkins, that will do," the duchess said crisply. "It is a good thing the girl has full hair, or you'd leave her looking like she was wearing a straggly wig."

The very superior upper servant muttered an answer beneath her breath, but she was far too used to the duchess's fits and starts to take any real offense. If the truth be told the two older women were both intensely uneasy, bothered by India's strange mood of abstraction all afternoon since her return from that wretched balloon ascension. Something had happened there, Hawkins was convinced, but there was no getting news from the coachman or anyone else beyond the fact that the Earl of Thornwood had also been in evidence.

Thornwood, the London servant thought. Now *there* was a man who could keep Miss India under tight reins, but she would have to make a push to hold him and right now the girl seemed anything but animated.

The dresser smiled faintly as an outrageous thought began to form in her mind. Yes, it just might work. Certainly the man would not be able to look upon India with indifference afterward. She studied India's elegant muslin chemise and then looked up to find the duchess's eyes similarly narrowed. The two nodded at each other, with the same thought in mind.

The duchess rapped on the floor with her silver-handled cane. "Very well. Up with you, gel, and out of that chemise."

India roused herself from her abstraction and frowned at the duchess. "Take it off? But I just put it on."

"Then you'll just have to take it off. Don't be stubborn with me, miss. And make it sharp. You have but two hours before you leave for Vauxhall."

"In two hours," India said mechanically, "I could have saved the lives of twenty men, passed out bread and tea to two hundred, and seen a whole regiment outfitted with clean linens."

The duchess clucked her tongue. "That was all very well and good, my love, but Waterloo is over. You're in London now. London at the height of the season." The old woman's eyes darkened. "And I'll tell you this, India Delamere, a more serious and dangerous battle takes place here every night among young ladies hoping to find suitable husbands."

"I'm not interested in a husband, Grandmama. I think I shall never marry. Luna and I shall return to Norfolk and there I shall dwindle into faded and shameless eccentricity, shunned by all my former acquaintances."

The duchess snorted. "Not if I can bloody help it," she snapped. She took India's shoulders and urged her to her feet. "Hurry, gel, off with that chemise."

Twenty minutes later India could only stare at herself in the cheval glass in utter astonishment. Her slender body was now covered by the thinnest sheath of white silk crepe, the single layer of fabric ghosting over her rich curves and soft hollows like a second skin. The bodice was cut low and square, fitted to emphasize the shape of her bosom. With every movement, the fabric coyly revealed then hid the shadows of her nipples.

Scandalized, India turned to the duchess. "But, Grandmama, I couldn't *possibly* wear this dress. It is utterly—"

"Ravishing," the old woman finished imperiously. "All the crack," she added, well pleased with her daring idea. In truth such soft fabrics were quite the rage among the faster females of the ton. Of course it would not have done for a young miss of sixteen during her first season upon the town, but India was a different kettle of fish entirely. She had the breeding and the countenance to carry off any sort of dress. And this, the duchess thought fiercely, was just the thing to make the Earl of Thornwood take a closer look.

She whirled her hand. India turned obediently, the soft silk fluttering about her body.

"But, Grandmama, it feels as if I'm wearing nothing."

It nearly looks like it too, the duchess thought. She cleared her throat. "Of course it doesn't, you silly thing. After lounging about in men's clothes so long, you naturally find it odd to be dressed as a female again. Within an hour or two you'll feel perfectly at ease again."

India fingered the soft fabric, unconvinced.

"Besides," the duchess added, "some females water their gowns thoroughly so that nothing at all is left to the imagination."

India, far too busy mourning the loss of the man she loved to spend time among the faster set of London society, raised her eyebrows in shock. "Nothing at all?"

"On my oath."

Beside her Hawkins nodded firmly. "And there's them that does more than that, my lady. I heard from my cousin Elizabeth, who is in service at Lady Tillingham's, that the countess's daughter puts gold paint on her toenails. And if that weren't enough . . ." The woman's voice rose in outrage. "Why then the terrible creature adds gold paint to other parts of her body in the most immoral way." As she spoke Hawkins's eyes fell to India's low bodice.

India's cheeks flushed. "You must be joking."

Hawkins shook her head. "I had it from my cousin's own lips."

The duchess snorted. "One thing I can tell you, it will take a great deal more than a little gold paint on Amelia Tillingham's scrawny chest to make any decent man offer her a proposal of marriage. The woman is a shrew, besides which I've heard that she's addicted to gaming."

The duchess's head cocked as she studied India thoughtfully. "On the other hand, I wonder if maybe a tiny bit of . . ."

"Grandmama," India said firmly, her hands crossed protectively at her chest. "You can't be serious!"

After a moment the duchess shrugged and waved her hand airily. "Perhaps not. Although in my day, gel, things went on that would make your hair curl."

Hawkins nodded conspiratorially. In her thirty years of domestic service she too had seen behavior that would have made India's eyes widen.

But India was not to be allowed to share in these confidential tales, for at that moment there was a light tap at the door and Ian Delamere appeared. His tall frame was exquisitely fitted out in crisp regimentals, and his jacket clung to his broad shoulders with perfect elegance. "Ready to go?"

"I suppose. But you'll completely eclipse me, Ian."

For a moment her brother's handsome face seemed to take on a stain of color and then he shrugged good-naturedly. "I think not, my love." His eyes narrowed. "Gad, you've never dampened that silk, have you? Fast is fast, but that would be rather beyond my powers of fighting off beaux, I believe."

The duchess snorted. "No, she hasn't dampened anything. More's the pity, because if she doesn't make some sort of a push to be noticed, she's bound to end an old maid on the shelf."

India's eyes took on a mutinous gleam. "And what if I do, Grandmama? I have no need to marry for money. I am perfectly well situated, thanks to Aunt Orelia's generous bequest. If I choose to dwindle into an eccentric old maid, so I shall."

For a moment it seemed as if the two of them would launch into an argument which was of long standing. But Ian laughed, caught up India's shawl of Norwich silk, and tossed it around her shoulders.

"No time for arguing," he said firmly. "It will be a devilish crush, since everyone who is anyone is expected to be at Vauxhall tonight, now that the prince has announced he'll be in attendance."

India nodded, slanting a final glance to the cheval glass. Passable, she decided. But what she did not see was that she looked far more than passable. In the candlelight her hair took on fiery sparks and her skin caught a golden glow. When she smiled, her face lit with an animation that would leave any man not yet senile breathless with admiration.

But India noticed none of this.

At the bottom of the staircase Ian turned to fetch his gloves from the impassive Beach. As he did, a small form darted from behind one of the Greek statues and grubby hands were thrown about India's waist.

"But what is this?" India looked down into Alexis's anxious face. The little girl's lower lip was trembling, but there was a look of determination in her eyes.

"I *had* to come. The earl was so very angry after what happened today that I know he said some very bad things to you. And it wasn't your fault. Andrew, Marianne, and I discussed it in our rooms after we got back from the trip with that nasty countess. We tried to tell him, but he refused to discuss it. Then that nasty creature dragged him off into the study and they were in there the longest time with the door closed." Alexis frowned. "What do you think they were doing? Marianne says that they probably drank that sparkling wine and acted silly. Andrew told me that I would learn soon enough about things like that." The little girl looked up at Ian. "Is it something terribly secret, do you think?"

Ian fought to keep a straight face. "Nothing so terrible, I expect. But your brother is probably right. You have a few years before you need to worry yourself about grown-ups' silly behavior."

"From all that I can see grown-ups act more like children than *we* do. Just look at the earl," Alexis explained. "One minute he's happy, the nicest sort of person, and the next minute he's cool and distant. I thought at first it was because of his shoulder. He hurt it, you know. And he has a scar there that he doesn't care to show anyone. But I don't think it's his shoulder that causes him to stamp and frown. You don't think he's coming down with some terrible disease, do you?" the little girl said anxiously.

Only with a case of chronic arrogance, India thought grimly. "No, I'm sure you're worrying about nothing, Alexis. I think your guardian is merely distracted with various responsibilities. He has been away from London for many months, you know. His business affairs must be attended to, after all."

Alexis's nose crinkled as she considered this possibility. "I suppose you're right. I only wish that nasty old widow weren't forever hanging about. I won't have her for a mama," the little girl said firmly. "She would lock us in a closet for the rest of our lives," she said tragically.

Ian laughed and ruffled the little enchantress's silky curls. "I doubt that your guardian would let such a thing happen. I think he cares very much about you."

"I used to think so." The little girl shook her head. "Now I'm not so certain. All he seems to do is go around looking cold and angry. I heard Cook say it was because he was lonely and needed someone to share his bed." The little girl studied Ian's face, perplexed. "But why? Do you think it's because his feet get cold?"

Ian cleared his throat. "Er, I suppose that might be the case." He took Alexis's arm gallantly, and led her outside. "But I suspect you will be missed. You wouldn't want to make everyone worry, would you?"

"Of course not. I simply wanted to explain to Lady Delamere how sorry we all were."

India brushed the little girl's cheek gently. "I'm very glad to know it, but you shouldn't have come out alone. London is very different from the countryside of Brussels."

The little girl's eyes widened. "Do you really think so? I find it very tame. There are not half so many gray people wandering about here as there were near the battlefield."

"Gray people?"

Alexis nodded soberly. "You know, the ones that come out of the bodies after they're dead. I saw any number of them near the fallen soldiers after Waterloo. Oh, they're harmless as a rule, simply as lost as we felt. I tried to make them see that their bodies were gone and they should find their way home, but they didn't seem to want to listen. I'm only a child, after all."

Something cold and tight gripped India's heart. Could this remarkable child, with a maturity far beyond her years, truly have strange powers of sight?

Ian moved away from them over to the carriage. India waited until he was out of hearing distance, then turned back to Alexis and asked softly, "Do you still see these people, Alexis—these gray people?"

The little girl looked anxiously at India. "I hope you won't tell. Andrew and Marianne say it's just my imagination, so I don't speak of it now."

"Your secret is safe, my dear."

"In that case, I'll tell you. I still see them some-times, but not so often now. Here in London there are ever so many little children. In Brussels it was usually the men. Soldiers, you know. But here it's the children and they all seem nothing but bones. Do you think they didn't have enough to eat?"

India thought that was quite likely the case. She struggled to find something wise to say to a child who had probably far more wisdom than she had. "You are right to be concerned, but perhaps you had better not think too much about this. Have you told your guardian?"

"The earl? No, he's too busy these days. I don't want to make him upset." The little girl studied In-dia closely. "He said to tell you not to cry," she said matter-of-factly.

"He? Do you mean the earl?"

"No, of course not. I mean the little boy. I see him around you sometimes—full of light, not like the others. And he always seems happy. His hair is short, with beautiful curls of dark auburn. His eyes are exactly like yours, my lady. He said to tell you it had to be. That the time was not right."

India's face had gone sheet white. Her arms tight-ened against her chest as if she were struggling to protect herself against a physical blow.

As of course she was.

No one knew the secret of her private torment, not until this little girl with the keen silver eyes looked deep and somehow plumbed the very core of her soul.

"You can't possibly know what you're saying," India said hoarsely. "This is some sort of cruel trick."

Instantly Alexis's eyes filled with tears and India realized it was no trick. She looked over at Ian, standing impatiently by the carriage. "I shall take her home, Ian. I must have . . . a little time alone."

Ian frowned. "I'll go with you."

"No!" India gripped his arm hard for a moment. "Just Alexis and I. Please, Ian."

After a moment her brother shook his head. "Very well, though I don't like it a bit. I'll send you ahead in the carriage with Brown, the footman. But I'll be along in fifteen minutes."

India knew it was as much as she could hope for from her protective brother.

"I hope you're not angry with me," Alexis whispered.

"No, not angry." India held the girl's fingers tightly. "Not angry at all."

"How did it happen?"

They bounced along toward Belgrave Square with Alexis's shoulder propped against India's as the girl toyed restlessly with the frayed edge of her dress.

"I don't quite know. There have always been other people around me, people that no one else could see. I think it was after the battle there in Brussels that I began to see the gray ones."

Even now India felt a little tremor of uneasiness at hearing such words spoken so casually. "And the little boy you mentioned?" She caught a breath to steady her voice. "Tell me about him, Alexis."

"Well, he was ever so nice. He has such kind eyes, deep and without bottom. Like a lake my parents once took me to see in Switzerland." The girl gnawed at her lip for a moment.

India fought to keep her voice level. "And . . . do you see him now?"

She could feel Alexis's head turn, studying the shadows of the carriage. After a moment the little girl sighed. "Not now. It happens that way. I never know when they are going to come. Maybe he doesn't want to disturb you, my lady. You look ever so beautiful in that gown—like a fairy princess. I'm certain he didn't want to spoil your evening."

India gripped the girl's fingers tightly, then sat back slowly, her heart pounding.

Of course it was all true. She had lost Devlyn's baby after Waterloo. She had been devastated by Devlyn's death, and the loss of the child had only driven her deeper into her grief. She had stayed on in Belgium for several months more, until she felt ready to face her family and hide the truth of her loss.

Afterward India had never mentioned her pain to anyone. To speak of it would have opened too many wounds. She had decided it was far better to bury all the sad memories as deep as she could.

And now this precocious child with the clever silver eyes looked deep inside her and saw what no one else ever had.

He said to say the time was not right.

India held tight to the words, feeling foolish, but at the same time taking comfort in what Alexis had told her.

"I'm sorry if what I said upset you, Lady Delamere. I didn't mean to bring you pain. Of course, no one ever believes me when I talk about the things I see. Especially about the man with the scar who comes sometimes at night."

India frowned. "You've really seen this person?"

"I wouldn't lie! I see him hiding in my room

sometimes. There is something cold about his eyes, as if he can look at you and turn you to a block of ice." The girl shivered.

"Think carefully, Alexis. Have you really seen this man or is he like—like the gray ones, the ones you see but cannot touch?"

The girl was silent for a moment. "I've never touched him, if that's what you mean. But I can see him there, as surely as I can see you right now in the shadows beside me." The little girl's voice fell. "As surely as I can see that you are crying." Her fingers stole up and brushed India's wet cheek.

"Thank you for telling me, Alexis. Don't feel bad. I . . . I'm glad to know. But I wish you would not speak of this to anyone else. It shall be our secret, just yours and mine. Could you do that?"

"Of course. I keep secrets from Andrew all the time. He doesn't like me to hide slices of cake from dinner, but I put them in my pinafore and take them upstairs to the nursery. I slide them behind a pile of books."

Suddenly Alexis was a normal six-year-old again, a rather sad and lonely young girl concerned with hiding sweets from her brother.

India reached out and gave her a tight hug. "And I promise I'll speak to your guardian. I shall see that you get to Astley's Amphitheater and Gunter's for ices. Do you think you would like that?"

"Oh *yes*. But we don't mean to bother you, especially not when the earl is acting like—like he has ale froth for brains."

"Alexis!"

"Well, he is. I heard Cook say so. And he's every bit in love with you. Whenever you're in the room, he gets what Andrew calls a dopey look on his face. But he hides it if he thinks you're looking."

India sighed. It was clear that the child had built a fantasy in her hopes to find a mother. "Let's not worry about that, my dear. Just look, we are back at your house."

The carriage creaked to a halt and the door was flung open by Ian, who stood outside to hand Alexis down to a waiting footman. "Stay there," he ordered India. "I shall see Alexis inside and deal with Thornwood."

India smiled slightly. When Ian was in his domineering mood, there was no crossing him. Besides, she was not looking forward to a discussion with Thorne, not after their last meeting.

So she sat back and let her brother escort Alexis gravely up the steps to the waiting butler.

As she sat in the darkness of the carriage, some strange compulsion made India look into the shadows, yearning for a sight of auburn curls and smoky blue eyes. "Are you there?" she asked softly. "My little lost love, are you truly there?"

As she spoke, the wind ruffled the linden trees in the small park across the square. For a moment India could have sworn the sound was just like the muted laughter of a small and very happy child.

18

Vauxhall was a glittering fairyland alight with thousands of dancing lanterns as India and her brother made their way past crowds of festive spectators. At ten o'clock there was a concert and at twelve o'clock the fireworks began, at which point the crowds in attendance usually turned quite rowdy.

The pleasure gardens to the south of London included narrow walks through half-hidden groves, which provided privacy for meetings of a more illicit sort. But Ian was careful to keep his sister to the lighted walkways and the laughing crowds where gay waltzes drifted through the cool air.

In one corner beneath a cluster of lanterns in the shape of stars, a tall man behind a black satin mask was holding forth before a crowd of enthusiastic listeners. "Lord," Ian muttered, "there's the Duke of Wellington thronged by admirers. Let's go the other way."

Smiling, India let him lead her off toward a row of hedges, her little satin slippers crunching over tiny pieces of gravel.

"I've reserved a place for us at a box not too far up

the hill," Ian explained. "We'll have a perfect view of the spectacles and the fireworks at midnight."

At that moment a raucous crowd of young bucks, clearly drunk, stumbled past laughing wildly. Ian drew India out of the way. "As you can see, this is no place for an unescorted female," he said grimly, "especially not the Dark Walk."

"I've never heard of it. It sounds wonderfully illicit, however."

"There's nothing wonderful about the place. It's damned dangerous and if you're found there it is commonly assumed that you're a woman in search of whatever she happens to find."

India snorted. "I dare one of those drunken louts to lay a hand on me." Her eyes sparkled behind the little golden mask that the duchess had given her, its color perfectly matching the edge of her sash. "Do you remember that time in Egypt, Ian? When we had to hold off a camp full of nomads who were bound and determined to take all our horses."

Her brother laughed softly. "How can I ever forget, hoyden? You stole the leader's horse and then ran off, with a lot of them howling in pursuit. That's when they discovered that I hobbled all the horses by tying together their legs."

Ian chuckled. As they stood laughing, a pair of women dressed in gowns even more translucent than India's wandered past arm and arm. The taller one, her face hidden beneath heavy rouge and a beauty patch, slanted Ian a seductive look.

"Heaven's, Ian, do not tell me that those two are—"

"Your suspicions are correct, India." Her brother cleared his throat. "And I really think it's time we moved on. I have a table reserved."

A pair of drunken soldiers ambled past, hot on

the heels of the two ladies of the evening. They
turned, caught sight of Ian in his regimentals, and
gave him a dashing salute. He shook his head,
laughing, but of course in Vauxhall any sort of in-
formality was permitted, perhaps even expected. It
was in fact one of the particular attractions of the
place, for here prince and pauper might stroll together casually, formality and virtue forgotten in
the fantasy of the dancing lanterns. It was a place
where one could be seen and at the same time be
entirely invisible, for whether one wore a mask or
not, whatever took place in the shadows would not
be commented upon the next day.

Nearby India heard low laughter spill over one of
the carved boxwood hedges where a pair of lovers
were having a quiet tryst. For a moment she felt a
pang of sadness, thinking of the fury on Devlyn's
face when he had left her at Hampstead Heath, but
she dismissed the thought, angry at him for disturbing her peace yet again.

Near the center of the gardens the orchestra was
tuning up. "Perhaps we had better take one more
turn around the orchestra area and then go look for
our box."

"Very well," India said.

But at that moment she saw a most disturbing
sight. Three small forms were creeping between a
row of tables behind the area where the orchestra
was playing. India's eyes narrowed as she caught a
glimpse of pale blond hair on the smallest one.

It was impossible, of course. It could not be—

The figure moved and beneath the light of a dancing lantern India had a perfect view of big gray eyes
and a very pale face.

Alexis's face.

"Oh no," she said to her brother. "It's the three

children. What in heaven's name are *they* doing here?"

Ian frowned. "They can't stay here, that's for certain." He studied the area beside the orchestra. "Those three over there?"

"I'm afraid so." A moment later the tallest of the shadows turned and India recognized Andrew beneath a hooded cloak that very nearly dragged on the ground. She waved quickly and gave a sigh of relief when the boy waved back.

"Thorne's here, you know," Ian said tightly. "I saw him by the grotto. He was with Lady Marchmont."

India's heart fell. If he saw the children he would no doubt punish them severely and India couldn't bear the thought. "Hurry, Ian, we can take a shortcut through the Dark Walk. There must be some quiet grotto where we can sit down and find out what they're doing here."

Her brother, ever the resolute campaigner, studied the shaded greenery. After a moment he nodded. "Just to the left of the oak tree, I think. Come along, my love."

True to his word, less than five minutes later they were assembled beside a gurgling fountain lit by lanterns, and Alexis was clinging to India's waist.

"We told her it was nothing but a foolish story, but she wouldn't listen." Andrew's face looked very grave. Despite his curiosity, he was out of his depth in this place and feeling reluctant he'd ever agreed to his sister's demands.

"But why in the world did you come here? It is not at all safe."

"I made them," Alexis explained, her voice trembling. "We had to come and warn you. You're in very great danger, Lady Delamere. You see I saw the

man again, the man with the scar. He was following
your carriage when you left Belgrave Square."

"What man is this, Alexis?"

"He's a bad man. I see him sometimes at the foot
of my bed. He wishes us all harm, and he's here
tonight."

India exchanged a quick look with her brother.

"You're sure that he was real, Alexis? Not like one
of the others, the ones we spoke about?"

The little girl shook her head sharply. "No, not
one of them. He was real. I know it." Her hands
tightened on India's. "You must believe me."

"Hush," India said softly, smoothing the girl's
hair tenderly. "Of course I believe you and I think
that you are all very, very brave to come here and
warn me. I shall be very careful, and of course I
have Ian to help keep me safe. But now that I know,
I think you must return home before your guardian
finds that you have slipped out." As she spoke,
laughter trilled past the high boxwood hedge that
ringed the grotto.

Lady Marchmont's laughter.

Alexis's hand rose to her mouth. "Oh, he's here!
He's here with *her*." The little girl looked up at her
brother anxiously. "He will be ever so angry if he
finds we disobeyed him, Andrew."

The boy looked clearly uncomfortable. "I dare say
we'd be put on bread and water for the rest of our
lives."

"All the more reason for him not to find you here
then," India said crisply.

"Fortunately I have just the solution." Ian had
moved to the back of the grotto and was holding
open a small door all but concealed behind the
hedge.

"How in the world did you know that was there, Ian?"

The soldier's lips curved. "It always pays to have an escape route, no matter where you are," he said jauntily. "Now, be quick about it, you three. I have the carriage not too far away. I'll take you there and have the coachman see you home."

Ian looked at India. "I'm afraid it means leaving you alone for a few minutes. I believe I saw Pendleworth back there, however. I'll track him down and send him to you."

"Don't worry about me. I shall send any drunken roués packing," India said firmly. "Just see the children to safety."

"But the man with the scar." Alexis shivered. "He's here! You must be very careful."

India patted the girl's head. "And so I will, my dear." She reached into her little reticule and pulled out a beautifully worked pistol with silver and golden mounts.

India smiled as Andrew gave a low whistle. "You don't think I'd come to a place like this unprepared, do you? After all, who would protect my big burly brother from all the women who would try and waylay him for their dastardly ends."

On the other side of the orchestra, Devlyn Carlisle was surveying the throngs of revelers, his lean features hidden by a black satin mask. "But I could swear I heard the children. They were here just a moment ago."

Beside him Helena Marchmont clicked her tongue and poured her lush body even closer. "Your devotion is the thing I like the most about you, my lord. But the children wouldn't dare come to a place like this at night. And if you keep on imagining them I should really begin to feel most slighted," she purred, her mouth taking on a luscious pout.

After a moment Devlin shrugged and turned back to his companion. "I suppose you're right. They wouldn't dream of flouting my orders, especially not after I told Andrew what punishment would await them if they were caught in another escapade like today's. Very well then, where shall it be next?"

The widow's eyes glittered. "Why not the Dark Walk?" Her hand toyed with the curve of his ear. "It would be so deliciously exciting to be there alone with you."

As Thorne stood undecided, a clock somewhere in the grounds struck the half-hour. He had another half an hour to wait until midnight, when he was to track his prey to a covert meeting at the far end of the pleasure grounds. Until then he needed a good excuse to be present and there could be none more obvious than the attractions of a woman such as Lady Marchmont.

"Very well, my lady," he said. "The Dark Walk it is."

"What are you doing here so early? You weren't supposed to meet me until midnight." A tall figure in a navy domino waited just outside the gazebo near the end of the Dark Walk. Hidden in the shadows across from him was another man.

"There's something strange going on," his companion said tightly. "There are guards at every gate. If I didn't know better I'd say somehow the news has gotten out."

"Nonsense. You're just imagining problems, the way you always do." The man's voice fell. "Now show me that diamond."

The two figures bent closer. Cloth rustled, and

then the lanterns sent light burning from a jewel twice the width of a man's finger.

"By God, this is it." The man in the navy domino leaned closer, his voice hoarse with excitement. "You've done it. How did you manage to get them safely out of France?"

"That's my business. Your business is seeing that they get to the right people here in England."

The man in the domino stared down at the priceless pink diamond, watching flames shoot from its beautiful facets. "L'Aurore. The one stone that the emperor would never be seen without." He looked at his companion. "When did you get it?"

"The details need not concern you," the other man said curtly. "There was chaos at Waterloo, and it was a time when many things went unnoticed. When it seemed clear that victory was lost, there were those of us who thought to take precautions. And now we mean to see our emperor restored. There's been an outpouring of sympathy in your country, even it is said from the Prince Regent's daughter herself."

"It is true. I have seen her myself. She is scandalized by the treatment of the man who once held Europe beneath his boot. Yes, with the right incentives, she can be convinced to help us. And this diamond will help us provide those incentives." He stroked the diamond gently, almost tenderly. "Where are the rest of the jewels?"

"In a ship docked in the Thames."

"Where in the Thames?"

"The exact location will remain my secret until you have performed your end of the bargain." The man in the shadows frowned. "What about Thornwood? He's said to be watching every port for the jewels."

"Thornwood is a fool. If he stands in my way I will simply kill him the way I did the other foolish pair of English in Brussels. I only wish I had managed to get those children at the same time." As he spoke the man in the domino turned slightly. Moonlight fell through the swaying oak leaves, and for a moment a jagged scar glinted hard at his mouth. He was a singularly tall man, his body broad and his shoulders heavily muscled. When he spoke it was with a voice utterly devoid of emotion.

"And what about the children? Did they see you last time?"

"Impossible. I was fully concealed and they were far too concerned with the discovery of their mother and father, who lay bleeding nearby. No, they will not recognize me. And by the time Thornwood has traced my tracks, our emperor will be restored to his rightful place on a throne at the head of all Europe." Smiling, the man reached beside him to raise a goblet filled to its brim with champagne. "A toast to the great man, then. May his victories ring through Europe once more." The diamond glinted in his other hand.

"To the emperor," his companion answered.

They had just clicked their glasses when there was a wild rustling in the shrubbery near their feet. A furry form shot through the greenery. Tail high, he raced across the table, knocked off the bottle of champagne, then snatched up the priceless pink diamond that the two men had been so keenly admiring.

And then he disappeared.

India was enjoying the lanterns that danced in the treetops when a servant in livery appeared at the entrance to the quiet bower lined by high hedges.

"For you, my lady," he said, placing a tray on the little table before her. "Champagne. The man in the uniform sent them."

So Ian had not forgotten she was here, after all. India smiled and thanked the man as the champagne bubbled up, its light, sweet fragrance clinging to her nose. It was smuggled, of course. No good wine was obtainable from France any other way these days, given the problems of the war.

Low laughter spilled from the neighboring alcoves and as India sipped her champagne she felt an odd sense of restlessness. A soft wind brushed her cheeks and she found herself wishing she had someone to share her enjoyment of the quiet beauty of the evening.

Then her peace was shattered.

"I thought I saw you in here. And those damnable brats with you." Lady Marchmont, resplendent in crimson satin that fit her like a second skin, glared at India from the break between the high hedges. The luscious gown made her skin gleam, enhancing the rouge so carefully applied to her thin lips. The widow smiled coldly. "And don't think to run away, my dear. If it's your brother you're looking for, he is occupied right now. The Prince Regent has him cornered by the orchestra, and I have no doubt he'll be captive there for hours."

India frowned. So that was what had been keeping Ian. She fixed an entirely false smile on her face. "Children? I'm certain I don't know what you're talking about. Oh, I believe there were several urchins lolling about by the gate, but—"

"You know *exactly* what children I'm talking about," the widow hissed. "It's those unruly wards of Thornwood's. When I saw them sneaking around the garden, I made certain that I followed."

India laughed carelessly. "I'm afraid your eyes have tricked you, my lady. I have no children in here." She waved her hands airily. "As even *you* can see."

The widow looked about suspiciously. After a moment she bent down and peered under the table. When she stood up her face was stiff with anger. "Don't think you'll fool me, Lady Delamere. You and all your family think you're above the rest of us, but you're not. One day the ton will tire of your eccentricities, and then you'll be cut dead. I for one will enjoy seeing it happen. Until them, I intend to hold onto what is mine and what is mine is Devlyn Carlisle."

India felt something hot and sharp burn at her throat. "I didn't realize Devlyn was anyone's possession. After all he is an adult male of reasonable intelligence."

"But he is taken. He has promised to marry me as soon as he has made arrangements for those ill-mannered brats of his."

India stood unmoving, her fingers locked on the cold crystal. Was it true? Could Dev possibly have promised marriage to another woman? He was married to *her!*

Anger made her hands tremble. "How very interesting. Am I expected to offer congratulations?"

The widow laughed coldly. "Hardly. But you will cease your interfering. Thornwood hates you after what happened at the balloon ascension. He's far too proud to stand being made to look a fool. Your endangering the children was the final nail in your coffin." The widow slanted her head, her eyes glittering as she ran her hands over her shimmering gown. "I expect the announcement will appear in the *Gazette* sometime next week. Until then, Lady

Delamere, you will stay well away from Lord Thorn-wood."

"Will I?" India stood unmoving, anger crackling through her. She was not about to be ordered about by this woman with no breeding and even less manners. "We shall see. And now if you're quite finished, I have just recalled an urgent appointment."

The widow's fingers lashed out, their red-tipped nails digging into India's hand. "Promise me that you'll stay away from him. Otherwise it will go very hard with you."

India pulled away from the widow's grip and laughed softly. "You must be very uncertain of your hold over the man."

"Not at all. I simply prefer to have a bit of insurance," the widow said tightly. "And if you disobey me I shall see that every person in the ton knows about your disgraceful behavior at the balloon ascension today. And also your disgusting masquerade as a cleaning wench."

India laughed coldly. "Do you think I care what the members of the ton have to say about me?"

"No?" The cool eyes narrowed. "But you do care about those children. The gossip will hurt them along with Thorne. You wouldn't care for that, would you?"

India fought back anger as triumph filled the widow's eyes. "If Devlyn finds out he will curse you for your interference."

"But he won't find out. I'm far too clever for him to discover where the gossip began," the widow said silkily. "No, they will begin as anonymous rumors. Of course, when I hear anything repeated around me, I will make certain to look utterly scandalized that someone would be so coldhearted as to attack three perfectly charming and innocent children."

There was nothing but cruel mockery in her voice now.

India realized then exactly how devious the woman was and how capable of evil. She was fighting a wave of uneasiness when she heard a noise in the greenery near her feet.

The countess took a jerky step back. "A rat, no doubt. This wretched place is full of them, along with the dregs of London society. Why Devlyn insisted that we come here is quite beyond me."

So Thorne had insisted on partnering Lady Marchmont tonight? India felt a little frisson of fury. Was he blind to the woman's cruelty?

Her pondering was abruptly cut short as a black shape emerged from the top of the hedge and sailed onto a nearby table. India's table trembled and her champagne glass went flying to the ground. A moment later a dark, furry body leaped through the air and landed on Lady Marchmont's elaborate, feather-encrusted coiffure.

"Get it off me!" The widow spun wildly, her hands flailing at empty space. "It's a rat, I'm sure of it. I shall die, I know it. Get the ghastly thing off me!"

But the new arrival was merely a small brown monkey clad in a neat red jacket heavy with gold braids and a dashing little shako hat. The animal's long tail was twitching, his eyes were wild, and he looked far more frightened than Lady Marchmont did at that moment.

"It's simply a monkey. You needn't shout so much."

But the countess was beyond comforting. She backed wildly into the hedge, desperate to dislodge her unwelcome passenger, who chattered and jumped nimbly to the top of the hedge, from whence he could survey the activity in safety.

"He's off now. You are perfectly fine."

"He's ruined my coiffure!" the countess shrieked. "And my beautiful gown is covered with muddy prints. I shall kill the wretched beast." She spun around and swung her reticule wildly. "Take that, you nasty thing. And that, and that."

As Lady Marchmont swung at the air, the monkey hissed protectively. The widow shrank back, then fled from the alcove, her crimson dress fluttering around her. India caught back a laugh, shaking her head at the small creature who had created such chaos.

But the monkey was no longer on the hedge. He had leaped to the ground and now was comfortably lapping up the pool of champagne left from India's overturned goblet.

"So you like champagne, do you? I fancy you have expensive tastes, little one." Bending down, India slowly held out one hand. With such a costume, the animal was probably a tamed performer escaped from somewhere on the grounds. After a moment the monkey shook his tail and walked up her arm. With great dignity he turned once, then settled on her shoulder. Chattering softly, he toyed with the jewels at her neck, then turned away, already eager for new discoveries.

"Savage beast indeed," India said, stroking the creature's head. He was frightened and dreadfully underfed, and she could feel ribs beneath his soft fur. She was just wondering what to do with him, when footsteps crunched over gravel on the far side of the hedge.

Low voices echoed on the still air. "That cursed animal must be somewhere close. I saw him run into this alcove. When I find him I'll get back what he stole, even if I have to cut out his stomach with this knife to do it."

India stared around her in horror. Where could they hide! The footsteps were crunching closer. They would be here any second.

Her eyes narrowed on the back of the bower, where a little door lay half hidden by greenery. She stroked the monkey, cautioning him to silence, then made her way to the door behind the curve of one hedge. "Steady now," she said softly. "A few more seconds and we'll—"

"You'll do what?" A man stood at the entrance to the bower, his face covered with a dark mask. A smaller man, his face concealed by a hat, stood close behind him.

India shoved the monkey up to a ledge made of stone, praying the overhanging greenery would hide him there. Then she raised her head imperiously. "You were speaking to *me*?"

"You heard me. Where did you think you were going with my monkey?"

"I have no monkey here. Now kindly step aside. I expect my gentleman friend will be looking for me any moment now."

The tall man in the mask did not move. "Maybe I don't believe you, my beauty. And maybe I'm wondering what you were at such pains to hide back near that hedge." He took a step closer. India saw his jaw tense beneath the edge of his mask.

The swaying lanterns cast a cold gleam of light on the pistol India pulled from her reticule. "I do not care for your attitude, sir. At the count of five I shall fire this thing. You would not care for that, I think."

The man cursed and took an unconscious step backward, slamming into his partner. "You don't know how to shoot that bleeding thing. No, I'm going nowhere. Not until I've found that cursed monkey."

India raised the pistol until it was level at the man's chest. "Now you shall see exactly how well I can shoot."

She was calculating just how far to the right she would have to fire to put a ball harmlessly into the stone wall above the man's shoulder when she heard a noise behind her. Without warning, a dark shape flew along the top of the boxwood hedge, leaped into the air, and landed on her arm.

The pistol wavered. She struggled wildly to hold her aim, but the monkey's weight thew her off balance and the pistol flew from her fingers. End over end it spun, clattering off the wrought-iron table and discharging noisily.

"There's the damned animal!" The two men bolted forward.

The monkey was clutching India's neck so tightly that she could barely see.

"Now we'll see what you have to say, my grand miss." The man in the dark domino circled the table slowly. His eyes glittered behind the slits of his mask.

India saw her chance and took it. Wildly, she shoved a chair forward and sent it crashing into her attacker's thighs. As he fell backward, cursing furiously, she tugged the quivering shape away from her face and charged toward the narrow gap in the boxwood hedge.

She heard the two men come crashing after her, but now the overturned table blocked her way.

Blast it, what was she to do now?

"You will be very sorry for this. The man I've come here to meet will not care for your behavior, I assure you. He will probably take out his cavalry saber and gut you from throat to thigh."

The two ruffians kept coming. Desperately, India fled around the table, inches before her pursuers, knowing any second they would have her. To right and left dark walks led back into the heart of the pleasure grounds.

She caught a ragged breath, running forward and praying that someone would come out of one of those quiet lanes.

A long shadow fell against the gravel path. A moment later a tall figure appeared, features veiled by a mask of black satin.

India threw herself forward and launched into a throaty greeting. "*There* you are, my love! I've just been telling these horrid men to leave me alone. Now you must drive them off, as I told them you would."

She spoke frantically, determined to cut off any sort of protest from the hapless stranger she had cornered all unknowing on the shaded walk. Of course, India knew her masquerade could not end here. Pushing to her toes, she threw her arms around the stranger's shoulders and pulled his head down to hers, softening her mouth for a convincingly passionate kiss.

Her heart was pounding. She felt the press of a hard male body and the quick check of the man's breath. Her fingers tightened on the crisp wool at his shoulders and she had the faint notion that there was something she was forgetting. But there was no time for idle speculation.

She pulled him closer still and slid her slender body full against his. "Kiss me," she whispered raggedly. *"Please."*

"Delighted. Except that I rather think you've welcomed me enough," came the dark and slightly mocking reply.

Abruptly India realized what had been bothering her. It was so very simple now. In fact, it was the very same thing that always seemed to be bothering her.

Devlyn Carlisle.

19

Thorne's silver eyes blazed with a mix of hunger and amusement. Why couldn't he have had the good fortune to fall in love with a normal, biddable female? Preferably, someone who knew the meaning of the word no.

But he lost track of his question a heartbeat later. The race of his heart swept away all rational concerns.

Because the woman in his arms was both innocent and seductress. She was summer's heat and autumn's calm. She was stubborn, volatile, rash, and utterly remarkable. Her death-defying antics at the balloon ascension had showed no less.

And Devlyn Carlisle knew he could not possibly resist her.

Dimly he heard the crunch of feet on gravel.

"Er, beg your pardon. Didn't realize this spot was taken." Two figures slipped past Devlyn, heading to the bower's mouth. They spoke quickly, and then were gone. But the thunder in Dev's blood was too intense for him to pull away as he should have. Not when India's fingers were buried deep in his hair and her body lay curved against him, supple as a young rowan tree in spring. He drew her to him, savoring the heat of her body. At this moment at least, she was opened to him, lushly welcoming. Her lips were softly tentative as she kissed his jaw, his cheek, and then the curve of his eye.

A shudder ran through him. The night was too tempting—*she* was too tempting. Her cheeks were vibrant, flushed. He smelled the rich sweetness of champagne on her lips and wondered how many glasses she had had. "I'll go away more often, my dear, if you promise to welcome me back like this every time."

He felt her stiffen, heard the sharp lurch of her breath. She drew back and closed her hands to fists. "Don't think it means a *thing*, Devlyn Carlisle. You were strictly the first convenient person at hand when I needed to escape those ruffians."

"Indeed?" The lantern played over the gossamer silk, molded lovingly to her splendid body. She was so beautiful that he ached, Thorne thought wryly. Silently, his fingers slid over the lush curve of her hips and he pulled her back against him.

"Stop that."

He paid not the slightest attention. Smiling lazily, he let his hand play through the magnificent red curls that covered her neck and coiled artlessly across the ripe swell of her breast. He caught one curl, warm and smooth as satin. Holding tightly, he drew her closer.

"Let me go, Devlyn. This is a reprehensible game you're playing. I won't stand for it, do you hear?"

His smile grew shred by shred. The lazy heat in his eyes flamed into unbridled hunger. But she did not move. The commanding power of his eyes did not permit it. She waited tensely, watching the vein that throbbed at his neck.

"Devlyn, this is dangerous. It is a bad idea for us even to think about—"

He pulled her the last few inches, hands claiming her waist. He took a step backward, searching for the cool stone bench that ran along one wall of the bower, but instead of granite he met something small and furry that screeched and darted away in the shadows. In the process, Thorne lost his footing and toppled backward onto the leaf-covered ground, cursing darkly.

Something sharp gouged into his back. "What in the devil is this?"

"My pistol, I imagine."

Her pistol. Of course, why hadn't he thought of that? "I suppose you were giving pistol lessons here?"

"I was defending myself, of course. Then I saw the monkey."

"The monkey." He sat up, wincing. "Don't tell me."

India frowned down at him. "Devlyn Carlisle, have you been drinking? You're making no sense at all."

"I make no sense? I am not the person who is talking about monkeys and pistols, my dear."

India glared down at him. "I suppose I should have let those two men paw me as they threatened?"

At this, Devlyn lunged to his feet. "Why didn't you say so! I'll kill them. I'll see the pair of them hung from the oak tree opposite the orchestra pit." As he lunged around the overturned table, his ankle caught on one of the wrought-iron chairs, throwing him forward so that his head struck the granite bench.

"Devlyn, are you all right?"

"Wonderful! In fact, I quite enjoy being attacked

by a feral monkey, spraining my ankle and then suffering severe trauma to the head when I trip over
your blasted pistol in the darkness."

India found her way to the long stone bench and
sat down heavily. A moment later she began to
laugh.

"I hardly see what's so funny," Thorne snapped,
rubbing his aching forehead.

"It—it's the sight of you, sprawled out on the
grass. First the pistol, then the monkey, now this.
Oh, I do beg your pardon, but it was really the end
of enough. And that dreadful creature has broken
the champagne goblet. Be careful that you don't sit
down on a piece of glass, won't you?" Her voice gur-
gled. "Here's another piece." She frowned down at
the bench. "It's very large. In fact, it's even bigger
than the first one." Her voice caught sharply.

"What is it now? Next you'll be telling me there's a
tiger in here with us."

When there was no answer, Devlyn moved carefully to India's side. What he saw next made his own
breath catch. In India's outstretched hand, lit by the
lanterns, lay a gem of unparalleled brightness, its
hundred facets gleaming like the first pale streaks of
dawn.

"It—it's beautiful," India said breathlessly. "But
how in the world did it get *here*?"

Thorne's eyes were locked on the pink stone.
"Those men, perhaps?"

India shook her head. "I doubt they were here
long enough. Of course, it was very dark and I did
have my mind on other things at the time."

"Like shooting them through the heart." Devlyn's
voice was grim as he studied the stone's gleam in
the restless light. "Sweet heaven, the thing must be
sixty karats at least." His voice hardened. "And pink.

A pink diamond. I know of only one like that. But it couldn't be . . ."

"Be what?" India frowned up at Devlyn as he removed his mask. "Devlin, what were you about to say?"

A thousand grim speculations flashed through Thornwood's head. Was it possible that the diamond shipment had already begun, and the first gems were to be exchanged here tonight? There could be few better places than Vauxhall for people to mix unobserved and unquestioned, rich and poor, English and foreign. And among them always, quiet and clever, passed some of the worst criminals of the London streets. Yes, Vauxhall would be the perfect location for a jewel exchange. Thornwood could only kick himself for not having thought of it sooner.

"Devlyn? Tell me what you meant."

He couldn't, of course. Meanwhile, his brain was raging to understand all the implications of this discovery. "What? It was nothing. And now if you don't mind I would like to have a better look at that jewel." He held out his hand.

But he was too late. The jewel had disappeared. Devlyn frowned. "What are you doing?"

"I've put it away for safekeeping."

"Then you can just dig into your recticule and bring it out again."

India's full lips curved. "But I didn't put it in my reticule," she said sweetly.

Thorne's eyes narrowed. There was no spot on that diaphanous gown where she could conceal a gem of such size. No place at all.

Except . . .

Throne's eyes locked on the luscious expanse of

her breasts. By God, she couldn't have had the utter gall to slip the thing into her bodice!

"India?"

"Yes, Devlyn?" came the sweet, purring reply.

"I'll find it, you know. It's only a matter of time. You can't hope to keep it hidden from me."

"You might if you dared, but somehow I don't think you will. You see, Dev, you're afraid of your emotions. You're afraid of what you see when you look at me and what you feel when you touch me. That's why I wager that the diamond will be perfectly safe where I've hidden it."

A muscle flashed at Thorne's jaw. The woman was worse than irritating! She was positively Machiavellian, just like her grandmother. And the fact that she was utterly right in her assessment only added to his irritation.

Yes, Thorne *was* afraid of what he was feeling at that moment. With one touch he would be lost, his control shattered, and he knew he couldn't risk the chance. Not here in this silent place of shadows and moonbeams, a place made just for lovers and for those who were fortunate enough to hold onto their dreams.

Which was something Devlyn Carlisle had lost long before in a muddy field in Belgium.

His voice fell. "Damn it, India, give me that diamond."

"Fetch it yourself, my lord."

So she thought he was a coward, did she? He cursed darkly and pulled her to her feet. Light danced over her reddish curls, making her dress shimmer like fairy wings. She was light in his arms, fragile, almost a creature of a fairy world herself, and his throat tightened as he caught her drifting scent of violets. "Don't make me do this, India. It will hurt you just as much as me."

"Do you really think so?" Her head slanted, her eyes agleam. "For myself, I can't agree at all. I believe I would enjoy myself very much."

"I'm trying to *protect* you! Why do you make it so difficult?"

"Maybe because . . . I don't want to be protected."

He gripped her shoulders. "I must have that stone, India. It is important—more important than you know."

"Why, Dev? What is so special about that particular gem?"

Devlyn bit back a curse, knowing he had already revealed too much. "I—I simply don't care to see a jewel of that size lost."

"I don't believe you. There is something you're not telling me. Quite a lot, I suspect."

Devlyn's eyes hardened. "The only thing I'm not telling you is what we both know. We're not right for each other and never have been. Why can't you accept that?" His hands slid along her bare arms and then cupped her waist. His jaw tightened as he brushed the slope of one breast, his actions in direct opposition to the force of his own words. "If this is a game, you're going to be damned sorry for playing it."

"This is no game, Dev. Of course, if I knew what you were really doing here and why you were so interested in that diamond, I might be more inclined to help you."

Thorne's eyes glittered as he pulled her back against him and ran his long fingers along the translucent silk. "I want that jewel." Beneath the cool fabric he felt the lush crests pebble at his touch. A dark groan gathered in his throat.

Dangerous, fool. Too soft—too tempting. Too close to everything you've ever wanted.

"India?"

No answer. Nothing but softness and heat. Nothing but danger.

At her slightest resistance, he would have let her go, but there was none. Her body was all suppleness and giving, and she knew it perfectly. It was that stubborn arrogance, coupled with her skill at knowing him even better than he did, that made Thorne respond in kind, planting his long hands around her creamy skin. There he found not diamonds but treasures of a more tormenting sort, their velvet heat more perfect than any of the hot fantasies he had brought back from Europe with him.

He felt her shiver against him. "Have you had enough?" he demanded hoarsely. "Say the word and I'll stop, India."

But she only laughed darkly. "Don't you know we Delameres never stop? It is not in our nature. Any hint of opposition is like a red flag to us." Her eyelashes veiled her smoky blue eyes. Slowly her back arched. Ever so gently she drew her body closer against his probing fingers.

That single seductive movement very nearly drove Devlyn over the edge. A thousand fantasies whirled through him, each one intensified by the knowledge that they were standing in a place of shadows and silence, a place meant for the baring of flesh to flesh. One movement and she would be his, lovers cushioned on the soft leaves while their bodies met in blind need. Devlyn Carlisle was far too experienced a connoisseur of women not to recognize all the symptoms of her racing pulse, husky voice, and unsteady breath.

But damned if he was going to fall for her again. Brussels had been one thing, the whole city swept up in madness. Then Devlyn had had an excuse for his blindness, but now—

Now he had no excuse for wanting her until he thought the pain would shred him up into tiny little pieces, for needing to hear her quick, sudden laughter, for yearning to feel her lips trail slowly over every inch of his hungry body.

He looked down, scowling to see one taut crest trapped beneath his fingers. "Damn it, India, I told you to—"

Outside the boxwood hedge voices drifted through the night. "But I'm certain I saw him over here just a few moments ago." There was no mistaking Helena Marchmont's high-pitched complaint.

"Perhaps you were mistaken. It is very dark along these walks, my lady." Ian Delamere spoke loudly as he walked beside the countess.

As Ian had planned, his words carried to India. She struggled to move away, but Devlyn held her still, pulling her back behind the boxwood hedge at the back of the bower.

"As you can see there's no one here." Ian's voice held a trace of lazy mockery. "Perhaps I should escort you back to the refreshment area?"

"That will hardly be necessary," the countess snapped. "And I *will* find him, you may count on that."

Her slippers crunched away over the gravel. After a moment Ian's soft laughter heralded his own departure.

India felt silence press around her. Then Thorne's

voice moved like wind through a spring meadow. "I need you, India. God help me, but I do."

His fingers tightened.

A kiss? Never so tame, this thing he gave her. The force of his body drove her back against the hedge, her back arching like a bow over his arm, her lips parting beneath the force of his possession. She did not try to fight him, knowing it was beyond her will-power. Instead she drove her body against his as his own control was tested as surely as her own. India knew that he would never hurt her. The anger radiating from his taut body was all for himself, for being unable to curb his desire.

And at that moment India's only thought was heightening the desire he struggled to deny.

Her neck arched. She touched her tongue to his and instantly his fingers tightened. Skin met, fought, joined, until India thought she would die of the melting heat that surged through her body. She wanted him and was too honest to deny it. Every harsh line of his own body told her that he was feeling the same need. With a sharp stab of woman's instinct she saw that something beside his lack of memories held him back from her.

Some new and dangerous mission that he had been called to fulfill?

Her eyes darkened as she used her very best weapon to answer that question. Her head fell back, offering him the sleek curve of her throat.

"India, don't. I'm trying to stop. For *both* our sakes."

"No." Her hand brushed his lips. "Not yet." *Not ever.*

His fingers tightened and he kissed a fierce path along the naked skin she had offered. He hesitated only a moment at the creamy expanse of her breasts

and then his lips closed over the thin barrier of silk.
Around them the night was rich and dark, all sound
lost in the fierce thunder of their hearts and the
pulse of their heated blood.

India didn't care about secret missions or convo-
luted responsibilities that would endanger Devlyn's
life. All she cared about were his hands sliding over
her. All she wanted was to know that he remembered what they had once shared and to find out
whether they could share such joy again.

Clearly he wanted her.

Clearly he needed her. Equally clearly, the man
was as honorable as both her brothers and as stubborn as the old rooster that terrorized every other
creature on her family's Norfolk estate.

She smiled darkly, knowing her campaign was
nearing success. She felt his fingers inch beneath
the shoulders of her gown and ease lower.

Silk trembled, giving way to heated skin. She
would have her answer at last, India thought. There
would be no more lies between them.

And then she gasped. The rogue had found the
edge of the diamond, hidden deep in the gusset beneath her arm. Damn the man! "Devlyn, stop," she
said hoarsely, fighting the rush of blood and heat.

But he didn't. His lips opened, searching her
mouth while his tongue tangled with hers. His body
was a fierce, unbroken line of need against her
while his heart beat in wild thunder like her own.

Then his fingers closed and the jewel was his.

At the same instant his other hand covered the
naked thrust of her breast.

India went entirely still, her body trembling, her
whole soul shivering in a wild rush of anger and
need and confusion. How did he always manage to

kindle such a storm of emotions? With any other man, she was cool and calm and detached.

His lips toyed with the sensitive skin. He laughed softly. "It seems I have found my treasure," he murmured. "And now I think it's time I had a better look."

With one final tug the silk slid free. Cool air swept over India's trembling skin.

"Beautiful." His fingers traced the perfect coral thrust of her. "I'd forgotten—" He caught back a curse.

She swayed, her hands buried in his hair as his mouth slid over her.

Heaven—and aching torment.

Memories washing over her.

"They must be here!" Feet crunched over gravel. "I'm sure I remember the turning."

"You can't even remember where you've left that doll of yours." This voice, drifting over the boxwood hedge, could belong only to Andrew.

India tensed. The children! She could not allow Devlyn to discover that they were here!

But it was too late. His body had hardened and there was a slow flare of anger in his eyes. "More of *your* work?"

"No, I—"

"Then they have disobeyed me on their own. They will soon know the penalty, I assure you."

India caught his arm desperately. "You mustn't be angry with them. They came because Alexis was convinced I was in danger. She saw that man, the one that she has dreams about."

Devlyn's brow hardened. "She has many nightmares after Waterloo. We all do," he added. "But I cannot allow them to endanger themselves this way."

He pulled away from India, distracted, and in that moment his fingers lost their grip on the diamond. "It seems that you have bested me yet again, but now I know where your treasure lies." There was a sensuous undercurrent to his words that made India's cheeks flame. "You may count on the fact that I shall remember—and be back to reclaim it."

Then, with a whoosh of greenery, he disappeared out the front of the bower.

India stood, breathless, letting her heartbeat slow. Beyond the high hedge the whispered voices moved away. Devlyn hadn't found them yet, but what he said was true. The children were in grave danger here.

She had just turned to the little door at the back of the greenery when it opened a crack. Dim light splintered through the hedges. Andrew moved stiffly inside, followed by Marianne.

Their faces were very pale.

"What are you doing?" India demanded. "You were to go with Ian to the carriage. Your guardian will be coming to look for you any second and you know *exactly* what he will say when he finds you."

But the children said nothing, their faces stiff. A moment later India saw why. Alexis had moved through the doorway, her small white hands locked tightly at her chest.

Behind her, his face covered with a dark mask, stood the man who had come in angry pursuit of the escaped monkey.

Only now one hand was locked around Alexis's neck.

The other held a pistol at her heart.

20

Something sharp twisted in India's throat as she stared at Alexis's terrified face. "Let her go."

"Not just yet, my lady." The man shoved Alexis into the bower and kicked the door shut behind him. "Not until I have that diamond you're hiding."

India edged along the hedge, thinking wildly. The light was poor. It might just be possible, if she could get close enough . . .

"You mean that silly piece of glass I found on the ground?" She made her voice utterly innocent.

"Not glass. A real diamond—as you damned well know!"

"A diamond? You don't say."

"Where is it?"

"Dear me, it was here just a moment ago." She peered owlishly about her. "But never tell me that it's yours? I assumed that a female of, er, uncertain morals must have dropped it from her necklace."

"Like bloody hell you did," the man growled. "But now who's laughing?" He shoved Alexis before him. "If you want to see her stay alive any longer, you'll hand it over now."

Out of the corner of her eye India saw a shadow

ease high onto the hedge. A little red shako hat with
a gold tassel jumped briskly.

India's eyes narrowed. Two feet closer and the
monkey would be nearly above the villain, she esti-
mated. With apparent carelessness she reached into
the bodice of her gown, knowing the man's eyes
would remain on her instead of the monkey inching
closer every second. "Of course, if it's yours I must
return it." She took her time, making a display of
searching for the jewel long after her fingers had
closed around it.

"You've hidden it well, I see," Alexis's captor muttered. "I'd be happy to search it out for myself, so I
would." He laughed harshly. "But I'm not such a
fool as to let this lovely child go free. Not until I
have my diamond back."

"Entirely understandable." India moved closer,
feeling his eyes lock upon the translucent silk that
tugged and pulled beneath her fingers. Meanwhile,
Andrew and Marianne had both seen the monkey
and they were waiting for India's lead. When the
monkey had progressed to the hedge directly behind the man's back, India gave a high titter. "How
utterly foolish. I remember now that I transferred
the jewel to my reticule for safekeeping. How can I
have forgotten?" She raised the little bag of satin
hanging on her wrist. "You will allow me?"

"Get on with it," the man growled.

India made a great display of opening the satin
handbag and delving into its depths. "Ah, yes, here
it is, safe and sound." She held out her hand, palm
closed. "Is this what you were looking for?"

The man in the mask pulled Alexis forward, his
eyes narrowed with greed. When Alexis was nearly
within reach India cried out threw her body sideways, to all appearances having tripped on the edge

of the table that lay overturned in the middle of the
enclosure.

"What in the devil do you think you're doing
now?"

Something glittered brightly on the ground, lit by
the lanterns in the trees. Attracted by the bright
bauble, the monkey launched its wiry body to the
nearest point of rest, which just happened to be the
ruffian's head. Furry arms closed, blinding the man
behind Alexis.

This was the moment India had been waiting for.
She leaped forward, drove the man's pistol to one
side and shoved Alexis back toward the wall of the
bower, protecting her with her own body. The girl's
captor cursed wildly, staggering as he tried to dislodge his unwanted passenger. Knowing she had
mere seconds to act, India caught Alexis's trembling
body up in her arms and circled to the front entrance, herding the two other children before her.

"You'll not escape me again, damn it! I'll have that
diamond or your life's not worth a ha' pence."

"Oh you will, will you?" The hedges shook. A
man's voice, flat and furious, barked from the shadows.

Thorne stood glaring as he motioned India and
his frightened wards past, then strode toward their
attacker, who had finally managed to dislodge the
monkey. The man cursed when he saw his chal-
lenger was another man, rather than an unarmed
woman and three helpless children.

Cowardice kept him motionless, and then his eyes
narrowed with cunning. "I'll have it back, damn
you. It's mine and you can't keep it from me." Bending down, he scooped his pistol up from the ground.

But he hadn't counted on the monkey. Recogniz-
ing his tormentor, the animal was determined to

settle an old score. With a shrill cry he flew from the
hedge and sank his teeth into the man's hand. A
bellow of pain filled the air and the man in the mask
sent the monkey flying, hurled against the high
hedges.

"A plague on the damn creature! Aye, a plague on
all of you." But when he saw Thorne striding
toward him, he cursed and charged out the same
way he had come.

Dev spun about, frowning. "Alexis, are you hurt?
Did that brute—"

The little girl hurtled into his arms. "No I'm fine,
Uncle Thorne. All thanks to Lady Delamere, you
know. She was ever so clever, throwing her mirror
on the ground where the monkey would find it."
Her voice broke as she buried her face against
Thorne's chest. "She could have been shot by that
terrible man. And I could have been, too . . ."

"Hush, Daffodil. You were all very brave. And
you're safe now." Thorne's head rose over Alexis's
curls. He studied India's face, nodding slowly. "Yes,
Lady Delamere is wonderfully clever, I agree with
you." There was something low and husky and endlessly tender in his voice, something that made India's blood race in the darkness. "All of you were
very clever. I should be terribly angry at you for
coming to a place like this." He waited for a moment, frowning, then shook his head. "But for some
unimaginable reason I find I can't be. The truth is,
I'm too glad to see you safe." His hands tightened
on Alexis's trembling shoulders. Closing his eyes, he
planted a kiss in her hair. "Thank God," he whispered.

India felt tears burn at her throat as she thought
of how close they had all come to serious harm. And
then she remembered the monkey. "Oh dear, I hope

our friend's not hurt." Followed by Marianne and
Andrew, she ran to the greenery and found the little
creature pushing clumsily to his feet. India picked
him up carefully and scratched his head. "Here's a
brave fellow. Even though he *was* the source of all
our problems." The monkey's tail arched wanly.
With a soft chatter he laid his head against India's
shoulder.

"He's bleeding." Marianne was staring down at a
dark blotch on her sleeve. "The poor thing. I'll take
him if you don't mind. I can bind his leg. I'm very
good at that sort of thing. I even stitched Andrew's
arm once."

Her brother winced at the memory, but said loy-
ally, "She did a good job of it, too, so the doctor
said."

Marianne lifted the monkey from India and held
him gently.

"He saved my life just now," Alexis said gravely.
"So did Lady Delamere. She saved Andrew's life yesterday and now she has saved mine."

"We owe her a great deal, Alexis." Thorne rose
slowly. While the children watched in fascination,
he caught India's hand and raised it to his lips.
"Either of those debts is beyond repaying. Together . . ." His eyes glistened suspiciously. "They
are sadly in need of manners, these three urchins of
mine," he said huskily. "But if anything had happened to them—" His jaw hardened and he seemed
to lose the ability to speak.

"Uncle Thorne?" Alexis asked softly.

Thorne cleared his throat. "What, Daffodil?"

"Lady Delamere has dropped her reticule. Hadn't
you better pick it up for her?"

Slowly Thorne bent to the bit of satin. Without a
word he handed it to India.

"She's dropped her shawl, too," Marianne said helpfully.

This, too, was retrieved in silence.

"Hadn't you better thank her?" This came from Alexis, who was studying Thorne curiously.

"I expect I should. I owe you a debt past repaying, my lady. The children are quite right."

Overhead the lanterns drifted, casting light in restless patterns over the high hedges. Somewhere a woman's laughter rose in a trill and the scent of roses and freshly cut grass spilled through the night.

"But, Uncle Thorne, shouldn't you *kiss* her?" Alexis's hands trembled with expectation.

"What do you say, Lady Delamere?" Thorne's eyes were unreadable. "*Shall* I kiss you?"

"That will hardly be necessary." India felt her face flush. "That is, I accept your thanks, my lord. There is really no need for—"

Her breath caught as he found her palm and raised it to his lips a second time. But the kiss he planted now fell at the soft center of her palm and his lips were slow, persuasive, a brush of heat and shadows and half-forgotten dreams. It was a warning—and an unmistakable promise.

"Never think it's over between us, Princess," he said huskily, too low for the children to hear. "You have managed to conceal that jewel, but I'll have your treasures from you yet, I warn you."

As he stood up, Alexis shook her head impatiently. "But Uncle Thorne, shouldn't you—?"

"I *know* he's here. He would not dream of leaving without me." There was no mistaking Helena Marchmont's shrill voice.

Thorne's eyes burned over India's face. "Soon," he said huskily. Herding the children before him, he moved toward the front of the enclosure, where Ian had appeared. "She's safe. And thanks to her, so are these three scamps."

Ian shot a questioning look at his sister.

But India didn't notice. She was too busy frowning thoughtfully at Thorne's back.

The ride back to Devonham House seemed to last forever.

India sat tensely, watching the streets pass in a blur and nursing the bruise that had begun to throb at her ankle, where she had struck the table. She was keenly conscious of the magnificent diamond nestled snugly in the bodice of her gown.

"But I don't understand what the man was after?" Ian frowned at his sister.

India shrugged. She had carefully avoided any mention of the diamond in her account of the night's events. Some instinct told her that her brother would forbid her to do the thing she had already set her mind on—exploring the mystery of the diamond, and why Thorne had acted so secretively after seeing the jewel.

"Where would I go to buy a diamond, Ian?" India's question came abruptly, cutting her brother off in the middle of a tirade about unruly females who refused to listen to their brothers and shot pistols in public places.

"Diamonds? Why in the world do you need a diamond? Grandmama has a nabob's fortune in jewels, as you well know. She has said she would turn them all over to you if you showed the slightest bit of interest. Which you never have." His gray eyes narrowed suspiciously. "What piece of mischief are you up to now, hornet?"

"No mischief, you silly great looby." India's eyes

narrowed thoughtfully. "I simply find I have a sudden yearning to buy a diamond. An *extraordinary* diamond. Who deals in such things?"

"As if I had any experience in buying jewelry! Ask me about dueling pistols or horseflesh and I could answer you. But diamonds?" He shrugged.

"Never mind. It was just a passing thought."

Ian studied his sister suspiciously. "Don't try and fob me off. I've seen that look on your face before, minx, and it means nothing but trouble."

India's expression could have melted the heart of the very sternest misanthrope. "Me, make trouble? My dearest brother, you must be *quite* mistaken."

"You're late."

Helena Marchmont pursed her well-rouged lips as she peered into the darkness of her boudoir. "*You!* I didn't know you were coming tonight." There was an edge in her voice. "When did you get here?"

The man seated in the wing chair before the dwindling fire smiled lazily. "Late enough to wonder what was keeping you, my dear."

"But you weren't supposed to be here until tomorrow. You said you wouldn't—"

Behind the countess there was a low laugh and a man appeared in the doorway. "My dear, luscious, Helena, I *do* hope you mean to make this evening worth my wait. After that sultry carriage ride, I am in unbearable pain." He frowned suddenly as he saw the shadowed figure in the wing chair. "Who are—?"

The countess spun around and pushed him back toward the door. "I've changed my mind after all, Richard. Go away. I'm in no mood for—"

The man in the wing chair pushed lazily to his

feet, his eyes dark and expressionless. "My dear Helena, it would be rude to send your guest away now. Show him in, do. I shall fix him a sherry."

Helena Marchmont stood poised, one hand to her throat, while her eyes flickered uneasily between the two men.

"I've seen you before." The countess's ardent companion stared in shock at the man before the fire. "But what are you doing here? I could have sworn that you—"

Firelight glinted off the polished silver butt of a perfectly balanced pistol. "How unfortunate that you have recognized me. For that particular mistake, you are going to pay—with your life."

The pistol cracked. A wisp of smoke drifted from its barrel.

Lady Marchmont's stunned suitor grabbed at the spot where a part of his chest had disappeared. Blood welled up over his fingers. "But you—Helena said that you were—were her *brother*—" He pitched forward with a groan. His big, muscled body convulsed once, then lay still against the rich Aubusson carpet, out of place among the dainty cabbage roses.

The countess sighed. "You do have a penchant for making simple things untidy. What in heaven's name am I to do with him now?"

"Heaven has very little to do with it." The man before the fire gave a lazy wave of his hand. "But I leave the details entirely up to you, my dear, as always."

"You are a most unnatural brother," Helena Marchmont snapped. "First you come back without warning, and now you leave me this—this nuisance. You think of no one but yourself!"

"Of course, my dear. It is what makes the two of

us so much alike." His thin lips lifted in a sneer.
"But then again I am not your brother, am I, Helena? I am only your stepbrother. So very convenient, is it not?" He stood back, his shoulders to the mantel. The firelight clearly exposed the rising evidence of his desire.

The countess watched, entranced. Her tongue slid delicately around her lips with anticipation. Her companion smiled, his eyes sweeping over the lush curves perfectly visible beneath the gown of dampened silk. His hand went to his cravat, loosening its knot. "Come here," he ordered softly.

Helena frowned. "But don't you want to know about Thorne? About what happened at Vauxhall?"

He smiled very coldly. The cravat hit the floor. "Later. *Much* later."

21

The next morning India awoke with faint shadows beneath her eyes and the sun slanting golden through the curtains. She hadn't slept well, her rest broken by a succession of dark dreams. The events at Vauxhall had left her shaken, worried about Thornwood and his three wards. And then she remembered the diamond.

She pulled a bird's nest from its shelf beside the bed in a sunny window. Digging deep into the moss lining the nest, she found what she was looking for.

An extraordinary, blush-pink diamond. In the morning sun dozens of glorious red facets winked and snapped on her hand. Whose was this stone of beauty, of incredible rarity? And how had the monkey at Vauxhall come to possess it?

India turned the jewel slowly, watching sparks play over her palm. A gem such as this had to have a history, but how was she to find it?

There was a soft tap at the door. Her dresser entered, lips pursed. "There's someone below who wants to see you, miss. Said as how he's a friend of your brother Luc's." The pursed lips grew even tighter.

"Dear Hawkins, you never approve of any man over the age of twelve and under the age of eighty."

"Not a bit of it. I only disapprove of men that are not your equal." Her lips twitched. "Which is to say any man between the age of twelve and eighty. Besides, there's something strange about this fellow. His eyes are different somehow—or maybe it's just that *he's* different. Something in his attitude—an air of silence and confidence."

"Connor MacKinnon!" The description could fit no one else. India shoved back the covers and jumped from the bed. "Do stop worrying about me for once and help me dress, Hawkins."

At that moment Connor MacKinnon was lounging in the sunny front drawing room. His broad shoulders filled the perfectly cut jacket by Weston, his polished riding boots were mirror-bright, and his hair, although longer than fashionable, lent a softness to the long and unusually chiseled planes of his face. Connor MacKinnon was indeed a friend of India's brother Luc, but few woman could have resisted the wish to make him more than a friend. Fortunately India, having seen too many women's hearts broken by one look, remained comfortably immune to his charms.

Pushing open the door, a vision in primrose muslin with a deep navy sash that brought out the clarity of her eyes, India stood tapping her toe as she studied her exotic visitor. "Come to check up on me, have you?"

The man at the window turned slowly, a lazy smile on his face. "I'm far too busy to act as *your* guardian, hoyden. I would be dragged from one end of London to the other in the process, beating off your suitors with a club. A very *large* club."

India chuckled. "Turning lazy in your old age, MacKinnon?"

"Old age?" One dark brow climbed lazily. "I'll see you pay for that particular comment, Lady Delamere." He crossed the room with the silent grace which always seemed to leave India breathless and bent over her palm, smiling faintly. "Do I need an excuse to come see my favorite friend's favorite sister?"

"I'm Luc's *only* sister. And I suspect Luc might be your only friend."

Connor clutched at his heart. "You wound me, woman. A mortal wound, and no mistake." He collapsed, choking, into the nearest chair and India sat down after him, laughing unsteadily.

"You are the most complete hand, Connor. I can't imagine what my brother sees in you."

But India knew, of course. Connor had saved her brother's life in the dangerous East, where Luc had been a captive of the pirates of Algiers. Several years later, when Luc had again fallen into danger, Connor had come to his aid once more. Remembering that time of danger, India's smile slowly faded. Her brother had trusted Connor with his life; she knew that she could trust him too.

Her hands locked at her waist. "What do you know about diamonds, Conn?"

"Diamonds?" Connor's eyes narrowed. "In India they were known as 'fragments of eternity.' In the Middle Ages they were said to cure everything from warts to infertility. Formed deep in the fires of the earth, they are among the most valued items of trade known to man." His lips curved. "In addition to that, what did you want to know?"

"Facts. Details."

"Only one is of any importance. They are beautiful, valuable—and very dangerous."

"Dangerous?"

"They are not always what they seem. One man's priceless treasure can be another man's paste replica."

"What about this?" India slowly raised her palm. Light danced over lush pink facets of crystal fire. "Is this a paste replica?"

Connor lifted the fine gem, studying it intently. He moved it from side to side, then turned it slowly.

"Well?" India asked breathlessly. "Is it real or isn't it?"

"It's real all right. And it's flawless—or as close as any diamond comes to being flawless. No clouds, no feathers, no knots."

"What?"

"Minute cracks or inclusions, things that would reduce the stone's value," Connor explained. "No abrasions or pitting, either. But it's that amazing color that gives the stone its value. Experts call a stone like this a fancy. A slight yellow tint is considered a flaw, but a stone with this kind of remarkable pink tone is priceless for its color. I have seen only two other gems like this—the Condé, which was part of Louis XIII's collection, and the Sancy diamond."

"Where did *you* find out so much about gems?" India asked suspiciously.

"In Brazil. I worked in a mine there for a while." His gaze settled on the window, his eyes shadowed, as if caught up in memories that were far from pleasant. "As a general rule, my dear India, when the world is in chaos and people lack faith in their governments, treasures like this diamond gain in value. That's why I make it my business to know

one or two things about separating good diamonds
from inferior ones."

India had the definite feeling that there was a
great deal more Connor wasn't telling her, but she
knew her brother's taciturn friend would reveal
only what he chose. "And what about this diamond?
Is it from Brazil?"

"Probably not. From India, more like. The most
fabulous diamonds come from there, stones like the
Koh-i-noor, the Hope Diamond, the Sancy, and of
course the Condé."

"Where would I go, Connor, if I wanted to sell a
jewel like this—or to buy one?"

"Montagu Street, for one. Possibly Rundell's, but
you'll pay through the teeth for the 'privilege' of
shopping at their select establishment. Why?"

"Just curious."

Connor's eyes narrowed. "I heard what happened
last night at Vauxhall. I don't imagine that had anything to do with this diamond, did it?"

India's expression was all innocence. "What gives
you that idea?"

Connor MacKinnon shook his head. "You would
lie to the king himself, wouldn't you?"

"Only if it were *very* necessary," India said softly.
"Rundell's, you say, and other's. Thank you, Connor."

Hard fingers shot around India's wrist. "Stay out
of it, India." MacKinnon's eyes were very dark.
"People who possess gems like this don't always live
long enough to enjoy them. All that fire and brilliance can kindle a terrible greed."

"Are you telling me the stone is cursed?"

"I'm saying nothing of the sort. What I'm saying is
that human minds can be cursed—cursed with
greed. A stone of this color and brilliance might

drive a weak mind over the edge." He studied India's face for a moment, then sighed. "Since I can
see you're so intent on finding out about the stone,
I'll go with you. How does two o'clock sound?"

India thought about protesting, but knew Connor
could be as relentless as he was charming. "Very
well, two o'clock will be perfect."

By the time her brother's friend left a few minutes
later, his fears had been entirely allayed.

Of course Connor didn't yet realize that India
planned to be gone at *least* an hour before he returned. And just to be sure he would be completely
distracted when he arrived, India sent a note
around to Thornwood, asking him to call at the very
same hour. By the time the two men stopped arguing and sorted out the situation, she would be safely
away.

A clock was just striking one when a dashing
youth in fashionable buckskins and a perfectly cut
gray jacket strode down the steps of Devonham
House. His cravat was exquisitely turned in the style
known as the Mathematical, and his Hessian boots
were polished to a jaunty shine. If his gait was slow
and bordering on the effeminate, it was a minor
flaw in an otherwise perfect appearance.

Of course the "boy" was not a boy at all, but India
Delamere draped in a pair of breeches long ago pil-
fered from her brother's wardrobe. Dealing with her
hair had been the hardest part, but she had twisted
it up and knotted it tightly, then covered the whole
beneath a broad-brimmed beaver hat set rakishly
askew.

Her first goal, the select establishment of Rundell's, was located on one of the finest shopping
streets in London, and India was properly im-

pressed when she stepped inside the heavily carpeted showroom. Jewels of all sizes and colors flashed from velvet-lined cases, and women in elegant dress sat speaking softly as they considered purchases worth more than a lifetime's wages for most of the residents of London. India's fingers tightened on the jewel hidden in the inner pocket of her embroidered waistcoat.

"May I help you, sir?" A man in a severe black jacket surveyed India from a rosewood desk near the door.

It would not do to make this too easy, India thought. After all, she wanted them to remember the name she left with them. "Perhaps," she said carelessly. "I was told that Rundell's is known to have a passably good selection."

The man's smile hardened. "Our selection is far more than passable, I assure you." He studied her slender frame, putting her down as a youth with more interest in fashion than common sense. "What in particular were you looking for?"

"Oh, I'm not looking to buy. I'm interested in selling. Of course only a person with a true depth of experience would appreciate the treasure that I'm offering."

"Indeed? Then again *everyone* believes that he has a treasure to sell," the man behind the desk said acidly.

India raised a quizzing glass from its cord around her neck and studied the man until his face flushed with anger. Only then did she settle herself in an elegant sprawl on the needlepoint cushion of a nearby chair. "It's a diamond, I'm selling. A rather unusual diamond," she continued lazily. "What I believe you fellows call a 'fancy.' " She saw the man's eyes flicker at that word, which could not fail to fuel a jeweler's greed.

"Fancy?" he said casually.

"Colored, don't you know? In this case a blush pink. Damned remarkable, so I'm told. Flawless, too."

By this time the man's pupils were noticeably dilated and his hands moved restlessly over the rosewood desk. India saw a speck of sweat break out along his brow. So Connor had been right.

"I don't suppose you happen to have this gem with you?"

"Of course I do. Useless to visit you without it, don't you know?" India reached into her waistcoat and removed the stone. As she set it casually on the desk before her, she heard the jeweler's breath check in a gasp.

He tenderly lifted the brilliant jewel onto a roll of black velvet. His hands were trembling, India saw.

"May I?"

"Of course."

"Well?" she demanded after a few moments.

"Rather unusual. A satisfying color, too."

"Satisfying?" India laughed coolly. "That color's damn near to making the stone priceless and you know it."

"It is unusual, I admit." His eyes narrowed. "Where did you acquire the stone?"

Again India raised her quizzing glass and gave him her haughtiest glare. "I do not believe that that is any business of yours, my good man."

"Of course, of course," the jeweler said hastily. "It is simply that in this business one cannot be too careful . . ."

"Are you implying this gem is stolen? Of all the damned impudence!" India shoved to her feet and grabbed up the jewel. "Jackanapes! I can see that I shall have to take my custom elsewhere."

Instantly the jeweler was around the desk, blocking her exit. "No need to be hasty, sir. If I gave offense, it was certainly not my intention. Come now, why don't we retire to my private office? I have a very good port that I've been saving for a special occasion. Perhaps you would enjoy a glass?"

India eyed the man haughtily. "Not today. Have to see about a piece of horseflesh at Tattersall's. Might be back tomorrow or maybe next week." She reached into her pocket and tugged out a card. "If you hear of someone interested in a diamond of this quality, it might be worth your while to contact the person on the card."

The jeweler squinted at the fine lettering. "Lady Delamere?"

"My cousin," India explained casually. "Wouldn't do for her to handle such transactions herself. Only a woman, you know."

The jeweler nodded. "Of course not. No female is to be trusted in a matter of such importance. I shall see what can be arranged for her."

By the time India sauntered out of Rundell's, the jeweler was having a positive storm of nerves.

Which, of course, was exactly what India had planned.

The second shop that Conn had mentioned was very different from Rundell's. Sandwiched between a candlemaker's and a public house, it lay on narrow street in one of the busiest parts of Piccadilly. A trio of noisy boys were rolling hoops along the cobblestones in front of the store while a wiry fellow made lazy sweeps with a rag over windows that carried years of grime.

India felt a moment of misgiving. What she was doing was dangerous, but it was the quickest way to gain information. Since she couldn't find the diamond's owner, she meant to see that the owner found *her*. Then she could begin solving the mystery of Thorne's interest in this remarkable stone.

Squaring her shoulders, she sauntered into the shop, blinking as her eyes adjusted to the semidarkness.

A balding man with a grayish face emerged from the shadows. "I was just closing for the day," he said querulously. "However, since you're here, you may as well state your business."

India affected her haughtiest demeanor. "My business, my good man, happens to be your business. That is, unless that shop sign outside is wrong, and you are not a dealer in diamonds, jewelry, and precious metals."

The man sighed. "My cup of tea and bowl of broth will have to wait, I see. Very well, what business have you brought me?"

India looked about the shop. There were only two glass-covered cases and each looked sparse in its contents. A few medium-size diamonds glinted on tattered velvet, and the necklaces beside them were made without elegance or grace. She raised her quizzing glass and studied the nearest piece of jewelry, a bracelet which contained a diamond far larger than anything else in the shop. She remembered what Connor had told her and took a chance. "I daresay we shall have *no* business together, if you try to interest me in trinkets made of worthless paste such as that bracelet there."

The man whisked a bead of sweat from his balding head. "Quite, quite. You know your jewels, I can see that. Of course, that particular bracelet was sim-

ply a copy, something I made up for a client by way
of a model."

India didn't believe it for a second, but she had
the man's interest now and she meant to take advantage of that. "Just so we understand each other."
She reached into her pocket and brought out the
jewel. "My business is this."

The jeweler's eyes widened as he saw the great
diamond winking on her palm. "As I live and
breathe," he whispered, reaching out toward the
stone.

India held it back, however. "I am thinking of selling this, Mr.—"

"Montagu. Mortimer Montagu. It would be a
pleasure to sell your diamond, but I'll have to take a
closer look."

India relinquished the gem and followed him to a
table covered with swatches of velvet and an array
of chisels and files. "Do you do your own cutting
here?"

"Some of it here, some elsewhere," the jeweler
said vaguely, as he caught up a small loupe and
drew a branch of candles closer. He stared intently
at the diamond, absolutely motionless. Somewhere
at the back of the shop a door closed and then a
crate was dragged across a stone floor.

The jeweler sat back slowly and let the loupe fall
to his lap. "Extraordinary. I don't think I've seen
anything like this. Not since . . ." His voice trailed
away.

Just the same way Thorne's had trailed away, India thought. "Well?" she said abruptly. "How much
will it fetch?"

"A king's ransom," the jeweler murmured. "If I
could find a buyer for it, that is."

"What do you mean?" India said sharply. "It's magnificent, you said so yourself."

"So I did. But a stone of that size and clarity will require a buyer with a great deal of ready capital." He turned the gem slowly, watching the facets reflect the light. "If you'll leave it here with me, I'll make some inquiries. In two or three days I should be able to—"

India laughed lazily. "Leave it here with you? You must think me an utter fool. No, the stone goes with me." She dropped a vellum card onto the sheet of black velvet. "If you find someone who is interested, send a message to that address. Meanwhile, I have other business in the area. I am looking for a jeweler several streets away," she said lazily. "You must know of it."

The jeweler was now a most unhealthy shade of gray. "Never tell me you mean to take that magnificent stone to Parrish Brothers? They'll rob you blind, so they will. Besides, they don't know diamonds from quartz," he protested.

So they would rob her blind? India smiled. Parrish Brothers sounded like an ideal place for her next stop. She pocketed her gem and strolled to the door. "Send me a message if you have interest. Until then, good day."

She felt the jeweler's eyes follow her all the way down the street. Somewhere nearby church bells tolled the hour of two.

Back at Devonham House, the Earl of Thornwood was standing beside the fireplace, glaring at Connor MacKinnon. "What do you mean, she was asking about diamonds?"

Connor shrugged, a lazy smile curving his lips. "Just what I said. Lady Delamere was interested in a special stone. I was to meet her at two o'clock and accompany her to several jewelers."

"Why in heaven's didn't she ask *me*?" Devlyn muttered. "And why did she tell me to come here, knowing she would already be gone? Of course it's that blasted gem. It *must* have to do with l'Aurore."

Connor went very still. "L'Aurore? Why would India Delamere be interested in Napoleon's favorite diamond?"

Devlyn's eyes narrowed. "You know of the stone?"

"Anyone with half an interest in jewels has heard of that particular pink diamond. Along with the Sancy and the Condé, it ranks as one of the three rarest pink diamonds in the world. l'Aurore was Napoleon's favorite, a stone that he credits for every victory he's ever had. What I want to know is how India came to possess it, for a more cursed jewel never existed."

"I'm not at liberty to discuss it," Dev said stiffly. "Besides, what is *your* connection with Ind—Lady Delamere?"

"I'm one of Luc Delamere's closest friends. Because of that, I choose to interest myself in India's happiness."

"Oh you do, do you? Well, so do I." Thorne's eyes flashed. "And I can keep her happy very well by myself."

The smile in Connor's eyes showed that he was enjoying himself immensely. "She's a rare sort of woman, but I suggest you take her in hand, Thornwood. Whoever lost that diamond is going to be very anxious to have it back."

"What do you know about l'Aurore?" Devlyn said grimly.

"Coupled with the Sancy and the Condé in the hands of one collector, the three stones would be beyond price. Certainly enough to raise armies and sway the destiny of all Europe." Connor's eyes narrowed. "I believe l'Aurore was once in the possession of the Dey of Algiers. He personally slit the throats of two of his own brothers to acquire it. I can only wonder how the stone came into Napoleon's keeping."

"You seem to know a great deal," Thorne muttered.

Connor shrugged. "I hear many things. Such information is helpful to me in my business."

"And just what sort of business is that, MacKinnon?"

"Gold, jewels, silks, and spices. I even deal in English woolens on occasion. My ships cover most of the globe and through their captains I collect information of all sorts."

"Such as?"

Connor smiled thinly. "Such as rumors that Napoleon's private treasure of jewels is about to be smuggled into England as ransom for his freedom."

Thorne frowned at the broad-shouldered warrior who had become famed for his exotic fighting techniques. "I think you know far too much, MacKinnon. And where would your loyalties lie if it came to a choice between Napoleon and the interests of England?"

There was absolutely no expression to be read in Connor's face. "My loyalties are . . . complicated. My blood must make it so. My background is part Manchu, part French, and part Scots, you see. But before you get your hackles up, Thornwood, let me point out that my greatest loyalty is to my friends, of which Luc Delamere is the oldest. You may count on my help in this affair, not because of patriotic zeal but because I shall do everything in my power

to protect India." His lips twitched for a moment.
"And perhaps, because Napoleon was always very,
very bad for business."

"He was bad for more than business," Thorne
said flatly. "Have you heard where these jewels are
to be brought into England?"

"Not yet. I was lucky to find out what little I did.
These men practice a hard code and any mistakes
are repaid with instant death. That's why I won't
have Luc's sister involved, Thornwood. Men who
would attempt such a scheme must be desperate."

"Don't you think I know that?" Devlyn turned to
pace the room angrily. "But I must find out why
that wretched jewel was at Vauxhall and how it
came into India's possession." He looked at Connor.
"I could lose my head for telling you any of this, you
know. Wellington was most explicit about that. Are
you to be trusted?"

"Sometimes." Connor smiled faintly. "Especially
when family or friends are involved." He studied
Thorne for a moment. "You're head over heels for
her, aren't you?"

Thorne ran his fingers through his hair, frowning.
"I *should* deny it. The woman's turned my life up-
side down since the first moment I set eyes on her.
She's reckless, impossible, infuriating. And yet—"

"And yet you can't live without her," Connor finished softly.

Devlyn sighed. "I can't keep my mind on my duties. I can't think straight half the time, and when I
can, it's India that fills my head, not the mission I've
sworn to complete."

Connor smiled. "A pathetic case, to be sure."

"Sometimes I think it would be better if we'd
never met. Then I think of all I'd have missed—the
laughter, the reckless adventures." Devlyn laughed

shakily. "As you can see, a truly *pathetic* case." He shook his head. "But why is she interested in jewelers?"

"No doubt she means to use that gemstone as a calling card. Since she can't find your enemies, she means to lure them out after *her*."

"I'm supposed to be protecting *her*, blast it! How does she always manage to stay one step ahead of me?"

"She's a Delamere, my friend. They live by different rules." Connor's eyes gleamed for a moment as he recalled several of Luc's past exploits. "It's no good arguing with a Delamere. They make the very best friends—and the very worst of enemies. But India is in gravest danger. Every cutthroat in London will be after her when they find out she has l'Aurore, and no jeweler of repute would dream of handling it, since it's far too easily identified."

"I was thinking something of the sort myself," Thorne said grimly. "You said she was to meet you here at two o'clock? I'd give a king's ransom to know where she went."

"I might be of some help," Connor said lazily. "If you'll tell me about this mission of yours."

"I'm under explicit orders to act in utter secrecy. There have already been too many leaks." Thorne cursed. "Orders bedamned! Where do you think she went?"

Laughing softly, Connor gripped Thorne's shoulder and motioned to the door. "Knowing India Delamere, she could have set off by hot air balloon for the mountain kingdom of Tibet. But I trust that between us we can track her down a little closer to home. It appears that she has taken her groom with her, at least."

"That doesn't reassure me." Thorne glared out at

the garden at the back of Devonham House. "No doubt India has the poor man wrapped around her finger like the rest of us."

Connor studied Thorne for a moment. "She'll lead you a merry dance, my friend. She'll give you no peace, no rest. And probably more joy than you thought life could ever hold."

Thorne gave a lopsided smile. He had already begun to suspect something of the sort himself. And at that moment the Earl of Thornwood would have given a great deal to see India's stubborn, irritating, and utterly beautiful face before him, instead of being torn apart with worry about her safety.

The sun was nearly lost behind the rooftops when India finally found her way to the narrow shop sign that read Parrish Brothers, Fine Jewels and Curiosities.'

A crowd of men lounged noisily in the alley beside the shop, in the company of two women who were definitely not ladies. Occasionally a carriage bearing a coat of arms sped past, but none of them stopped outside the grimy windows of Parrish Brothers. Only twice did someone enter the shop, each time a man with rumpled clothing and cunning eyes.

India looked uncertainly at her tough-faced old groom, whom she had persuaded to accompany her on this unorthodox mission. "Well, Froggett, what do you think?"

"I think, Miss India, that those breeches of Ian's are very near the most ill-fitting piece of clothing I've ever clapped eyes on."

"Not about my breeches, Froggett. About Parrish Brothers."

"Looks havey-cavey to me." The old groom

crossed his arms defiantly. "And if you think I'm letting *you* stroll into that den of thieves, then you are sorely mistaken. And so will your backside be."

"I rather think you're right, Froggett. It does not look like an entirely respectable place of business, I think. But that is the last shop I know of. What am I to do if—"

At that moment the proprietor of Montagu's pounded up behind her, puffing loudly. "My lord— so glad to have—have found you in time—" Pulling at his waistcoat, the jeweler stopped beside India and caught his breath. His face was a sickly gray after his exertions. "I felt it my duty to warn you about Parrish Brothers'. Not at all respectable, you see. In fact, should they set eyes on that jewel which you showed me, it would go very hard with you." He shook his head expressively and ran a finger across his neck.

"That's the bloody end of this," Froggett said curtly. "We'll consider the business over and done with and be making our way back home, in that case."

"But there *is* one more possibility," Montagu said quickly. "Nothing fancy you understand, but perhaps it will be of use to you. There is a man who is most unusual, but he pays the highest prices for quality merchandise. You will find him east of London, in a small town called Evesham, not far from the Thames. He is called the Frenchman, but I know nothing more about him. No one does, in fact. But he pays and pays well, and the word is that he is especially looking for rare diamonds these days. You'll have to be careful, however, for bands of ruffians are working all that area of the river."

India felt excitement race through her. Could this Frenchman be the man who had lost the diamond?

The man who had attacked Alexis at Vauxhall? "It is very good of you to tell me," she said crisply. "And now, Froggett, we must—"

"Just what manner of tradesman is this Frenchman?" the groom demanded. "I've never heard of any banker conducting business in a village on the banks of the Thames."

Montagu shook his head. "Oh, the Frenchman's no banker. Not a jeweler either. He is whispered to be many things, you understand, and it is not precisely healthy to speculate about his past. But he will not harm you unless you attempt to trick him, and I am sure a gentleman of your obvious quality would never attempt to do that."

The more India heard, the more she was certain that *this* was the clue she had been waiting for. She dug into her pocket and tossed Montagu a half crown for his help. "My dear Montagu," she said lazily, "I assure you that trickery is the very *last* thing on my mind. In fact, I am as honest as my name is Edward Fairchild, cousin of Lady Delamere."

Beside her Froggett broke into a fit of hoarse coughing.

"It is not a great distance from London," Montagu said, politely ignoring the groom, who was having trouble recovering his composure. He pocketed the half crown and bowed. "A word of caution, however. Keep the nature of your business to yourself. There are those who are not so scrupulous about how they would possess such a jewel. And now I must return to my shop. My broth will be gone cold."

Froggett watched the man hurry back down the street. "She won't listen to nobody. I don't expect she'll start listening to *you* either," he muttered.

"Remember your rheumatism, Froggett," India said absently. When she grabbed the groom's arm and pulled him back toward Devonham House, she was already laying plans for their upcoming ride to a little village called Evesham.

Two hours later India sat her white gelding, looking at the whole of London spread below them to the south. "It's a fine evening for a ride, don't you think, Froggett?"

"A fine night to die by a cutthroat's knife," the old groom said gloomily. "Should never ha' let you talk me into this madness."

"Nonsense. It's wonderful to be out of London and back into the fresh air again." India patted the gelding's neck and cocked her head. "It reminds me of a time in Calcutta when Ian and I finally managed to escape from an awful governess Mama had saddled us with. With the help of our Parsi groom, we rode hell for leather for hours. It was the most perfect fun—until we were stopped by a band of dacoits in the hills, that is. One nasty fellow wanted to string Ian up by his toes and see how long it took the vultures to finish him off. The others wanted to doing something that sounded even more painful. Since our Hindi was limited, we never were sure what they had in mind." She shrugged cheerfully. "Then they discovered I was a female and turned more horrible still. But I began to spin about and wave my hands, chanting strangely. Of course they wanted nothing to do with a madwoman, since they were very superstitious."

"Lucky for you, else they never would ha' been fooled by a green girl like *you*."

"Don't be gloomy, Froggett. It only makes your rheumatism flare up, you know. As I was saying, everything turned out well in the end. Finally they paid *Ian* to take me away from their camp, because they were convinced that I was possessed by *rakshas* and would bring them nothing but bad luck."

"And so you would have, for a person with a greater aptitude for trouble I have yet to meet." The groom sniffed. "What in heaven's a *raksha*?"

"An evil spirit. You see, I found a packet of fireworks that Father had brought back for me from Macao. I tossed them into the fire when the camp was asleep, startling all the horses. Ian caught on and began demanding more and more money to take me off their hands. He was enjoying himself immensely." She smiled. "In the end they offerred a lordly sum and threw in two lovely Marathi daggers into the bargain. Very good steel they were, too."

"No need of heathen weapons to see us murdered tonight. Good, plain English steel will see us dead well enough," Froggett predicted grimly.

"Why? I've pistols in my cuff and a dagger in my boot. I am not at all worried." India smoothed Ian's old jacket about her slender hips. "We are simply a groom and his assistant, off to view some prime horseflesh at Norwich."

"Who's the groom and who's the assistant, that's what I want to know?"

"I'm the assistant, of course," India said loftily. "What could possibly be dangerous about *that*?"

"Ain't enough time in the day to list all the things," Froggett muttered.

Nor did his face grow any happier as the miles sped past. With the city behind them, they plunged on into lonely countryside, where danger lay behind every tree and shrub. Froggett envisioned a dozen smugglers or highwaymen lying in wait behind every bend in the road.

"Admit it's a fine adventure," India said as she reined in her great gelding and pulled out a chunk of Cheshire cheese wrapped in oiled paper. She broke off a piece for Froggett.

"Oh, it's fine all right. Many's the man who's found danger on a fine night when he least expected it. And there'll be the devil to pay when your grandmother and brothers hear about this, Miss India. Lucky if I don't get sacked for *this* piece of madness."

"Bosh," India said, chewing thoughtfully on the other half of the cheese. "No blame will be laid at your door, dearest Froggett. My brothers know me too well to think anyone else planned this." She studied the horizon to the east, where the night sky lay like velvet over the deeper black of the hills. "Besides, the Red Lion is just over that hill, unless I miss my guess. We'll put up there for a few hours before we push on to Suffolk."

"Rest or not, I still say as this is a stupid idea. The whole area's rife with footpads and highwaymen."

"Which is why I'm carrying two loaded pistols."

"Who's to say this Frenchman ain't a highwayman himself?"

"He wouldn't *buy* gems in that case, would he?" India studied the moon, just creeping over the horizon. "He would simply hunt down a carriage and take what he wanted, like Luc used to do. No, my intuition tells me that this Frenchman's the man we want."

Froggett snorted. "Heaven help us if we're relying on *your* intuition."

India laughed and brought her magnificent mount to the little stream bubbling down the hillside. The great animal neighed and bent low to drink. "Just a few miles more, Froggett. Then it's a nice bed for you and a rasher of oats for Hannibal to—"

Suddenly the great gelding's head rose. Whinnying, he stepped back from the stream and pranced skittishly.

Up the bank a dozen shadows edged from the greenery. The furtive way they moved reminded India of a windy night and a band of angry dacoits.

One man inched in front of the others. "Now just fancy what we've got here," he said coldly, raising a pistol. "Mebbe our luck's about to change."

22

"Stop where you are, cur." Froggett pulled a pistol from his pocket and spurred in front of India. "Unless you want a gaping hole between those ugly eyes of yours, that is."

Instantly a dozen more pistols leveled on Froggett.

"Put your weapons down, all of you," India said quickly. "I'm sure we can discuss this in a civilized fashion."

"In a pig's eye," the groom muttered.

The leader of the sullen band pointed at India. "Get down off that horse, whelp. Otherwise the old man dies."

India slid her hand along her shirt cuff, reassured by the outline of the pistol hidden there. "No reason for threats. My friend and I mean you no harm."

"No harm!" The man threw back his head and roared with laughter. "They mean us no harm, did you hear that, lads?" Laughter rang over the hillside, making India's mount dance restlessly. "Now climb down from that horse and turn it over."

"I don't think you want me to do that."

"No? And just why is that?"

India shrugged. "You'll see."

The man's eyes narrowed. "Talk damned careful for a stable boy. Where do you come from?"

"I don't believe that's any of your business."

A pistol glinted in the moonlight. "Mebbe I'm *making* it my business, whelp. Let's have your name."

"Jeremiah," India said coolly.

"Big name for a mighty scrawny creature," the man said thoughtfully. "A sight too big for that horse, too. Now climb off, boy, like I told you."

"If you insist." India slid from the horse and took a step back, her face expressionless.

"Going to ride the big brute, are you, Will?" someone called from the ragged circle of followers.

"What if I am?" the man growled. He moved to the big gelding and patted the animal's muscled neck. Emboldened when the horse did not pull away, he slid a foot into the stirrups.

Still no reaction.

Another second and he was in the saddle, smiling in triumph.

But the smile did not last. Neighing loudly, the horse reared, throwing his hapless rider head over heels into a row of thornbushes. He landed to the accompaniment of loud laughter from his band.

The bushes rustled and the man named Will reappeared, his steps pained. "I'll teach you," he swore, pulling a whip from his threadbare jacket. "You'll not try that trick on me again, you great brute."

"It won't work, you know," India said coolly. "He's trained to my bit and no one else can ride him."

"Then he'll soon learn better manners, won't he?"

One of the others put a restraining hand on his shoulder. "Looks a damned expensive piece of horseflesh, Will Colton. Why not take him to the Frenchman?"

The band muttered uneasily.

"He deals in anything of rarity. This horse would fetch a nice guinea or two."

The muttering grew to clear assent.

"Oh? And just how d'you expect to get the beast to the Frenchman's ship?" Will demanded.

"Make the whelp ride him, since he's so cocky."

The leader smiled coldly, struck by the reasonableness of this plan. "Aye, you're right. Let the Frenchman teach these three some manners." He laughed coldly and pointed his pistol at India. "You heard the man. Mount up, boy."

"We're not going anywhere," Froggett snapped. "You can just take yourselves off to hell and toast your eyebrows!"

The leader's eyes hardened. "Is it a fight you're after, old man? If so, you've got one."

India slid into the saddle and kneed the great gelding between the two men. She thought of putting a bullet through the man's head here and now, but one wrong move and the others would shoot her and Froggett. Far better to wait until they were spread out on the trail. Then there would be any number of chances to bolt. "Who is this Frenchman you're muttering about?"

Will Colton smiled coldly. "Not healthy to ask too many questions of that sort, boy. Besides, you'll be meeting the man soon enough. Reckon you can ask him all about hisself then," he sneered. He waved sharply, and India was swallowed up by a circle of riders.

And at the front of the line rode Froggett, with the Colton's pistol trained dead on his back.

*   *   *

They rode until the moon disappeared and the eastern sky had turned the color of ripe plums smudged with crimson. After galloping east for several hours, Colton directed them south toward the river. Aside from muttered threats, India had so far suffered no ill. None of the riders was brave enough to come close to Hannibal's hooves and contented themselves with warning India to keep up, on threat of shooting the old man.

No one showed any curiosity about where she and Froggett had come from. Being criminals themselves, the men obviously assumed that the pair had stolen the fine horse from the stables where they had formerly been employed.

At the top of a rise, Will Colton wheeled about and ordered a halt. Below them the Thames curled east, a restless ribbon threaded through a patchwork quilt of small farms and villages.

"Are we there, yet?" India demanded.

"Right down there."

"Then why are we stopping?"

"Close yer mouth, boy. Not healthy to ask so many questions," the man behind her snarled. "Fine horse or not, I can still put a ball through your cocky head."

The rest of his words were swallowed up by the sounds of a rising argument. Half of the band wanted to stay where they were, while the other half insisted on going ahead to keep an appointment with the pirate and smuggler who paid the best price for quality merchandise and information—but whose wrath was awful if he was duped.

They were still arguing the point when the man at India's side sat forward with a growl. "I thought as how that animal looked familiar!" He stared coldly at India. "Seen him once at Newmarket when I was picking pockets." He inched his mount closer. "Damned fine piece o' horseflesh. Look here, Will. That horse belongs to the duke of Devonham," he finished triumphantly.

"The duke what lives in Norfolk?" Will cantered closer. "Damned if these two ain't had the barefaced gall to steal that horse out from under his nose." He frowned. "But I heard stories about this horse. They say as how only the duke's daughter can ride the brute. Her father bought her the animal in Egypt, where she picked him out herself, I hear tell."

India sat stiffly as a row of angry eyes locked on her. *Bloody hell, what was she going to do now? She couldn't bolt, not with Froggett caught in the cold sights of a pistol.*

Hiding her fear, she inched toward Froggett. "I had the stabling of the horse. Couldn't a done that if I didn't ride the animal, could I?" she said scornfully. But fear was what they would expect, so she gave a nervous laugh. "You won't turn us back, will ye? He'll have a reward out for us by now. A fat reward, if I know the bloody duke. And he's got a hard hand with that heathen whip what he brung back from India."

But her ploy failed.

The leader laughed sullenly. "Reward? Aye, the reward of a noose around all our necks, most like. No, I reckon we'll not try the duke's hospitality, not when we're almost at the Frenchman's doorstep. I hear tell he's looking for treasures of all sorts these days—jewels, gold, silk. Mebbe a nice bit of horseflesh like this will interest him just as well."

"What if they come after the horse?" one of his men muttered. "The duke's son is damned handy with a pistol."

"They'll have to find us first," Will said coldly.

"How are they going to know where to look? Not like these two left a bleeding message, seeing as how they was sneaking off in the dead of night with the duke's most valuable horse."

"Oh, they'll find you," India said fiercely. "And when they do, that soldier fellow who's the duke's son will split you from neck to knee. He's damned protective about his property."

A Babel of worried voices followed these words, but the leader quelled them with a harsh curse. "Shut up, the pack of you! The whelp's just trying to frighten us. We been on the trail for four hours and seen no trace of anyone following us. We're *safe*, I tell you. And the Frenchman'll pay a tidy sum for that horse. Now who's with me?"

Again the voices rose in angry discord.

India saw Froggett jerk his head, ordering her to break free and leave him, but she refused to consider it. They would shoot him in a second if she got away. Her only choice was to stay. She had been hoping to meet this mysterious pirate, after all.

But she fingered the knife in her boot grimly. Just let the man try to lay a single finger on her!

Their destination was a two-masted sloop called the *Gypsy* rocking at anchor in a wooded loop of the Thames near the border of Suffolk. Clustered along the nearby pier were a dozen skiffs and dinghies. On the bank a crowd of merrymakers danced in the firelight.

India had a very bad feeling about this. But they wouldn't get her or Froggett without a fight!

The man riding guard beside her laughed coldly. "Starting to sweat, are you?"

"It will take more than a wine-swilling, whey-faced foreigner to frighten me!"

"And I'm the bleedin' king of England. But we'll see if you're so clever when you're facing the Frenchman. He's got unnatural tastes, so they say." At the head of the pier, men and women danced drunkenly around Colton as he jumped down and strode toward the sloop.

But his way was blocked by a tall man with one arm caught in a greasy sling. "Where do y' think *yer* going?"

"To see the Frenchman."

"By whose invitation?"

"His, o' course."

"What property ye got to show him?"

"This fine piece of horseflesh, for one."

The man with the sling studied India and the horse. "That so. I reckon I'll take the beast down to him."

"No good," Will said quickly. "The horse don't let a soul on his back except the boy. And where the boy goes, I go."

The man scowled, but reluctantly stepped aside.

Colton shoved Froggett in front of him. "Hurry up, boy," he called to India, who slid down and led the gelding carefully along the dock, reins tight in her fingers. At that same moment a man bounced down the gangway and landed in a heap at the bottom. A box of gold coins and jewelry came hurtling after him, landing on the wood with a crack.

"Nothing but worthless zinc and copper," a voice cried from the deck. "And those 'diamonds' only rock crystal! Try that again and you'll leave without the front of your head, *mon ami*."

The man gathered up his merchandise and skittered away, cursing.

"See," Will said glumly. "Don't do no good to try fobbing false goods off on the Frenchman. Still, he

pays the best, when he's satisfied." He moved closer
to Froggett, his pistol now hidden in one pocket. "I
got the barker right here, old man, and it can still
put a ball through your worthless head, so remember your manners. It's the horse to sell and no
tricks."

Froggett scowled, but nodded.

Female laughter echoed over the gangplank.
Aboard the *Gypsy* an argument was clearly in progress. It seemed to revolve around the question of
whether female garters ought to be red or pink.

India swallowed. Yes, she *definitely* had a bad feeling about this. The instinct grew even sharper when
a buxom female appeared at the top of the gangway, her lush form barely restrained by a clinging
gown of crimson satin. She tittered loudly. "Here's
more come to see the Frenchman. Said it would be
a busy night, didn't I just!" She rubbed her hands
greedily while Colton pushed Froggett before him
up the wooden planks. India stayed behind, sooth-
ing the great gelding, which was growing steadily
more nervous with the wild activity and the loud
voices.

"No use for horses," a voice called harshly. "Send
the pack of 'em away."

"But, yer honor, yer ain't even seen what I got for
you."

"No need to see it," the heavily accented voice
said. "I've seen my fill for the night. Now be off with
you."

India's fingers tightened on Hannibal's mane. She
knew exactly what the band would do next. If the
horse had no value, they would dispose of it—along
with the two travelers.

That left her only one alternative.

In one swift movement, she swung up into the

saddle. As Hannibal reared and danced beneath her, she caught him back, drove him up the gangway, and charged onto the deck.

"Good sweet God above! The boy's rode the horse right onto the *Gypsy!*" Torches flicked over the polished wood of the deck where men lolled on coiled ropes and overturned barrels. "Here now," one of the men growled. "You can't bring no animal on board. Bleedin' bad luck, it is!"

"How much for the horse?" a hard voice demanded.

Around India the men went still.

"The horse is not for sale," she said flatly.

All noise faded away on the deck.

"No? If he isn't for sale, why have you brought him here, *mon gars?*"

All eyes swung to the tall figure leaning against the forward mast. His broad shoulders were covered by a thick wool sweater and his face was in shadow.

"I didn't. These *brutes* waylaid us and tried to steal the horse."

" 'Tis a lie," Colton protested. "I hired the whelp to ride the horse, and then the cunning little snake tried to steal him from me."

"You begin to interest me, boy." A long shadow fell across the deck, slashing across India and her prancing mount. Something about that bar of darkness made her shiver. She frowned, trying to make out the features of the man by the mast.

Black hair, tied back in an unfashionable queue. A black eye patch. Swarthy skin half hidden by grime and a heavy beard. Her eyes locked with fascination on the gold ring that dangled from his ear.

She swallowed.

"And just whose horse is it that I have the great

honor of viewing?" The voice was liquid, heavily accented, and darkly compelling.

"I am—Jeremiah."

"Jeremiah who?"

"Er, Froggett. Your honor," she added. "But like I said, the horse ain't for sale. These villains was trying to steal him from me."

Instantly Will Colton shouldered his way through the crowd. " 'Tis a lie, yer honor. The thievin' little wretch only rode the beast down here from London for me. Paid him proper to do the job, too, so I did."

"*He's* the one who's lying!" India protested. In an instant a fierce argument ensued. It was halted by a pistol ball striking the *Gypsy's* deck.

"Enough," the captain growled. "It is easy to determine if the horse is stolen. Off the horse, boy." India slid to the deck, though she kept her fingers locked on the gelding's mane.

"Move apart now."

Colton moved back, scowling.

"You, sir, call the horse."

After a moment's hesitation Will raised one grimy hand. "Here, er, fellow. Come to me now, come like a good fellow."

The great horse raised his head and nickered, unmoving.

"Now you, boy."

"Come, love," India called softly. "There's a sweet fellow." Instantly the gelding danced across the deck and moved behind her, butting her softly. "Ho," she said, but the horse kept moving, shoving her toward the man at the mast. "Stop that, you irritating creature!"

But the gelding had ideas of his own. A moment later India was pitched against the tall, unsmiling figure by the mast.

Her breath caught. Hard ridges of muscle drove into her hips. The pirate's low laugh made her cheeks flame. She tried to step back, only to find his hands clenched at her waist.

"*Voyons,* the night, she has turned interesting."

Her head was wrenched back. The lantern rose above her.

The captain gave a low, muttered curse. "Perkins?"

"Aye, Cap'n?"

"Take the horse away and rub him down," the Frenchman ordered harshly.

"I'll not leave! Not without my money!" Colton bellowed. "You'll not get the animal past my men neither."

The pirate waved his hand as if knocking away a fly. "Take this fellow away, too, Perkins."

A fight broke out on deck. During the chaos that ensued, India slid onto Hannibal's back, determined to protect Froggett while he escaped overboard.

But she never got the opportunity.

Strong hands closed over her waist. She was yanked from the horse and flung over a brawny shoulder.

"Let me go, you—you pirate scum!"

Her protests were met with a low chuckle.

"He'll do you no good! Only I can ride Hannibal. He'll toss you on your face the second you touch his back."

"But no, I have a way with animals—and with people."

Something in that cool, fluid voice made India's pulse quicken. She fought furiously as the Frenchman's hard hands slid along her back and covered her twisting hips.

Abruptly his long fingers tightened. India heard him curse.

Dear God, he couldn't know! Not after one brief contact!

From somewhere in the night came the shrill cry of a seabird. Ragged clouds ran before the moon.

India was having a *very* bad feeling about this.

But she wouldn't let this grimy pirate see her fear. "Let me go! He'll be no good to you, I tell you."

By now every man on deck was silent, watching rapt as their captain struggled with this cocky new arrival.

"Stop fighting me," the Frenchman hissed.

"Like hell I will!"

Her captor's voice fell. "Do you wish for me to reveal you to all my men? Right now, my dear?" he added silkily.

He knew. Sweet heaven, he'd found her out! India caught a ragged breath. What was she to do now?

But the answer was taken from her as the deck pitched. She was shoved low and carried as ignominiously as a sack of oats across the deck.

"Keep the horse safe, Perkins. No one is to touch him until I have the facts of this matter. No doubt a few blows with my strap will work the truth out of the boy."

"Just you try it," India hissed, kicking furiously.

"Oh, you may count on that. Beating you is *exactly* what I mean to do, my dear. Or should I say *Lady Delamere*?" the harsh voice hissed back.

23

"Blasted thief! Rotten scoundrel!"

India's angry shouts echoed over the deck. But anger was just a defense. The pirate knew her sex and her identity. What in heaven's name would he do with her now?

Confronted with a problem, India did as she had always done since she was able to walk. She followed the example of her two beloved and thoroughly unruly brothers.

She raised her fists and prepared to fight. "Stay away from me."

The Frenchman closed the door of the cabin and slid the bolt home.

"Don't come near me. You'll be sorry if you do, I warn you!"

He turned slowly and angled his back against the door, arms crossed across his broad chest. A single candle flickered on an ornate, brass-bound chest, casting his bearded features into shadow.

India felt a rising wave of panic. "The horse is no good to you."

No answer.

"You'll *never* be able to ride him."

Still no answer.

"So you won't listen to reason." She tugged her pistol from her cuff. "Then this will have to convince you." She leveled the silver barrels. "Stay away. I'll shoot if you touch me," she said fiercely.

"Will you, indeed?" the Frenchman said softly. He took a step closer.

India's fingers tensed. She aimed carefully and sent a bullet cracking off the wall over his shoulder.

"I suggest you be careful where you're pointing that thing."

"Where I'm pointing is at *you!*"

Silently the pirate closed the gap, shadows dancing around him.

Grimly, India sent a second ball hurtling from the pistol. It took a nick out of the wall and sent a sliver of wood slicing across the Frenchman's arm.

He just kept coming.

"Don't you have ears? The next ball will go through your heart!"

He smiled faintly. "But now you have no bullets left, *petite.*"

He was right, India realized too late. She tossed down the pistol and tugged a knife from her boots. "Then you'll taste my steel instead."

"Such fire for a woman—and an Englishwoman at that. *C'est fort amusant.*"

"Oh, I'm funny, am I? Well, you won't think so in a minute, cur."

"No? *Mille pardons.* And me, I thought I was being so chivalrous."

Scowling, India leveled the knife, but the Frenchman caught it away with one smooth lunge. "I have no intention of touching you, little fool."

"Hah! And I suppose those men out there are in training for a life in the church."

"My men are well enough. Neither they—nor I—will hurt you."

India looked at him suspiciously. "You won't? Why not?"

"Because I like my women to look like women, for one thing. And also because taking partners to bed by force is not a good entertainment."

India swallowed. "Then what do you intend to do with me?"

"I haven't the slightest idea." Shrugging philosophically, he opened a drawer in the desk and pulled out a decanter and two tumblers. "Brandy?"

India crossed her arms at her chest and studied him defiantly. "I see right through your tricks, snake. You couldn't frighten me so now you're going to poison me instead!"

"Poison, you fear." The Frenchman filled two glasses and then drained one. "Like that?"

India bit her lip. "You must be trying to make me foxed. That won't work either."

He shrugged again, took the glass he'd poured for her, and drained it as well. "Now then, tell me what you're doing among those ruffians."

"My groom was with me, so I *wasn't* alone."

"*Voyons,* that makes it all different, of course. So let me ask you what you are doing dressed in boy's breeches and riding a horse that would cost a lifetime of work for any of my men?"

"None of your business," India said sharply. "I won't tell you. Not even if you *torture* me."

Across the cabin the shadowed face hardened. "There is torture, *petite.*" His voice fell, low and seductive. "And then there is *torture.*"

India sensed the tension in his body. Even more she felt the power of his will, a power that kept a score of villainous men in tight check. She swallowed. "And just what is that supposed to mean?"

"What do you choose to make of it, *ma mie?*"

India's fingers tightened. "You're threatening me."

"Merely stating a fact of the most evident."

"Well, you don't frighten me. I won't be badgered and bullied." She yanked the second pistol from her other boot and leveled the sights.

The Frenchman's brow rose. "I don't? How interesting." His hands went to his shirt. One button slid free.

"What are you doing?" India rasped.

"I'm giving you a chance to satisfy your English threats." The shirt parted slightly.

"You"—India swallowed—"are?"

"Of course, *anglaise*. One must never make a threat which one does not wish to carry through." There was an edge of warning to his voice. He moved closer, mere inches from the pistol now, his face draped in shadow. "*Alors,* you have your opportunity. I offer you my chest as a target. Shoot me now."

"Sh-shoot?"

"You forget how? Simply aim and press the little trigger with your finger."

"I *know* how to shoot a gun!"

"*Eh bien,* then shoot me."

India glared at him.

"Ah. Then it is not lack of skill that holds your finger back?" he asked innocently.

His innocence only added to India's fury. "Nothing's holding my finger back! I am simply—taking time to aim."

"But of course. I make a difficult target at this distance, to be sure."

India muttered harshly. All she had to do was

squeeze the trigger of the pistol her father had given to her in Egypt.

But she couldn't. Her finger wouldn't move. She could not shoot an unarmed, unresisting man. Every instinct forbade it.

"No?" He gave a Gallic shrug. "Your nerves are—how do you say—in a crisis?"

"*I am not having any crisis of nerves!* It's simply—well, unsporting to shoot someone who is unarmed."

"Ah, now you speak of sport. You English concern yourselves too much with this. Me, I find it most incomprehensible."

"You would," India muttered. "And now I'll show you exactly how I mean to—"

With a quick chop the Frenchman struck her wrist and sent her second pistol clattering to the floor. "Let that be your first lesson aboard the *Gypsy.* Never hold a pistol unless you're prepared to fire it. And you, *ma belle,* though very brave, are not prepared to kill a man. Consider it a blessing that you have never had the need." The pirate's voice was grim as he picked up India's pistol and slid it into his pocket. "And now, we commence again. *Ton nom, ma belle.* You are a Delamere, *non?*"

"I won't tell you. Not my name or a single word."

"No?" The full lips hardened. "But perhaps there is no need," he said coldly in his heavily accented English. "After all, I've seen that arrogant nose and those cool eyes before. All you Delameres have them."

India tried to hide her shock. Dear God, he hadn't been bluffing. He *knew.* Now there would be no escaping. He would demand a vast amount of ransom money. Maybe he would demand even more than money.

She couldn't let that happen.

Her chin rose. "So you've noted the likeness. It's been the curse of my life, for I'm no Delamere, not in the way it counts. They've only given me reason to hate the lot of them."

"I think I do not understand."

"I'm one of the duke's by-blows, blast it! I was fathered on a servant girl!"

The Frenchman turned away and refilled the glasses. India thought she heard him cough. "A by-blow, you say. By that you mean a natural child?"

"Just so." India warmed to her tale. "For years I've been snubbed and mocked. Everyone knows I was born on the wrong side of the blanket. I hate the whole lot of them!"

"Now it is all of the most clear. And of course you stole that beautiful animal from their stables for revenge."

"I didn't steal him," India snapped. "That is, I didn't steal him right away. I worked there for several years first."

"Years? *Pardieu*, and here I was thinking how young you look."

"Well, it *seemed* like years," India said firmly. "And in a manner of speaking the horse is mine, because of the bond between us. Besides the duke's daughter, only I can ride the great animal. So he might as well be mine."

"I dare say the magistrate might not see it in quite the same light," her captor said dryly.

"What would a ruffian like you know about magistrates or King's Officers?"

"Only that they make my life troublesome." The Frenchman made a sharp, dismissing gesture with his hand. "But you present me a dilemma. I can hardly permit you to leave without retribution. My crew will expect it, you understand, for I am most bloodthirsty." He studied her thoughtfully. "I have a reputation to uphold."

"Don't look at me for suggestions," India said sulkily. "You'll have to devise your horrible torments without my help."

"Horrible torments. Yes, I rather think you've hit the hammer on the head. Or is it nail? Your English tongue is *fort ennuyeux, enfin.*"

"Not as *ennuyeux* as you are, villain!" India snapped. "Let me go and we will both feel much better, I assure you."

For a moment something played over that shadowed face. "Alas, I cannot oblige you, *ma mie.* It is the men, you understand. They would turn most unpleasant at the loss of such a fine catch."

"The devil fly away with your men!"

"Me, I've thought the same words myself. It is of a most surprising thing how your thoughts run like mine. Are you sure we are never met before?"

"Are you implying that I think like a vile cutthroat and thief! I'll have your tongue for that."

"But you have neither pistol nor knife. You must learn your lesson about making threats you can't deliver."

India caught up one of the empty glasses. "No, it's you who'll learn about making threats, Frenchman!"

"Oh? Do you mean to drown me in my own wine?" he said lazily.

"No, I'm going to leave. Right here and now."

The dark brow arched. "And how are you going to do that?"

"Because *you're* going to open the door for me."

He laughed softly. "There you're quite wrong."

"Am I?" India cracked the goblet against the

chest, leaving a razor-like rim of glass exposed. With this before her, she began to drive her captor backward. "I'm not afraid to cut your throat, I warn you." He was at the wall now and India's blade was at his chest. "Well?"

"I have a great curiosity to see you slice through my throat," he said coolly, as if he were discussing the merits of a new kind of rigging knot.

"Damn you, I'm *not* lying. I'll do it, I swear."

"I am all at your convenience, *anglaise*."

Muttering, India closed her eyes and lunged. She felt the brush of skin and then his hand at her wrist. She heard the quick check of his breath as the glass was pulled from her fingers.

She opened her eyes and gasped. A two-inch gash ran across his shirt, where blood now oozed. "Now see what you made me do! Why did you have to move?"

"A thousand apologies." the pirate said dryly. "But it is a mere prick of a pin."

"Prick? You're bleeding like a pig!"

"Bah, me, I once faced down a dozen Barbary vessels that hove up like a great tropical wind. I fought twenty men at one time without a single weapon until every inch of my body flowed with blood."

"Off the Barbary coast?" India said, intrigued in spite of herself. "My father and I sailed there once, while we looked for the lost city of Dido in the Aeneid. Carthage, you know." She frowned. "Probably you don't know. On the way, we were trailed for three days by a pirate sloop."

"Then you are lucky you're still alive," the Frenchman said grimly.

"But it turned out to be an English frigate sent to protect us. I had met the captain in Cádiz, you see,

and he fancied—" Abruptly, India blushed and
looked away.

The Frenchman touched her chin and lifted her
face, scanning her crimson cheeks. "Yes, *sauvage*?
He fancied what?" His voice was dangerously soft.

"He—had conceived a tendre for me. It was most
foolish of him, for I was barely thirteen at the time."

"And what became of this crude captain with the
foolish tendre?"

"Oh, he wasn't crude. He was quite handsome, in
fact, and his manners were very elegant. His family,
too, was most respectable. From Berkshire, I believe."

"Yes, yes," the Frenchman interrupted coldly,
"but what of his pursuit of you?"

"Oh, there was no pursuit. My father told him I
could not wed until I was at least thirty, since I was
far too useful to him in his research. The captain
was regretful, but made his leave. I understand he
has five sons now."

The Frenchman's fingers relaxed on her chin.
"Me, I think this tendre of the most paltry kind. A
true man of sentiment would never have been so
easily turned away. He would have swept you onto
his schooner, carried you off, and then had his way
with you. After that you would have been his forever."

"Life doesn't happen like that," India said tightly.
There was a faint note of sadness in her voice. "Only
in poetry or books. No, life is—" She sighed, looking
down at his chest. "Very different."

"Is it, *ma mie*?" The voice grew rough. "I think
you are wrong." The calloused edge of one finger
traced India's cheeks and then gently crossed the
high arch of her mouth.

"Wh-What are you doing?"

"Wondering."

"Wondering what?"

"Why your captain gave up so easily. Me, I would not have given you up. Not even for a whole fleet of English frigates snapping at my bow."

"N-No?" India tried to make out his expression in the shadows cast by the cabin's single candle. "What would *you* have done?"

"Something very dangerous, I think." The Frenchman's thumb feathered the center of her mouth and India felt a curious urge to open her lips to him. Of course it was an urge she resolutely ignored. "First I would have touched her, oh, *comme ça*." He brushed a fringe of hair from her cheek. "And here, I think." His head bent.

India swayed for a moment, then stiffened. What was she doing? Could she actually be accepting the advances of this villainous river pirate? "Stand away, snake! You'll not trick me!"

But somehow she found herself gathered tightly against her captor's chest. "B-Besides," she sputtered, "you're *bleeding*!"

"Perhaps I am," he said roughly. "In places you cannot see," he muttered. He looked down and sniffed. "This, she is nothing."

Even as he spoke blood inched down his chest over the slit shirt.

"You enjoy making sport of me. It is very low of you." India's voice was tight. "A plague on you and all men!" Angry at her mortifying moment of weakness, she twisted free and grabbed the last goblets, hurling them against the wall, where they exploded with a satisfying crack. Then she saw her knife, within easy reach now, balanced on the edge of the bed where the pirate had tossed it.

India ran to seize it, and in her haste, she stumbled on the scattered glass shards.

Pain bit through her hip as she landed on a jagged piece of glass. Squeezing her eyes, she fought back tears.

"*Farouche,*" the Frenchman said, but the word was a caress. "Wild, just like that hair of yours. You seem not at all English to me, *enfin.*"

"I *am* English. And I am *not* wild. Oh, just go away."

The Frenchman's eyes narrowed as he saw how she cupped her hip. "You have hurt yourself?" Quickly, he pulled her to her feet and carried her to the bed. "You are every bit as wild as that horse you claim is not yours."

"I'm not wild." But the protest was weaker now as she fought back tears.

"You are both wild and reckless." The pirate shoved away her trembling fingers and tugged at the old breeches. The shard of glass was deeply imbedded in her skin, he saw. "*Merde.*" Carefully, he freed the jagged piece of glass, then tossed it up onto the chest. After rummaging through a drawer, he came back with a clean piece of flannel soaked in brandy. "This may hurt."

"Bah," India mumbled, her face on fire with embarrassment.

But the hard fingers slid relentlessly over her bared skin, and something in that touch made her heart lurch drunkenly. "Enough," she croaked. "I— will be fine."

Keen eyes studied her for a moment, taking in the lines of exhaustion in her face. "You will sleep now, *mon Inde.*"

My India.

Something about his caressing tone set India's

blood to the boil. "You have no right to my name, you snake."

"No? I believe I do have that right—and any other I choose to take." Laughing darkly, he made her a mocking bow. "Now I will leave you to think over what I have taught you this night." He strode to the door. "Sleep well, *ma mie.*"

He slid open the bolt and strode outside. The length of iron shot home behind him, locking her in.

"Let me out!" India screamed, jerking at the door latch.

"Tomorrow perhaps. Until then, cease this howling or I will return and beat you some more, boy. And you shall pay for all that broken Irish crystal in the morning."

This time one of the drawers hit the door. "Not if you were Barbarossa himself!"

She paced.
She cursed.
She hammered angrily at the door.

After a few moments, she sank back against one wall and dug deep into her pocket. Her palm opened, revealing a circle of dawn-pink flames. At least she still had her jewel.

India scowled at the barred door. She had come to find the Frenchman, of course, but something made her wary of mentioning the priceless gem. Not yet, she decided. In the end the stone might be the only way of escape from this cutthroat.

After pocketing the jewel and fuming for another quarter hour, she decided to conserve her energy for the infuriating pirate's return. She sniffed suspiciously at the blanket across the narrow bed, relieved to find it surprisingly clean.

With an angry hiss, she slid down against the soft blanket, the hours of strain finally taking their toll. She closed her eyes and almost instantly was swept into darkness and dreams.

The dream began as it always did, with drums and shouts and marching feet. Suddenly India was there again, in a Brussels thronged with carts and wagons while soldiers marched to join their regiments.

She ran through the crowds, looking for a pair of broad shoulders, looking for a tall lean body and a devil-may-care smile. But the faces were always wrong and she could never find him.

Artillery thundered in the distance and terrified villagers rushed past. The first wounded stragglers made their way through the streets, their weary eyes haunted by nightmares of blood and hate and fear among the mud.

She tossed, struggling to push the memories away.

And all the time India told herself everything would be good and safe and fine if only she kept searching. If only she looked long enough, she must finally find him. . . .

The Frenchman stood with the lantern in his hand, watching his beautiful English captive murmur restlessly and twist in her sleep. His eyes were locked on the slim fingers clutching at shadows and ghosts he could not see.

His jaw hardened as she tossed the blanket aside and cried out, her hand flung wide, one lush breast outlined against the soft cambric of the old shirt she wore.

He swore beneath his breath, blasted by a storm of desire, hungry to push her beneath him and drown himself in her sweetness.

His hands clenched with the need to have her. He could smell her scent, fine and soft like bergamot and violets. His groin was heavy, blood squeezing hot and slow through his veins as he studied the dusky point of one nipple molded against the white cambric.

So near. So bloody near.

He could ease her to pleasure as she slept. When she woke she would be wet and welcoming, his name a husky prayer on her lips.

Suddenly he realized just how much he wanted her ragged cries of desire filling his ears as he buried himself inside her.

Cursing sharply, the *Gypsy*'s captain turned and set down the lantern. With fingers not quite steady he filled a glass with brandy and drained it in one gulp.

Fire burned down his throat, hot and furious.

But not half so furious as the fire that burned at his groin.

He watched India's hand catch in the tangled sheets. He did not move, as if paralyzed.

Or perhaps he was afraid.

24

*I*ndia was running, fire on her right and fire on her left. Voices called out, high and shrill and mocking, but she did not stop. Because he was there, somewhere in the darkness, somewhere in the night. And she had to find him.

She called his name, but no answer came. She was alone, as she always was, trapped in a place of darkness and dreams.

And then a voice. A single word.

It was her name, whispered low and hoarse, as it always was on his lips. She shivered, feeling the shadows close around her. And then he was there, sprung from her dreams, his eyes urgent with desire, his body tight with need.

There was no time for fear or protest. She wanted him too much for that. She molded herself close and tasted the fire of his body, wanting more. Wanting to feel his scent on her skin and his breath as ragged with need as hers was.

"Please," she whispered, not knowing quite what she wanted.

But he knew.

"So I shall, my love."

With a soft hiss of silk, her gown loosened and slid inch by inch down her fevered skin.

Not fast enough. She shoved it away, gasping when she met him heat to heat.

It was like coming home. It was like grabbing a wild breath after swimming too long underwater. It was taking the creek at Swallow Hill in one bound.

She'd found Devlyn at last. Tall and strong and laughing. Clear eyes burning, sweet as heaven itself. Somehow she'd found him again.

Her breath caught. She knew a greed to taste him everywhere, to worship the body she had never had time to know. She laughed with the heady joy of discovery and pressed him back, her fingers toying with the mahogany hair that swirled across his chest.

And then there was no softness, only blood in a thin line that trailed over bronze skin. There was low laughter and a fine gold earring glinting in the light of a single lantern.

India sat up with a ragged cry, sleep still clutching at her. "No, not him. It was only a dream."

A dream. But why did it feel like so much more?

She tugged the blanket to her chest as if that could hold back her horror and her own forbidden thoughts.

"So, Perkins, what business have we so far today?" The captain of the *Gypsy* stood high on the foredeck, letting wind rake his hair as he studied the great restless track of the river stretching east to the sea. Today the same kind of restlessness flashed in the Frenchman's eyes.

Perched on a coil of rope, the first mate scratched wind-hardened cheeks and frowned. "Someone to see you about a set of diamonds. Fabulous, he swears. Someone else who says he can show you a secret passage through the Tower to the Crown Jewels. For a price, of course. An offer to buy that white horse from you." The man's lips twitched. "And three offers to buy the boy what rode in on the great beast."

"Buy? Perkins, you astound me."

"I bloody doubt it, Captain. Beggin' yer pardon."

"And who were these, er, buyers?"

"Oh, the usual river scum, along with a man from a bordello up by Whitechapel."

The captain laughed bitterly. "We are now a thorough nest of vice, to be sure. And how much did they offer for the boy?"

"The highest? Two hundred pounds for the horse and twenty pounds for the boy. For work in the bordello, that is." Perkins's eyes narrowed. "As if you'd consider selling the lad."

"No? I am a man of vile reputation, Perkins."

The first mate snorted.

"You are in a black mood today, Perkins."

"Not as black as I outta be. Since when are we taking in captives aboard the *Gypsy*—especially boys what ain't boys?"

The Frenchman's brow rose and he scratched thoughtfully at his heavy black beard. "Is there a point to your question, I ask myself?"

"What are we doing with a female below deck? Is that clear enough for you?"

"*Doucement*," the captain said quickly, looking about to be sure they were alone.

"Well, I'm tired of *douce* this and *patience* that. I keep things quiet here while you go running off to London and God's knows where else, and all for what, I'm asking? You've found three sets of diamonds already, and another two of emeralds. But that isn't what you want, is it? So what are we doing here, pitching at anchor when we could be hauling fine burgundy over the Channel or horses from Galway Bay."

The Frenchman's face went very hard. "No questions, my friend. It was our agreement when the voyage began, and it must remain a condition still."

"Oh, I ain't asking outright, Captain. You'll tell me when the time's right. But I can't be patient forever. Meanwhile, I don't hold with *no* females on board. Nothing but trouble will come from it, mark my words."

"Trouble. This one, she will be that, of a certainty." The pirate took out the knife he'd taken from India and studied its honed blade. "But she stays awhile longer, my friend. Bad luck or no."

Perkins scrubbed at a grimy corner of the deck with his toe. "So what do I tell them that's waiting to see you?"

"No to the emeralds. No to the Crown Jewels in the Tower. And no to the first two offers to buy my cocky red-haired boy. Who will *remain* a boy," he said warningly to Perkins.

"Aye, Cap'n. It's your game. But what about that last rogue? Him that's from the bordello?"

The Frenchman's eyes hardened. "Tell our friend from Whitechapel that if he ever shows his face along this stretch of the river again, I will personally see to it that his filthy ears are shaved from his equally filthy head. I'll see the fellow about the diamonds in ten minutes."

Perkins chuckled. "Any other orders?"

"Just one, *enfin*. The door to my cabin stays locked, no matter what. Do you understand me?"

"Aye. But there's trouble to come," the wiry sailor said darkly. "You'll see. As sure as there's a wind from the east and fog before nightfall."

* * *

India was lying in wait for the captain an hour
later, with the last drawer from the chest clutched
in her fist.

When the door bolt hissed free, she aimed for
where the captain's head would be.

And barely had time to catch herself as Froggett
appeared in the doorway.

"Whatever are you doing now, Mis—" The old
man cleared his throat. "Er, Jeremiah." He was
shoved into the cabin and the door bolted behind
him.

"I was trying to escape! Have they hurt you, Froggett?"

The groom stood studying the maps tossed over
the chest, the broken glass on the floor, and the un-
made bed. "No, I was treated well enough. So was
that white horse of yours. But what in thunder's
been going on *here*? Did that Frenchman—"

"No," India said quickly. "Not that he didn't want
to. And not that he won't try again," she said darkly.
"The arrogant snake knows I'm a woman, Froggett.
And somehow he knows I'm a Delamere. We *must*
escape."

"What about your great plan to get information
from the Frenchman? Told you how it would be,
didn't I? Deviltry and mayhem, and us left prisoners
in the middle of the bleeding river with no one to
know we're even gone."

India sighed. "You were right, Froggett, I admit
it."

"That Frenchman's a cunning sort, all right. Sees
everything, though he acts like he doesn't. And all
the while there's a bad lot of people coming in and
out." Froggett looked at India, who was rubbing her
sore hip. "What's amiss?"

"It's nothing. I hurt my side when I fell on a piece of glass."

"Don't know who's more dangerous—you or that pirate," the groom muttered.

"Stop being so gloomy and help me think how we are going to get away from here."

"Reckon you'll have to use that stone you've got hidden in your boot."

"I was thinking the same thing. A pity to waste it."

"A bigger pity *not* to waste it," the groom said darkly. "I don't care to stay here and rot. Or worse."

India sighed. "I suppose you're right. But he mustn't know it's here, or he'll never let us go. I'll tell him that I hid it ashore. He'll have to send me to find it, and I'll insist that you come. Then we'll escape."

The old groom looked skyward. "Heaven help us both, if *that's* your plan."

"Do you have anything better in mind?"

Froggett scowled.

"I thought not. So we may as well get it over with." India strode to the door and banged loudly. "You, out there! Fetch the captain and look lively about it!"

"It's the boy, Captain." Perkins moved closer to the Frenchman, who was just climbing down from the rigging. "The boy what *ain't* a boy," he muttered.

"What does he want now, a bath and a hot meal? Or maybe a presentation at court?"

"He wants *you*."

The Frenchman smiled faintly. "One can only wish, Perkins." He shouted an order to one of his crew, wincing as he dropped back onto the deck.

"You've hurt your shoulder again."

"It's nothing."

"Like hell, it is."

The Frenchman scowled at his first mate. "What does my captive want me *for*?"

"He didn't happen to confide in me. But before you go, you'd better speak to that man called Frasier who just arrived from London. He said he was from a jeweler called Parrish Brothers and has some important information. Something about diamonds," the mate added.

"Show him aboard," the captain said tightly.

The interview was conducted between two coils of rope and a mass of torn canvas sail. The Frenchman didn't trust his visitor, a swarthy man with more teeth than hair, who seemed more interested in the *Gypsy* than in his discussion.

"What about these diamonds you mention?"

The Londoner pulled a knife from his boot and toyed with its silver hilt. "I heard you're looking for good stones. Very special stones."

"I might be."

"Then I've got what you want. Diamonds you've never seen the like of before."

The Frenchman's eyes narrowed. "When can I see them?"

A shrug. "Maybe tomorrow. Maybe next week. It's a matter of some . . . delicacy."

"Delicacy be damned. Do you have jewels to sell or don't you?"

"No call to get angry. I'm here, ain't I? You'll get word when they're ready to show. But it's solid sterling at time of sale." His eyes hardened. "And no questions asked, understand?"

"You'll find I pay better than anyone. And I'm not overly concerned with who the stones' last owner was."

"In that case, it will be a pleasure doing business with you." Frasier stood up and resheathed his knife in his boot. "I'll send word when it's time to meet."

"I am a busy man. How will I know when to expect you."

The man smiled thinly. "You won't. Meanwhile, it sounds like you have your hands full keeping control of your crew, Captain."

The Frenchman frowned, hearing muffled shouts from the other side of the deck. He looked up and saw half of the *Gypsy*'s crew huddled by the companionway.

"Or maybe it's some of your *human* cargo you're having trouble with." His eyes narrowed. "Maybe that slender fellow with red hair who rode in on a finer horse than this sorry stretch of river has ever seen before."

"Make your point."

"My point? That a young gentleman of that description was recently seen in London, trying to sell one of the finest pink diamonds in the world. Curious, don't you think?"

The Frenchman leaned back against the deck railing. "Curiosity, my friend, is what killed your English cat, *n'est-ce pas*? It might be better if you remember that."

As the shouts grew louder, Frasier pushed to his feet. "Just don't get yourself taken up by the magistrate for murder." His lips curved. "Or unnatural acts."

The Frenchman scowled as he watched Frasier walk cockily from the ship. Something about the man irritated him, but if the offer was genuine, it could be of extraordinary importance. He would have to lay his plans carefully.

But first, he had one shouting, intractable Englishwoman to deal with.

When the captain strode across the deck toward his cabin, his crew scattered hastily. "What the devil's going on here?" he growled.

"It's the boy, Captain," someone said helpfully. "Going to beat him some more, are you?"

The Frenchman's scowl grew blacker. "About your business!"

"Aye, Captain."

Outside his cabin the shouts were ear-splitting. The captain flung open the door. "Cease your howling!"

"It's about time you came!"

The captain ignored her. He looked at Froggett, and motioned to the door. "Out."

"Now, just you listen here—"

"Do not tax my patience, old man," the Frenchman snapped.

"Go on, Froggett. I'm not afraid of this snake."

The old groom glared at the two grinning crewmen waiting to usher him back onto the deck. "You sure, er, Jeremiah?"

"I'm sure."

The old man was pulled away. The captain waited until the door was bolted and advanced toward his captive.

"Stay back." India hefted a drawer from the chest.

"I don't believe I will, *ma mie*." The captain ducked as the drawer hurtled past his shoulder and hit the wall. His best powder horn and two score iron pistol balls went flying all over the floor.

His captive stumbled on the scattered balls and was thrown back against the bed. "S-Stay away. I'll start screaming again otherwise. And *then* I'll break your neck."

The Frenchman was right behind her. His fingers feathered gently over her neck. "You've hurt your own neck, little fool."

"I'm fine," India said tightly.

Hard fingers eased over her bruised skin. Then his lips slid over her ear.

India swallowed, feeling a curious heat unravel through her legs and inch upward. She tried to shove free of him, as her throat went hot and dry. "Stop doing that."

He found the pulse that beat at her neck and palmed the skin gently. "Is it because you fear me?"

"No," India lied. "I—I simply do not care to be mauled about, with a tongue thrust between my lips and, oh, cold fingers poking everywhere."

"Who has done this?" The voice came sharp and angry as a gunshot.

"A great many, I suppose." She shrugged. "I cannot remember."

"You let these *imbéciles* with hands like hooves take such freedoms?"

"I was merely curious. There are things I wanted to know," India said irritably. "What business is it of *yours*?"

"What did you want to know?"

"What it felt like—that is, whether I would know if—" She broke off, unable to frame such thoughts in words. "Oh, you are only a pirate. How could you understand?"

"Perhaps I do," came the silken answer. "And perhaps I can answer your questions." His hands slid into her hair. "You want to know if you can feel the heat of a man, *non*? And whether you can make him feel that same heat."

"Rubbish," India said sharply. But she stood still just the same. The heat had begun to skitter up to

her knees and showed definite signs of making its
way even higher. "It is simply that moving around
as we did, with my father always on the scent of
some treasure or new discovery, I never had a
chance to—that is, I never got to know if—"

"If you are a woman desirable, yes? If the sight of
your lips can make a man's legs go weak with wanting you? If the touch of your lovely breasts could
send heat to his groin?"

"No! I never said—"

But the quest had gone too far. His fingers were
deep in her hair and she was molded against his
unrelenting body. "Shall I answer you now, *ma
belle*? Shall I tell you that you can find your own
answer here in my body?" he said hoarsely.

A thousand questions plagued India, questions
that she had never had time to explore with Devlyn
before he'd gone off to Waterloo. And there was
something else, something that pricked at her even
more than those questions. She stiffened. "Release
me."

"You want answers, don't you?"

"Not from you."

"You want me, *ma sauvage*. Your blood already
sings for my touch."

"No!"

"You can find your answers right now. Kiss me
and read them on my lips."

India could not move, mesmerized by the heat of
his eyes, the hoarse urgency in his voice. She tasted
desire, hot and sweet.

For a stranger. For a pirate.

For a villain of the lowest sort.

And she—

She wanted him, wanted his lips on her mouth,
his hands on her naked skin.

She tried to pull away, but he laughed darkly and tugged her closer against him, while the candle glinted on his golden earring. Angry, she struck out, her fingers trembling.

But they met only hot skin.

"No," she cried, as desire whined through her blood. "Not for you."

His laughter echoed around her. His calloused hand slid around her hips and welded them together, hardness to heat, male to female, as love had always been given.

His fingers massaged the tensed muscles at her spine then splayed open at her ribs. India shivered in spite of herself, knotted muscles turning to jelly at his clever, knowing ministrations. How many woman had he touched to know such dark skill?

"And what of these other imbeciles with hands like hooves. Do you stop them? Do you cry your pleasure sounds for them, when they touch you just so?" His hand slid lower, molded to the swell of her hips.

"No," she rasped.

"Me, I do not understand. No, you do not stop them or no, you do not cry out with pleasure for your English lovers?"

"Neither, you pig. You abject, depraved, infuriating goat carcass."

Soft laughter teased her skin, heated air that played through her hair. "How glad I am to hear it, *sauvage*. For it must be only for me, *comprends tu*? Only us together like this, one dawn to the next."

"You are mad! When my father and brothers find what you've done, they'll murder you. But first they'll tie you up and strip away your skin, the way the dacoits do in India. Then they'll take hot coals and—"

She was stopped by the pressure of his hard body, squarely atop her, driving her down into the mattress. He clicked his tongue softly. "Your tongue is like a whip. You must scare away many men this way, *non?*"

His barb hit her with shocking force, because it was far too true. She had always had to guard her tongue, to hide her temper and her adventurous nature. Otherwise, there was constant censure and tittering, along with the endless, draining gossip that London society seemed to thrive upon.

"So it is true, *enfin.*"

Damn the man, did he miss nothing? "No, it's not true, curse your villainous reptilian heart!" India struggled furiously, trying to dislodge his powerful body, but it was as pointless as trying to capture the Thames in a sieve. He only gave slightly, moving with easy power.

"I think you must make up your mind. Either I am a goat carcass or I have the heart of a reptile. Even me, who is ignorant of science, knows I cannot be both, my beauty."

India twisted wildly, but the effort only drove her into the heated length of him, where straining muscle could no longer be mistaken.

Her breath caught.

"But I have given you your answer. You read it in my body, which already rises hot and hard for you. *Enfin,* you are a woman in every sense desirable."

She caught back an angry cry and wrenched one hand free, then drove it straight to his chin, where it landed with an angry crack. When he pulled away, she scrambled wildly to her feet.

"Very beautiful, you are," he whispered. But now there was a hint of danger in the words.

India followed his gaze and blushed furious crimson to see that her shirt had worked free in her struggles. Now the pearl buttons gaped open over the creamy sweep of her breast, where one rose-pink nipple rose taut and bold.

"And judging by the look of that lovely bloom, your blood has been just as fired as mine."

Cursing furiously, India jerked the shirt closed and backed toward the door. "With fury. With contempt. Nothing more, on my honor."

In the cold gray light of dawn, his eye patch lay black as the road to Waterloo, black as the cannonballs lined up in the carts rattling to the front. His voice hardened. "Honor? Now there is a strange word to hear on a woman's lips. Have you honor, my *anglaise*? Do you keep your vows sworn in honor?"

"Always!"

"Ah." His fingers quivered faintly. "And when you give your vow to the man you will one day marry, you will make your answer with honor?"

His single uncovered eye mocked her.

Marriage would be the very thing for her. Her mother and grandmother had told her so often enough. Yes, it would put Devlyn Carlisle into the past, where he belonged. "Yes," India said flatly. "I will."

Why should she feel so cold when she said the words?

"And this, it is a bond of honor?"

"Of course. Why do you stare at me like that?"

"Because, you will not find joy in the arms of any proper English lord. There is too much fire in you, too much need. He will never make you cry out in passion. If you marry such a man, you will soon make him a cuckold."

"Never. When I marry, it will be out of love. I will

be honest and faithful, and, oh, the most *dutiful* sort of wife!"

He gave a hard laugh. "But a man does not want *duty* in his bed."

"Have you no decency?"

He looked very thoughtful, then shook his head. "No, I think I have not. It vanished when I left my country and tried to learn your cold, hard English ways." There was bitterness in his voice. Then he shrugged, a most Gallic, philosophical gesture. "Decency, she does not fill my stomach. Nor does she warm my bed. Not like you, *sauvage*. No, we will speak no more of decency. Perhaps not even of *honneur* will we speak. We will speak only of heat and blindness. Of the *coup de foudre*, for the thunderbolt is what I felt when I first saw you, wild and splendid on that great white horse you stole."

"I didn't steal—"

The Frenchman laughed darkly. "Yes, I forgot. You simply removed that which was yours from the duke's stable."

"You can't hold me here! And I won't have you as you want me. Never! Not if you were the last living specimen of manhood on earth."

"*Par Dieu*, such a tongue. But soon I will feel a different lash of its soft velvet."

"Never! And if you don't open this door right now—"

"Captain! Open up!" Rough hands banged at the cabin door. At the same time boots hammered across the deck.

Scowling, the Frenchman crossed the room and threw open the door. "Well?"

His first mate stood in the hallway, frowning. "It's those scum from downstream, Cap'n. They decided it was time to drive you out of their territory once and for all. There must be fifty of them, and every one armed."

The Frenchman cursed. He took the saber Perkins was holding out and strode off toward the companionway.

"Aren't you forgetting something, Captain?"

"What?"

"The boy. The boy what *ain't* a boy," he added quietly.

The Frenchman turned.

But it was too late. India Delamere flew through the door, rammed the first mate and sent him stumbling sideways, then hammered up the stairs toward the *Gypsy's* noisy deck.

25

The deck was covered with clouds of smoke and the air boomed from the volleys of the cannons on the rival vessel. Through the smoke and chaos of fighting bodies the Frenchman finally made out his captive's slender figure running toward the starboard railing. Mid-deck she was waylaid, but she twisted away from her attacker, kicked him in the groin, and wrenched his pistol from his hand. This she tossed to her companion and then the two of them started toward the side of the boat. When another pair of snarling river pirates attempted to stop her, she waved the gun until they retreated.

The Frenchman watched in horror as four more men began to circle her slowly. Now there was only one way to reach her in time.

Grabbing a cable, he launched into the air, swung wide and dropped onto the deck. In the process he knocked out two cursing sailors and kicked a pistol out of the hands of a third.

But he was too late. His captive was already perched nervously on the edge of the *Gypsy*'s aft railing, waving wildly to her companion back on the deck.

"Jump, Froggett! Jump now!" And then her slender form went hurtling toward the foam-streaked waves below.

By the time the Frenchman reached the railing, she was a small figure bobbing up and down in the water.

Her friend was standing white-faced at the rail. "I couldn't go. I can't swim. Never learned how." He looked pleadingly at the captain. "You have to understand. You can't hurt her. She's—"

Perkins grabbed his arm. "Quiet, now." His voice fell. "The captain will have a care for the woman."

The Frenchman only hoped he could. Wincing, he touched his shoulder, feeling pain gnaw at the joint. Hardly an auspicious start. Grimly, he tossed his pistol to his first mate. "See that they don't destroy my ship while I'm gone, Perkins."

And then he sailed down into the river after her.

The force of the impact slammed through him, yanking his breath away. When his head broke from the waves, the *Gypsy*'s captain saw the woman already had twenty yards on him. He watched her cut through the water with sure, fast strokes and maneuver past three more rowdy sailors looking for a fight.

The fool was lucky to be alive, the captain thought, grimly closing the distance until she was mere yards before him. But when he had almost reached her, she spun about and aimed a punishing blow with her right heel on his shoulder.

He fought a crashing wave of pain, gulping water and going under for a moment. When he came up, his jaw was hard. She was going to *pay* for that.

Of course, that was if he could ever manage to use his arm again. At that moment, the bone felt as if it were being pulled from its joint.

He cradled his shoulder for a moment. It had

been a stupid move to swing across the deck. Clearly, he wasn't the man he had once been, the Frenchman thought bitterly. Meanwhile, he had a captive to catch. A captive who was halfway to the shore, while he was here gasping for air.

He put the pain out of his mind and cut a straight path toward the rocky cove. Years of practice had made him a strong swimmer, so the Englishwoman was barely working her way along the top of the bank when the pirate heaved himself out of the water.

Now she would learn a lesson, he vowed. With a running dive he shot forward, tackling her not ten feet up the bank. In the process she slammed into his chest and he was thrown shoulder first onto a row of rocks.

This time the pain was blinding. He closed his eyes, white-faced and sweating.

"You're hurt!"

She sounded surprised, he thought irritably. "Of course I'm hurt. This is the second time today you've nearly castrated me. I hope you're enjoying your success."

But her face showed no triumph. She was shivering a little and her eyes were anxious.

For him?

A strange ache invaded his heart. "Why did you run away?"

"To get your attention."

"*What?*"

"To get your—"

"I *heard* you." He eyed her shivering, bedraggled figure, auburn hair slicked to her neck. "Now, you have it, little fool, but we can't stand here and argue while you freeze to death. And we can't go back to the ship. One look at you in that wet shirt and every man in my crew will know you're no boy."

India's head slanted down toward the soft cambric. After her swim it lay damp, molded to her chest like a second skin. She flushed, then studied him, frowning.

"Waiting for a carriage, are you? If so, you're flat out of luck." He shook his head, muttering. "Let's go."

The Frenchman felt her eyes on him as she followed him through a scattering of trees that bordered a winding stream. Beyond stood an old stone cottage, now covered by wild brambles. The green vines hung lush with berries, red against the weathered stone. Together the two of them managed to clear away the overgrown foliage and push open the front door. "I keep this cottage for safety, just in case things grow too difficult aboard the *Gypsy*," he explained. "There's wood over here." He winced as he bent toward the grate. "I'll make up a fire."

"No, *I'll* make the fire." India was studying his arm, frowning.

Without giving him time to protest, she expertly stacked the logs in the fireplace, then struck the flint she had found on the dusty mantel overhead. Soon the fire gave a comforting crackle and heat began to fill the room.

The Frenchman closed his eyes and eased his long body back against a pile of grain sacks. Yes, it had been amazingly stupid to swing that way across the deck. His only excuse was that he had been worried about her, surrounded by four grinning sea vermin. "Where did you learn to lay a fire so well?" he asked.

"Egypt, India, Greece." She smiled faintly. "A

small schooner pitching in a very rough sea off the coast of the Hebrides."

"You've led a busy life, *anglaise*. Busier than I, it seems. But leave the rest of those logs. I'll tend to them."

"Why?"

"Because I'm *supposed* to, that's why."

"Who said?"

"Nature says. Society says. *I said.*" He turned slightly, cupping his shoulder. "I'm the man, after all."

Her eyes were thoughtful as she studied the planes of muscle where his shirt had billowed open. "You're hurt. I'm probably better at making fires, anyway." After settling a final log on the now snapping fire, she turned to study his long body slanted against a pile of grain sacks. "In my family we all help each other. It's the Delamere way." Her eyes darkened with challenge. "And we help each other *equally*, male or female."

"Then you're . . . very lucky, *sauvage.*" The Frenchman's jaw hardened. "I would be a fool to argue over something I would not be half as good at. But you must be freezing." He patted the sack next to him. "Come and sit here." When India sat down gingerly beside him, he tugged an old cloak around her shoulders.

It was dangerous to be here with her like this, he knew, but suddenly he didn't care. The room was quiet except for the cracking of the fire and the heat that left him increasingly drowsy. He was only half awake when her hand moved over his shoulder. "What are you doing?"

Her fingers traced an old, jagged scar, which glistened copper in the firelight. "Looking." Her voice was husky. "How did this happen?"

He shrugged. "It was . . . a long time ago." He rubbed his beard, which had begun to itch from the saltwater.

She looked at him oddly. "Don't you want to talk about it?"

"No." Flat. Unrelenting.

"When?" She turned to study the hard lines of his chest as he stripped off his wet shirt and tossed it over a wooden crate before the fire to dry.

He sighed. "Later, *anglaise*. And you should take off those damp things too."

There was an odd intensity to her face. "Should I?" she asked softly. "When I'm alone with you, a pirate? A total stranger? Would that—give you pleasure, Captain?"

"If I wanted to have my barbaric way with you, *anglaise*, I could have done it long before this," the Frenchman said dryly.

"Yes, you could have. And that's exactly what's been bothering me." India's fingers slid over the warm planes of his chest. "Do you like this?"

The Frenchman frowned. "I might."

"And do you like this?" She teased the hard ridge of his stomach, until heat gnawed at his groin. "No," he lied.

"Indeed." Smiling, India raised her hands to the dark strands of his beard.

And there they jerked sharply.

The Frenchman sat up with a shout. *"Mille diables!* What in the name of all that's sacred was *that* for?"

But India barely heard him. Her body was tense and her fingers were locked tight.

Over something dark and stiff.

"That was for lying to me," she rasped as her

palm opened to reveal a strand of thick black hair.
"You bloody, bloody fool!" she cried.

To the man whose false beard had begun to dissi-
pate in the saltwater.

To the man whose shoulder still pained him, as
Alexis had said.

To her *husband*.

"Did you think you could hide your identity from
me, Devlyn Carlisle? I remember every inch of your
body and always will. Now I want the truth. Every
single bloody word of it!"

The Duchess of Cranford paced her sunlit conservatory, while Beach hovered anxiously behind her.
"Where can that impossible creature have gone
now? I visit a friend for one night and return to find
the whole house in turmoil. What happened here,
Beach?"

"She didn't return last night, Your Grace, and
there's been no sign of her today."

The duchess's cane struck the floor. "If we were in
Norfolk, I wouldn't mind. There India can run as
free as Luna, if she likes. But this is London . . ."
The duchess returned to her pacing.

"Your Grace." The butler cleared his throat.
"There's something else, I'm afraid."

"What now?"

The butler reached into his pocket and pulled out
a clump of auburn hair.

"She's cut her hair?" The duchess frowned. "What
in heaven's name was the girl planning?"

Abruptly she stiffened. No, India would never
dream of carrying her masculine masquerade so
far. The duchess refused to believe it. Then again,
she *had* been acting very strangely ever since Lord
Thornwood's return to London.

The duchess's eyes narrowed. There were clearly sparks between the two of them, and where there were sparks there was usually fire.

"Begging Your Grace's pardon, but I also found this, shoved in a drawer of Miss India's desk." The butler held out a creased piece of paper.

The duchess opened the folded sheet, and her face paled. *"Stay away from Voksal or youl b sory,"* she read.

"This one was half hidden beneath a curtain in her room," Beach went on nervously. "I found it an hour ago."

The second note the butler held out was even worse. Ragged letters raced across the page in angry slashes. "Leve London or die," the duchess read.

Her hands closed tightly over the sheets and she looked up at her butler and friend. "Oh, Beach, what kind of danger has the little fool gotten into now?"

"It's done."

The man looked up from the fire, which colored his face an angry copper. "The cargo is secure?"

"Exactly as you wished."

"And the location?"

"Just as you indicated. Somewhere in which the—cargo—will attract no attention at all." Helena Marchmont frowned. "But what about Thornwood? What if—"

Her companion smiled coldly. "Thorne is no threat to us, not with his memory gone. And I will dispose of him long before his memory returns."

"But what if he—"

"Forget about Thorne," the man before the fire said harshly.

He turned, his body hard and pulsing. "Now come here."

The widow toyed with the sash trailing at her waist. "But it's barely been an hour since—"

He moved across the room and was shoving up her skirt before she could finish.

A moment later her sultry laughter filled the darkness.

26

The man dangling half of a thick black beard, the man who was India's husband, went very still. "How did you know?" he said hoarsely.

"I didn't—not at first. You did a fine job with your wretched masquerade, but that scar made me wonder. And then it all fell into place. You're very good at being a pirate."

"I've had a fair amount of practice."

"But *why*, Dev? Why didn't you tell me? What sort of danger are you involved in?"

Thorne's jaw hardened. "I think the fire is going out. Perhaps you'd better stir it up."

"Don't think you're going to avoid my questions, Dev! You've kidnapped me and my groom, and I have a strong suspicion that indirectly you've brought those children of yours into real danger. I want to know why."

Devlyn watched the flames dance and leap, thinking about a diamond that could sway the fortunes of all Europe. "For a fortune in diamonds, India. Or maybe I should say for a king's ransom—or an *emperor's* ransom. A madman could fight his way back to power if I let them slip through my fingers. Again," he added bitterly.

"Do you mean the diamond I found at Vauxhall?"

"That one and many many others. I'm sworn to silence and I shouldn't have told you this much, but you're involved now and whether I like it or not, the children are too. Those gems were part of Napoleon's private collection, but they went missing after Waterloo, though it was my responsibility to see they didn't. Now our reports indicate that they will be brought into England very soon. It's my job to find them—and whoever is behind this."

"So Devlyn Carlisle is transformed into the notorious, cutthroat river pirate known as the Frenchman." After a moment India nodded. "It's very clever, Devlyn. I congratulate you."

"Do you? Most women would have flayed the skin off my back by now, then sunk into a fit of shrieking hysterics. You're not furious?"

"Oh, I'm furious all right. I'm furious at you for lying to me and for putting those children in danger. You were entirely effective as a pirate." Her eyes darkened. "Too effective."

"Come to me, *ma mie.*"

India felt the little hairs stir along her neck. A slow sweetness uncoiled through her. "No, I don't think I will. Not until we finally have the truth between us."

"Maybe there are different kinds of truth, India. Maybe there's the truth that comes heart to heart, body to body. Otherwise words are too easy to twist."

"You have an answer for everything, don't you? It doesn't matter whether you're Devlyn Carlisle, the returned war hero, or the notorious Thames River pirate!" She strode to the hut's single window and stood looking out at the shifting water. "They're still fighting," she said after a moment, watching distant figures twist and leap over the *Gypsy*'s deck.

"They'll fight that way till morning. They need their few entertainments, the poor beggars, for it's a grim life on the river. The few left standing at dawn will break open the rum and suddenly be the finest of friends. It's the way of the river."

India turned slowly. "And what about us, Dev? Can *we* be the best of friends? We married in blindness and haste, in the shadow of war. We loved before we even knew each other. We were young, we were strangers, and we had so much to learn—but we had no time to learn in. And then you came back, with all the memories gone." An arrested look filled her face. "But that was a lie too, wasn't it? You *did* remember. That was just another part of the masquerade."

"I had to do it, India. It was the only way I could—"

She spun about, her hands clenched. "How do you do it? How do you lie so easily? How do you twist the truth again and again to suit your ends?"

"They're not *my* ends, India, they're England's. This is for the benefit of you and me and every man who died bloody and blind at Waterloo. It's for the good of every child who hopes to have a free and decent life on English soil."

"Very fine words, Devlyn. But for me it's a far simpler issue. All I see is one man who has lied to me and betrayed me, in spite of the fact that I loved him so much that I—"

She spun away, biting back a sob.

Thorne strode across the floor and pulled her against him. His hands slid deep into her hair. "You gave me your heart. You gave me your trust. It was a treasure I didn't deserve." Slowly his chin fell until it rested on the crown of her head. "But things were different before Waterloo, and I was a different man, India. That wasn't a lie. I can never go back to being what I was. Just as you were changed by the horrors you saw after the battle, so was I. And I *must* see that Napoleon never has a chance to inflict those horrors again."

"What about us?"

His hands tightened, and his breath slid out in a bitter sigh. "I loved you then. You must believe that."

"And . . . now?"

"Now I'm not sure I can love anyone. I have three children to protect and I've made a bloody mull of it so far, as you've pointed out only too clearly. In the few days they've known you, I think those three brats have come to care for you far more than they will *ever* care for me."

"That's not true! Andrew worships you, and Marianne hangs breathless for a single word of praise. And Alexis? Sometimes I think that child is the wisest person I know," India finished softly.

"Strange, but I've felt the same. It's almost as if she can look right through you and see your deepest thoughts. But today I nearly landed flat on my back on that deck and my shoulder is—well, not in prime shape. That nearly lost us both our lives." He sighed. "What I'm saying, India, is that we can't go back. Maybe you can never go back. Or maybe I'm finding it's harder to be friends than to be lovers. But I want that. I'm jealous whenever you laugh with Monkton or Pendleworth—and especially with that arrogant snake Connor MacKinnon."

India turned slowly, a gleam in her eye. "Connor MacKinnon? You're jealous of *him*?"

"I wanted to tear out his fingers joint by joint

when he helped you into your carriage. And when I
see you look up at him, slanting your head and giving him the kind of sunny smile that I've never gotten . . ." His fingers tightened in her hair. Slowly
he eased her head backward. "I want that too. It's
damnably greedy, I know, but I want all the fire and
madness we had in Brussels. I also want the trust."
His voice fell. "I want *everything*, damn it. You've
made me like this. Blind and greedy. Limitlessly
greedy." His eyes burned over her slender body, outlined clearly in the damp cambric shirt. He pulled
her closer, feeling her heart pound against his chest.
"Well?"

Silence.

"Are you going to answer me sometime in this
century, or is this your way of repaying me for all
my treachery?"

"I'm thinking." India's hand stole up to his cheek.
Her finger traced the outline of his ear. As she eased
closer, a shudder ran through him.

Her eyes narrowed. "How could I be certain you
wouldn't lie to me again? Because that's *my* condition, Dev. No more lies. No more holding back.
That's the Delamere way. It's also *my* way."

He stared at her, his heart pounding and his
blood on fire. For a moment all he could think of
was her beneath him stripped of every shred of
clothing.

Instead, Devlyn Carlisle took a deep breath and
eased his arms around her back, savoring the
warmth of her breath and the slide of her body
against his.

Maybe, in the end, *this* was what coming home
was all about. "I'll try, as much as it is within my
power. But there are other people involved, India,
and you will have to accept that. This mission is of

crucial importance." He frowned suddenly. "Speaking of deceptions, what about you? You left a calling card as broad as Regent's Park when you showed that bloody diamond all over London."

"Since you wouldn't tell me about your enemies, I decided to find out myself. It was the most logical thing to do."

He shook his head as he studied her, tenderness filling his eyes. "You are entirely impossible, you know. Stubborn, reckless, and with no sense of fear. You'll make a most unbiddable sort of wife." His hands drew her closer against him, and he savored her instant softening. "But the damnable thing is that I'm starting to like the thought. In fact, I'm starting to find it the most natural thing in the world." He sighed. "And since we're about plain speaking, there's something else I'd better tell you."

Her hands traced the scar at his jaw. "Maybe it's time we tried different ways of talking, Dev. The kind of talking you mentioned earlier." Her hands moved upward into his hair. "The kind of talking with bodies that doesn't require words."

Fire filled Devlyn's eyes. "Don't tempt me, woman. It's been too bloody long. For months, I've dreamed of nothing else. No matter where I was or what I did, there was always the thought of you, the memories sweet and lush. But we were lovers once and that wasn't enough. *This* time it's going to be different. It's going to be trust, equal trust as friends." He smiled wryly. "Although whether I can manage to keep my hands off you for more than five minutes at a time is something I'm finding impossible to contemplate right now."

"I don't mean to make it easy for you either," India said softly. "Because I remember too, Dev. I have the same memories to torment me." Her hand brushed the soft hair at his chest, and she delighted in the instant darkening of his eyes.

Outside a horse whinnied. A moment later footsteps pounded along the slope outside the hut.

Someone hammered at the door. "Thorne? Damn it, are you in there?"

Devlyn cursed sharply. "I was going to tell you, but . . ." He strode to the door and pulled it open. India stood staring at the man outside, a man with dark hair and an angular jaw.

A man with her husband's face.

She was looking at Devlyn Carlisle—or what looked like Devlyn Carlisle.

Thornwood laughed grimly. "Meet James Herrington, my love. That's the *other* thing I was trying to tell you."

India looked from one man to the other, shock in her face. "But he—that is, he looks just like—"

"That's the general idea," Thorne said dryly. He grabbed Herrington's arm and pulled him inside. "But what are you doing here? I told you never to come to this hideaway except in an emergency."

"I had to come." Herrington swallowed. "It's—it's Alexis. She's been kidnapped."

27

Devlyn swayed, almost as if an invisible hand had struck him. "She's been *what*?"

"The other two children are safe, but I—I lost Alexis. We had just come out of a hackney and she'd forgotten that wretched doll of hers. She ran back to the carriage before I knew it and—" He looked away and ran a hand through his hair.

"And she never came out," Devlyn finished harshly. "It's an old trick, Herrington. The oldest in the book." He moved awkwardly across the room, as if his legs would not work properly, then sank down on one of the grain sacks without quite being aware it was there. "Dear God, Alexis." His head fell to his hands. "Alexis, sweet Alexis." After a moment his fists tightened and he looked up again, his face hard with fury. "Has there been a note of ransom yet?"

India gasped. "But surely you don't expect—"

"On the contrary, it is exactly what I expect," Dev said flatly. "They couldn't get you, so they chose the easiest alternative. A helpless, innocent girl of six." He pushed to his feet and grabbed awkwardly for his shirt, the movement showing how much his shoulder still pained him. As he did, India fetched a jug of water and doused the fire.

"What are you doing?" Dev said sharply.

"I'm coming with you, of course."

For a moment he looked as if he would argue. His shoulders tensed, each muscle flexed. Then he nodded curtly, jamming the buttons of his shirt closed. "I won't lie and say I can't use you. You'll be a treasure. And they will be expecting that diamond to be on you."

India reached into her boot and held out the blush-pink jewel. "Take it," she said. "I never wanted it, nor was meant to have it. If it will help Alexis in any way, then of course you must have it."

Devlyn's fingers closed over the cold, hard facets. For a moment their hands met and his fingers twined through hers, locking the stone between them. Slowly it picked up the heat of their bodies and cast it back between them. "Thank you for offering so freely. And thank you for being exactly the person you are."

But there was no time to say more. Their questions would hang and their future linger unresolved. Now a far greater question loomed.

A child's fate at the hands of madmen.

After a quick word with Perkins, Devlyn reemerged from the *Gypsy* with Froggett in tow. The old man looked as confused as he was happy to be freed from the vessel.

He scowled at India. "What's amiss, Jeremiah?"

"There's no need for the deception, Froggett." Thornwood strode past him and down the pier toward the shore. "I know everything about your mistress's wild masquerade, just as she knows about my own. But there's no time for explanations now. A child has been kidnapped and I fear it will require all our skills to see her freed." He looked at Herrington. "Where are the other children?"

"The Duchess of Cranford collected them and took them off to her estate in Norfolk. She insisted it would be the safest place for them until Alexis was found."

"She's probably right," Devlyn said grimly. "It appears that I cannot keep them safe in London."

"What do we do now?" Herrington was white, his face a mask of guilt and unhappiness.

"We return to London. And then we wait. Have you brought a carriage? Lady Delamere will require—"

"Lady Delamere will require no more than what she had when she came. Hannibal will carry me back. We'll make far better time that way."

After a moment Devlyn nodded. "As usual you're right. I only wish we'd had you with us at Waterloo." But the brief warmth left his eyes almost as quickly as it had come. When the great white gelding was brought around from the snug stables in the village, Thornwood's face was bleak and lined once more.

For India the ride to London was a nightmare. The four riders pressed their mounts and made excellent time, stopping only once at a small inn just outside Tottenham. The sky was streaked with red and purple clouds when they finally turned into the bustling thoroughfares near Belgrave Square. Though India ached to ponder the revelations of the last hours, at that moment all her thoughts were fixed on the innocent child caught in a web of danger.

As soon as they entered the mews, Dev jumped

down and tossed his reins to a waiting groom. India knew he was praying for a message from Alexis's captors.

He strode through the little garden and up the back steps to the house. "The longer we wait, the less likely it becomes that . . ." He stopped and his fist slammed down against the door. His eyes held the blind pain of a wounded animal, a pain such as India had never seen before.

She yearned to touch him and comfort him, but she knew it was beyond her power. Only bringing Alexis home would drive that look from Thorne's eyes. And if they failed, if it was already too late . . .

India refused to consider the possibility.

The place where she was lying was dark and cold. Somewhere over her head water dripped, loud and incessant. There were no voices, no footsteps, nothing but the water to keep her company.

And Alexis was frightened, terribly frightened.

At six o'clock that night everyone clustered in Thorne's study. Grim-faced, Chilton told them there had still been no messages. He himself had stayed by the front door every second since the child had been taken.

Devlyn's jaw hardened at the news. He moved awkwardly from the room, almost like a man reeling under a killing blow. When he returned ten minutes later, his beard was gone and he was dressed in fresh clothes. The horror still hung about his eyes, but now there was a granite resolve in his stride.

"I've some messages to send. This hand is far from played, as these brutes will soon discover." He looked at India. "Meanwhile, you'd better get some

rest. You look exhausted. If they're after the diamond, they might demand your presence, since you
were last seen with the stone."

India nodded numbly and turned away, wishing
she had never seen the cursed gem. A moment later
she felt Thorne's hands on her shoulders. "And don't
be taking the stubborn notion into your head that
you are somehow to blame, for you aren't. It's my
own fault, every bloody bit of it. If not the diamond,
it would have been over something else, for I've no
doubt that they have watched my house ever since I
set foot in London. That's why having Herrington
here was so valuable, allowing me the liberty to
come and go at will." His fingers covered India's
pale cheek. "Chilton will take you up. Never fear, I'll
call you as soon as we have any news."

India gently combed back the dark lock of hair
that had fallen over his brow. "You're so different. I
wondered at first how I could possibly have been so
fooled, but now I know. It's changed both of us,
Dev. You *didn't* come back home from Waterloo,
not as the same man. And even if you had, I
wouldn't have been here to meet you because I'm no
longer the same woman. But I pray that we're
stronger now, because that strength must somehow
help us save Alexis."

"Believe it." Thorne's fingers locked around hers,
pressing tightly. "Never, never stop believing it."

At nine o'clock the three men were still scouring
London in search of anyone who had seen a girl of
Alexis's description. India rested fitfully upstairs,
while Chilton manned the front door and two
grooms guarded the mews.

But no message of any sort came from Alexis's
captors.

Herrington and Froggett returned, weary and unsmiling. They took a meal of cold meat and very
strong tea served by Chilton in grim silence.

When India came downstairs, some of the pallor
had left her cheeks, but the lines of worry remained.
She read all too clearly from the men's faces that
there had been no word about the girl.

At the last stroke of eleven the front door was
thrown open and a hard step echoed through the
hall. A tall figure with a hooked nose appeared in
the door of Thornwood's study. "What's this I hear
about the child being kidnapped?" the Duke of Wellington demanded as he strode into the room. "It's a
barbaric act, that's what it is! We shall run those
wolves to ground, I make you my solemn vow on
that." He shrugged off his greatcoat and tossed it to
the man behind him. "I'll need those papers, Stevens. Both sets, including the maps."

"Of course, Your Grace." His secretary immediately produced a thick sheaf of documents from a
leather satchel.

"Excellent. Now, Thorne, tell me what you've discovered so far."

Alexis shivered.

She looked around her at the darkness, fighting to
keep from crying. In her hands was clutched the old
doll that she had carried through half of Europe
and on to England after the horrors of Brussels.

It was her only companion now, except for the
dripping water and the occasional noises in the
darkness. It was just as well Alexis did not know
those low muffled sounds came from rats. And so
she waited, her thin body shivering, drawn up into a
tight ball in the darkness.

But as the hours crept past, she found she was no

longer alone. There were drifting shapes around her. Tall, bright figures with comforting smiles. Sometimes Alexis had seen them before, when loneliness and fear threatened to overcome her.

Now the bright shapes drew close and ringed her in the darkness, a determined army who would keep her from harm.

Or so Alexis thought, half dreaming with the old doll clutched in her fingers. And then she grew aware of another figure beside her, a smiling boy whose eyes glinted, full of happiness as he looked at her.

And Alexis knew this was the child she had seen near India.

Anyone else would have thought this merely a trick of the imagination, a phantom summoned up by an unhappy mind, but to Alexis the images were as real as the cold ground she lay on. And they gave her a world of hope.

When the door to her dark room rattled and slowly squeaked open, she was ready and did not flinch. She already knew who her visitor would be.

He strode through the shadows, a single candle in his hand. His face was the face the girl had seen so often in her dreams, a garish mask with a long pointed nose, and of course the jagged scar along one cheek. Alexis had seen a mask like this before, worn by the wandering street players in Europe. But the man who wore it now was deadly serious, she knew.

And then her breath caught. Around him in the darkness Alexis began to see faint tendrils of movement, the cold twisting shapes of people.

Gray people.

People who had died.

As they coiled around his chest, their fingers jabbing at his eyes and clutching at his throat, Alexis knew that these were people this man had killed; like angry shadows, they circled, waiting for him in death.

She shrank back, horrified. As she did, cold laughter filled the empty room.

"So you begin to show some fear? It is good, silly girl." His voice hardened. "Where is Lady Delamere?"

Alexis's hands tightened on her doll. "I don't know. She's been gone."

"So she has." He laughed softly. "But your answers are unnecessary. It is you we need, *you* who will summon your solicitous guardian and the adventurous Lady Delamere. Then everything we want will be ours."

"Don't do it!" Alexis's eyes were wide as she watched the gray shapes twist and coil about the man in the mask. "They're waiting for you right now. If you change, if you speak to them nicely, they might go away." She knew it was not true, but her pure spirit rebelled against the sight of such evil. Somehow she had to try to change his dark fate.

But her captor merely threw back his head and laughed. "Be *nice*?" he sneered. "Bide my time, do my work, and don't ask questions?" He bent before her, in the candlelight his mask a horrible, misshapen gargoyle. "But I won't wait, my dear, not any longer. The game is nearly ours. All that we require now is the diamond, and your friend, Lady Delamere, will soon bring that to us. Thanks to *you*."

Alexis shrank back, out of reach of the drifting gray shapes. With every angry word her captor spoke, their numbers grew. But she knew there was no way this man would believe her.

Not until it was too late.

She could only stare at him in fright, the doll clutched to her trembling body, while he slammed the door behind him and strode laughing back into the darkness.

It was after midnight when the Duke of Wellington gathered up his greatcoat and prepared to leave. He studied the tense faces before him and nodded. "We are close now. We will find the girl and through her the rest of this barbarous cabal. Meanwhile, my men are at your command, Thornwood." He turned, brisk as he had been among the firing cannons at Waterloo, and motioned to his secretary. "My satchel, Stevens."

And with that he was gone.

Gradually the city stilled. The carriages thinned out, the footsteps ceased, and the night grew as quiet as it ever could in the restless giant that was London.

Devlyn sat in his study, watching the last red sparks flicker and die in the grate. He could not sleep. He could not plan. All that he could think of was Alexis's face, white and terrified somewhere in the night.

And that vision was going to drive him mad. He ran his hands through his hair, tensing when he heard a noise at the door.

It was India, her face showing the same strains that his did. "I couldn't sleep."

Thornwood gestured to the chair beside the fire. "Nor could I. Come and join me. Sherry?"

After a moment India nodded. But when he

brought the drink, she made no move to take it, only looked at him, her eyes haunted. "Devlyn, do you think that they will—"

"*Don't*. It doesn't do any good to imagine the worst. I know, because I've done nothing else for the last hour." His hands gripped the mantel, each joint outlined in white and his eyes burned as he looked down into the fire. "India, I know I have no right to ask this. In fact, I know I'm a cur even to think of it, but—" He looked up, a world of torment in his face. "Do you think we could—that is, could you possibly—"

Her eyes were liquid in the dying firelight. "Say it, Dev. Tell me what you want from me." She couldn't make it easy for him, not now, not after all the shadows between them. This time it had to be clear, entirely without question.

"Could you stay with me? Just for tonight, India? As my wife and as my love? As the one fine and stable thing in this bloody world that has any chance of keeping me sane until tomorrow?"

She could.

In a heartbeat, she moved. In aching silence her hands were on his shoulders, her body warm against his.

No time, he prayed. No time for thinking or remembering. No time for anything but her skin, soft as a rose petal. To touch her left him hard with desperation.

Her hands were trembling.

Lord, his were too.

He closed his eyes tight, letting the first brush of her skin warm him as brandy never could. Maybe if he tried very hard, he could block out the thought of Alexis, shivering and afraid somewhere in the night.

But Devlyn could never forget that. His low, hoarse cry was like a wound.

India caught him then, fierce in her generosity. She would *not* lose him again, not after so long. During the dark months since Waterloo she had learned her own lessons of survival. "*Now,* Devlyn. Make me remember. Make the days slide away until it's spring again and there are rose petals beneath us on the ground."

His eyes burned over her face. "You believe in me, don't you? You always have," he said wonderingly. "Even when I didn't believe in myself."

"It's another Delamere trait," India said softly. Her hands slid across his chest and began opening his shirt.

And Devlyn Carlisle was utterly lost.

They were both too urgent to be careful. Her hands yanked at his shirt. She inched to the floor and pulled him down against her. His body was already hot and hard, red-tinged in the firelight. Frowning, Thorne caught her face and stared into her eyes as if he could see all the way to forever. "India? Is this what you truly want?"

She nodded. "Please, Dev," she whispered. Her eyes did not leave his face as she found his hardness and took him in the span of her hand.

"God, woman. I only hope you won't regret it," Thorne said hoarsely. He slid his fingers into her heat and stroked her until she shuddered. "Tell me that you won't."

"I—oh, Dev—"

Pleasure, moving in a blind crest.

Heat and need and endless, aching homecoming. "Dev, *now.*"

He paused above her, his hard, aroused body like forged copper in the glowing light. Only when India was hot and hungry, her body stretched taut with desire, did he part her legs deeply.

He wanted her.

He needed her.

But he was going to be damned sure that she needed *him*, too.

Silver eyes burning, Thorne teased the sleek petals so familiar from a thousand nights of fantasies. She caught him tight, rippling velvet in her desire. Her body arched and she drove blindly against him, her fists angry. "Now, Dev. Now, or I'll—"

Thorne closed his eyes. With a groan he held her still as he buried himself deep inside her. Like silk she spread, holding him, savoring him, wrapping him in unspeakable pleasure. Dimly he felt her long legs rise to grip his back.

"Closer, India," he ordered hoarsely. "Don't spare me. Don't spare *us*. Not tonight, Princess. I need you wild and unquenchable tonight."

Her nails gripped his shoulders as she rocked beneath his shuddering thrusts, lost in a shimmering haze of need.

As wild as even he could wish.

It was no gentle, poignant claiming. They knew each other too well for that. Tonight each touch was wild and rough, each kiss full of blindness and need. There were no soft words or muted whispers, only the urgent slide of skin on naked skin.

But there before the dying fire, they blocked out the night. Between them they made their own dawn, where war and loneliness and the thought of a young girl's frightened face disappeared for at least a few minutes.

Dev's fingers locked in India's hair. He watched her back arch and heard a ragged cry of pleasure spill from her lips. His eyes were ablaze with triumph when she shuddered and arched beneath him a second time, her fingers twined with his.

A single tear glistened on the curve of her shoulder. It might have been hers or it might have been his—perhaps it was both of theirs.

But when India's eyes opened, they were accusing. "Damn your honor, Dev. I don't want duty or restraint, I want you with me. I want to feel your hot seed drive up inside me and know that there's no room for thoughts of any other woman but me. If you can't give me that, I'll just have to find another man who—"

He cut her off with a curse, his fingers locking around her thighs and holding her still, willing captive to the dark fury her words had unleashed. "*No* other man. Not now or ever."

A log hissed, exploding with a shower of sparks inside the grate.

India's eyes glinted. "No?"

"No, damn it." Thorne's jaw hardened as he proved his claim, sliding half-hilt in her hot folds.

She wriggled.

He did not budge.

"No?" It was half whisper, half challenge.

"No." And then the word was a groan as she closed tight, urging him home, urging him to the dawn their need would kindle. "Never," he rasped, moving deeper, finding the core of her sweetness.

She shuddered. "Don't—spare me, Dev. Don't spare *us*."

He was lost, just as he had been lost in the crowded Brussels street when her silly hat with the silk strawberries had blown away before him. Just as he had been lost in the moonlit garden while the scent of roses drifted around her. "I won't."

And he didn't. Breath harsh, he pounded deep,

each thrust moving her across the fine old carpet. She met him, matched him, goaded him.

Completed him.

And she screamed when the pleasure rocked through her yet again.

Her eyes were hazy and her hands were buried in his hair when he found his own hammering release, bare seconds after hers.

Even then his fingers did not loosen, nor his body pull away. He only dropped his head slowly, then rolled to his side and pulled her tight against him.

Much later, when the fear returned, when the thoughts of Alexis could no longer be kept at bay, he took her beneath him and their bodies met again, urgent and blind, driven by a force more primitive even than fear.

The end of lies.

The dawn of all their tomorrows.

And when they finally slept, her head drawn to his chest, it was the most natural thing in the world.

But even then they were aware of dim shadows creeping closer.

28

The ransom note came at dawn.

The significance of the time was not lost on Devlyn, amid the words so simple yet chilling. "Hyde Park, near the Serpentine. Just before daybreak tomorrow. Lady Delamere brings the diamond—if you ever want to see the little girl again."

Dev looked down at the crumpled sheet, a pulse throbbing at his temple. "Tomorrow," he said hoarsely. "Just before dawn in Hyde Park." His eyes hardened on the scrawled commands.

India watched the emotion go out of him as he became all cold soldier. Only in that moment did she realize exactly how much Devlyn Carlisle had changed. This part of him, too, he had hidden from her.

"Ian and I will choose the point of greatest advantage. We'll make our plans carefully—and hope we'll have a chance to use them."

"Hope?" India said.

"If they have any sense, Alexis's captors will be making their *own* plans, too," Thorne explained grimly.

* * *

342

"And Froggett will be hiding here, five feet to the right, just behind a clump of brambles." Dev, Ian, Connor MacKinnon, and Froggett sat in the kitchen beside India, with Dev's sketch of the park before them. An X marked the spot where India was to wait for Alexis's kidnappers. If they tried to draw her elsewhere, it was crucial that she think of a way to hold them in place.

"Do you understand? Right here by the oak tree." Thorne tapped at the dark X. "It all depends on your bringing them here." He looked at India then, a flicker of warmth in his eyes. His hand brushed hers for the space of a heartbeat. And then he was all soldier again, hard and impersonal. "We'll need two carriages and blankets and food for Alexis. She's bound to be—upset."

No one contradicted him, though they all knew the word was far too gentle for the terror she would be feeling when they freed her.

If they freed her.

An hour before dawn India was waiting at the base of a giant oak tree in Hyde Park. Below her stretched the gleaming Serpentine. To her right lay a dark tangle of berry bushes. A single lantern in the tree boughs shone down, outlining India's pale features.

Connor and Ian were hidden in the tree's dense foliage, ready to leap down as soon as Alexis was brought into view. Froggett was concealed five feet away behind the thicket, and the diamond, the blush-pink gem that was the source of all their troubles, rested safely in India's shoe.

India's eyes went to the top of the hill. Each time she'd asked about Dev, Ian had whispered that he would be there later and not to worry. She frowned

at the dense shadows running along a stony rise.
Where was Devlyn?

Through the trees the first streaks of dawn brightened the eastern sky. Suddenly, leaves crunched behind India. "Lady Delamere?"

India swung about, her heart pounding wildly.
"I'm here."

A man stood up on the hillside, his features hidden beneath a broad-brimmed hat. "Where's the diamond?"

India tried to swallow the lump of fear in her
throat. "In a safe place. Where's the child?"

The man pointed behind him. "In a carriage up
the hill, where we can keep an eye on her. Come
along and we'll turn her over to you."

India shook her head. She and Dev had gone
through this possibility carefully. Somehow she had
to persuade the man to bring Alexis here, or all their
preparations would be ruined. "No," she said flatly.
"Right here, right out in the open. Otherwise there's
no telling what you cutthroats will do to her."

The man moved closer. "And there's no telling
what arrangements *you* have made," he hissed. "If
you want to see the child alive, my lady, you'll do
exactly as I say."

But India had heard the edge of uneasiness in his
voice. She prayed her own voice was convincing.
"You want the diamond and I want the child. We
can both have what we want. But only here and
now, while no one is about. The sooner done," she
added, "the sooner you can be off to freedom."

The man looked behind him for a moment. India
saw his hand move in a sharp gesture. Then he
turned back and started down the hill toward her.
"Very well, but if you've deceived me in any way," he

growled, "the two of you are going to find your throats slit."

With the sheer force of willpower, India kept her eyes from drifting up where Ian and Connor were hidden. Her knees were trembling, but she kept her voice level. "Where is Alexis? You'll get nothing from me until I see the child safe and sound."

"She'll be along soon enough. Where's the *diamond*?"

He was nearly to the tree now. India moved off the path, hoping to stop him in perfect range beneath the branch where Ian was hidden. "You'll have everything you want, everything you deserve, just as soon as the girl is brought here safely." The wind fluttered the leaves and an acorn broke free and went *pinging* off a branch. For one terrified moment India thought the man was going to look up into the foliage, but he simply cursed as the tiny missile hit him on the head.

Then there was a muffled cry and two figures were coming toward India. Her heart lurched when she saw that one of them was Alexis, her mouth bound with a cloth.

The man in the hat took a step closer. "Now you've seen the girl. Let's have that diamond!"

India knew that this was the moment of greatest danger, the moment when all would have to act as one. Carefully she bent down to the ground, every motion larger than life. "It's in my boot for safekeeping, but I'll get it for you now. It will just take me a moment."

Carefully she bent to one knee and tugged at the soft leather. With every step Alexis came closer. Almost time . . .

Her fingers closed over the cold stone. If only the

second man would get close enough to Froggett, hidden just behind the bushes . . .

"Damn it, what's holding you up?"

"I'm done now." India stood up slowly, palm closed. The man on the hill inched closer, hoping for a better view of the stone.

Slowly India opened her hand.

The first pink rays of dawn glinted over the hillside, tossing bright sparks off the diamond in her fingers. The man on the hill shoved Alexis forward, while his accomplice made a low sound of satisfaction. "It's a pleasure doing business with you, my lady," he said mockingly. "And now if you don't mind, I think I'll take that diamond and ask you to come along up here while we—"

India heard Alexis scream, and then the crack of a gun. In an instant both Ian and Connor had dropped to the ground and were running toward their targets. Froggett, meanwhile, had tackled Alexis's captor and the two were struggling on the ground.

Alexis was stumbling toward India when a third man appeared on the slope, moving in a direct line for the little girl.

India's heart lurched. She yanked her pistol from her reticule and tried to focus, but he was too close to Alexis. She couldn't risk a shot, not with the possibility of hitting the child. She could only watch, horrified, as the man closed in on his captive.

And then in a wild storm of leaves, Devlyn catapulted from the bank on the far side of the oak tree, where he had been hiding. In a second his great whip coiled through the air, snaking out toward the man behind Alexis. There was a loud crack and a man's wail of pain.

A moment later Alexis was in India's arms, her body shaking.

"Did they hurt you, Alexis? My little love, are you safe and well?"

The little girl nodded, her face covered with tears. "I was brave. I only cried once. You would have been proud of me."

"I *am* proud of you. Very, very proud," India said hoarsely.

"And I didn't forget my doll either," the girl said, holding up the battered figure that accompanied her everywhere. It was dustier now, and the skirt more ragged than ever, but like Alexis it was in one piece.

"You were very clever to have saved her," India said, hugging the girl close.

Up the hill Ian and Connor had their prisoners in tow, while Devlyn wrapped his whip around the third man and dragged him none too gently down the hill.

"Did you see Uncle Thorne?" Alexis asked breathlessly. "I told you he could do wonderful things with his whip."

"You were right." Suddenly India felt Alexis tug at her hand.

"But there was something else, something I should have remembered." The little girl's lip quivered. "I remembered when I was there in the dark with nothing to do but think. It was very important." Her eyes filled with tears. "Now I've forgotten again."

India caught her in a tight hug. "Don't worry, little one. Whenever you need to remember, you will. Now just rest, and think about how happy Andrew and Marianne will be to see you again."

"I was brave even when I saw the gray people,"

Alexis said softly. "They were everywhere, all around the man in that mask. It was the same man with the scar that I kept telling Uncle Thorne about."

India frowned. Were these more nightmares, or had the girl's visions been true all along? "The man with the scar was there with you?"

Alexis nodded. "Just the same. Only he was more evil than I thought. And then the gray people came around him, full of hate, hoping for revenge. It was t-terrible. They are waiting for him, just waiting."

The girl shuddered and India smoothed her hair. "Don't talk, my love. It's over now. You're safe again."

On the way back from the park, Alexis was the center of all attention. The little girl sat between India and Thorne, tightly wrapped in a warm blanket and the duchess's best fur muff.

They traveled straight from London, heading east to Norfolk and the Delamere estate, where Alexis would be reunited with her brother and sister. Dev decided this was the best way to put Alexis's bad memories behind her. The cheerful gaiety of her siblings would help her most now.

Dev did not talk to the child about what had happened. There would be time for that when the harrowed look left her face and her body stopped its trembling. For now they only talked of silly, inconsequential things, like the way the Prince Regent's corset creaked whenever he bent over to kiss a woman's hand and Ian's exploits as a boy at Eton, where he had been sent down for hiding a cow in the master's chambers.

Finally the little girl began to relax. As the green countryside sped past, her eyes blinked shut, she

rested her head against India's shoulder and fell
asleep. India's eyes met Thorne's and he nodded.
Lifting Alexis up into his arms, he cradled her the
rest of the way. The fierceness in his eyes told India
that he meant to see nothing ever happened to
Alexis again.

The little girl was still asleep when the rolling
hills gave way to a shining emerald valley. Then
Swallow Hill was before them, a tangle of turrets
and chimneys, without symmetry or order, almost
as if the house had grown in unruly bursts right out
of that green sweep of hillside. But there was a
beauty to the sunlit walls, and a vitality that few
other homes could match.

And as India stared at Swallow Hill's pink granite
walls glowing in the morning sunlight, she thought
there was no more beautiful sight in the world.

She was going home.

Two rows of servants were lined up at Swallow
Hill's broad front steps, waiting to greet the carriage. Thorne carried Alexis in his arms and from
her safe perch the little girl stared in sleepy awe at
the ranks of liveried servants. Only when Andrew
and Marianne ran out was her awe forgotten amid a
host of noisy, tearful embraces.

The three children were still chattering when they
settled in a magnificent yellow sitting room at the
rear of the house, overlooking Swallow Hill's vast
rolling lawns.

"So, my little imp, I see you managed to work
your way out of disaster again." The Duchess of
Cranford smiled at the girl, who nodded happily,
her face covered with crumbs from a lemon tart.
The duchess had arranged for several of the London
servants to come to Swallow Hill, thinking it would

make Alexis more comfortable, since the staff had already fallen in love with the little girl. So far Beach, Mrs. Harrison, and Albert, the footman, had all been by to say hello to the child.

But Alexis suddenly shook her head. "Oh, it wasn't I who was clever. It was Uncle Thorne and those three other nice men." She bestowed a queenly smile on Ian, Froggett, and Connor Mac-Kinnon, who sat beaming on the other side of the settee. "And, of course, Lady Delamere. She was *so* brave, even when that nasty man was growling at her to follow him to his carriage. I heard them say they meant to drive away with her after she gave them the diamond," she explained breathlessly.

Thorne sat beside the girl, brushing her hair gently. "Did you recognize any of them, Alexis? Their names, their voices, or anything at all?"

The little girl shook her head. "I only saw one up close, and that was the man in the mask. The other three men only came at the very end. By then I was already in the carriage with my eyes covered." Her body began to grow tense again.

Dev pulled her closer. "No more questions, Daffodil. By the way, are you sure you won't have another lemon tart? Cook has worked so hard, and you have only eaten *four*."

The little girl giggled. "I was ever so hungry, Uncle Thorne. They didn't feed me, except for one moldy piece of bread. And I gave that to the rats, because I realized they were hungrier than I was."

Dev's eyes hardened. India saw a look of fury shoot through them. "No more rats, Daffodil." As Alexis's eyes began to close, he picked her up in his arms. "And no more talk either, I think. If the duchess wouldn't mind, I think it is time for you to rest."

"Of course," the Duchess of Cranford said. "Beach

will show you upstairs." It had been settled that
Alexis would sleep on a couch in India's room, in
case she woke up in the night.

After carrying the drowsy child upstairs, Dev
went off to fetch a glass of hot milk, while India
tucked Alexis beneath a thick down comforter.
"You'll sleep well here. You have Josephine, don't
you?"

Alexis nodded sleepily and held up the battered
doll. "Safe and sound, just like I am." Her eyes narrowed for a moment. "I saw him again, you know.
He was there to help me when I felt like crying."

"Who was, Alexis?"

"The child," Alexis said impatiently. "The nice boy
with the sparkling eyes and glossy curls." She studied India, blinking sleepily. "He is here now, too. He
is trying to tell me something. Something very important I think, but I'm so tired . . . and I'm falling
asleep . . ." The little girl's eyes closed and her
head slid back against India's arm.

India sat frozen, her heart pounding. A prickle
worked along the back of her neck, and she had the
odd sense that she was being watched.

Which was absurd, of course, since the room was
empty except for Alexis, who was now asleep.

But in spite of all of the cool, clear arguments
that her mind was posing, India did not move. Her
hands locked, she prayed to feel the smiling spirit
that Alexis had seen so clearly.

And as India sat with Alexis cradled beside her, a
ray of sunlight broke from behind a cloud, casting a
bright, golden beam down the center of the bed. At
that same moment a thrush began to sing merrily
on a bough outside her window.

And India was unable to stop the hot slide of tears
over her cheeks.

*   *   *

"Grandmama, may I ask you a question? An *important* question?"

The duchess looked up from a half-filled basket of rose cuttings. "Of course you can, child. Are you still worried about Alexis?"

"No, this has to do with me, Grandmama. With what I have been feeling these last months. You must have noticed."

The duchess carefully placed the last rose in her basket and sat back, studying India's face. "I have noticed many things, my love. The way you let your words trail away in the middle of a sentence and look out at the setting sun. The way you smile when someone tells you a story, but the smile never quite extends to your eyes. Yes, I have noticed many things since you came back from Europe. Are you finally going to tell me the truth?"

"I never could keep a secret very well, could I?" Then India was in her arms, her head in the duchess's lap. "Oh, Grandmama, It was Dev, of course, Dev all along. When we met in Brussels, it was blind and reckless and utterly wonderful. And then we—" She caught back a low sob. "We were married. In the chaotic days before Waterloo, it was not too difficult to arrange. I know I should have sent you word, but there was no time. He was to leave so soon for war, and I didn't know if I would ever see him again."

"And then it was too late to tell us," the duchess said softly. "Because he was dead, lost at Waterloo. And instead of opening up the wound all over again, you simply kept it your secret."

India nodded, her face a pale line of pain.

"But it didn't work, did it, my love?" The duchess looked off into the distance, wrestling with her own sad memories. "Painful secrets never go away. Sometimes I think they must be shared for them to loose their sting." The old woman sighed, then turned India's face upward, so she could look into her eyes. "And now that Thornwood is back?"

"I don't know, Grandmama. Sometimes I love him. But he is a different man now. He can be so cold and secretive. When he is distant and aloof, I want to pound him on the head, and that is *not* the way a person in love should feel."

The duchess laughed. "It's very healthy, if you ask me. I have never held with these simpering misses who swear that they're going to languish away for the sake of love. Utter rubbish," she said soundly. "Love is no time for die-away airs. Love is fighting and scheming and growing. It's time that both of you learned that," she added.

India brushed at her eyes. "I don't know if we can, Grandmama. It's not smooth or always sweet, the way I thought love would be. What's wrong with us?"

The duchess patted India's hand. "Nothing at all."

"But there is something else, something I couldn't bring myself to tell him. Now maybe it's too late."

The duchess looked up at the house and smiled. "Don't you think you'd better go and ask your *husband* whether it is too late?"

Thornwood muttered angrily, twisting through corridor after corridor. He despaired of finding his way through this great house. His own estate, Thornwood Hall, less than ten miles to the north, was elegant but not half so large as Swallow Hill.

There was a soft cough behind him.

"If you are looking for Miss India, I believe she is

with Her Grace in the rose garden," Beach said impassively. "Shall I fetch her for you?"

"I believe that's my job, Beach. And unless I am mistaken, I have a great deal of groveling to do. I have to explain why I haven't been exactly honest with her, you see."

The butler's eyes took on a gleam. "I believe groveling is something that all the Delamere men learn to do while quite young, my lord. Something about the Delamere women has demanded it of them. I am sure you will manage it superbly."

But by the time Devlyn found his way to the rose garden, India was gone. "She is not here? Blast!"

The duchess studied him closely. "You missed her by only a few minutes, which seems to be a pattern for you, Thornwood. India is not like your other women, you know. She is stubborn and independent, but vulnerable on the inside, where it counts. And I won't have her hurt again, do you hear? She has been through enough," the old woman said fiercely.

Thornwood's hands tightened. "Hurting her was the last thing I ever meant to do. Even now, if I knew it would be better for me to leave, you may be certain I would do just that. But I'm hoping desperately that there is a chance for us." He jammed his fingers through his hair, looking confused. "I suppose none of this makes any sense."

"More than you might expect, you young scapegrace. And if I had known sooner what the two of you had done, I would have traveled to Brussels and dragged you both back by the scruff of your neck," the duchess said curtly.

"You know? She told you?" Dev looked shocked.

"We keep few secrets in this family, Thornwood.

If you are to be one of us, you will have to accept that."

Thorne shook his head. "How could you have me, after the deception I played on you? First I let your granddaughter accept a hole-in-the-wall wedding on the eve of war, then I was gone for all those months."

A faint smile played around the duchess's mouth. "It hardly matters what I think, only what India thinks. Hadn't you better ask her?"

Devlyn's eyes widened. He caught up a bunch of roses from the duchess's basket. "You don't mind, do you?" he called, already dashing toward the house.

"Be gone with you," the duchess said huskily. "You'll find her in the attic, I believe. She often goes there. Her thinking place, she calls it."

The attic at Swallow Hill was a cavernous place with eaves on two sides that let in the streaming Norfolk sun. India had come here since she was a child whenever she needed a place to escape from her unruly brothers or simply time to dream her wild, adventurous dreams.

And she came to the old attic now, trying to sort through her conflicting emotions. As if in a dream she moved past the huge four-poster bed where Charles II was said to have slept, past the priceless Gobelin tapestries and the huge antique oak trestle table where some of her family whispered that the Magna Carta had been signed.

But today India did not look to right or left. Her eyes were fixed on the great, brass-bound chest angled beneath a dormer window.

Her hands trembled as she slid open the heavy lid. The clean scent of lavender filled her lungs. She looked down at layers of neat white cambric, carefully wrapped in fine paper.

She did not move. A tear eased from her eye and dropped onto the top piece of fabric, an exquisite length of linen, hand embroidered and tucked with bits of lace and ribbon. It was a child's christening robe.

The robe that her infant son had worn in the village ceremony in Brussels, a week before his death.

India's fingers trembled as she brought the fragrant linen to her face, inhaling its crisp scent, remembering the last time she had seen the child she had called Devlyn Ryan Carlisle.

His dark curls had been shining and his eyes were bright as he played with the simple wooden rattle her landlady's husband had carved for him. His laughter had filled her days with joy.

But tragedy had struck without warning. Whether it had been one of the dozens of diseases that had swept over Brussels in the aftermath of battle, India had never found out. The child had simply sickened, growing weaker by the hour, his little body listless and wan.

Up to the end, he had never cried once.

Frantic, India had done everything the Belgian doctor could suggest, but bathing and herbal tisanes had been of no use. It was almost as if the child had lost his will to live. He had seemed to regain his strength just before dawn on the fifth night. He had blinked, his little fingers locked on India's palm.

And then he had closed his eyes and breathed his last, while India clutched him to her heart.

The loss had been crushing to India, who had already been dealt the news of Dev's death in battle. For three weeks she had not gone out of her rooms, only sat looking out the window at the muddy fields and the new grave in the churchyard with the little stone cherubs on its headstone.

India had thought she might die then—she had even thought she wanted to die. But a strange thing had happened. A sudden rainstorm had brought gusts hammering from the east, knocking away all the flowers she had laid on Ryan's fresh grave. With the wind had come torrential rain, digging up soil and grass in deep furrows.

That storm had tested India's very sanity. She had run across the churchyard and flung herself on her knees, trying to hold back the rich earth, fighting to keep the water from tearing away the neat flowers and soft grass she had been so careful to tend through the first bleak days of spring.

But all of her desperate clawing was to no avail. Nature moved in its courses, implacable and relentless. Beneath her hands the mud slid free, the grass tore asunder, no matter how hard she tried to hold them in place. As she knelt in the dirt, arms dark to the elbow, her face white with anger, she began to cry for the very first time since losing her beautiful, beloved child.

No one had bothered her. She was simply the strange Englishwoman who haunted the churchyard and she was left alone to grieve in peace.

When she had finally come to her feet, trembling and exhausted, three hours later, for the first time some measure of peace had filled the jagged hole in her heart.

Her child was gone. She accepted that now.

Her husband was lost. That, too, India had come to accept.

And she knew that there was nothing for her to do but go home, back to the family who loved her.

There in Norfolk she would try to make some kind of life for herself.

Now as India stood before Swallow Hill's high dormer window, reliving those sad days in Europe, a bar of sunlight slanted through the glass and glistened over the tears scattered across the baby clothes her husband had never seen and her son had never had a chance to wear.

In her reverie, she did not hear the light step behind her, nor the check of indrawn breath.

Two hands settled at her shoulders. "India, what are you doing up here? Your grandmother said . . ." Thorne's voice trailed away as he heard her shuddering breath. "India, are you crying?"

"No." She spun away, putting the high lid between them. "I—I just need to be alone."

"Why? There's nothing you can't tell me. Besides," Thorne said harshly, "I have some serious explaining of my own to do."

"Maybe it's too late for explanations, Dev. Maybe what we had last night, all that fire and passion, is the most we can ever have." India's face was a pale oval of uncertainty. "Maybe that's the lesson Brussels was supposed to teach us."

"Damn it, India, don't turn away from me!" He caught her waist and pulled her back to face him. "What happened last night was wonderful, but it was only part of what I feel for you. I love your spirit and your innocence. I love your determination and your honesty. I even love your recklessness, though it frightens me half to death sometimes." He ran his hand over her moist cheek. "What I'm trying to say is that I love all that you are, India Delamere. And I always will."

"Will you?" Her voice was a trembling whisper. "Sometimes the past seems so far away that it might as well be a dream. And other times it all feels like yesterday, the pain still bleeding like a raw wound."

"What are you saying, India? Damn it, what are you trying to tell me?"

She looked down without thinking, her eyes pools of sadness. Thorne followed her gaze to the tears glinting like jewels on the white fabric.

On the neat layers of pristine baby clothing.

Suddenly his fingers tightened. "My—my God." His voice was strangled. "You didn't tell me. I never knew—never even suspected—"

A shudder went through him, a great wrenching of muscle and tendon and cartilage that felt as if a giant hand had reached into his chest and torn everything inside out. "Is it true? *Was* there a child?" he asked hoarsely.

India did not answer. Her hand simply continued to stroke the fine white linen.

Devlyn pulled her back against him fiercely. His voice broke. "What happened, India? Dear God, I have to know the truth."

India felt something hot fall on her shoulder and knew it was Devlyn's tears. She knew, too, that it was time for her husband to taste the grief that she had carried so long in silence. "He was . . . a beautiful little boy, with eyes as wise as his father's. He was the joy of my life for the short time I had him. And I don't regret anything, not even one second of time I had with him, do you hear? Even though I lost his so—so suddenly."

"He died so young. I never even had a chance to see him." Devlyn's lips locked in a tight line. "And I left you alone in a strange city. With a child, my child . . ." He looked away, his voice ragged. "What kind of a monster was I?" He shook his head. "Why didn't I wait? Why didn't I have the control to hold back until I'd come home from battle? My blindness meant the loss of my son. *Our* son." His fingers clenched.

"Don't, Dev. I don't regret *anything* about Brussels," India said fiercely. "It was only luck that you came back to me. Don't try to carry the weight of those choices on your shoulders."

"How can you look at me without hating me when I missed so bloody much? Everything of any importance." His hand fell to her slender waist. "I missed the sight of you full with my child. I missed the sight of your joy and radiance, as you bloomed every day. And I missed the sight of a boy with wise eyes, smiling as you held him in your arms. And all for what?" He laughed bitterly. "For an empty notion of honor and a country that cares less for heroes than it does for gold guineas and noisy parades," he growled.

"You had your duty, and I had mine. You can't go back and change that."

"If only I could!" Dev looked down at the neat layers of clothes. He held up a tiny shirt, his eyes glistening. When he turned, the sun was slanting golden through India's hair, glinting over the tears on her cheek. The sight made him catch a ragged breath. "I want another chance, India. I want you. I want *this*." He rested the fragrant linen against his cheek. "I want a house full of laughter and children spilling everywhere. Even if I am terrified whether I can be any fit sort of father." He smiled crookedly. "It's not as if I had a normal childhood. My father was an inveterate gamester and my mother was . . ." He cleared his throat. "Perhaps I'd better not give her a name."

"You won't be like that."

"No?" Dev laughed bitterly. "I'm damnably afraid I'll never be able to put down roots. What if I find I'm no good as a father or a husband? What if I cut line and run, like the worst kind of coward?"

"Then we'll all run away with you. I *do* know most of Turkestan, after all. And there is still that Bedouin leader who would be only too happy to—"

"You've made your point," Thorne said darkly.

"But I don't want him. I want you." India stared up into his eyes, needing. Wanting.

Suddenly there was a universe of wanting for both of them.

Her voice came low and husky. "I warned you, Dev. I never promised to make this easy for you." Her hand drifted along his chest and slid between the folds of his shirt, nestling against the warm planes of taut muscle.

"Any more of that, woman, and I'll—"

India eased sleekly against him. "You'll what?"

A muscle flashed at Thorne's jaw as he read the hunger in her eyes. "I think," he said huskily, "that I will give you anything you want, my lady."

"What I want is this." India eased to her toes and slid her tongue against his ear.

Dev's hands clenched against her soft hips as she whispered lingeringly. "Sweet God, India, I'll die of pain right here and now."

"You can't die of what I suggested." She frowned. "At least I don't *think* you can. I've never tried it of course, though I suspect there were any number of men who would have been happy to show me how to—"

Dev caught her up against his chest, his expression thunderous. "I don't want to hear about the other men who have fallen in love with you. Don't cast my stupidity up in my face. For me you were the only one, ever since I saw you in that muddy street in Brussels."

"And what about the notorious river pirate?"

"He was never as notorious as he seemed. And he was simply a role, another of those I have learned to play too well in this chameleon's life of mine. Only *you* seem to have the uncanny ability to get past my facade and find the truth of me."

India bent her head and nuzzled the warm skin at his neck, delighting in his instant shudder. "Prove it to me then. I want to feel your heart pounding against mine. I want to see your eyes blind with desire. And then I want to feel you against me. Driving inside me."

Devlyn groaned. His hands shook as he kissed her.

They didn't make it to the bed where Charles II had slept. Thorne lifted her back against the nearest stable surface, which happened to be the great trestle table.

Never mind that the Magna Carta had been signed there. They had their own momentous history to make, history of a more intimate sort, against those polished wooden planes.

In a flurry of black broadcloth and peach satin, they struggled against layers of unwanted clothes.

"Dev, I—I can't breathe."

"Neither can I, *sauvage.*" He tossed away her damask sash, eased her foot around his waist and slid up her skirts, his eyes dark with the sight of her creamy skin. "It will be here, *ma mie.* I can't wait. It feels like forever already."

"Yes, here. *Now.*"

And it was there, right at that moment. India met him halfway, supple and perfect, smooth heat against his hard male need. Her hands gripped his shoulders and she eased him deeper inside her.

"*Doucement*, beauty," he said hoarsely. "Too fast and I'll hurt you."

But India burned in his touch, burned with months of fantasies and the raw reality of the prior night. Her Delamere blood was on fire and there was not a shred of patience left to her. "Give me tomorrow, Dev. Here in this square of sunshine help me make another child. He would want that of us, I think."

Her husky plea slammed through Thorne. His hands tightened and he drove deeper, feeling her clench around him. Fighting for control, he kissed her face, her hands, her neck.

And then her hands slid low and circled him and he was lost.

He closed his eyes. His hands were shaking as he laid her back, moving hard and fast, as deep as a man could go.

They were both lost then, lost to everything but the desire that raged free, unbound and unfettered, in the wake of confidences shared. Thorne whispered to her with every hard stroke, hoarse words that worshiped her beauty and adored her wild courage. With his words he loved her, as much as with body and heart.

And his prize was her wild yielding.

He smiled darkly when she tensed against him, back arched, hands clinging to his shoulders. And when her breath had stilled, he brought her high and blind again, through a dark landscape of magic forged anew.

She shuddered her way back down to the quiet square of sunlight in the quiet room in a quiet corner of Norfolk. When she opened her eyes, slumberous and hazy with desire, her mouth took on a determined force. "And now, you rogue, I've had enough of your charm." She moved against him, her hands doing painful, extraordinary things to all his muscles.

Thorne shuddered with each erotic slide of movement. "I meant to show you I was serious. I meant to show you how well I could grovel."

India's eyes glinted as she studied their joined bodies. "You grovel, my dearest husband, *quite* wonderfully," she purred. "But did I tell you about that dashing young officer who tried to convince me to elope with him after—"

As she'd hoped, Thorne's response was instant and fierce. His hands dug into her soft hips and with a low curse he drove hard against her, all restraints forgotten. Now they were just two people burying sad memories and forging the first of many happy tomorrows.

Two people who had by some wondrous miracle discovered that death could sometimes hold the seeds of life.

29

Two counties away in London the Duke of Wellington looked up from his crowded desk at the secretary holding out a sealed message. "Not another death threat, I trust, Stevens?" Three such letters had already arrived in the last week, and one angry ex-soldier had even attacked his carriage. "I must be back to the Continent soon."

But this time when the duke opened the vellum sheet, his face broke into a broad smile. "Damned good work by the lot of them! The little girl is safe, Stevens. We must drink a toast of thanks."

"Of course, Your Grace." Wellington's aide turned away. With the meticulous movements that had first caught the eye of his superior officer, he slid open a decanter of brandy and carefully tipped the mellow spirits into a cut crystal tumbler.

"Take one for yourself, Stevens. This is an event worth celebrating. With any luck, Thornwood will have caught the rest of the brutes at one stroke, and we'll have no more trouble from this group called l'Aurore."

Glasses clinked. The two men savored their drinks in silence. Then with a long sigh, Wellington turned back to his desk and the mound of paper-

work that seemed to grow higher during his visits to
London. Meanwhile, his aide turned away to
straighten up some outgoing correspondence carrying Wellington's signature.

Silently Stevens pulled back his cuff, revealing an
odd curving scar just above his wrist. It was not the
jagged mark of an accidental wound, but precise
and sharp, almost as if made by design. The pattern
was simple, a straight line running beneath a half
circle. The crown of radiant lines at the top might
have depicted the sun setting in the west.

Or the sun rising.

At dawn.

After smoothing back the cuff, Stevens looked out
at the small garden, remembering how that scar
had hurt him when it was cut into his skin five years
ago. Their numbers had been far fewer then. Stevens had been among the very first to obtain access
to Wellington's select circle, and he had used his
position carefully and cleverly. No one had guessed
his real beliefs—or his secret identity as the leader
of the group known as l'Aurore.

His jaw hardened. No matter that Waterloo was
done, they would *still* win. His whole existence was
dedicated to that goal. One day soon, Napoleon
would walk down the hillside at St. Helena and
board a boat for France. When he did, his supporters would return to Paris in grandeur, and the
course of Europe would be changed once more.

And *he* would be there to watch it, glorying in his
triumph.

Stevens thought of his father, a graceless, impov-
erished younger son openly mocked in his village.
Jonah Stevens, his only son, had also been an outsider, first in the Hampshire village where he was
born, then in the lonely halls of the school where

his father had scrimped and saved to send him. The loneliness had only grown worse when Stevens entered the tight, clubbish world of the officers who surrounded Wellington. Soon his efficiency and skill for organization had been noticed, resulting in access to more secret materials.

Now he would show them all. This time, he *would* belong! Soon everyone else would be made to suffer the pain he had known all his life.

"Stevens, are you forgetting those letters must be out within the hour?" Wellington's voice had an edge to it.

Dangerous, the aide thought angrily. He must be especially careful not to draw suspicion now. "I was simply looking over the rear garden, Your Grace. I thought I saw someone hanging about near the gate. They have asked you to make a public appearance at Hyde Park, but it is hardly advisable after all these threats you have been receiving."

Wellington laughed harshly. "The day that it is too dangerous to walk in Hyde Park is the day in which Waterloo might as well not have been won," the general said fiercely.

Stevens shrugged. "One cannot be too careful, you know." His face held a thin smile as he turned away to complete his tasks for the duke.

It was true, he thought. These *were* dangerous times. No one knew that better than he.

And as he picked up the duke's silver letter opener, he was thinking with cool delight of Wellington's impending death.

30

Devlyn and India walked slowly down the stairs, hand in hand. En route from the attic they passed at least seven servants. All were too well trained to reveal any surprise at seeing the two walking hand in hand; obviously in love and obviously disheveled. But India knew that within five minutes rumors would be raging through Swallow Hill.

She looked at Dev and smiled. "You know they will be talking about us. They will say the most outrageous things. That you held me at gunpoint. That I held *you* at gunpoint. Will you mind?"

Thorne slid a curl of auburn hair away from her cheek. "I doubt, my sweet, that they could say *anything* as amazing as what I'm thinking right now."

"You're sure? You didn't care for gossip after the balloon ascension."

"Let them talk," Devlyn said huskily. "In fact, let the whole *world* talk. I think I'd like to figure in a few sordid Delamere scandals. Besides, we have a great deal of making up to do, you and I."

India bit her lip. "I wonder what the children will think."

Devlyn laughed dryly. "The children? *They* will be

ecstatic, no doubt. They've loved you from the first second they saw you." His eyes darkened. "Just as I have."

"Rake," India scoffed.

"*Reformed* rake," Thorne corrected gently. Their fingers tightened.

"But what about the rest of the diamonds?"

They had come to the bottom of the staircase now, and Devlyn stood looking down the sunny, polished corridors of marble, in a house that was filled with the treasures of five centuries, acquired by a buoyant, stubborn family whose history was a good part of the history of England itself.

He smiled to himself for a moment. He only hoped he was smart enough and strong enough to keep pace with these Delamere women. "Now that we have three of the band, we'll soon have all the rest. They're not the sort to hold their tongues. Besides, we have another clue. We are told they carry a peculiar scar above their right wrists."

"A rising sun," India said thoughtfully. "L'Aurore."

"Very quick, my wife. You have a natural flare for this kind of work."

"I must remember that. Unless you keep me very well occupied, I might just disappear on some dangerous mission or other."

Dev's face darkened with a scowl. "Not if you value your life, you won't. There'll be no more jaunting off in the middle of the night to interview river pirates, I warn you."

"Not even if they are *very* handsome? Not even if they hurt their shoulder swinging across the deck trying to rescue me from problems of my own creating?"

Dev studied her thoughtfully. "I suppose something might be arranged, *ma mie.* The crew of the *Gypsy* took quite a liking to you, as a matter of fact. Perhaps a run downriver could be arranged." A smile played over his lips. "If the terms were favorable, of course."

India ran her hand lightly along his shoulder. "Oh, I suspect that the terms could be *very* favorable." They were nearly at the end of the marble corridor when a ripple of sultry laughter drifted out of one of the salons at the rear of the house.

Dev stiffened. His eyes locked on India's. "It couldn't be—"

But it was. At that moment Lady Helena Marchmont sat next to the Duchess of Cranford drinking tea from a fragile Sèvres porcelain cup.

"Let's go back," Devlyn muttered. "If we hurry, she'll never see us." But it was too late.

"Ah, there you are," the duchess said, rising imperiously to her feet. "Lady Marchmont and I were just talking about you." A devilish gleam lit the duchess's keen blue eyes. "I was telling her how delighted we all were to hear of your upcoming marriage."

Lady Helena studied the two figures in the doorway, her expression unreadable. "It did seem rather sudden to me, but then I suppose that's the soldier in Lord Thornwood. It is the soldier's way, to see a target, plan a campaign, and move forward without thinking."

"It worked well enough for us in Brussels," Dev muttered. He looked down at India, smiling. "I find it has worked well again."

The countess rose to her feet in a flurry of lace and satin ribbons. "I must not intrude. I merely came up from London because I was concerned about the children. I have brought a gift for Alexis, if I may see her."

After a look at Thorne, the duchess nodded. "I believe you'll find her in the rose garden. She was playing hide-and-seek with Ian and the other two ragamuffins."

The countess smiled at India. "I wish you every happiness," she murmured before turning toward the open french doors. Her heavy perfume seemed to hang on the air long after she had gone off in search of Alexis.

"I wonder what *she* wanted?" India looked thoughtfully after the countess's retreating form.

"She wanted to see you of course," the duchess said crisply. "*And* to see if she still had any chance with Thornwood." The duchess's eyes crinkled. "I hope I was not too far off in my reading of the situation?"

"You were dead on target, as always," Dev said dryly. "I can see I shall have to be on my toes in this family." He looked out at the garden. "I suppose it will do Alexis no harm to speak with the countess for a few minutes. I will herd her away after that."

"It won't do to coddle the girl, you know," the duchess said firmly. "She's had a terrible ordeal, but the memory is already fading fast. My advice is not to treat her differently from the other two."

"I suppose you're right," Dev said slowly. "All the same, there's something about the countess that leaves me unsettled."

"Yes, Chilton, what is it?" The duchess looked up as the butler entered the room. "Another disappointed female to see Thornwood?"

Chilton shook his head. "This message has just come from London, Your Grace. It was directed to Lord Thornwood. There is a carriage waiting, too."

As Dev scanned the note, a frown grew between his brows. "I have to go back," he said harshly.

India went very still. "Does it have to do with—?"

"Exactly," Thorne growled. "And until this business is completed there will be no peace for any of us." He circled India's hands and gripped them tightly. "I'll be back as soon as I can. It's not my choice, you must understand that."

India managed the semblance of a smile. "I know that. Do you have the—lost merchandise?"

"Safe and sound," Dev said, thinking of the diamond hidden in his boot.

"I'll have Cook pack you a lunch. I'm afraid you missed it."

"But I feel entirely satisfied, my lady," Thorne said with a wolfish grin.

For a moment India's fingers tightened on his. "Come back to me, Dev. I've lost you twice now, and I don't want to lose you again."

Her husband kissed her with hot, thorough skill and they were both breathless when he finished. "You'll never lose me again. Not even if you *want* to," he vowed hoarsely.

The Duke of Wellington's private secretary waited calmly in the shadowed interior of the traveling coach. He was neatly dressed, careful in this as in everything else. In fact, all of his plans were immaculate.

He fingered the pistol well hidden beneath his cloak and smiled. There would be no more thwarting of his plans this time. Within hours the Duke of Wellington would be dead, the diamond known as l'Aurore once more in his possession, and the emperor of France on his way to being restored to his throne.

Thornwood pulled open the carriage door. "Ah, Stevens, is that you? There was no need for you to come and see me back personally, I assure you."

"His Grace had some reports he wanted me to show you. And there were some other things which he did not care for me to mention, but I thought you should know anyway."

Dev swung easily into the carriage and dropped a satchel on the opposite seat. "What sort of things?"

"The four recent threats against his life, for example."

"He never said a word to me."

Wellington's aide nodded. "He never says a word to anyone. He should not be going about, not until these malcontents lose their interest in him." He called to the coachman, who put the horses into motion. "You've brought the diamond?"

Dev patted his boot. "It won't escape me again."

The secretary sat back and smiled. "Excellent. His Grace will be delighted." Outside the carriage the green lawns of Swallow Hill rushed past in a blur. "And congratulations on the safe return of your ward. It was cleverly done."

Devlyn shook his head. "Not clever enough. Our timing was far too close. Damnable how these madmen seem to know our every move before it comes. Still, we'll have them all soon. Those three in custody will be happy enough to reveal everything they know."

The secretary's hands gently smoothed the folds of his cloak. "Oh, haven't you heard? There has been a bit of bad news. One of the men jumped from the window of the house where he was being held. The other two were found poisoned. It appears their compatriots did not wish them to reveal any of their secrets."

Devlyn's eyes hardened. "So it's not finished after all."

"I'm afraid not, Lord Thornwood." Stevens drew the pistol from beneath his cloak and trained it on the earl's chest. "Not finished at all."

A moment later a gun cracked harshly. But the carriage raced on, heading relentlessly toward London and the carefully planned assassination that would mark the beginning of a new dawn.

"Did you hear that?" India frowned out at the green hills, watching a hot air balloon bob up and down. Its red and blue silk canopy was half filled in preparation for the afternoon ride Thorne had arranged for his three wards. Outside India could see the amiable Mr. Smithson checking the ballast and securing lines.

"Hear what?" her brother said, finishing off a second slice of Cook's best caraway cake.

India frowned. "Something that sounded like a pistol."

"Love has gone to her head," Ian muttered, shaking his head in a great display of sadness. "Such a pity, too, since she used to be *so* levelheaded."

"No, I'm serious, Ian. I heard something, and it was coming from down the hill. Down the hill toward Devlyn's carriage." India's eyes followed the carriage fast disappearing into the trees at the foot of Swallow Hill's broad lawns. "I hope Dev remembers about the problem with the bridge."

"It's well marked."

"The sign might be gone. Or the coachman might not notice."

"It *must* be love," her brother said teasingly. "Thorne's barely been gone two minutes and already the woman's imagining a thousand kinds of danger." Then he frowned. "You're not serious, are you? You don't really think there's something wrong?"

India pushed to her feet and moved restlessly about the room, straightening a picture frame and then a pair of Chinese porcelain vases. "I don't know, Ian. Maybe it's just my imagination, but something is worrying me about that sound I heard."

"If it's bothering you, I'll ride after them. It will be easy enough."

"Would you, Ian? I know I'm acting like a silly goose, but—" She sighed. "Would you mind terribly?"

Her brother ruffled her hair. "Not at all, hoyden. Maybe now you'll finally consider the debt repaid for my tossing you into the pond."

Out in Swallow Hill's beautiful rose garden, Lady Marchmont toyed with a spray of crimson roses, trying to hold a one-sided conversation with Alexis. "It is very pleasant to see you safe again, my dear."

Alexis simply nodded, her hands tight on her battered doll.

"You seem to be very happy here."

Another nod.

"Alexis, it would help a great deal if you would look at me."

The little girl's head rose slowly. "Very well," she said softly.

"That's better. I don't suppose you remember anything about your kidnapping, do you? Anything about the people who took you or the place where you were held?"

Alexis shook her head. Her hands clenched her doll. Lady Marchmont reached out suddenly, intent on the old battered toy, but Alexis pushed to her feet and shrank away. "Don't touch Josephine! And don't touch me. I'm frightened of you. Can't you see them?"

"See whom?"

"The gray people, of course. They're all around you. Just like they were around *him*!"

Helena Marchmont advanced on the little girl, her eyes filled with hate. "Gray people?" She laughed coldly. "Whatever silly stories are you spinning now, you little brat?"

Alexis retreated a step. "Stay away. They want *you*, not me. And they're getting angrier all the time." The little girl shuddered.

"I'm sure these tales are perfect to frighten your unruly brother and sister, but you can't expect them to frighten *me*. Now give me that doll. Then I will be on my way."

"Why do you w—want Josephine?"

"Because I have been told it might contain something very interesting, something lost since the night your parents died."

The little girl turned and began to run. "I *won't*! You are one of them, and Uncle Thorne will take care of you."

"I think not," the countess said harshly. "I'm very sad to say that your Uncle Thorne will not be taking care of anything. Not *ever* again."

31

India was staring through the window at the bright silk canopy of the hot air balloon when she heard Alexis's frightened cry from the rose garden. A moment later the little girl hurtled through the open french doors, her face white. "She is one of them! I saw them all around her."

"Who?"

"The gray people." The girl shuddered. "They were all around her, just like the man with the scar. Something terrible is going to happen, I know it." Alexis twisted convulsively, burying her face in India's skirt.

The duchess frowned at India. "Gray people? What does she mean?"

"I'll explain later, Grandmama."

At that moment another figure appeared in the french doors. "Lady Delamere, I must speak with you. No, I must plead with you." A woman in a simple traveling cloak stood on the threshold, ringing her hands. Behind her stood Albert, the footman who had come from London.

"Perhaps now is not quite the best time," India began diplomatically, but the woman hurried into the room just the same.

"This has to do with Miss Alexis. It's that horrible Lady Marchmont, you see. I've worked in her employ for six months, and every second of it was an agony. Such things she does and says, and now she's planning something horrible, I know it. But I don't care, I've run away and good riddance to the lot of them. And I had to tell you, since Albert and I, we—" The young woman's face filled with color.

The footman stepped forward, squaring his shoulders. "We're wishing to be married, my lady, and that's the fact of it. I told Eliza that you would not be against the match, for you are not like Lady Marchmont. But she has something to confess, and she must do it herself."

The woman's hands trembled. "*I* was the one what sent those warning letters to you, my lady. I knew Lady Marchmont had something bad in store for you, and it was the only way I could think of to warn you. She never let me out of her sight, you see. Albert and I only got to meet when I was doing errands. But I begged him to leave the messages for you, and he did, good-hearted man that he is. He didn't know what was in them, I swear it."

That mystery, at least, was solved, India thought. She smiled at the anxious young woman. "Oh, I doubt we will be sacking Albert anytime in the next twenty years. He's far too efficient a footman for that. As for you, Eliza, I'm quite certain we can find a place for you, either here at Swallow Hill or back at Devonham House. Would you like that?"

"Oh, miss, *would* you? Could you possibly, in spite of the deceit I've played on you?"

"You tried to warn me, Eliza. How can I be angry for that?"

Alexis scrubbed at her cheeks. "You worked for

Lady Marchmont? She *was* evil, just like I thought, wasn't she?"

The young woman nodded vigorously. "Everything you said about her was true and I think you were ever so clever to notice it." She looked at India. "I've always been wishing to work as a governess, my lady. I thought perhaps . . ." Her voice trailed off wistfully.

India laughed. "As it happens, I know three ragamuffins who are in need of a firm but loving hand."

The young woman smiled at Alexis and reached for her hand. "Well, then, Miss Alexis, why don't you and I see if we can't find something to do for Cook in the kitchen? Mr. Albert will show us the way."

India watched in amazement as Alexis trotted off happily, the traumas of the last hour forgotten in her eagerness to "help" Cook by tasting one of her superb confections.

"But where has Ian gotten to?" India asked her grandmother. "I asked him to ride and check on Devlyn in the carriage. He still hasn't come back after a quarter of an hour?"

The old woman frowned. In the curve of the valley the balloon dipped and swayed in the steady eastern wind. "That's not like your brother," she said slowly. "Maybe the little girl was right. Maybe we *ought* to be worried . . ."

Stevens trained his pistol on Dev's chest. "And now, Thornwood, I believe you will hand that diamond over to me."

"If I did, I'd be a fool. As soon as you have it, you'll most certainly shoot me." Dev had trouble keeping his voice even as sharp pains from Stevens's first bullet burned down his arm.

"But I shall shoot you *either* way, Lord Thornwood. Not a thing you do now will make any difference."

A horse thundered alongside the coach. Ian's face appeared in the carriage window. "Everything all right in there? India was concerned and asked me to—"

The cloak slid from Stevens's arm. Ian's eyes widened as he saw the gleam of a polished barrel.

The weapon cracked and a ball grazed his thigh. The force sent him reeling backward to the ground in a crumpled heap.

"Such a pity about India's brother." Stevens smiled coldly. "But we don't want to be disturbed, do we, Thornwood?"

Dev did not speak. He was fighting to stay upright, while blood soaked through his shirt. But now would be his only chance at escape.

Abruptly he threw himself forward, shoving Stevens back against the side of the carriage and dislodging the pistol. Cursing, he turned and wrenched open the carriage doors, tensing his body to jump. Outside the ground rushed past in a blinding blur, for the team was at full gallop now.

And that moment of hesitation was Thorne's undoing.

"You'll pay for that, Thornwood," Stevens growled. And then his boot slammed into Thorne's side.

India stood up abruptly. "I'm going after them. Something's wrong, Grandmama, I can *feel* it."

"But they have over a half-hour's start. Even on Hannibal, you could never catch up."

India's eyes locked on the brightly colored silk canopy outside the window. She lifted her skirts, revealing the breeches she had put on at her first suspicion of trouble. "But I'll go by balloon, of course."

Frowning, the Duchess of Cranford summoned Connor MacKinnon. "The hoyden's gone after Devlyn. She's convinced something's happened to him, and I can't say that I am not a little worried myself. You'll find her down the slope of the hill."

MacKinnon's brow rose. "How can she hope to catch up with him?" As he looked out the windows, Connor's face took on a rather sickly pallor. "Surely not by balloon?" When he met the duchess's eyes, his worst fears were confirmed. He swallowed and summoned up a smile. "By hot air balloon. Why not? After all, how much more difficult can it be than standing a wave-swept deck in pitching seas?"

But he didn't look at all convinced as he set out after his friend's sister.

Henry Smithson was just checking the last of the rigging, with India at his side, when Connor reached them. MacKinnon looked dubiously at the full canopy, then shook his head. "Give me a slippery deck in a gale-force storm any day," he muttered.

"Connor, what are you doing here?" India was straightening sandbags along the edge of the basket.

"Your grandmother thought I could use the broadening experience of a balloon flight."

"Bosh. You've come to keep an eye on me."

"If that balloon looks half as shaky as it appears, it's *you* who will have to keep an eye on me, minx."

Smithson, however, was eyeing the clouds gathering in the north. "Time we should be going, miss. Those clouds mean a change of winds, and I don't care to be bucking crosswinds, not over this valley. But we'll catch your carriage, never you fear." He

looked at Connor MacKinnon's tall frame. "You'll be
stretching our weight to come with us. Are you sure
about this?"

"Having lived through the English bombardment
of Algiers, I suppose I can manage one hot air balloon ride." MacKinnon frowned at the basket. "How
do I get into this thing?"

India hid a smile, shoved him over the edge, and
followed him in. A moment later Smithson cast off
the lines, and the balloon began to rise over the
sweeping lawns. As the ground grew smaller, India
watched the hills to the south. "I see them!" A carriage crawled along the twisting road. She said a
silent prayer of thanks that she had also sent Luna
off in pursuit, guided by the scent of one of Devlyn's
boots. Already she could make out the wolf loping
through the meadows far below them.

India only prayed they would not be too late.

"So, Stevens, how is it that you first became a
traitor to your country?" Thornwood eased back
against the side of the carriage, cradling his bleeding arm. "Was it money that turned you, or was it
sheer lust for power?"

"What would you know about wanting power or
money?" His captor scowled. "You, who have had
nothing but privilege your whole life?"

"You might be surprised," Devlyn said softly.

"None of that matters anyway. When I have that
diamond back in my keeping, everything will
change. We have many powerful supporters now.
Even the Prince Regent's daughter is sympathetic. A
few gold guineas in the right hands and their loyalty
will be ensured."

"You think so? Does it take gold to buy the loyalty
of these men who bear the scar on their wrist?"

"Very astute, Thornwood, as was your masquerade with James Herrington. You outmaneuvered us again with the exchange of the little brat in Hyde Park. But in the end it does not matter. Our cause will *still* triumph."

Thornwood laughed coldly. "While the emperor is in exile at St. Helena?"

"Not for long," Stevens said fiercely. "We already have two cabinet ministers favorable to our cause. Fox and Wilcox are entirely committed. Not all are in awe of your sainted Wellington, you see."

Devlyn hid his shock. How could these madmen have possibly garnered support at such high levels? His expression did not change, however, as he studied Wellington's aide. "And what plans do you have for the Great Man? Is he too to be sacrificed for your great and honorable cause?"

"There have already been a number of attempts on his life. L'Aurore shall simply complete what the other malcontents have not been able to do. Soon all England will resound with our name, and Paris will throw open its doors to welcome its heroes home."

Thornwood looked at Stevens and realized he was looking into the eyes of a madman. No amount of arguing would change the man's mind by one whit. Thorne's only hope was to escape from the carriage. Out of the corner of his eye, he saw a silver shape loping over the hill in an easy pace parallel to the carriage.

Luna! Had India somehow grown suspicious and sent the wolf after him?

Something exploded against the top of the carriage, making Stevens sit forward and curse.

Thornwood smiled at the man training the pistol on his chest. "They are closing in, Stevens. Do you hear that?" Another sandbag hit the carriage, rock-ing the frame. "Whatever plans you have are fin-ished."

"Hardly. A tragic carriage accident is in store for you, Thornwood. I understand there is a bridge out somewhere in the area. Most unfortunate, given your obvious reconciliation with Lady Delamere. But then these are dangerous times," he said, smil-ing thinly. "Of course there's no need to try shouting to the coachman. He is one of *our* men, entirely loyal. You will find no help from him."

Out the carriage window, high above the treetops, Devlyn caught a glimpse of bright red silk. Only with great effort did he keep a smile from his face at the thought of India flying overhead, aloft in the hot air balloon. Now the rest was up to him.

He looked at Stevens and shrugged. "It appears you have thought of every possibility, Stevens. I must applaud you. But we might still strike a bar-gain. If I give you the diamond, you can count on me to keep my mouth shut. There is no necessity for murder. Assuming you would succeed, of course."

His captor laughed coldly. "You don't convince me for a second, Thornwood. You would never keep your mouth shut. You are too much a man of honor, though you chose to hide it from the world. Now give me the diamond. There is no need to drag this out."

Thornwood cursed and bent down to his boot. Slowly he drew out the huge diamond called l'Aurore.

When Stevens sat forward, eyes narrowed with greed, Devlyn cast the diamond with all his might against the far wall of the carriage and then flung himself backward, jamming open the door and pushing toward the ground.

But he got only halfway. Lips curled, Stevens seized his legs and held him blindly. "You'll not escape me *now*, damn you!"

Outside there was a low growl. Without warning a powerful gray form hurtled through the open carriage door and slammed against Stevens's chest. Growling, India's wolf knocked the pistol free and drove Stevens to the carriage floor.

"Get the creature off! It'll tear out my throat!"

Devlyn wondered whether it might be true. He had never seen Luna so fierce before.

But there was no time to think. Another sandbag hit the carriage as the great wolf turned and shoved hard at Dev's shoulder, forcing him over the edge of the door toward the ground.

To his death?

The next moment Devlyn spun backwards. Head over heels, he crashed down blindly against the ground.

He was still shaking, his vision blurred, when he saw Stevens appear in the carriage door. Wellington's aide fired one desperate shot, which went wild and hissed through a nearby hedgerow.

And then Devlyn's eyes narrowed as he realized exactly where the carriage was headed. Due south was a sharp rise, and beyond that lay the river.

There was no time to warn Stevens or the coachman. The horses pounded on, straining up the rise, unable to see what lay before them, where the road gave way to the deadly space of a washed-out bridge.

Time seemed to hang suspended as Stevens disappeared, no doubt to search for the lost diamond.

And then he reappeared in the window.

Dev had one brief glimpse of his terrified face before the carriage sailed forward out of sight and exploded against the rocky bank far below.

"She knew." Dev stood on the riverbank, cradling his arm as he stared down at the shattered chaos of the carriage. "Somehow Luna knew."

India had landed in a whoosh of silk and now the two stood hand in hand overlooking the river and the carnage below. At their feet Luna sat expectantly, well pleased as Thorne stroked her velvet fur.

"She tried to shove me from the carriage. At first I thought she had turned wild and was trying to kill me." He shook his head. "But she knew. She saved my life. Or *you* did, by sending her."

"You're very good, my precious," India whispered, and at her words both Luna and Thorne looked up. The similarity of their expressions made India laugh.

She threw her arms around both of them. "Thank God you're safe, Dev. Something about that message coming so abruptly left me suspicious."

Thorne cursed. "Stevens got a shot at Ian. He fell from his horse several miles back. Do you think that balloon could take us—" The drum of hoofbeats drowned out his words.

"Don't move a step, *either* of you! I've barely got Ian in tow, and I don't intend to lose you know." The two turned to see the Duchess of Cranford's carriage careening over the hill. At the river's edge the door was thrown open and India's grandmother descended imperiously, silver cane in hand. "There you are! I was wondering what was keeping you." When she saw the remains of the shattered carriage, she shook her head. "My granddaughter was right to be worried about you, Thornwood. I hope you know that you owe her your life."

"I've just been telling her the same thing," Dev said. "I was on the verge of asking what I could do to repay her."

"I'll answer that question for her, you young jackanapes! You can marry India in Swallow Hill's chapel, with all the countryside to look on, the way it should have been done the first time! She'll wear her mother's antique wedding gown and carry a bouquet of my finest roses in her hands when you do it, too." The duchess struck the ground with her cane. "And if I hear even one tiny sound of protest from you, I'll—"

Thornwood's brow rose haughtily. "If you don't mind, Your Grace, I prefer to do my own proposing." He turned to India and slid his good arm around her waist. "It's late in coming, but I beg you will have me for good, my love. We'll do it right this time, too." The earl awkwardly maneuvered down onto one knee, ignoring the pain where Stevens's bullet had gored his arm. "I'll be the devil's own husband and I suspect you'll be an equal sort of wife, but I think together we might make a fair job of it. Perhaps between us we can even tame those children and give them some of the joy their lives have been missing for so long."

Tears filled India's eyes. She thought of another child who had missed this happiness, and as they stood in the clearing, the sun pouring golden over their shoulders, she thought she felt a warm, laughing presence nearby. "Of course I'll marry you again, you silly great thing. But for no other reason than to keep you from reverting to your terrible ways as a river pirate."

"And what about *you*, storming through London dressed in men's clothing? A walking invitation to every footpad and larcenist in Whitechapel, if I ever saw one!" Thorne swayed for a minute, fighting a stab of pain. "But you'll really have me? For good this time? There'll be no more marching off to war and no more of me being called away on dangerous missions. The only missions I mean to accept in the future are rescuing Alexis from the top of the apple tree, or perhaps that great silver wolf of yours from some angry villager."

"My answer is yes," India said huskily. "Just as it has always been." She frowned. "Dev?"

"So glad," Thorne said unsteadily. "So very glad . . . to hear it . . ."

And then he collapsed in a heap at her feet.

MacKinnon was just making his way toward them, wobbly-kneed after his balloon ride, and Ian, his leg covered by a strip of linen, was climbing stiffly from the duchess's carriage. The old woman eyed both men with disfavor. "Isn't that just to be expected," she muttered. "MacKinnon is white as a ghost and Ian refuses to stay put in the carriage, though he can barely walk. Now *your* husband passes out cold at your feet, India." She shook her head in disgust. "Men! Utterly no use when a woman needs them most. See you remember that, gel."

And then a faraway look entered the duchess's eyes, making her smile faintly. "Of course, I have found there are a *few* things that they can do passably well."

32

On the following day the duchess had lined her patients up in Luc's old bedroom in three camp beds ranged against the wall. From her campaign position in a large wing chair by the window she dispensed broth, noxious herbal brews, and evil-smelling poultices along with general hygienic advice. Luc and his wife, Silver, had traveled up from London as soon as they heard the news and were watching the duchess's campaign with vast enjoyment. At least this gave Silver some freedom, for usually the duchess made her a prime target, ordering strengthening broths, brisk walks, and an array of other exotic remedies for what the duchess called the rigors of motherhood.

Never mind that Luc's wife was clearly in glowing health and strong as an ox.

That very morning the so estimable lords Pendleworth and Monkton had also arrived from London looking relieved to see their friend safe. They, too, were enjoying the sight of three brawny men, Ian, Connor, and Thornwood, held captive under the iron fist of one fragile and diminutive old woman.

"I rather think Connor's too pale, don't you,

Grandmama?" Luc stood grinning, one shoulder propped against the mantel as he studied his friend, confined to bed with the other two. "I'm afraid that jaunt on the hot air balloon has overtaxed him more than he lets on."

"You men," said the duchess. "More trouble than you're worth most of the time." She gestured to the butler. "Beach?"

"Yes, Your Grace?"

"Fetch me that jar from the side table, if you please." Well armed, the duchess moved off to Connor's bedside. "Open your mouth and take your medicine like a man," she ordered.

A look of revulsion filled MacKinnon's face as he stared down at the clotted brown concoction. "But truly, Your Grace, I am fine. It was merely a temporary bout of dizziness from the flight."

"I won't hear of it. You've been looking pallid for hours, and this calf's foot jelly is just the restorative you need. Don't go cowardly before all these spectators."

Scowling, Connor opened his mouth and swallowed the appallingly distasteful remedy.

"Excellent." The duchess turned to choose her next victim. "Now it will be your turn, Ian. That wound at your thigh has been coming along nicely, but you haven't been eating enough." Never mind that her strapping grandson had just consumed three rashers of bacon, half a loaf of bread, and two of Cook's best plum tarts.

But Ian knew it was no use to argue when his grandmother was in one of her managing moods. "Very well, Grandmama," he said, opening his mouth and swallowing with an audible clenching of teeth.

Now it was to be Thorne's turn. "Bring that jar

over here, Alexis, my child. It is time for your uncle Thorne to have his medicine," she said briskly.

The little girl promptly obeyed the duchess's directive, her eyes wide with wonder at the sight of the three very large men molded like clay in the hands of one old woman.

Thorne eyed the jar mutinously. His arm was paining him a great deal, though he refused to acknowledge it and now he was experiencing the flush of a slight fever. "I won't have any more of that potion today. You've already forced it three times down my gullet."

Alexis's eyes grew even rounder.

But the duchess only laughed and stamped her cane against the floor. "Here's a man with spunk. I like that, so I do. You'll make a fine match for my granddaughter, Thornwood. But *first* you're going to finish every bit of this restorative jelly. Then if you're very good, I'll let you have some of the garlic paste I've made for you."

Thorne's brow furrowed. But he saw India's pleading look and bit back a curt comment, swallowing the distasteful mix obediently while his friends Pendleworth and Monkton tried to hold back their laughter.

It was at this point that Alexis set her battered doll on the bed beside Thornwood. "Uncle Thorne, in all the excitement, I nearly forgot. I have something very important to tell you!" She looked at the duchess questioningly. "May I, Your Grace?"

"Of course, my child. I'm sure your uncle is in need of some distraction. His temper is lamentably surly of late," she murmured.

The old woman's knees were aching, her hands were stiff, but she was enjoying herself more than she had for months.

Alexis turned breathlessly and tugged at the doll's
shoes. "It all happened when Josephine fell down
the stairs this morning," she explained. "One of her
legs came off and I discovered she was hollow inside." Her excitement rose as she tossed off the
doll's, tattered gown and pinafore, revealing a battered wooden body beneath. "And then I found the
rest of her was hollow too. When I looked inside, I
found the most amazing thing." With a quick yank,
the girl pulled off one of the doll's legs and shook
the body over Thorne's lap. "Do you see now, Uncle
Thorne?"

A gray tangle landed on the coverlet, and then
two more. Thorne looked up, one brow crooked.
"You mean these lumps of dirty cloth?"

"More than that. Open one of them!" Alexis was
fairly dancing with excitement now.

Slowly Thorne picked apart the tangle and
opened one of the frayed lengths of cloth. And then
he caught a sharp breath.

A dozen glinting jewels lay shining on the satin
coverlet.

Several were at least as big as l'Aurore.

"At first I didn't understand what they were,"
Alexis said breathlessly. "Then it began to make
sense. I finally remembered about that night in
Brussels." The girl's eyes clouded for a moment, but
she resolutely raised her chin. "That night my parents died, my father had just given me something to
hide inside Josephine, when there was a hammering at the door. He seemed very anxious and said I
was never to tell anyone, that our lives depended on
my keeping the secret. Then he sent me off with
Andrew and Marianne to hide in a secret room. But
first he told me he knew I would be a good soldier.
And I *was*," she said fiercely. "I never told a single

soul. Not until now." She gnawed at her lip for a moment. "Of course, I did forget for a great while and I'm sorry for that. But now I've remembered and here are the jewels all safe again, just as my father wished."

Dev stared down in disbelief as one after another of the frayed rags came open to reveal an array of jewels long hidden in the old doll. A king's ransom, they were.

Or an *emperor's* ransom.

Ian gave a long, low whistle. "So that's where they were hidden all this time. I think you're quite extraordinary, Alexis."

The little girl beamed. Her brother and sister crowded close, staring at the jewels in awe while Thornwood picked up one of the gems and studied it closely. "Unless I miss my guess, these are Napoleon's lost hoard, each one as priceless as that pink diamond we found clutched in Stevens's hands in the shattered carriage." His face went grim for a moment. "We examined the rest of the pieces he had brought in, but they were fakes. Only l'Aurore was real, which explains why he went to such trouble to recapture it. Without that one, he could never have hoodwinked a jeweler into buying the rest, and his plan was nothing but a wild bluff. But here are the real ones, hidden inside Josephine all this time. It was your father's final act of bravery to manage to switch the real jewels with the false ones, Alexis. If only we'd known . . ." Dev smiled at the girl. "He was a very courageous man." He squeezed Alexis's hand tightly. "And he would be very proud of you right now."

"He is," the girl said softly.

Not was, but *is*.

India looked at Alexis and understood. She was

glad the little girl had such a gift to give her comfort after all the losses in her life.

"L'Aurore is dead," Thorne said gravely. "Thank God we've seen the last of that crew of madmen."

"Good lord, Thorne, never tell me *this* is what you've been chasing down since your return to London." Pendleworth shook his head, staring at the treasure trove of jewels. "Been deceiving us all the time! It's the outside of enough when a man don't tell his best friends what he's up to."

"But all that is about to change," the duchess said firmly. "Remove these jewels, if you please, Beach. We have more *important* matters to discuss now." In one stroke she consigned months of an important English campaign to utter obscurity. "You may store them in that Sèvres teapot on the mantel. It was a gift from my late husband's mother, and a more ugly piece of porcelain I have yet to see."

Without the slightest quiver of a smile, Beach swept up the priceless gems as if they were glass and disposed of them as directed. The duchess, meanwhile, continued without a pause. "I've been trying to find a date for your wedding, India. I expect you both will wish to make it soon, even though you are already married."

"Already *what*?" Ian, Luc, and Pendleworth spoke in tandem.

The duchess smiled from her wing chair, delighted with her explosive revelation. "Unfortunately, there might be some difficulty in finding a day. There are endless arrangements to be made, flowers to be organized, and invitations to issue. I shall have to contact those footloose parents of yours, too, India. They are somewhere between Greece and Cairo, I believe, which is not altogether a great deal of help. It will probably take six months for them to come home."

Devlyn scowled. "If you think I'm waiting *six months*—"

The duchess cut in smoothly. "Of course, that might be a trifle too long. Let me see now." She picked up a little leather-bound book and frowned down at a crowded page. "Possibly *here*." Then she shook her head. "No, I'm afraid that is a Tuesday, which presents a problem for Beach."

The butler stood impassive.

"After that will be the second week of the month, which will pose problems for Mrs. Harrison with a house full of guests. Of course Albert and his new bride will wish to be here, except that *they* will not be back from Yorkshire for several more weeks. I sent them up to visit the bride's family, you know. Which means . . ."

Thorne watched her, frowning.

"Six weeks hence *might* be possible."

"If you think I'm waiting *six weeks*, then you're—"

The duchess's eyes twinkled as she savored Thornwood's impatience. "No, I supposed you would not. Perhaps five then."

"Your Grace," Thorne growled.

India decided it was time to intervene. She slid closer and whispered in her husband's ear. "Never fear, Dev. If all else fails, I know a certain oak trestle table in the attic, which we might always call into use. If your impatience grows too great, that is."

Thorne's eyes darkened. He shifted, fighting a wave of heat.

"Is something the matter, Thornwood?" the duchess demanded.

"It's my, er, arm. Yes, my wound is paining me,"

the Earl of Thornwood lied, watching his wife bite back a laugh.

"Then you certainly *must* have some more calf's foot jelly. And some of the duchess's excellent tea," Alexis said anxiously.

Thornwood sighed. "Utterly Machiavellian. Soon Alexis and Marianne will be just like you."

Ian and MacKinnon grinned, while Luc and Silver relished the sight of this new member of the family falling victim to the duchess's managing ways.

"Now as I was saying, we might just be able to whittle off a few days and plan for one month hence." The duchess studied her grandson-in-law. "That is assuming that you will be physically competent by then, Thornwood. You are looking rather pale and it would never do for you to be out of sorts on your wedding night."

Luc chuckled.

Ian cleared his throat.

India flushed crimson.

But the Earl of Thornwood merely laughed lazily as he gazed at India. "Oh, I expect I will manage to bungle through, Your Grace." Heat filled his eyes as he studied this woman he knew would admonish and irritate and inspire and torment him for the rest of his life.

The woman he loved above all else in the world.

The woman he prayed would soon bear his child.

Ian laughed, but found the duchess's gaze turned thoughtfully upon him. "And now that I've dealt with your impossible sister, I believe it's *your* turn, Ian Delamere. Though what female could find *any* interest in a great hulking figure like you is beyond me." She frowned and tapped her pale cheek. "Of course there is the Townshende chit. Impeccable bloodlines, and that squint of hers isn't *too* notice-able."

India's brother held up his hands hastily. "Now, *Grandmama* . . ."

Three nights later India and Dev finally managed to slip away from a noisy masquerade being held in Swallow Hill's ballroom to celebrate Marianne's birthday. The candles had been blown out and the cake consumed, and Marianne was now happily immersed in opening a sea of presents.

By then Thorne deemed it safe to fetch away his wife.

"But what about the rest of the presents, Thorne?"

"She'll never even notice we're gone," Thorne said. "Besides, I have something I want to show you."

India's lips curved. "Your set of rare etchings, my lord?" she asked silkily.

"I just might at that," the earl growled. "It's been hell being near you for the last three days and not being able to have any privacy. Today I almost locked the door in the library and started shucking your clothes."

India's eyes glinted. "You had the same idea I had, I see."

Thorne took her hand and pulled her to the stables, where his great black gelding stood waiting, already saddled.

"But Thorne, your arm."

"My arm is fine, wife, except for a few twinges. I only wish the *rest* of me felt so good."

India knew exactly what parts he was talking about. She was feeling fairly restless herself. "But where are you taking me, Thorne? Back to the *Gypsy* perhaps?"

"Reprobate," he murmured. "No, I want you to see the house where we're going to raise all those children. Carlisle Hall is not like Swallow Hill, you know," he said gravely. "The roof is in disrepair and everything is sadly in need of a woman's touch." He looked uncertainly at India. "It will be a change for you. Not necessarily a pleasant one."

"A wonderful change. With a wonderful man and three wonderful children," India said firmly, sliding her hands around his waist. When they were both mounted, she snuggled closer, catching up her satin skirts before her. "Well, what are we waiting for?"

Thorne swallowed as one long white leg was thrust against his hip. "For me to regain some fragment of my sanity, I think." Shaking his head, he guided their mount out over dark fields lit by the warm silver glow of a full moon.

They rode slowly, each acutely conscious of the brush of the other's body. They shared slow, lazy kisses, their fingers taking any excuse to twine and mingle. Their soft, intimate laughter drifted through the still, warm air when Thorne finally reined in his mount on a hill overlooking the gabled roofs of Carlisle Hall.

Moonlight melted through the tall windows and painted the stone walks of the garden a ghostly white. What Thorne had said was true, India saw. The grand old Tudor house was in need of care, but immediately she envisioned a thousand projects that would keep them busy for the next fifty years or so, while they raised a dozen unruly children.

She sighed happily and raised her hand to Thorne's neck, well pleased at the thought.

"Do you—dislike it too much? After Swallow Hill, it's very small, I know, but—"

"I love it," she said firmly.

"You do? In spite of the leaking roofs? But you haven't even seen the bedrooms."

"I've slept in far worse while on caravan with my father, I assure you." India turned, sliding her hand down her husband's broad chest. Beneath them the great gelding neighed softly, then bent to nibble at a clump of tender grass. "The house will be fine, my love. I only hope that a certain treacherous French pirate will come to visit once in a while," she said wistfully.

Thorne's eyes darkened with desire. "Perhaps he is closer than you imagine, my lady."

"Do you think so?" India reached lower and found the hard length of male muscle rising hungrily to meet her. Her eyes took on a heated gleam. "Permission to come aboard, Captain?" she murmured as she closed around her goal.

"Sweet God." Thorne groaned, his face a mask of pain. Without another word he caught her tight and slid from the horse. There, beside a bank of flowers, he stared at India's creamy skin molded by her satin gown, at the auburn curls spilling loose around her shoulders. "This pirate is a dangerous man, you know. He takes whatever he wants."

India's tongue slid over her parted lips. "So do I."

Thorne closed his eyes, fighting for the control that was fast slipping past him. When he opened them again, India was pulling the first button free at his neck. "Exactly *who* is the pirate here, madam?"

"Shall we draw lots?" India purred.

"God help me," Thorne said in a vain prayer.

"Actually, I think we both are." The white linen pulled free and India bared her husband's powerful shoulders. Her lips moved over the rippling muscles. "I'm in the mood to do some very dangerous things tonight, I warn you."

Thorne muttered softly. His hands closed over her hips as he brought their bodies together.

India's fingers lingered slowly over the hot, throbbing skin captive in her hand. She smiled at his response, which was instant and fierce. "Amazing. Far better than I remembered, actually." She smiled up at her husband. "Almost as good as that notorious river pirate who once tried to seduce me."

"Almost?" Thorne slid one satin sleeve from her shoulder. "You'll murder me, woman. I swear, you're more dangerous than any pirate I ever had to fight." He found one tight coral crest peeping between the ruffled white lace at her bodice. "I'm most certainly close to dying. Still," he said appreciatively as he heard her breathless sigh, "I suppose there *are* worse ways to die. . . ."

The next week passed in a glorious blaze of early fall color.

Ian recuperated, Thorne grumbled incessantly, and Alexis seemed to be everywhere at once, tending to everyone's needs.

At last the duchess pronounced Thornwood fit to be out of bed for a whole day, and immediately he swept India off to Swallow Hill's rose gardens.

Alexis sat happily on the other side of a wall of blooms and watched Thorne bend down and kiss India. "He's very handsome, isn't he, Josephine? Of course, you've missed a great deal of activity since Uncle Ian's had you off to finish your repairs. Now let's see." She frowned. "First, there is the duchess. She has been so kind. She is even going to give me my very own gown of real silk. Of course, Marianne

will have a finer one, because she is older, but I
don't mind. She will look lovely in pink with her
dark curls. And then there is Cook. She has promised to teach me to make plum tarts. Then I will be
very happy."

Alexis gave a contented sigh as she smoothed the
doll's silk floss hair. She studied India and Thorne's
shadowed figures through the greenery. "They are
so happy together. It is almost as if every good
dream I've ever had has come true." She hugged
Josephine and smiled a secretive little smile. "Of
course, there is one dream that they don't know
about yet." She looked over her shoulder, where a
beam of sunlight spilled over the grassy bank. "This
is Ryan. I thought you might like to meet him, Josephine." Her eyes widened. "And he's brought someone else with him this time. A new friend. She is
going to be his baby sister, you see." Alexis turned
and studied the laughing couple beyond the hedge.
"Yes, they are going to be very happy. *We* are going
to be very happy," she added softly.

She moved away toward the house, old doll in
tow. "And if you are very good, Josephine, I'll let
you go with me to Uncle Ian's workshop. Do you
know, he can whittle frogs and all kinds of wonderful things out of wood . . . ?"

In the rose garden in the shadow of a pergola
dark with damask roses, Thornwood pulled his
smiling wife against him. "And now, my *sauvage* . . ."

"But, Dev, you're *sure* your arm isn't too sore?"
India looked anxiously at Thorne. "You really
shouldn't exert yourself so much."

"It must be the duchess's restorative jelly," the
earl murmured huskily, tugging at her sash.

"And, Dev, about the child. About Ryan, I mean. Sometimes I can feel him close by. I almost hear him laughing. I know it's silly, but—"

"No." His finger touched her lips. "It's not silly. And I'm very glad you do, my heart. But maybe it's time we gave him a brother."

India smiled slowly. "Or a sister."

Dev looked skyward and rolled his eyes. "God help the rest of us poor, benighted males then."

But he didn't look at all unhappy when his wife pulled him down beside her beneath a lush bank of roses and climbing lilies. In their urgent intensity, neither seemed to notice the wind rustling through the great, sweeping willow tree, nor the whisper of the flowers.

The sound was *almost* like the soft laughter of a very young child.

Dearest Reader,

I hope you have enjoyed this second foray into the lives of the dauntless and unpredictable Delameres. India and Dev were a perfectly matched pair, even if it *did* take two balloon ascensions and a kidnapping to make them realize that for themselves.

The theft of the French Crown diamonds? Entirely historical fact, I swear it. In 1792, robbers climbed a lamppost, vaulted onto a balcony, and broke into the French treasury in the Place de la Concorde, making off with over 8,000 diamonds. In their haste to get away, they scattered jewels all over the square and along the adjoining streets. Eventually, about 1,500 of the stolen gems were recovered, including the Regent and the Sancy diamonds. Another stone that disappeared in the robbery, the Hope Diamond, was later recut and passed to various owners. The fate of the other stones remains a mystery to this day, although another famous set of jewels—the parure of sapphires and diamonds belonging to Marie Antoinette—also vanished during the turmoil of the Revolution, but mysteriously resurfaced in the possession of Napoleon.

Food for thought, indeed.

Nor does the history of Napoleon end with Waterloo. The French emperor's popularity grew steadily in England, fueled by rumors of cruel treatment and poisoning attempts at St. Helena. Several attempts were made on the life of the Duke of Wellington, who remained a very visible and conservative figure in English political life for nearly half a century after Waterloo. Had any one of the plots to reinstate Napoleon succeeded, the fate of Europe would have been very different. (History buffs will note that I have moved up Wellington's return to England. Officially, this did not occur until 1818. But suppose he had made several *covert* trips, in a desperate effort to deal with a cache of lost diamonds. Who can say that it did *not* happen?)

Hot-air ballooning?

The first hot-air flight took place in 1783 in France, where the Montgolfier brothers launched an unmanned canopy of paper and linen. Manned flight began five months later from a starting point in the center of Paris. In spite of the danger of explosion, hydrogen was preferred because of its superior buoyancy. At the end of the eighteenth century, Europe and the United States were swept up in a craze for ballooning, commemorated in prints, paintings, and enthusiastic journal accounts.

As for that blush-pink stone called l'Aurore, *that* is purely a product of my imagination. Ah, but what if such a jewel had been among those stolen from the French treasury and was used by zealots to finance Napoleon's freedom? Who can say?

I hope you have enjoyed *Come the Dawn*. As you have probably guessed, the Duchess of Cranford has more matchmaking schemes in store for her helpless victims. I believe that she has already slated Ian and Connor MacKinnon as her next targets. In the meantime, I must confess that Alexis has turned out to be an intriguing character. What mayhem and havoc *she* will create among the ton! No rake will be safe, and no charming scoundrel immune to her singular abilities of sight. Yum. I *can't* wait.

If you would like a copy of my next newsletter and a signed bookmark, please send a self-addressed stamped envelope (legal-size works best) to me at:

111 East 14th Street, #277D
New York, New York 10003

As always, I would love to hear from you. And please let me know whose story *you* would like to see next.

With best wishes,

Christina Skye

Christina Skye

Joan Johnston

"Joan Johnston continually gives us everything we want... fabulous details and atmosphere, memorable characters, and lots of tension and sensuality."

—Romantic Times

☐ 22201-X	AFTER THE KISS		$5.99
☐ 21129-8	THE BAREFOOT BRIDE		$5.99
☐ 21280-4	KID CALHOUN		$5.99
☐ 20561-1	SWEETWATER SEDUCTION		$4.50
☐ 21278-2	OUTLAW'S BRIDE		$5.99
☐ 21759-8	THE INHERITANCE		$5.99
☐ 21762-8	MAVERICK HEART		$5.99
☐ 22200-1	CAPTIVE		$5.99

"WHAT DO YOU THINK YOU'RE *DOING*?"

"Testing your resolve, my lord. After all, you assured me your control was complete." Her eyes glittered, belying the careful calm of her voice. "But I must satisfy myself that it's true." Her hand rose, sliding into the dark depths of his hair. As she did, his hands locked about her shoulders.

"Don't," Thorne said harshly.

"But where is all that wonderful control you spoke of?" It was reckless and dangerous, but at that moment India didn't care. All she knew was a blind urge to see Thorne's control shattered. Only that way could she glimpse the real man hidden beneath the layers of reserve.

"Afraid you won't succeed? You say you're indifferent. You say you remember nothing. I begin to doubt that, my lord."

"Don't do this. You will only make us both sorry."

But India closed her ears, reckless as only a Delamere could be. Silently she raised her finger and traced the full curve of his lower lip.

And in that instant her plan began to backfire. What had begun as reckless provocation had become ragged need. . . .

The Ruby

"*The Ruby* intoxicates the senses. The characters and plot are constantly fascinating and darkly seductive. Ms. Skye builds danger and sexual tension with the turn of every page until the reader is drawn into her wondrous web of danger, intrigue and wild passion."
— *Romantic Times*

"Sensuous, swashbuckling, and wildly romantic! *The Ruby* is a gem of a read!"
— Bertrice Small, author of *Wild Jasmine*

The Black Rose

"As powerful, emotional, and sensual as *Defiant Captive*, *The Black Rose* will delight and enthrall Ms. Skye's fans. . . . Cleverly constructed, riveting, and breathtaking, *The Black Rose* ensures Ms. Skye's reputation as a writer of strong romances for . . . readers who like their heroes bold, their heroines daring, and their sex hot."
— *Romantic Times*

Defiant Captive

"From page one, Ms. Skye captures the essence of London as it could only have been in 1816. . . . This book is an absolute must to tuck in with the suntan lotion for a steamy romantic holiday. Five stars!"
— *Affaire de Coeur*

Books by Christina Skye

Defiant Captive
The Black Rose
East of Forever
The Ruby
Come the Night
Come the Dawn